*Barbara Villiers, Countess of Castlemaine
and Duchess of Cleveland.*

Photo by Mansell after the painting by Sir Peter Lely at Hampton Court.

My Lady Castlemaine

Being a Life of Barbara Villiers
Countess of Castlemaine, afterwards
Duchess of Cleveland ::   ::   ::

By Philip W. Sergeant, B.A.,

Author of "The Empress Josephine, Napoleon's Enchantress,"
"The Courtships of Catherine the Great," &c. ::   ::

With 19 *Illustrations including*
a Photogravure Frontispiece

LONDON: HUTCHINSON & CO.
PATERNOSTER ROW ::   ::   1912

PREFACE

IT may perhaps be maintained that, if Barbara
Villiers, Countess of Castlemaine and Duchess
of Cleveland, has not been written about in many
books, it is for a good and sufficient reason, that she
is not worth writing about. That is not an argument
to be lightly decided. But certainly less interesting
women have been the subjects of numerous books,
worse women, less influential—and less beautiful
than this lady of the dark auburn hair and deep blue
eyes. We know that Mr. G. K. Chesterton says that
Charles II attracts him morally. (His words are
" attracts us," but this must be the semi-editorial
" we.") If King Charles can attract morally Mr.
Chesterton, may not his favourite attract others?
Or let us be repelled, and as we view the lady acting
her part at Whitehall let us exclaim, " How different from the Court of . . . good King William III,"
if we like.

Undoubtedly the career of Barbara Villiers furnishes
a picture of one side at least of life in the Caroline
period ; of the life of pleasure unrestrained, unfalter-
ing—unless through lack of cash—and unrepentant.
For Barbara did not die, like her great rival Louise de
Keroualle (according to Saint-Simon), " very old,

v

very penitent, and very poor "; or, like another
rival, Hortense Mancini (according to Saint-Evremond), " seriously, with Christian indifference toward
life." On the principle *humani nil a me alienum
puto* even the Duchess of Cleveland cannot be considered unworthy of attention ; but, as being more
extreme in type, therefore more interesting than the
competing beauties of her day.

A few words are necessary concerning the method
of this book. The idea has been to let contemporaries
tell the story as far as possible, and usually in their
own language. This involves a plentiful use of in-
verted commas ; but it appears to me that thus a
more vivid and faithful presentation is made of the
spirit—or spirits—of the times than if all the material
had been transformed into Twentieth Century shape.
What could bring the volcanic Barbara more clearly
before our eyes than Pepys's tale, in chapter VII, of
her departure from Whitehall Palace, after a threat
to murder her child before Charles's eyes, making
" a slighting ' puh ' with her mouth " ; or Mrs.
Manley's, in chapter IX, of her fit after Churchill
had refused to lend her money, when " her resentment burst out into a bleeding at her nose and breaking
of her lace, without which aid, it is believed, her
vexation had killed her upon the spot " ? Even the
mis-spellings have their value ; as when the Duchess
tells Charles that " this prosiding of yours is so jenoros
and obliging that I must be the werst wooman alive
ware I not sensible ; no S^r my hart and soule is toucht
with this genoriste of yours."

Another point in the method adopted will, I fear, be unfavourably criticised by all except the general reader.   Practically all the footnotes except those which can be read without a distraction of the attention from the thread of the narrative have been banished to the end of the book.   Almost every reference to the pages of the authorities has been thus treated.   Those readers, therefore, who do not care (for instance) on what page of what volume of the Historical MSS. Commission reports a certain letter is to be found, will not have their eyes irritated by asterisks drawing attention to " H.M.C. Rep. 15, App., Pt. 4." Those, on the other hand, who wish to verify a quotation or to read a passage which illustrates, without directly belonging to, the narrative may do so without more labour than is involved by turning to the Notes at the end of the book.

As these Notes quote my sources of information, it is unnecessary here to make special acknowledgment of indebtedness to particular authorities.   But it would be ungracious not to mention the authors of the three [1] previous biographies of Barbara Villiers— the complete and careful *Memoir* by Mr. G. S. Steinman, privately printed in 1871, with *Addenda* in 1874 and 1878 ; the attractive sketch in Mr. Allan Fea's *Some Beauties of the Seventeenth Century ;* and the wholly admirable article by Mr. Thomas Seccombe in the *Dictionary of National Biography.*

---

[1] Since the above was written my attention has been called to a fourth biography, by Mr. Alfred Kalisch, included in *The Lives of Twelve Bad Women.*

With regard to the title of this book, "My Lady Castlemaine" was chosen in preference to others because it is so that the lady is always called by Samuel Pepys; and he (who has surely more right than Euripides to the name of "the human") has taught us how she may be looked upon with a kindly eye.

PHILIP W. SERGEANT.

November, 1911.

CONTENTS

LIST OF ILLUSTRATIONS

MY LADY CASTLEMAINE

CHAPTER I

BARBARA VILLIERS

" O Barbara, thy execrable name
Is sure embalmed with everlasting shame."

CHARLES, EARL OF DORSET.

" I LOVE not to give characters of women, especially where there is nothing that is good to be said of them," says Bishop Burnet, in a fragment which perhaps he intended originally to incorporate in his famous *History of My Own Time*. He does, however, so far overcome his reluctance to attempt feminine character-drawing as to devote a few lines, both here and in the *History*, to her who was at the time he wrote Duchess of Cleveland. The latter of the two passages has been quoted by almost every writer who has had occasion to allude to the Duchess. What Burnet says in the fragment will be less familiar to most readers. It is brief and much to the point : " Indeed, I never heard any commend her but for her beauty, which was very extraordinary and has been now of long continuance." (Her Grace was forty-two years of age when Burnet wrote this.) " In short, she was a woman of pleasure, and stuck at nothing that would either serve her appetites or her passions; she was vastly expensive, and by consequence very covetous; she was weak, and so was easily managed."

The Bishop's opinion of the lady's beauty was generally shared by his and her contemporaries. To Sir John Reresby she is " the finest woman of her age "; to Boyer, " by far the handsomest of all King Charles's mistresses, and, taking her person every way, perhaps the finest woman in England in her time." In the course of this book we shall see many other tributes of the same kind from writers of all sorts. Among the painters, Lely in particular paid her a still greater compliment, for he did her picture so often and so admirably that her handsome features are better known to us nowadays than those of any of her rivals. There are in existence at the present time, in England and abroad, enough portraits of her to fill a small gallery.

If her bodily loveliness was universally recognised in her lifetime and is incontestable to-day, her moral character was a byword while she lived and has never found an apologist since her death. Horace Walpole in a letter to his friend George Montagu, it is true, puts her among " the historically noble "; but, as he classes together under this heading " the Clevelands, Portsmouths, and Yarmouths " as opposed to ladies like " Madam Lucy Walters," it is clear to what sort of nobility he is referring. Except Samuel Pepys and King Charles II nobody appears to have discovered a good point about her. What Burnet thought of her was thought also by nearly all who came in contact with her. But the majority of them in committing their judgment to paper used much stronger language. The satirists, indeed, went so far that their verses seldom permit of quotation. Some discount must be allowed in the lady's favour on account of the violent hatred stored up against her during her long rule at Whitehall, and breaking forth as soon as it was reasonably safe to give vent to it. It can scarcely be doubted, however, that she deserved the substance of what was said about her. And if the language of her censors was excessively vehement, she could not justly complain. She was herself such a shrew that we may apply to her what Pope said of a certain Oldham, " a very indelicate writer " : " He has a strong rage, but it is too much like Billingsgate ! "

It would not be quite true to say that Barbara Villiers was a female incarnation of the spirit of Restoration England ; for it is a popular fallacy which makes the Restoration the starting-point of a change not merely in the externals of life, but also in the inner morality of this country. But she may fairly be said to be a distinctive product of her time, fostered to rank luxuriance by the special circumstances of her early girlhood, rather than the off-shoot of a bad stock growing up like a weed in a garden where it has no rightful place.

Barbara was indeed of very honourable descent through both of her parents. Her father, William Villiers, second Lord Grandison, was the eldest son of Sir Edward Villiers ; and of Barbara St. John, to whose descendants the title of her childless uncle,

Oliver St. John, Viscount Grandison of Limerick, was
transmitted. To this grandmother Barbara, no doubt,
the subject of the present biography, owed her name.
Sir Edward Villiers, who himself had a family of
seven, was one of the nine children of Sir George
Villiers of Brokesby, Leicestershire. Sir George was
twice married, Edward being the second son of the
first marriage, while from the second sprang the
famous George, first Duke of Buckingham, two other
sons, and a daughter. Going further back, the family
of Villiers were entitled to make the boast that they
came over with the Conqueror, and their origin was
referred to the Norman house of Villiers, Seigneurs de
l'Isle Adam, which gave France a famous marshal in
the fourteenth century, a celebrated Grand Master of
the Knights of St. John of Jerusalem in the sixteenth,
and, in modern days, a notable poet. After their arrival
in England the family settled in the North Midlands,
their estates in the early Norman times being in
Lancashire, Nottinghamshire and Leicestershire. As
we reach the Stuart period we find them closely
connected with the last-named county, of which Sir
George Villiers was Sheriff in 1591. The wonderful
favour to which Sir George's son and namesake attained
at the Court of James I led to the advancement of the
whole of this branch, and even the children of Sir
George's first marriage benefited by the reflected
glory of the brilliant Duke of Buckingham ; Sir
Edward, Barbara's grandfather, being made in turn
English Ambassador to Bohemia and President of the
province of Munster, in the latter of which posts he died.

Succeeding first to his father's estate in 1626 and then to his great-uncle's Irish viscounty of Grandison, William Villiers made an apparently good match with the young Mary Bayning, one of the four daughters of Paul, first Viscount Bayning, of Sudbury, Suffolk. The Baynings were a wealthy commercial family, Paul's father having been Sheriff of London, and having married an Essex heiress ; while Paul himself took to wife Anne Glemham, granddaughter of the first Earl of Dorset. Of Mary Bayning we hear little beyond the fact that she married two more husbands after William Villiers. But from the early profligacy of her daughter it may be gathered that she was a bad mother, whatever her character may have been in other respects. If she bore the responsibilities of married life ill, there is perhaps this excuse, that she undertook them before attaining full womanhood. When she bore her only daughter Barbara, she was apparently no more than sixteen, and she was left a widow for the first time at the age of eighteen ; although that was by no means extraordinarily young for a widow in those days of very early marriages.

Barbara Villiers was born in 1641 in the parish of St. Margaret's, Westminster, in which her father presumably had at this time a house. The register of St. Margaret's Church contains an entry, showing that the child was baptised there on November 27th, 1641. From this it has been concluded that her birth took place in the autumn of the year ; but no record exists of the actual date and, curiously, there is no mention in the writings of her contemporaries of any

celebration of her birthday after she had become so
notorious. There is extremely little known, too, of the
fortunes of her family in the first years of her life.
Before she was one year old there broke out what
Evelyn calls " that bloody difference between the King
and Parliament," in which her father, as a Villiers,
naturally ranged himself on the side of the King.
Viscount Grandison received a commission as " Colonel-
General," and raised a regiment for the Royalist
Army. At the opening of the war he captured Nant-
wich for the King. He fell into the hands of the
Parliamentarians at Winchester, but escaped ; took
part in the battle of Edgehill ; and in the following
year was at the siege of Bristol by the royal forces.
Here he received a fatal wound on July 26th. From
Bristol he was carried to Oxford and died in August,
being buried in the Cathedral. His daughter some
years after the Restoration raised above his remains
the white marble monument which may still be seen
at Christ Church, with a highly eulogistic epitaph
upon it.

But a more glorious tribute to the memory of
Barbara's father is to be found in the words of his
friend Clarendon, Lord Chancellor of England and
author of two of the most valuable works on the
Commonwealth and the reign of Charles II. Lord
Grandison's loss, he declares, could never be enough
lamented. " He was a young man of so virtuous a
habit of mind that no temptation or provocation could
corrupt him ; so great a lover of justice and integrity
that no example, necessity, or even the barbarities of

From an engraving after a painting by Van Dyck

WILLIAM VILLIERS, SECOND VISCOUNT GRANDISON

this war could make him swerve from the most precise
rules of it; and of that rare piety and devotion that the
court or camp could not shew a more faultless person,
or to whose example young men might more reasonably
conform themselves. His personal valour and courage
of all kinds (for he had sometimes indulged so much
to the corrupt opinion of honour as to venture himself
in duels) was very eminent, insomuch as he was accused
of being too prodigal of his person; his affection, zeal,
and obedience to the King was such as became a branch
of that family. And he was wont to say that if he had
not understanding enough to know the uprightness
of the cause nor loyalty enough to inform him of the
duty of a subject, yet the very obligations of gratitude
to the King, on the behalf of his house, were such as
his life was but a due sacrifice. And therefore he no
sooner saw the war unavoidable than he engaged all his
brethren as well as himself in the service; and there
were three more of them in command in the army,
where he was so unfortunately cut off."

So Grandison fell a victim to the war, followed to
the grave five years later by his cousin, called by
Aubrey " the beautiful Francis Villiers," shortly before
the cause for which so many of the name fought was
lost for ever by the death on the scaffold at Whitehall
of the Royal Martyr. The widowed Viscountess, on
April 25th, 1648, married her late husband's cousin
Charles, second Earl of Anglesea, the undistinguished
son of an undistinguished father, who owed his earldom
purely to the talents and influence of his brother
George, favourite of James I and Charles I.

After this wedding we hear no more of the mother, stepfather, or daughter until 1656. But Abel Boyer, in his *Annals of Queen Anne's Reign*, which began publication in 1703, in the course of his obituary notice of the Duchess of Cleveland in 1709 says : " This Lady being left destitute of a Father when not above Two or Three year old, I cannot learn who had the Care of her, but have been informed that the Circumstances of the Family was Mean, and that when she came first to London, she appeared in a very plain Country dress, which being soon altered into the Gaiety and Mode of the Town, added a new lustre to that Blooming Beauty, of which she has as great a share as any lady in her time."

This is the nearest approach which we can find to a contemporary account of Barbara's first years. Boyer continues : " Thus furnished by bounteous Nature and by Art, she soon became the Object of divers young Gentlemen's Affections." Concerning the affections of one of these young gentlemen we are fortunate enough to have some testimony, most thoughtfully preserved by himself for the information of future generations.

Philip Stanhope, second Earl of Chesterfield, is undoubtedly less known to popular fame than his grandson, the fourth Earl. Nevertheless, if it comes to a question of comparison of character, the earlier Chesterfield is the more remarkable man of the two. In his lifetime and immediately after his death, people's judgment upon him was chiefly dependent on the view which they took of his politics. He was a loyal

gentleman or an arrant knave, according as his critic
was an adherent of the Stuarts or not. Beside his
attachment to the Royal Family, his other most striking
trait—his contemptuous and promiscuous devotion to
woman—was scarcely taken into consideration. His
value was estimated apart from the matter of his
sexual morality ; which was, in effect, to judge but
half the man. Seen by us to-day, as portrayed in the
letters and autobiographical notes which he left behind
him, he produces a very mixed impression on the mind.
As his last thought would have been to betray his
sovereign (whether he were Charles or James), so his
last thought also would have been not to betray a lady,
if he had the chance and she (as he wrote to one of
them) were " neither ould nor ugly."

When he came into the life of Barbara Villiers, Lord
Chesterfield was twenty-three years of age and had
been a widower three years. His career so far had
been a very adventurous one. Born in 1633, he
was only son to Henry Stanhope and Catherine,
daughter of Lord Wotton. His paternal grandfather
had been created Earl of Chesterfield by Charles I, on
whose behalf he and his numerous sons fought bravely
during the Civil War. When Philip was in his second
year his father died and was buried at Becton Malherbe,
Kent, the home of the Wottons. Here the child was
brought up until the age of seven, when his mother
married a second time. Her new husband was " John
Poliander Kirkhoven, Lord of Hemfleet," ambassador
of the Prince of Orange at the Court of Charles I.
With him she went to Holland, taking her little son,

who during his eighth and ninth years was under the
tuition of his stepfather's father, "Monsieur Poliander,"
Professor of Divinity at the University of Leyden.
" His new disciple," says the editor of the memoir
prefixed to the Chesterfield Letters,[1] " seems to have
conceived a deep respect for the religious and erudite
character of his instructor." He appears to have gone
no further than admiring M. Poliander's character.
Had he been bigger at the time when he was under the
Professor's care we might have looked for the explanation of Chesterfield's moral lapses in some lines of an
epitaph upon the old gentleman, written by Dr.
Browne, who was esteemed by His Lordship " a fine
poet." These lines ran :

> " Sinn hee reproved with so much Art
>   That hee both smote and strok'd the harte ;
>   And men seem'd fond of their back slyding
>   For the pleasure of a chiding."

After leaving the delightful care of M. Poliander,
the boy spent his next six years partly in Holland,
partly in France. Three months of this time he was
attached to the Court of the exiled Queen-Mother
Henrietta Maria in Paris. For two periods, one as long
as twelve months, he was at the Court of the Princess
of Orange, formerly Princess Royal of England, to
whom his mother was Governess. At the age of

---

[1] *Letters of Philip, Second Earl of Chesterfield* (London : 1829).
Lord Chesterfield preserved these letters, copied out by himself in a
manuscript volume, which included also what he calls " Some short
Notes for my remembrance of things and actidents, as they yearly
happened to mee."

sixteen he was at an academy in Paris, where, as he
explains in his *Short Notes*, " I chanced to have a
quarrel with Monsieur Morvay, since captaine of the
French king's guards, who I hurt and disarmed in a duel,
and thereupon I left the academy." A visit to Italy
followed, whence he returned to his native land, which
he had not seen since he was seven, and married in
1650 Lady Anne Percy, eldest daughter of the Earl of
Northumberland. After three apparently peaceful
years he lost his wife by smallpox, following childbirth,
and went abroad again, being now only twenty-one
years of age. His second visit to the Continent was
marked by many adventures and great straits of
fortune. For, as we learn from his *Notes*, in the year
he left England a decree in Chancery was given against
him and " my unkle Arthur "—Arthur Stanhope,
sixth son of the first Earl of Chesterfield, and Member
for Nottingham in the Convention Parliament—
seized his estate, claiming that his nephew owed him
ten thousand pounds. Arthur Stanhope stood very
well with Cromwell, it appears. In the midst of
Philip's distress, however, after he had actually been
reduced to begging on the way from Lyon to Paris,
news came of the death of his grandfather on September 12th, 1656, and of his own succession to the
earldom.

Hurrying home at once, the new Earl not only
managed to make up the quarrel with his uncle, but
was so well received by the Protector that he had the
offer of the hand of one of his daughters—either Mary,
afterwards Countess of Falconberg, or Frances,

afterwards wife first of Robert Rich, and then of her
relative Sir John Russell—with a dowry of twenty
thousand pounds, and a high command for himself,
naval or military according to his preference. From
the matrimonial alliances which he either made
or might have made during his life, it is clear that
Chesterfield was looked upon as a most desirable match.
But he refused the present offer, which, he says, so
offended Cromwell that " it turned his kindness into
hatred," the force of which he was soon destined to
experience.

For declining Cromwell's proposal Chesterfield had
a good enough personal reason, since he was desirous
at this time of marrying Mary, the only daughter of
Lord Fairfax, who a year later became the wife of
George Villiers, second Duke of Buckingham, after he
had first refused the hand of Frances Cromwell, it was
said. In fact, the *Short Notes* state that Chesterfield
and Mary Fairfax were " thrise asked in St. Martin's
church at London " (St. Martin's, Westminster).
What was the cause of the engagement being
broken off when it had got so far, we are not
informed. But we do know, from the date which
Chesterfield puts on the first letter in his collection endorsed as " To Mrs. Villiers, afterwards Mrs.
Pamer, since Dutches of Cleaveland," that, during
the brief period of little more than six months between
his return to England on his grandfather's death and
the legal end of 1656,[1] the gallant Earl not only

---

[1] Chesterfield reckons the year in the old style, as ending on March
25th.   See p. 325.

refused Cromwell's daughter and engaged himself to
Mary Fairfax, but also made the acquaintance of
Barbara Villiers.

Barbara can but recently have attained her fifteenth
birthday when she met her first lover known to history.
She was living in the house of her stepfather, which is
conjectured to have been somewhere in the neighbourhood of St. Paul's. Lord and Lady Anglesea may have
been in straitened circumstances, but they were too
well connected to sink entirely out of sight. A close
friend of Barbara, as we shall see, was a daughter of the
Duke of Hamilton. Whether or not there was any
previous acquaintance between Chesterfield and the
Angleseas, before he had been back in England six
months he was sufficiently intimate with Mistress
Villiers to send her a letter which, if more formal
than those which followed on either side, argues a
friendship of exceedingly rapid growth.

" Madam," wrote Chesterfield, who was probably
at the time on a visit to his estate at Bretby, near the
Peak in Derbyshire, " Cruelty and absence have ever
been thought the most infallible remidies for such a
distemper as mine, and yet I find both of them so
ineffectuall that they make mee but the more incur-
able ; seriously, Madam, you ought at least to afford
some compassion to one in so desperat a condition, for
by only wishing mee more fortunat you will make mee
so. Is it not a strang magick in love, which gives so
powerfull a charme to the least of your cruel words,
that they indanger to kill a man at a hundered miles
distance ; but why doe I complaine of so pleasant a

death, or repine at those sufferings which I would not change for a diadem ?   No, Madam, the idea I have of your perfections is to glorious to be shadowed either by absence or time ; and if I should never more see the sun, yet I should not cease from admiring the light ; therefore doe not seeck to darken my weake sence by endeavoring to make mee adore you less ;

> For if you decree that I must dy,
> faling is nobler, then retiring,
> and in the glory of aspiring
> it is brave to tumble from the sky."

Chesterfield was a better judge of lovemaking than of poetry, it must be admitted.   But no doubt his letter gave satisfaction to the maiden heart of her to whom it was addressed.   The affair progressed rapidly, and the next letters in the series preserved by His Lordship—it is easy to imagine with what pride this coxcomb of love endorsed them, " From Mrs. Villars, since Dutches of Cleaveland "—show Barbara writing in a most passionate strain, in spite of a formality of style which we do not find in her letters later in life.

" MY LORD [she says in the first],

" I would fain have had the happyness to have seen you at church this day, but I was not suffered to goe.   I am never so well pleased as when I am with you, though I find you are better when you are with other ladyes ; for you were yesterday all the afternoune with the person I am most jealous of, and I know I have so little merit that I am suspitious you love all women better than my selfe.   I sent you yesterday a

PHILIP STANHOPE, SECOND EARL OF CHESTERFIELD

letter that I think might convince you that I loved
nothing besides your selfe, nor will I ever, though you
should hate mee; but if you should, I would never
give you the trouble of telling you how much I loved
you, but keep it to my selfe till it had broke my hart.
I will importune you no longer than to say, that I am,
and will ever be, your constant and faithfull humble
servant."

Her next note is even more formal, almost Chester-
fieldian [1] in tone.

" My Lord,

" I doe highly regret my own misfortune of
being out of town, since it made mee uncapable of the
honour you intended mee. I assure you nothing is
likelier to make mee sett to high rate of my selfe, than
the esteem you are pleasd to say you have for mee.
You cannot bestow your favours and obligations on any
that has a more pationat resentment of them, nor can
they ever of any receive a more sincere reception than
from,
" My Lord,
" Yours, &c."

If the wording of her second letter suggests that
Barbara had been taking a lesson in literary style from
him to whom she was writing, it is plain from her third

---

[1] "No man," says the author of the memoir prefixed to Chesterfield's
letters, "has left more elegant specimens of that peculiar courtesy, with
which an object of the passions only is intreated with the semblance
of respect." It seems, from a comparison of these early letters of
Barbara Villiers with those which she wrote to Charles II in 1678, for
instance, that Chesterfield must have edited and improved the letters
which he transcribed into his collection.

that he had commenced to instruct her in the art of
which she was to become so notorious a professor before
many more years had gone by.

"My Lord [she says],

"It is ever my ill fortune to be disappointed of
what I most desire, for this afternoon I did promis to
myselfe the satisfaction of your company; but I
feare I am disappointed, which I assure you is no small
affliction to mee; but I hope the faits may yet be so
kind as to let me see you about five a clock; if you will
be at your private lodgings in Lincoln's Inn feilds,
I will endeavour to come, and assure you of my
being,
                              "My Lord,
                                        "Yours, &c."

It is not in accordance with the usual picture of life
in England under the Commonwealth to find a girl
between fifteen and sixteen being allowed by her
parents, or being able without her parents' knowledge,
to visit a young man in his private lodgings; but we
know of nothing to the credit of Barbara's mother except that her first husband was William Villiers, nor of
anything at all to that of Lord Anglesea. The super-
vision which they exercised over Barbara was evidently
very slight. The next letter preserved by Chesterfield
is written jointly by her and her chief girl friend,
"the Lady Ann Hambleton," as he calls her. This
Lady Anne was one of the five daughters of the
Duchess of Hamilton, whom the battle of Worcester
left a widow. As Lady Carnegy, and afterwards

Countess of Southesk, she figures in the *Gramont Memoirs* in a very unfavourable light. About a year older than Barbara, she seems at the age of seventeen already to have laid the foundation of her future ill name.

These two young ladies write to Chesterfield, clearly before rising in the morning, that they are " just now abed together contriving how to have your company this afternoune," and making an appointment " at Ludgate Hill, about three a clock, at Butler's shop," which was no doubt sufficiently close to Lord Anglesea's house as well as to Lincoln's Inn Fields to be convenient to all parties. The Lady Anne may be presumed to have been on a visit to her friend's home. She was, equally with Barbara Villiers, an admirer of Lord Chesterfield and equally a willing victim to the wiles of the rake. But retribution overtook the elder of the two girls. Chesterfield for some reason went to " Tunbridg," as he spells it, and there he received a letter from Barbara in which she said : " I came just now from the Dutches of Hambleton, and there I found, to my great affliction, that the Lady Ann was sent to Windsor, and the world sayes that you are the occation of it. I am sorry to hear that the having a kindness for you is so great a crime that people are to suffer for it; the only satisfaction that one doth receive is, that their cause is so glorious that it is suffitient to preserve a tranquillity of mind, that all their malice can never discompose."

It was true that the Lady Anne was sent away in disgrace. Chesterfield preserved a note from her, also

c

written in the courtly style of which he himself was
the great exponent. " I have to good an oppinion of
you," she says, " not to believe you gratefull, and that
made mee think you would not be satisfied if I should
leave you for ever without a farewell." She sends
" this advertisement "—her note—" that you may
give mee some Adieus with your eyes, since it is to be
done noe other way."

Chesterfield's reply is interesting as showing how the
gallants of either sex met, even as early as 1657, in
places that after the Restoration became scandalous
for assignations and encounters :

" MADAM,

" Soon after your ladyship's departure, I came
to town, and went to the Park and Spring Garden, just
as some doe to Westminster to see those monuments,
that have contained such great and lovely persons.
Seriously, Madam, I may well make the comparison,
since you, that were the soul of this little world, have
carried all the life of it with you, and left us so dull,
that I have quite left of the making love to five or six
at a time, and doe wholly content myselfe with the
being as much as is possible,

" Madam,
" Yours, &c.,
" C."

To what extent Lord Chesterfield " left of the
making love to five or six at a time " may be gathered
from the warmth of a letter to him from " Mrs.
Villars," in which she speaks of doing nothing but

dream of him. "My life is never pleasant to mee," she continues, "but when I am with you or talking of you ; yet the discourses of the world must make mee a little more circumspect ; therefore I desire you not to come tomorrow, but to stay till the party be come to town. I will not faile to meet you on Sathurday morning, till when I remain your humble servant."

Could he set down all he thought (upon the subject of the kindness which he should show to her), says Chesterfield in his turn, all the paper of the town were too little ; " for having an object so transcending all that ever was before, it coins new thoughts, which want fresh words, to speak the language of a soul that might jusly teach all others how to love."

As if to make sure that posterity should be in no doubt as to his ability to carry on simultaneously a number of affairs, Chesterfield made copies of letters addressed to him by other ladies about the same period, including one from the Lady Elizabeth Howard, daughter of the Earl of Berkshire and afterwards wife of Dryden, whose patron Chesterfield became later in life. He also copied a letter which he received from Lady Capel, sister of his late wife, in which she remonstrated with him in a kindly but serious tone about the rumours which reached her in the country as to his misdoings. "Though I live here where I know very little of what is done in the world," she wrote, "yet I hear so much of your exceeding wildness, that I am confident I am more censible of it than any freind you have ; you treate all the mad drinking lords, you sweare, you game, and

commit all the extravagances that are insident to
untamed youths, to such a degree that you make your
selfe the talke of all places, and the wonder of those who
thought otherwise of you, and of all sober people ;
and the worst of all is, I heare there is a hansom young
lady (to both your shames) with child by you."

Chesterfield replied impenitently, complaining that
the world was " strangly giving to lying," saying that
since she had not credited his former professions he
could not now expect to be more fortunate, and
desiring her to forbear censuring on his account one of
the most virtuous persons living—presumably " the
hansom young lady." Two more letters passed
between them, from which it is evident that Lady
Capel's esteem for her brother-in-law was forfeited
for ever.

Lord Chesterfield, however, had other matters to
engage his attention as well as affairs of the heart. In
the year after his introduction to Barbara Villiers he
had a quarrel with a Captain John Whalley, on account
of a piece of impertinence which he (Chesterfield)
offered to a lady, fought a duel with him, wounded him,
and was arrested and sent to the Tower. In 1658 he was
three times in prison again, on political charges, " the
fruit of his attachment to the exiled Royal Family," his
biographer says. Cromwell was by no means inclined to
be friendly with him now, and the charge of treason
against the existing Government was pressed so far
that at first his estate was sequestered. But in the end,
" with great charge and trouble," as he expresses it
himself, he got off.

In this stormy year Chesterfield's intimacy with Barbara Villiers may well have been interrupted ; and, indeed, he preserves no letters between himself and her which bear the date 1658. Moreover, apart from the misfortunes which befell him, an obstacle arose which temporarily, at least, stood in the way of their meeting. What this was must be left to the next chapter to describe.

CHAPTER II

BARBARA'S MARRIAGE

"FURNISHED by bounteous nature and by art," says Boyer in a passage already quoted, Barbara Villiers " soon became the object of divers young gentlemen's affections ; and among the rest Roger Palmer, Esq., then a student in the Temple and heir to a good fortune, was so enamoured with her that nothing would satisfy him less than to have the jewel to be his own. It was reported that his father, then living, having strong apprehensions upon him, foreboding the misfortunes that would ensue, used all the arguments that a paternal affection could suggest to him, to disuade his son from prosecuting his suit that way, adding, *That if he was resolved to marry her, he foresaw he should be one of the most miserable men in the world.* The predominancy of the son's passion was such, that the authority and dissuasions of the father availed nothing ; so that the marriage between him and Mrs. Villiers was consummated, not long before the Restoration of King Charles II."

The Roger Palmer who now enters into the story was born on September 3rd, 1634, at Dorney Court, Buckinghamshire, being son of Sir James Palmer by

From an engraving by Faithorne

ROGER PALMER, EARL OF CASTLEMAINE

his second wife Catherine. On both sides of the
family his ancestry was good. Sir James Palmer was
a Gentleman of the Bedchamber to James I, and an
intimate friend of the Prince of Wales, afterwards
Charles I ; his father was Sir Thomas Palmer, known
as " the Travailer " on account of a book he published
in 1606 entitled, *An Essay of the Meanes how to make
our Travailes into forraine Countries the more profitable
and honourable ;* and his grandfather and great-
grandfather, Sir Henry and Sir Edward, both soldiers
of repute. Sir James, after the death of his first wife,
leaving him a son and a daughter, took as his second
Catherine, widow of Sir Robert Vaughan. This lady
was daughter to William Herbert, first Baron Powis,
a leading Roman Catholic nobleman, whose grandson,
the third Lord Powis, was destined to experience many
tribulations in the company of Roger Palmer in the
reign of terror set up by Titus Oates and his friends.

The Palmers were well off, and Roger received his
education at Eton and at King's College, Cambridge,
entering the latter at the age of seventeen. Soon
after leaving Cambridge—as it happened, just about
the time when his future wife made the acquaintance
of Lord Chesterfield—he was admitted a student of
the Inner Temple, but he was never called to the Bar,
fate having other things in store for him. How he
came to meet the Anglesea family and to enrol himself
among the " divers young gentlemen " who set their
affections upon Barbara Villiers does not appear. At
the Temple he must have been within easy reach of her
stepfather's house, and no doubt to the ill-provided

Angleseas he appeared in the light of a most welcome suitor for Barbara's hand ; especially if her name was already compromised by her affair with Chesterfield, as her mention of " the discourses of the world " seems to show. Sir James Palmer did not necessarily exhibit great foresight in auguring misfortunes for his son arising out of the marriage, if Barbara had caused herself to be talked about scandalously at the age of sixteen.

But Roger was not to be denied, and on April 14th, 1659, he and Barbara Villiers were married at the church of St. Gregory by St. Paul's, one of the buildings totally destroyed by the Great Fire of London seven years later.

The character of Roger Palmer is difficult to esti-mate. Jesse, in his *Memoirs of the Court of England*, is certainly not justified in summing it up in the words, " He figures through a long life as an author, a bigot, and a fool." The fact that he became a Roman Catholic and was employed by King James II in positions of trust, including that of special ambassador to the Pope, caused a prejudice against him in the minds of many of those who wrote about him during his lifetime or soon after his death. His narrow escape from being one of the victims of Titus Oates, and his persecution again after William of Orange had mounted the English throne, were typical of the treat-ment of which he was thought worthy by his enemies. It is not surprising, therefore, that he should by some of them have been classed among those husbands who, Gramont's friend Saint-Evremond told him, were typical of England—docile with regard to their wives ; but by no means tolerant of the inconstancy of their mistresses, he added. This is a question to which we must return later, but it may be said here that what Boyer calls " the misfortunes of his bed " would seem naturally to demand sympathy for him rather than contempt. That he was a fool to marry a bad woman cannot be denied. But he did not do so wittingly, nor was he the first or last man to do so. At any rate, after his discovery of his wife's worthlessness, we do not find him seeking consolation in the usual method in vogue at the Court of Charles II with the husbands of meretricious beauties. There is a singular absence of scandal about him, in an age when scandal left few indeed untouched.

Apart from the question of sexual morality, what we hear of him attracts rather than repels. Those who were not utterly biased against him by his religion could not deny him some merits. Boyer says in his obituary notice of him : " He was a learned person, well vers'd in the Mathematicks. For he was the inventor of a horizontal globe, and wrote a book of the use of it." This was a pamphlet published in 1679, entitled *The English Globe: being a stable and im-mobil one, performing what ordinary Globes do and much more.* He was also the author of *An Account of the Present War between the Venetians and the Turks ; with the State of Candie,* based on his experiences with the Venetian squadron in the Levant in 1664 ; of a history, in French, of the Anglo-Dutch war of 1665–1667 ; and of several works in defence of the

Roman Catholic faith and the loyalty of the Roman Catholics in England, including *The Catholique Apology,* which Pepys had a sight of on December 1st, 1666, and, without knowing who was the writer, found " very well writ indeed."

Of the first months of the married life of Roger and Barbara Palmer nothing is known until we come once more upon a letter preserved by Lord Chesterfield. From this it appears that within less than a year of her marriage Barbara had renewed acquaintance with her lover, and that Palmer was aware of the fact and resented it.   Under the date 1659 Chesterfield has a letter "from Mrs. Pamer, since Dutches of Cleaveland," which runs thus :

" My Lord,

" Since I saw you, I have been at home, and I find the *mounser* [*sc.* monsieur] in a very ill humer, for he sayes that he is resolved never to bring mee to town againe, and that nobody shall see me when I am in the country.   I would not have you come to day, for that would displease him more ; but send mee word presently what you would advise me to doe, for I am ready and willing to goe all over the world with you, and I will obey your commands, that am whilst I live,
" Yours."

Barbara did not, however, elope with Lord Chester-field.   Doubtless he had not the slightest desire that she should, she being only one of his very numerous flames.   And for a time all possibility of her doing so was removed.   Within the same year, 1659, she was

attacked by that fearful scourge of the period, smallpox, which (as can be seen from any contemporary
diary or collection of letters) ravaged almost every
family in England without distinction of rank. As
there is no subsequent mention of any blemish on
Barbara's beauty, it may be gathered that she was
not marked by the disease ; but she makes herself out to
have a bad attack. From her sick-bed she writes to
Chesterfield :

"MY DEAR LIFE" [this is the only occasion on which
she departs from the formal My Lord],
    " I have been this day extreamly ill, and the
not hearing from you hath made mee much worse
then otherwayes I should have been. The doctor doth
believe mee in a desperat condition, and I must
confess, that the unwillingness I have to leave you,
makes mee not intertaine the thoughts of deathe so
willingly as otherwais I should ; for there is nothing
besides yourselfe that could make me desire to live a
day ; and, if I am never so happy as to see you more,
yet the last words I will say shall be a praire for your
happyness, and so I will live and dey loving you above
all other things, who am,
" My Lord,
" Yours, &c."

In other circumstances the utter abandonment of
this letter might seem pathetic. But Chesterfield's
reply hardly suggests that he was deeply touched. It
is very courtly in tone. He " will not believe that you
are not well, for the certain newse of your being sick
would infalibly make me so ; and I doe not find

myselfe yet fitt for another world." And so on, with
no expression of anxiety beyond the request that she
should send him word that she was in perfect health.

Barbara recovered in due course,[1] and announced
the fact, in a letter not preserved. Chesterfield, in the
country at the time, thanked her for the news—" tho
it was but a peece of justice in you to lessen the
apprehentions of a person who doth more participate
in your good and bad fortune, than all the rest of
mortals." Had he thought his coming to town, he
added, could have been either serviceable or acceptable to her, she should have seen him in London
instead of his name at the bottom of a letter.

And now, after smallpox on Barbara's side had interrupted the intimacy, a misfortune befell Chesterfield
which abruptly removed him from England. Near the
beginning of Pepys's *Diary*, under the date of January,
1660, the writer tells how he, when taking his wife
and the young Edward Montagu by coach to Twickenham, on the way, " at Kensington, understood how
that my Lord Chesterfield had killed another gentleman about half an hour before, and was fled."

Without waiting for arrest and trial—as a matter of
fact he might have done so safely, for the jury found
it " chance-medley," it is recorded—Chesterfield made
for Chelsea and escaped thence by water to France.

---

[1] In later years she was apparently emboldened by her early
attack to be without dread of smallpox. In the midst of an epidemic
in London, Moll Davis, her actress rival, endeavoured to alarm her
with the suggestion that she might contract the disease and lose her
beauty; whereon she scornfully replied that she had no fear, for she
had had what would prevent her from catching it.

From here he wrote to King Charles, then at Brussels, asking the Royal pardon for what he had done, and affirming that he begged a forfeited life " to noe other end then to venter it on all occations in your Majesties service and quarrel." Charles replied in a most friendly strain, concluding : " I hope the time is at hand that will put an end to our calamities, therefore pull up your spirits to wellcome that good time, and be assured I will be allwayes very kind to you as Your most affectionat friend CHARLES R." Moreover, the King received him in audience at Breda in April, and granted him full forgiveness for his crime. Chesterfield departed for Paris and soon afterwards was at Bourbon (Bourbonne), drinking the waters, whence he wrote a letter, of which he kept a copy, to Mrs. Palmer. Then, hearing of Charles's intention of proceeding to England, he made for Calais, took a boat, joined the *Naseby*, which had the King on board, and with him landed again at Dover on May 26th.

After Barbara's recovery from her attack of smallpox, the movements of the Palmers are not certainly known. Mrs. Jameson, in her *Beauties of the Court of King Charles the Second*, published in 1833, says that Barbara's " first acquaintance with Charles probably commenced in Holland, whither she accompanied her husband in 1659, when he carried to the King a considerable sum of money, to aid in his restoration, and assisted him also by his personal services." Similarly Jesse, writing in 1840, says that in the following year after their marriage the Palmers " joined the Court of Charles in the Low Countries, where the husband made himself acceptable by his loans, and the lady by her charms." Neither of these late writers mentions any authority for their statements, and contemporaries, so far as is known, are silent upon the matter. There is nothing improbable, however, in a visit of Roger Palmer and his wife to Holland at the beginning of 1660. Hither Charles moved in April, thinking it advisable to leave the Spanish Netherlands at this period, and being assured of a benevolent attitude on the part of the Dutch toward his attempt on England. Palmer's loyalty, like that of all his family, was well known, and he was in the expectation, shared by so many other Royalists in England, of a good post when the Restoration should come about. Being a wealthy man, he had every inducement to help King Charles with his money when money was all that was required to make Charles's prospects brilliant. In a petition which he made to the King in the following June for the Marshalship of the King's Bench Prison, he represented that he had " promoted the Royal cause at the outmost hazard of life and great loss of fortune." We cannot tell what was the hazard of life to which he was exposed. The great loss of fortune may well have been in the shape of loans to the King, who certainly needed cash. Do we not know from Pepys "in what a sad, poor condition for clothes and money the King was, and all his attendants . . . their clothes not being worth forty shillings the best of them " ?

With regard to Barbara's acquaintance with His Majesty, it is certainly curious, in view of the notoriety of their relations from the very commencement of

his reign, that no writer of the period should have
recorded the time or place of their earliest meeting.
Boyer and the author of a scurrilous tract entitled
*The Secret History of the Reigns of King Charles II
and King James II*, printed in 1690, both state that
Mrs. Palmer was with the King at Whitehall Palace
on the night of his Restoration. Another account
makes the King withdraw from the Palace to Sir
Samuel Morland's house in Lambeth to spend the
night after his arrival. But loyal observers of the
entry of King Charles into London did not see Mrs.
Palmer. Evelyn stood in the Strand on May 29th and
beheld " a triumph of above 20,000 horse and foote,
brandishing their swords and shouting with inexpressible joy ; the wayes strew'd with flowers, the
bells ringing, the streetes hung with tapistry, foun-
tains running with wine ; the Maior, Aldermen, and
all the Companies in their liveries, chaines of gold, and
banners ; Lords and Nobles clad in cloth of silver, gold,
and velvet ; the windowes and balconies well set
with ladies ; trumpets, music, and myriads of people
flocking, even so far as from Rochester, so as they were
seven houres in passing the Citty, even from 2 in the
afternoone till 9 at night." He saw, too, at Whitehall,
when he went to present letters from Queen Henrietta
Maria a few days later, " the eagerness of men, women,
and children to see His Majesty and kisse his hands . . .
so greate that he had scarce leisure to eate for some
dayes, coming as they did from all parts of the Nation ;
and the King being as willing to give them that satisfaction, would have none kept out, but gave accesse to

all sorts of people." But he, who is so outspoken in
his opinion of the royal mistress in later years, has
nothing to say about her now. Other writers are
equally silent. The only positive evidence in favour of
Barbara's intimacy with King Charles at this date is
that, in her second letter to him from Paris in 1678 [1]
she speaks to him of Lady Sussex, her daughter born
on February 25th, 1661, nine months after the
Restoration, being his child.

Amid the throng about Whitehall, in these first
days, of loyalists and pretended loyalists, benefactors of
the King during his famous flight from Worcester, and
place-hunters who could allege little or no reason why
they should receive the honours which they coveted,
one might think it difficult for His Majesty to carry
on an intrigue secretly. But amid the enthusiastic
rejoicings of the Restoration there was no inclination
to be censorious. The time for reflection was yet to
come, when the hopes of a Golden Age for all were
seen to be baseless, and a fair but grasping hand was
discovered to have a grip that none could relax on the
royal purse.

The Chancellor, Lord Clarendon, puts forward a
theory of the reason of Charles's abandonment of
himself to dissipation now which does credit to his
loyalty. He says that the " unhappy temper and
constitution of the royal party "—rent by " jealousies,
murmurs, and disaffections amongst themselves and
against each other," and all scrambling for places—
" did wonderfully displease and trouble the king;

[1] See p. 232.

From an engraving after a miniature by Samuel Cooper

BARBARA VILLIERS, COUNTESS OF CASTLEMAINE
AND DUCHESS OF CLEVELAND

and . . . did so break his mind, and had that opera-
tion upon his spirits that finding he could not propose
any such method to himself by which he might extri-
cate himself out of those many difficulties and laby-
rinths in which he was involved, nor expedite those
important matters which depended upon the goodwill
and despatch of the parliament, which would proceed
by its own rules and with its accustomed formalities,
he grew more disposed to leave all things to their
natural course and God's providence ; and by degrees
unbent his mind from the knotty and ungrateful part
of his business, grew more remiss in his application to
it, and indulged to his youth and appetite that license
and satisfaction that it desired, and for which he
had opportunity enough, and could not be without
ministers abundant for any such negotiations ; the
time itself, and the young people thereof of either sex
having been educated in all the liberty of vice, without
reprehension or restraint."

The last words appear to apply with singular
propriety to the case of Barbara Palmer ; though
throughout his works the Chancellor carefully avoids
mentioning her name, never designating her otherwise
than as " the lady " when, later, he is compelled to
allude to her. But the unfortunate Roger, at any rate,
could not be included among the young people indicted
by Clarendon. He was, on the other hand, one of
those who besieged the King with requests for a
reward for services rendered. As has been mentioned, there survives a petition which he made in
the June after Charles's return for the Marshalship of

D

the King's Bench Prison, representing that he had " promoted the Royal cause at the utmost hazard of life and great loss of fortune." It appears from the Domestic State Papers of Charles II that it was not until November 1661 that the warrant was made out for a grant to Palmer of the reversion of this coveted office after Sir John Lenthall ; and by that time much had happened to make the King inclined to be generous to him.

If he had to wait for the royal recognition of his services, Roger Palmer in the meanwhile had a position of some credit. In the Parliament which met for the first time on April 25th, and played its part in welcoming the King back to England, he was the representative for New Windsor. He took a house, at what date is not known, in King's Street, Westminster, described by Pepys as the " house which was Whally's " ; that is to say, it was formerly occupied by Major-General Edward Whalley the regicide, who had fled to America on the Restoration. Here Palmer resided in the early days of the Restoration summer with his wife, within easy reach of the Palace at Whitehall ; " My Lord's lodgings " (as Pepys calls Sir Edward Montagu's town house in King's Street) which were next door to the Palmers', giving access to the Privy Garden of the Palace.

It was strange, even at the first, that Roger should have been ignorant of his wife's familiarity with the King, if it commenced at the end of May ; but such seems to have been the case. The earliest contemporary indication of a scandal is to be found in Pepys,

writing on July 13th, 1660. The diarist had gone to
the house of his kinsman and patron on business.
" Late writing letters," he says ; " and great doings of
music at the next house, which was Whally's ; the
King and Dukes there with Madame Palmer, a pretty
woman that they have taken a fancy to, to make her
husband a cuckold. Here at the old door that did go
into his lodgings, my Lord, I, and W. Howe, did stand
listening a great while to the music."

Three months afterwards, Pepys went on a Sunday
to the Chapel Royal attached to Whitehall Palace,
" where one Dr. Crofts [the Dean] made an indifferent
sermon, and after it an anthem, ill sung, which made
the King laugh." Here also he " observed how the
Duke of York and Mrs. Palmer did talk to one another
very wantonly through the hangings that parts the
King's closet and the closet where the ladies sit."
Charles and James had forgotten their upbringing ;
for in a fragment of diary for 1677–8 kept by Dr.
Edward Lake, chaplain and tutor to the Princesses
Mary and Anne, we are told how " the Bishop of
Exeter, discoursing of and lamenting the debaucherys
of the nation, and particularly of the Court, imputed
them to the untimely death of the old King, who was
always very severe in the education of his present
Majesty : insomuch that at St. Mary's in Oxford, hee
did once hit him on the head with his staffe when he did
observe him to laugh (at sermon time) upon the ladys
who sat against him."

Pepys had not yet, it appears, conceived that vast
admiration for the royal favourite to which he so

amusingly confesses later. But the beginning of it can be seen in his entry for the following April, when " by the favour of one Mr. Bowman " he was admitted to a performance before the Court, in the Cockpit, of *The Humorous Lieutenant,* by Beaumont and Fletcher. The play Pepys found " not very well done." " But," he says, " my pleasure was great to see the manner of it, and so many great beauties, but above all Mrs. Palmer, with whom the King do discover a great deal of familiarity."

It is not until three months later that Pepys actually styles the lady " the King's mistress." Yet an event had occurred which might have put the matter beyond all question, had not Barbara Palmer's conduct nearly always left room for an element of doubt in such cases.

About the end of January 1661 Barbara lost her stepfather. His death does not appear to have attracted much attention. In fact, its exact date is not recorded, though his burial took place on February 4th. The Earl of Anglesea made no impression on the affairs of his lifetime, and his stepdaughter had no reason to be grateful to him for any care he had bestowed upon her during the years when she lived under his roof. Had he survived a few weeks longer he would have seen her the mother of a child to whom different people assigned three fathers. Anne, afterwards Countess of Sussex, was born on February 25th, and was accepted by Roger Palmer as his daughter. It is only Palmer's subsequent behaviour which prevents us from regarding him now as one of Saint-Evremond's " docile English husbands." As

for the King—whether it was that he really thought
Anne was Palmer's or that he was precluded from
recognising her as his child, the mother not yet having
had her position made regular even after the manner
of such connections—he did not definitely acknow-
ledge the paternity until the time of Anne's marriage
to Lord Dacre in 1674. In that year he treated her
and his undisputed daughter Charlotte on precisely
the same footing.

But there were many who said that the real father
of the first child was Lord Chesterfield, claiming that
Anne Palmer (or Fitzroy) resembled him in face and
person. The supposed likeness, however, is the only
evidence put forward in support of the theory.
Chesterfield's published remains do not give any hint
of his fatherhood to Anne. Early in 1660 he had
married his second wife Lady Elizabeth Butler, eldest
daughter of Charles's trusted counsellor and Clarendon's friend, the Duke of Ormonde. In the following
year we find him writing to Barbara two letters somewhat cautiously worded, from which it is clear that he
has somehow offended her. "After so many years'
service, fidelity, and respect," he says in one, " to be
banished for the first offence is very hard, especially
after my asking so many pardons." " Let me not
live," begins the other, " if I did believe that all the
women on earth could have given mee so great an
affliction as I have suffer'd by your displeasure. . . .
If you will neither answer my letters, nor speak to mee
before I goe out of town, it is more than an even lay I
shall never come into it againe."

As to what aroused Barbara's extreme displeasure there is no indication. Perhaps it was the mere fact of Chesterfield's marriage, ladies of her kind being apt, when they have once really bestowed their affection (as undoubtedly Barbara had on Chesterfield), to demand in return a constancy as strict as though they were themselves immaculate. But it was assuredly not her first lover's devotion to his wife which stirred her to anger; for of the three ladies whom he married during the course of his life, the beautiful Elizabeth Butler was the one for whom Chesterfield felt the least affection. The lively and malicious *Memoirs of Gramont* adduce some reason for this, stating that the second Lady Chesterfield's heart, " ever open to tender sentiments, was neither scrupulous in point of constancy nor nice in point of sincerity." Anthony Hamilton, who wrote the Memoirs for his brother-in-law, the Comte de Gramont, was cousin to the lady, and should have known what her character was like. He represents her as being on very intimate terms with his brother James, of whom we shall hear again.

After the birth of her daughter, Barbara Palmer was in stronger favour than ever with the King. Pepys records various appearances of hers at the theatre. We have already seen her at the Cockpit in April. On July 23rd Pepys, in the afternoon, finding himself unfit for business, goes to see Suckling's *Brennoralt* for the first time. " It seemed a good play, but ill acted," he comments ; " only I sat before Mrs. Palmer, the King's mistress, and filled my eyes with her, which much pleased me." He was now fully

under the spell of her beauty. Again on August 27th
he goes with his wife to *The Jovial Crew*, the King,
the Duke and Duchess of York, and Madame Palmer
being present; " and my wife, to her great content,
had a full sight of them all the while." On September
7th he is with his wife at " Bartholomew Fayre with
the puppet-show, acted to-day, which had not been
these forty years." The Pepyses seated themselves
" close by the King, and Duke of York, and Madame
Palmer, which was great content; and, indeed, I
can never enough admire her beauty." Yet only a
week earlier the writer is lamenting the condition of
affairs at Court, where " things are in a very ill
condition, there being so much emulacion, poverty,
and the vices of drinking, swearing, and loose amours,
that I know not what will be the end of it, but confusion " ! Pepys very successfully managed to admire
the sinner and (in words at least) abhor the sin. But
as it is owing to his admiration of this particular
sinner's beauty that we owe his frequent allusions to her
appearances in public, when other writers are silent,
we can but feel grateful to him for his weakness.

One more allusion to the lady is to be found in the
Diary for the year 1661. On December 7th Pepys
sees at the office of the Privy Seal " a patent for Roger
Palmer (Madam Palmer's husband) to be Earl of
Castlemaine and Baron of Limbricke in Ireland."
He continues : " The honour is tied up to the males
got of the body of this wife, the Lady Barbary : the
reason whereof every body knows."

There have come down to the present day two

short autograph notes from King Charles to Sir William Morrice, one of his Secretaries of State. In the first, dated " Whitehall, 16 Octr.," Charles says : " Prepare a warrant for Mr. Roger Palmer to be an Irish Earle, to him and his heirs of his body gotten on Barbara Palmer, his now wife, with the date blank "— a postscript adding : " Let me have it as soon as you can." The second message has the date " Whitehall, 8 Nov., morning," and runs : " Prepare a warrant for Mr. Roger Palmer to be barron of Limbericke and Earle of Castlemaine, in the same forme as the last was, and let me have it before dinner."

The King was about to bestow upon her whom Bishop Burnet calls " his first and longest mistress " the earliest of the public manifestations of his feelings for her—and the only one in which her husband was to share. There was a reason, or perhaps it should be said that there were two reasons, why he should specially wish to afford her gratification at this time. In the first place, he was preparing to take to himself a lawful consort ; and, secondly, Barbara was now in expectation of a child about whose paternity there was never any discussion.

On the afternoon of Sunday, November 10th, 1661, Pepys went and sat with Mr. Turner in his pew at St. Gregory's—the church which, nineteen months pre- viously, had witnessed the wedding of Roger Palmer and Barbara Villiers—and there he heard " our Queen Katherine, the first time by name as such, publickly prayed for." The proposal of a marriage between Charles, then Prince of Wales, and Catherine of

Braganza had been made as far back as sixteen years
previously by the lady's father, King Juan of Portugal,
when she was but seven years old. It was renewed
tentatively by the Portuguese Ambassador in England
as soon as the Restoration looked probable, and on
Charles's return took definite shape. Portugal, poor as
she was through her struggle with her late masters the
Spaniards, offered a very handsome dowry, including
two million crusados (about £300,000) and the
settlements of Tangier and Bombay. The idea of the
marriage was very popular with the Portuguese. But
the Spanish Court was very strongly against it, and
attempts were made to dissuade Charles from it
through the agency of the Earl of Bristol, a Roman
Catholic peer in high favour at Madrid, and Baron de
Watteville, the Spanish Ambassador in London.
Catherine was declared to be incapable of bearing
children, while as good a dowry as Portugal offered
was promised with any princess whom Charles might
marry in her stead with the approval of Spain.
Moreover, the Vatican was, so to speak, in the pocket
of Spain at this time, and therefore Rome's blessing on
the Anglo-Portuguese union was not to be expected.

In the end, however, France threw her weight into
the scale in support of Portugal, and Charles made
up his mind to enter upon the marriage. On May
8th, 1661, the opening day of the first Parliament
elected during his reign, he announced to the two
Houses his intention of wedding Catherine of
Braganza. Six weeks later the marriage treaty was
signed, to Sir Edward Montagu, now Lord Sandwich,

being assigned the duty of bringing over the Princess in the following spring.

To no one could the signing of the treaty of marriage be of more serious importance than to the royal mistress, and the grant of a title to the Palmers has all the appearance of an attempt at consolation on the part of the King. His Majesty, however, in his desire to confer this honour on his favourite was met by a great difficulty. His Chancellor and Treasurer, both indispensable to him, would have nothing to do with Mrs. Palmer, and united together by a fast friendship stood out against Charles's designs in her regard. They resolved, says Bishop Burnet, " never to make application to her nor to let anything pass in which her name was mentioned." Burnet finds this conduct " noble in both these lords," but especially in Clarendon. Southampton was not much concerned whether he lost his office or not, and had not such powerful enemies. But the Chancellor " was both more pushed at and was more concerned to preserve himself, so that his firmness was truly heroical."

Clarendon himself tells us, with regard to Barbara's mortal hatred for him, that she well knew " that there had been an inviolable friendship between her father and him to his death . . . and that he was an implacable enemy to the power and interest she had with the King, and had used all the endeavours he could to destroy it."

In concert with the lady the King devised a way of circumventing the opposition which he knew that the Chancellor would offer to the conferring of a title upon

Roger Palmer. As we have seen, he asked his Secretary of State for a warrant for Palmer to be an *Irish* earl. According to Burnet, this plan was first suggested by Lord Orrery, one of the Lords Justices of Ireland. Its advantage was that the patent would not have to come before the Lord Chancellor of England. It was sent over to Ireland to pass the Great Seal there. For the present, the matter was kept secret from Clarendon and other hostile persons. What the Chancellor thought when the news was divulged to him by the King we shall see below. Here we may mention a story told by him of an attempt by the Earl of Bristol (who hated him) to make capital of the delay. Bristol went to the favourite and asked her whether the patent was passed. She answered no, whereon he told her that it had been taken to the Chancellor ready for the Great Seal, but that he, " according to his custom, had superciliously said that he would first speak with the King of it, and that in the meantime it would not pass ; and that if she did not make the King very sensible of this his insolence, His Majesty should never be judge of his own bounty." The lady laughed and " made sharp reflections on the principles of the Earl of Bristol. Then, pulling the warrant out of her pocket, where she said it had remained ever since it was signed, and she believed the Chancellor had heard of it : she was sure there was no patent prepared, and therefore he could not stop it at the Seal."

Barbara, therefore, although she had the satisfaction of knowing that she would before long be called Lady Castlemaine, was compelled to wait for a while. As for the prospective Earl, there is no ground for assuming that he felt any pleasure at the bestowal of this public mark of the King's affection for his wife. Clarendon, indeed, represents Barbara as being in fear that he would try to stop the passing of the patent.[1] He was clearly now at last "sensible of his wife's infidelity," though until the birth, which was soon expected, of her first son by Charles he made no open break with her.

[1] Clarendon, calling Palmer "a private gentleman of a competent fortune, that had not the ambition to be a better man than he was born," says that he "knew too well the consideration that he paid for it [his earldom], and abhorred the brand of such a nobility and did not in a long time assume the title." He is said never to have taken his seat in the Irish House of Lords.

From a painting by Sir Peter Lely

BARBARA VILLIERS, COUNTESS OF CASTLEMAINE
AND DUCHESS OF CLEVELAND

CHAPTER III

THE AFFAIR OF THE QUEEN'S
BEDCHAMBER

THE period preceding the arrival in England of
Catherine of Braganza was one of anxiety to the
newly created Countess. She had her title, it was
true, and probably had already extracted from Charles
a promise of a further honour, about which we shall
hear soon. But the approach of the royal marriage
encouraged the tongues of those who disliked her
ascendancy over the King to greater boldness against
her. Pepys, on January 22nd, 1662, hears of "factions
(private ones at Court) about Madam Palmer."
"What it is about I know not," he adds. " But it is
something about the King's favour to her now that
the Queen is coming." On April 13th Mr. Pickering
tells him how all the ladies " envy my Lady Castlemaine," presumably on account of her title, which
seems now coming into general use. And on the 21st
of the same month the diarist gets hold of a choicer
piece of gossip from Sir Thomas Crew, how that " my
Lady Duchess of Richmond and Castlemaine had a
falling out the other day ; and she did call the latter
Jane Shore, and did hope to see her come to the same
end that she did."

This was not the only time that the name of Jane

Shore was to be coupled with the Countess's; and the comparison could scarcely be gratifying to her. But my Lady Castlemaine probably was at no loss for a retort, if we may judge by her powers of abuse at other times.

The uncharitable lady who made the remark on the present occasion was a kinswoman of Barbara, by birth Mary Villiers, daughter of the first Duke of Buckingham, and married first to Lord Herbert and secondly to the Duke of Richmond and Lennox, by whom she was left again a widow in 1655. The reason for the Duchess's enmity toward the Royal mistress is nowhere stated; but her brother George was also hostile to Barbara during the greater part of his career at Court, so that there may have been some family quarrel of which we do not know the particulars.

The ladies at Court made a shrewd guess that King Charles would find it difficult to shake off his mistress's yoke. Lady Sandwich, talking to Pepys on May 14th, is " afeared that my Lady Castlemaine will keep with the King." " And I am afeard she will not," writes Pepys ingenuously, " for I love her well." Seven days later the entry in his *Diary* is more artless still. He goes with Mrs. Pepys to Lord Sandwich's lodgings and walks with her in Whitehall Privy Garden. " And in the Privy Garden saw the finest smocks and linnen petticoats of my Lady Castlemaine's, laced with rich lace at the bottom, that ever I saw; and did me good to look upon them." Going out to dinner the same day with his wife and Sarah, Lord Sandwich's housekeeper, he is told by the latter " how the King dined

at my Lady Castlemaine's, and supped, every day and
night the last week; and the night that the bonfires
were made for joy of the Queen's arrivall, the King was
there; but there was no fire at her door, though at all
the rest of the doors almost in the street; which was
much observed. . . . But she is now a most disconsolate creature, and comes not out of doors since the
King's going." After dinner they proceeded to the
theatre and " there with much pleasure gazed upon
her "—out of doors after all, it seems, in spite of her
disconsolate state—" but it troubles us to see her look
dejectedly and slighted by people already."

The King left London and the disconsolate lady
on May 19th, having been unable to proceed to
Portsmouth hitherto owing to the necessity of pro-
roguing Parliament before he went. But Catherine
had reached England as early as the 13th. Her departure from Lisbon with Lord Sandwich, on board
The Royal Charles, had been delayed by a dispute as
to the form in which a most important part of her
dowry should be paid (Portugal offering " sugars and
other commoditys and bills of exchange " in lieu of
the promised crusados), or she would have arrived
earlier still. Off the Isle of Wight the *Royal Charles*
was boarded by the Duke of York, accompanied by
Lord Chesterfield among others, whom Charles had
appointed chamberlain to his bride. In his *Notes*
Chesterfield records that His Royal Highness, out of
compliment to the King, would not salute—that is,
kiss—Catherine, " to the end that His Majesty might
be the first man that ever received that favour, she

coming out of a country where it was not the fashion."
In his *Letters* there is one to his friend Mr. Bates
(written after the King had reached Portsmouth),
which contains a description of Catherine worth transcribing :

"You may credit her being a very extraordinary
woman," he writes ; "that is, extreamly devout,
extreamly discreet, very fond of her husband, and the
owner of a good understanding. As to her person,
she is exactly shaped, and has lovely hands, excellent
eyes, a good countenance, a pleasing voice, fine haire,
and, in a word, is what an understanding man would
wish a wife. Yet, I fear all this will hardly make
things run in the right channel ; but, if it should, I
suppose our Court will require a new modelling."

Charles was at Portsmouth on May 20th, and on the
following day was married to Catherine, first secretly
in her bedchamber, according to the Roman Catholic
rites (on which she insisted), and then publicly by the
Bishop of London. On his wedding day he wrote
to the Lord Chancellor : "If I have any skill in
visiognomy, which I think I have, she must be as good
a woman as was ever borne." On the 25th he wrote
again : "I cannot easily tell you how happy I think
myselfe ; and I must be the worst man living (which
I hope I am not) if I be not a good husband. I am
confident never two humors were better fitted together than ours are." How he proceeded to prove
himself a good husband will shortly appear. In the
meantime it may be noted that Reresby says that,
though at Portsmouth "everything was gay and

splendid and profusely joyful, it was easy to discern
that the King was not excessively charmed with his
new bride"; and, according to Lord Dartmouth, the
King told old Colonel Legge (i.e. William Legge, Dartmouth's father) that when he first saw the Queen " he
thought they had brought him a bat instead of a woman."

Clarendon, recipient of his King's good resolutions
concerning his behaviour to his wife, has much to say
concerning Charles and Catherine during the period
immediately following their meeting at Portsmouth.
Speaking of the " full presumption " which there was
that the King after his marriage would contain himself within the strict bounds of virtue and conscience,
he continues : " And that His Majesty himself had
that firm resolution, there want not many arguments,
as well from the excellent temper and justice of his
own nature as from the professions he had made with
some solemnity to persons who were believed to have
much credit, and who had not failed to do their duty,
in putting him in mind ' of the infinite obligations he
had to God Almighty, and that he expected another
kind of return from him, in the purity of mind and
integrity of life ' ; of which His Majesty was piously
sensible, albeit there was all possible pains taken by
that company which were admitted to his hours of
pleasure, to divert and corrupt all those impressions
and principles, which his own conscience and reverent
esteem of Providence did suggest to him."

As for the Queen, Clarendon says that she " had
beauty and wit enough to make herself very agreeable "
to Charles, and that " it is very certain that at their

E

first meeting, and for some time after, the King had very good satisfaction in her, and without doubt made very good resolutions within himself and promised himself a happy and innocent life in her company, without any such uxoriousness as might draw the reputation upon him of being governed by his wife." Charles had observed the inconvenient effects of such uxoriousness as this and had protested against it, according to Clarendon; though "they who knew him well did not think him so much superior to such a condescension" himself, had only the Queen been like some of her predecessors on the throne. The writer might have mentioned, and no doubt had in mind, Queen Henrietta Maria, the inconvenient effects of whose influence over her husband he had only too good reason to appreciate.

But Catherine of Braganza was of a very different stamp from that of her mother-in-law. "Bred, according to the mode and discipline of her country, in a monastery, where she had only seen the women who attended her and conversed with the religious who resided there, and without doubt in her inclinations . . . enough disposed to have been one of that number," she brought with her from Portugal a large suite of men and women whom Clarendon considered "the most improper to promote that conformity in the Queen that was necessary for her condition and future happiness that could be chosen : the women for the most part old and ugly and proud, incapable of any conversation with persons of quality and a liberal education." (We are reminded of Evelyn's

description of the Queen's " traine of Portuguese
ladies in their monstrous fardingals or guard-infantas,
their complexions olivader and sufficiently unagree-
able " ; and of Pepys's " Portugall ladys, which are come
to town before the Queen, . . . not handsome, and
their farthingales a strange dress.") These ladies,
whom the English critics found so unpleasing to the
eye, desired to keep the Queen under their own control and to prevent her from learning the language or
adopting the manners and fashions of her new country.
On reaching Portsmouth, Catherine had been met by
some of the ladies of honour assigned to her by Charles,
but had refused to receive them until the King himself came ; " nor then with any grace or the liberty
which belonged to their places and offices." [1] His
Majesty had sent also a wardrobe of English clothes to
Portsmouth, which at first Catherine declined to wear,
preferring the farthingales in which she had arrived.
But, finding that the King was displeased and would
be obeyed, she conformed to his wishes, much to the
disgust of her Portuguese women. They persisted in
dressing in their accustomed mode, regardless of the
offence to English taste.

On May 25th, at once his birthday and the anni-
versary of his Restoration, Charles brought his bride
to Hampton Court, where it was intended to pass the

---

[1] It is only fair to state that the Portuguese side of the case, which
is given by Miss Strickland in *Lives of the Queens of England* Vol. V,
represents Catherine as gracious to the English ladies and quite docile
in the matter of dress. It is difficult to see, however, why Clarendon
should misrepresent the Queen, to whom he was a better friend than
most at the English Court.

greater part of the summer. And here he planned to introduce to Catherine the lady who had illicitly occupied her place before her arrival in England. He had doubtless promised Lady Castlemaine to do so as early as the matter could be arranged. But the Countess's bodily condition prevented the introduction from taking place at once. At some time in the first half of June she gave birth to her eldest son Charles " Palmer," afterwards called Fitzroy. She had had the assurance, according to what Lady Sandwich told Pepys in May, to talk of going to Hampton Court for the birth. But this, perhaps, was more than even Charles II could tolerate at the time of his marriage, and the event accordingly took place at Lord Castlemaine's house in King Street.

If the day of the little Charles's birth is not known, the register of St. Margaret's, Westminster, gives the date of his christening. Here we read : " 1662 June 18 Charles Palmer Ld Limbricke, s. to ye right honor^{ble} Roger Earl of Castlemaine by Barbara." This entry is a monument to the last act but one in the married life of Lord and Lady Castlemaine. The Earl some time before the child's birth became a Roman Catholic, and now insisted upon his being baptized by a priest—which is curious, as he can have been under no impression that Charles was his son. He got his way, but at the cost of a falling out with his wife. Of this " Mrs. Sarah " told Pepys next month ; and, living next door to the Castlemaines, she was doubtless fully informed of all that went on there. Lady Castlemaine " had it again christened by a minister ;

the King, and Lord of Oxford, and Duchesse of
Suffolk, being witnesses; and christened with a proviso
that it had not already been christened." Pepys here
writes Duchess for Countess, the godmother being
Barbara, Countess of Suffolk, eldest daughter of Sir
Edward Villiers, and therefore Lady Castlemaine's
aunt. Otherwise his information was right.

The King had practically made public acknowledgment of his fatherhood of the so-called Charles
Palmer. He now proceeded to carry out his promise
of presenting the mother to his wife. We cannot do
better than give Clarendon's celebrated account of
the scene which took place, noting that the date given
—within a day or two after Her Majesty's being
at Hampton Court—cannot be correct. The presentation must have taken place after Lady Castlemaine
had arisen from bed, and it is not likely to have preceded the christening.

"When the Queen came to Hampton-court," says
Clarendon, " she brought with her a formed resolution,
that she would never suffer the lady who was so much
spoken of to be in her presence : and afterwards to
those she would trust she said, ' her mother had en-
joined her so to do.' On the other hand, the King
thought that he had so well prepared her to give her a
civil reception, that within a day or two after Her
Majesty's being there, himself led her into her chamber, and presented her to the Queen, who received her
with the same grace as she had done the rest ; there
being many lords and other ladies at the same time
there. But whether Her Majesty in the instant knew

who she was, or upon recollection found it afterwards, she was no sooner sat in her chair, but her colour changed, and tears gushed out of her eyes, and her nose bled, and she fainted ; so that she was forthwith removed into another room, and all the company retired out of that where she was before. And this falling out so notoriously when so many persons were present, the King looked upon it with wonderful indignation, and as an earnest of defiance for the decision of the supremacy and who should govern, upon which point he was the most jealous and the most resolute of any man ; and the answer he received from the Queen, which kept up the obstinacy, displeased him more."

One of the principal sufferers from this Royal quarrel was the Portuguese Ambassador, Dom Francisco de Mello de Torres, who had done so much to promote the match between them and had been made a marquis as a reward. Already there had been some difficulty through the inability of Portugal to pay more than half the portion promised with Catherine. Now Charles was indignant with him " for having said so much in Portugal to provoke the Queen, and not instructing her enough to make her unconcerned in what had been before her time, and in which she could not reasonably be concerned " ; and Catherine, who was god-daughter to de Mello, still more for " the character he had given of the King, of his virtue and good nature." The poor Ambassador fell ill and nearly died before he was forgiven for the blunders which he had made under the impression that he was acting for the best.

*From a photograph by W. A. Mansell & Co., after a painting
in the National Portrait Gallery by Jacob Huysmans*

CATHERINE OF BRAGANZA, QUEEN OF CHARLES II

After the scene described above, Charles, according to the Chancellor's account, " forebore Her Majesty's company, and sought ease and refreshment in that jolly company to which in the evenings he grew every day more indulgent, and in which there were some who desired rather to inflame than to pacify his discontent. And they found an expedient to vindicate his royal jurisdiction, and to make it manifest to the world that he would not be governed." This expedient was to magnify the temper and constitution of his grandfather ! His Majesty King James I, they pointed out, " when he was enamoured, and found a return answerable to his merit, did not dissemble his passion, nor suffered it to be matter of reproach to the persons whom he loved ; but made all others pay them that respect which he thought them worthy of : brought them to the court, and obliged his own wife the Queen to treat them with grace and favour ; gave them the highest titles of honour, to draw reverence and application to them from all the court and all the kingdom ; raised the children he had by them to the reputation, state, and degree of princes of the blood, and conferred fortunes and offices upon them accordingly." They reproached the present King, who had the same passions as his grandfather, for lacking " the gratitude and noble inclination to make returns proportionable to the obligations he received," and said : " That he had, by the charms of his person and his professions, prevailed upon the affections and heart of a young and beautiful lady of a noble extraction, whose father had lost his life in the service of the crown. That she had provoked the jealousy and rage of her husband to that degree, that he had separated himself from her : and now the Queen's indignation had made the matter so notorious to the world, that the disconsolate lady had no place of retreat left, but must be made an object of infamy and contempt to all her sex, and to the whole world."

This touching picture of the wronged lady (which, by the way, seems premature, as Lord and Lady Castlemaine did not definitely separate until July 14th, if Pepys is correct) did its part in spurring Charles on to bestow a fresh honour upon her. He " resolved, for the vindication of her honour and innocence, that she should be admitted of the bedchamber of the Queen, as the only means to convince the world that all aspersions upon her had been without ground. The King used all the ways he could, by treating the Queen with all caresses, to dispose her to gratify him in this particular, as a matter in which his honour was concerned and engaged ; and protested unto her, which at that time he did intend to observe, ' that he had not the least familiarity with her since Her Majesty's arrival, nor would ever after be guilty of it again, but would live always with Her Majesty in all fidelity for conscience sake.' The Queen, who was naturally more transported with choler than her countenance declared her to be, had not the temper to entertain him with those discourses which the vivacity of her wit could very plentifully have suggested to her ; but broke out into a torrent of rage, which increased the former prejudice, confirmed the King in the resolution he had

taken, gave ill people more credit to mention her dis-
respectfully, and more increased his aversion from her
company, and, which was worse, his delight in those
who meant that he should neither love his wife or his
business, or anything but their conversation."

When did Charles first resolve to have Lady Castlemaine appointed to the Queen's Bedchamber ? Clarendon, we see, makes him treat the appointment as a
kind of reparation for the scorn of the world, which
she had incurred through her connection with him.
Did he make up his mind after the Hampton Court
scene, or had she herself suggested the idea to him
before Catherine's arrival in England ? Among the
State Papers of the year 1662 there is preserved a
warrant, dated April 2nd, for the Countess of Suffolk
to be " Groomess of the Stole," First Lady of the
Bedchamber, Mistress of the Robes, and Keeper of
the Privy Purse to the Queen when her Household
should be established ; and we read in a letter from
Lord Sandwich to Clarendon on May 15th of
Catherine's reception of " my Lady Suffolke and the
ladies." But we find no warrant appointing sub-
ordinate Ladies of the Bedchamber until as late as
June 1663.

It looks as if Charles, having already decided on
Lady Castlemaine's inclusion in the Queen's Household, but anticipating trouble over it, had kept back
the appointment of all the ladies (except the indispensable Countess of Suffolk) until he could coerce the
Queen into accepting the whole suite.

Now, met by Catherine's point-blank refusal to

accept the Countess of Castlemaine, Charles called upon his Chancellor to take a hand in the affair. It would have been better for Clarendon had he declined the commission. But could he do so except by resigning his office and retiring into private life, to expose himself to the assaults of his foes? The King was insistent that he should undertake the task, and when Charles set his mind to get a thing done it was hardly possible to contradict him. " You and I know what a spark he is at going through with anything," wrote Anne, Countess of Sunderland, about Charles on a later occasion to her friend Henry Sidney.

Clarendon is at great pains to prove his friendly intention toward the Queen in going to her from the King and to report his plain speaking in the presence of His Majesty before he set out on his errand. He represents himself as not having heard before this " of the honour the King had done that lady "—the lady's name is, as always, unmentioned—" nor of the purpose he had to make her of his wife's bedchamber." With regard to the latter resolve, he says that he spoke to Charles about " the hard-heartedness and cruelty in laying such a command upon the Queen, which flesh and blood could not comply with." He reminded him how he himself had censured " the like excess which a neighbour King had lately used, in making his mistress live in the court, and in the presence of the Queen," which Charles had declared a piece of ill-nature that he could never be guilty of. In his righteous indignation at the French King's conduct Charles, it appears, had said that, if ever he should be guilty of having a mistress after he had a wife (which he hoped he never should be), she should never come where his wife was ; for he would never add that to the vexation of which she would have enough without it ! After some truly English reflections upon the lower state of morality in France, the Chancellor warned his master that there was no surer way to lose the affections of his people than by indulging himself, after his marriage, in that excess which had already lost him some ground. He concluded by asking His Majesty's pardon for speaking so plainly and beseeching him " to remember the wonderful things which God had done for him, and for which he expected other returns than he had yet received."

Few kings have been better able to bear a rating with good humour than Charles II. Clarendon says now : " The King heard him with patience enough, yet with those little interruptions which were natural to him, especially to that part where he had levelled the mistresses of kings and princes with other lewd women, at which he expressed some indignation, being an argument often debated before him by those who would have them looked upon above any other men's wives. He did not appear displeased with the liberty he had taken, but said he knew it proceeded from the affection he had for him ; and then proceeded upon the several parts of what he had said, more volubly than he used to do, as upon points in which he was conversant and had heard well debated."

The most interesting part of the King's argument, however, was the impassioned appeal with which he

concluded on behalf of his favourite ; which, indeed,
is so curious that no apology need be offered for
quoting it in full from the pages of Clarendon.
Charles said : " That he had undone this lady, and
ruined her reputation, which had been fair and un-
tainted till her friendship for him ; and that he was
obliged in conscience and honour to repair her to the
utmost of his power. That he would always avow to
have a great friendship for her, which he owed as well
to the memory of her father as to her own person ;
and that he would look upon it as the highest disrespect
to him in anybody who should treat her otherwise than
was due to her own birth and the dignity to which
he had raised her. That he liked her company and
conversation, from which he would not be restrained,
because he knew there was and should be all innocence
in it : and that his wife should never have cause to
complain that he brake his vows to her, if she would
live towards him as a good wife ought to do, in
rendering herself grateful and acceptable to him, which
it was in her power to do ; but if she would continue
uneasy to him, he could not answer for himself that
he should not endeavour to seek content in other company. That he had proceeded so far in the business
that concerned the lady, and was so deeply engaged
in it, that she would not only be exposed to all imaginable contempt, if it succeeded not ; but his own
honour would suffer so much that he should become
ridiculous to the world and be thought too in pupilage
under a governor ; and therefore he would expect and
exact a conformity from his wife herein, which should

be the only hard thing he would ever require from
her, and which she herself might make very easy, for
the lady would behave herself with all possible duty
and humility unto her, which if she should fail to do
in the least degree, she should never see the King's
face again : and that he would never be engaged to
put any other servant about her, without first con-
sulting with her and receiving her consent and appro-
bation. Upon the whole," he said, " he would never
recede from any part of the resolution he had taken
and expressed to him : and therefore he required him
to use all those arguments to the Queen which were
necessary to induce her to a full compliance with what
the King desired."

Clarendon's account of the King's obstinate determination to gain his end is supplemented by a letter
which survives in the British Museum from Charles
to his Chancellor, which, though undated, obviously
belongs to this period and may have been written
immediately after the interview above described. It
runs as follows :

" I forgott, when you weare heere last, to desire you
to give Brodericke[1] good councell, not to meddle any
more with what concerns my Lady Castlemaine, and
to lett him have a care how he is the authorre of any
scandalous reports ; for if I find him guilty of any
such thing, I will make him repent it to the last
moment of his life. And now I am entered on this
matter, I think it very necessary to give you a little

---

[1] "Brodericke" is Sir Alan Broderick, appointed about this time
Provost-Marshal of Munster.

good councell in it, least you may think that, by
making a further stirr in the businesse, you may
deverte me from my resolution, which all the world
shall never do : and I wish I may be unhappy in this
world and the world to come, if I faile in the least
degree what I have resolved ; which is, of making my
Lady Castlemaine of my wives bedchamber : and
whosoever I find use any endeavour to hinder this
resolution of myne (except it be only to myselfe), I
will be his enemy to the last moment of my life. You
know how true a friend I have been to you. If you
will oblige me eternally, make this businesse as easy
as you can, of what opinion soever you are of ; for I
am resolved to go through with this matter, lett what
will come of it ; which againe I solemnly sweare before
Almighty God. Therefore, if you desire to have the
continuance of my friendship, meddle no more with
this businesse, except it be to beare down all false
scandalous reports, and to facilitate what I am sure
my honour is so much concerned in : and whosoever
I finde to be my Lady Castlemaines enimy in this
matter, I do promise, upon my word, to be his enimy
as long as I live. You may show this letter to my
Ld. Lnt.[1]; and if you have both a minde to oblige me,
carry yourselves like friends to me in this matter.

" CHARLES R."

To execute his commission from the King, it was
necessary for Clarendon to have two interviews with
the Queen. When he first approached her, before he
could do more than express his regrets about the royal

---

[1] The Lord-Lieutenant of Ireland, namely, the Duke of Ormonde,
who went to take up his post at the beginning of July 1662. Evelyn
visited London to take leave of him and the Duchess on July 8th.

misunderstanding, Catherine gave way to so much
passion and such a torrent of tears that he retired,
telling her he would wait upon her in a fitter season.
Next day he made a second attempt, which promised
well at the start. Clarendon reports the dialogue with
more humour than usually is to be found in his pages.
When he had explained that if he said to her what
was fit for her to hear rather than what pleased her,
she must take it as evidence of his devotion to her, the
Queen assured him he should never be more welcome
to her than when he told her of her faults. " To
which he replied that it was the province that he was
accused of usurping with reference to all his friends."
And so his lecture began. " He told her that he
doubted she was little beholden to her education, that
had given her no better information of the follies and
iniquities of mankind, of which he presumed the
climate from whence she came could have given more
instances than this cold region would afford "—though
at that time, adds Clarendon, it was indeed very hot
in England !

Had Her Majesty been fairly dealt with in the matter
of education, continued the Chancellor, she would not
now think her condition so insupportable. He could
not comprehend the ground of her complaint. With
" some blushing and confusion and some tears,"
Catherine explained that she did not think she should
have found the King engaged in his affections to
another lady. Did she then expect, asked Clarendon,
to find the King, at his age, of so innocent a constitution as to be reserved for her whom he had never

seen ? And did she believe that when it should please
God to send a queen to Portugal she would find that
court so full of chaste affections ? " Upon which Her
Majesty smiled, and spake pleasantly enough, but as
if she thought it did not concern her case, and as if
the King's affection had not wandered, but remained
fixed."

The Chancellor appeared to be gaining his end.
Assuring Catherine that, of whatever excesses His
Majesty had been guilty in the past, he was now
dedicating himself entirely and without reserve to
her, and that her good fortune was in her own power,
he persuaded her to express her gratitude toward the
King, her desire to be pardoned for any passion or
peevishness in the past, and her assurance of obedience
in the future.

With what feelings Clarendon now approached the
second part of his task, he does not tell us. Having
brought the Queen to so good a temper, he lost no
time in urging her to show her resignation to whatsoever His Majesty should desire of her. He then " in-
sinuated what would be acceptable with reference to
the lady." No sooner had he done this than the
storm burst. Catherine exhibited " all the rage and
fury of yesterday, with fewer tears, the fire appearing
in her eyes where the water was." Rather than submit to the insult of having Lady Castlemaine attached
to her Bedchamber, she declared, she would get on
board any little boat and go to Lisbon. Clarendon
interrupted her with the reminder that she had not
the disposal of her own person and with a warning not

to speak any more about Portugal, since there were
plenty who wished her there. He then left her with
the doubtless admirable advice, if she denied anything to the King, " to deny in such a manner as
should look rather like a deferring than an utter
refusal."

It is true that the attitude assumed by the Chancellor
toward Catherine, somewhat resembling that of master
toward school-child, would have been more appro-
priate had he been counselling her to the practice of
virtue rather than the overlooking of vice. Yet we
can see from his account of the whole affair that he
was really much more sympathetic toward the Queen
than he allowed himself to seem in his speech ; and
he appears to have believed Charles's promises of
amendment of life, if only his debt to Lady Castlemaine could first be paid by giving her a suitable post
at Court. In reporting to Charles the result of his
labours he asked him not to press the Queen in the
matter for a day or two, but to let him first have
another interview with her, from which he hoped to
get better satisfaction.

The King, however, had other advisers, who were
anxious to see him insist on immediate submission.
Playing upon his fear of being governed, they soon
counteracted the Chancellor's influence, and in consequence the crisis was precipitated that very night at
Hampton Court; and of course the matter was soon
known to all there. The royal couple began with
mutual reproaches, Charles alleging stubbornness and
want of duty ; Catherine tyranny and want of affec-

F

tion. Then came threats, on Charles's part, of conduct which, according to Clarendon, he never meant
to put into execution ; on Catherine's, of a return to
Portugal. The Queen had disregarded the Chancellor's advice about the mention of her country, and
was at once put in a position to appreciate her folly.
Charles told her that she would do well first to know
how her mother would receive her ; in order to let
her discover which he would send home all her Portuguese servants, to whose counsels he imputed her
perverseness.

After this outburst, the relations between King
and Queen were very strained during the remainder
of their stay at Hampton Court. The Queen sat
weeping in her chamber—that chamber which Evelyn
visited on June 9th of this summer and found so
magnificently furnished, with its state bed costing
£8000, its toilet-set of beaten and massive gold, and
the Indian cabinets brought by Catherine herself
from Portugal, such as had never before been seen in
England. Or, if she were not weeping, she was indulging in violent talk over her wrongs. The King
spent all his nights in merriment with the company
which he preferred, and only came to the Queen's
chamber in the morning ; " for," says Clarendon,
" he never slept in any other place." This concession
to his wife, however, seems to have had little effect.
The courtiers noticed that King and Queen never
spoke and hardly looked at one another. It is rather
curious to read Pepys's " Observations " set down in
his *Diary* at the end of June 1662. " This I take to

be as bad a juncture as ever I observed," he says. " The King and his new Queen minding their pleasures at Hampton Court. All people discontented," etc.

Clearly Pepys was for the moment out of touch with Court affairs, for otherwise he could not have written of Catherine, at least, " minding her pleasures at Hampton Court." A few days after he had penned his Observations he was given some further insight into affairs at Hampton Court, since on July 6th Lady Sandwich told him, " with much trouble, that my Lady Castlemaine is still as great with the King, and that the King comes as often to her as ever he did." " At which, God forgive me," adds the diarist, " I am well pleased." The fears which he expresses earlier of the admired one's nose being put " out of joynt " are allayed, and he appears not to give a thought to the Queen.

Charles determined to make another effort to bend Catherine to his will with the aid of the Chancellor, and a few days after the quarrel sent for him and informed him—though Clarendon could hardly be in any doubt upon the point—of the unalterableness of his resolution. In reply to his minister's remonstrances on the anger and precipitation with which he had acted, he allowed that he might have done better had he listened to advice, but said that, " besides the uneasiness and pain within himself, the thing was more spoken of in all places and more to his disadvantage, whilst it was in this suspense, than it would be when it was once executed, which would put a final end to all debates, and all would be forgotten."

So the Chancellor set off once again on his errand to Her Majesty, and engaged with her in an argument which he reports very fully. But Catherine remained obdurate. Beginning with tears, as she acknowledged her excessive passion at the former interviews, and then listening with an incredulous smile to the Chancellor's protestations of the King's sincerity of purpose with regard to his future conduct, she finally declared that " the King might do what he pleased, but she would not consent to it." Her face, as she said this, showed Clarendon that she both hoped and believed that her obstinacy would in the end prevail over the King's importunity. Accordingly he left her, proceeded to Charles with his account of his ill success, and, after expressing his opinion that both parties were very much to blame and that " the most excusable would be the one who yielded first," begged to be excused from further employment in the affair. It was indeed an ill day for him when he consented to take any part in it whatever. Not only did his reputation suffer thereby at the hands of his critics, but his lack of success with the Queen caused a coolness toward him on the part of Charles and certainly no kindlier feeling on the part of Lady Castlemaine.

When Clarendon retired from the ungrateful business, the King promptly put into execution his threat against the Queen's Portuguese suite. As Charles I, but in very different circumstances, had driven out Henrietta Maria's French priests and women, so now his son named a day for Catherine's Portuguese to leave England ; and he insisted on his orders being carried out, only relenting so far as to allow her to retain the invalid Countess of Penalva, sister of the Ambassador Francisco de Mello, who had been her companion from a child, a few priests, and some inferior servants. Moreover, he avoided meeting her as much as he could, refused to speak to her when they did meet, and spent his time with those who, in Clarendon's words, " made it their business to laugh at all the world and were as bold with God Almighty as with any of his creatures."

Apart from his desire to be as soon as possible governor in his own home, Charles seems to have had one reason for hastening Catherine's acquiescence in his demand which is not directly mentioned in any of the contemporary accounts of the affair. The Queen-Dowager, Henrietta Maria, was expected from France on a visit to congratulate her son and her new daughter-in-law on their marriage. Charles must have been anxious to bring about a state of peace in his household before his mother's arrival. He took the step of bringing Lady Castlemaine into Catherine's presence a second time, without waiting for her consent to the Bedchamber appointment.

This we learn through a letter from Clarendon to Ormonde on July 17th. " The Kinge is perfectly recovered of his indisposiċons in which you left him," says the Chancellor. " I wish he were as free from all other. I have had, since I saw you, 3 or 4 full long conferences, with much better temper than before. I have likewise twice spoken at large with the Queene. The Lady hath beene at courte, and kissed her hande, and returned that night. I cannot tell you ther was no discomposure. . . ."

Now we know that, four days before this letter was written, a great change had taken place in Lady Castlemaine's life. She had left her husband's house in King Street, and gone to the home of her uncle, Colonel Sir Edward Villiers, knight-marshal of the royal household, who lived at Richmond Palace. Pepys gives July 15th as the date on which " my Lady Castlemaine (being quite fallen out with her husband) did go away from him with her plate, jewels, and other best things." To confirm this date of the separation, there is in existence a bond, dated July 16th, 1662, which the Earl obtained from two of his wife's uncles, the Lords Suffolk and Grandison, binding them in the sum of ten thousand pounds to indemnify him " from all and every manner of debts, contracts, sum and sums of money now due, or that shall hereafter grow due, from any contract or bargain made by the Right Honourable Barbara, Countess of Castlemaine, or by any person or persons authorised by her."

In this move of the lady to Richmond Pepys sees a design to get out of town that the King might come at her the better. " But strange it is," he comments, " how for her beauty I am willing to construe all this to the best and to pity her wherein it is to her hurt, though I know well enough she is "—not what she should be. On the 26th of the same month Mrs. Sarah gives Pepys some further information about the falling out of my Lord and my Lady, and how the latter had taken away from King Street " so much as every

dish and cloth and servant, except the porter." Pepys
continues : " He is gone discontented into France,
they say, to enter a monastery ; and now she is coming
back again to her house in King Street. But I hear
that the Queen did prick her out of the list presented
her by the King; desiring that she might have that
favour done her, or that he would send her from
whence she came ; and that the King was angry and
the Queen discontented a whole day and night upon
it ; but that the King hath promised to have nothing
to do with her hereafter. But I cannot believe that
the King can fling her off so, he loving her too well."

If Castlemaine went to France at all in July, it
must have been on a very brief visit, for he was in
London again before the end of August. But the
break with his faithless wife was permanent, nevertheless. They lived together no more after the day of
her departure for Richmond. The husband effaced
himself, as soon as he was allowed, from the scene of
his disgrace.[1] It was not long before, as Boyer expresses it, " the misfortunes of his bed put him into
a vein of travelling," which continued with but occasional interruptions until late in the reign of Charles II.
As for the wife, she carried all before her. After he
had for the second time forced her presence on the
Queen, Charles seems to have felt that the victory
was won.

We read in Clarendon that " the lady came to the
Court, was lodged there, was every day in the Queen's
presence, and the King in continual conference with

[1] See below, p. 82.

her; while the Queen sat untaken notice of: and if
Her Majesty rose at the indignity and retired into her
chamber, it may be one or two attended her; but
all the company remained in the room she left, and
too often said those things aloud which nobody ought
to have whispered." Charles himself threw off the
troubled looks which he had worn at the beginning of
the quarrel and "appeared every day more gay and
pleasant, without any clouds in his face, and full of
good humour." This only increased poor Catherine's
humiliation. She saw mirth around her everywhere,
except in her own immediate neighbourhood, and
"the lady" being treated with more respect than
herself, even by her own personal servants, who found
her less able to do anything for them than the favourite.
As for the King, all that she had of his company each
day was "those few hours which remained of the
preceding night and which were too little for sleep."

The Queen-Dowager had, in the meantime, arrived
at Hampton Court. On July 19th the King went
down the Thames in his barge, on his way to the
Downs, whither the Duke of York had already gone,
to meet her. "Methought," observes Pepys, "it
lessened my esteem of a king, that he should not be
able to command the rain," the weather just now
being so wet that the diarist, who was having the top
of his house at the Navy Office reconstructed, was
sadly inconvenienced by the superabundance of water.
The King's impotence where the weather was concerned was to be further manifested; for the royal
yacht and its escorts were very roughly treated by

a storm, and Henrietta Maria's crossing was so delayed
that it was not until the 28th that she reached Green-
wich and awaited at the Palace there the first call from
Charles and his bride.   By the end of the month the
whole Court was gathered together again at Hampton
Court preparatory to the return to Whitehall for the
winter.

What Henrietta Maria thought of the state of
affairs between her son and her daughter-in-law, we
do not hear.   But, as we are not told so, we may assume
that she did not intervene on Catherine's behalf.   The
young Queen—her twenty-fourth birthday had yet
to come—was left entirely without any influential
supporter in a strange land, and it speaks highly for
her courage and determination that she could hold
out so long in the unequal struggle.

The move from Hampton Court to Whitehall was
now made.   Fortunately for posterity, the spectacle-
loving Pepys was an eye-witness of the scene on
August 23rd, in which Lady Castlemaine played a
notable part—at least in his admiring eyes.   He and
his friend Mr. Creed vainly tried to get a boat to
convey them from Upper Thames Street to Whitehall,
the boatmen refusing to be tempted by an offer of
eight shillings on such an occasion.

" So we fairly walked it to Whitehall," he writes,
" and through my Lord's lodgings we got into Whitehall garden, and so to the Bowling-green, and up to
the top of the new Banqueting House there, over the
Thames, which was a most pleasant place as any I
could have got. . . . Anon come the King and Queen

in a barge under a canopy with 10,000 barges and boats, I think, for we could see no water for them, nor discern the King nor Queen. And so they landed at Whitehall Bridge, and the great guns on the other side went off. But that which pleased me best was that my Lady Castlemaine stood over against us upon a piece of Whitehall, where I glutted myself with looking on her. But methought it was strange to see her Lord and her upon the same place walking up and down without taking notice one of another, only at first entry he put off his hat, and she made him a very civil salute, but afterwards took no notice one of another; but both of them now and then would take their child, which the nurse held in her armes, and dandle it. One thing more; there happened a scaffold below to fall, and we feared some hurt, but there was none but she of all the great ladies only run down among the common rabble to see what hurt was done, and did take care of a child that received some little hurt, which methought was so noble. Anon came one there booted and spurred that she talked long with. And by and by, she being in her hair, she put on his hat, which was but an ordinary one, to keep the wind off. But methinks it became her mightily, as everything else do. The show being over, I went away, not weary with looking at her."

This account is interesting in many ways, and not least for its record of an amiable trait in Lady Castlemaine's character which her other critics nowhere discover. We can hardly accuse Pepys of inventing it, however, in spite of his partiality for her whom it so delighted him to have Lady Sandwich call " your lady."

The Court had hardly settled down at Whitehall before the victory of the mistress over the Queen was the talk of everyone. In the Bodleian Library at Oxford there is preserved an instructive letter from Clarendon to Ormonde, dated September 9th, 1662, part of which is as follows : " All things are bad with reference to the Lady ; but I think not so bad as you heare. Every body takes her to be of the bedchamber ; for she is always there, and goes abrode in the coach. But the Queene tells me that the King promised her, on condition she would use her as she doth others, that she should never live in Court : yet lodgings, I hear, she hath. I heare of no back staires."

In spite of the fact, however, that everybody took her to be of the Bedchamber, Lady Castlemaine was not definitely appointed until nine months later. Among the Domestic State Papers of Charles II there is a warrant dated June 1st, 1663, to admit " Lady Chesterfield, the Countess of Bath, the Duchess of Buckingham, Countess Marishal, and of Countess Castlemaine " as Ladies of the Bedchamber to the Queen. The reason for the delay in the issue of the warrant, after Catherine's surrender, we do not know ; but that she had really given way is proved by the scene at Somerset House mentioned at the beginning of the next chapter.

Clarendon—having told how the Queen " at last, when it was least expected or suspected, on a sudden let herself fall first to conversation and then to familiarity, and even in the same instant to a confidence with the lady ; was merry with her in public, talked kindly of her, and in private used nobody more friendly "—sees her injured in the general esteem by her condescension, and says that " this sudden downfall and total abandoning her own greatness, this low demeanour and even application to a person she had justly abhorred and worthily contemned, made all men conclude that it was a hard matter to know her and consequently to serve her."

Poor Catherine ! What chance had she of pleasing anyone at such a Court as that of her husband ? And what wonder can there be that a deterioration in her character followed her early years in England. She arrived with piety and modesty her most marked traits. She became flighty (not in morals, be it said, but in general deportment), fond of excitement, and avaricious. Not having the makings of a saint, she refrained from becoming a sinner, but failed, in attempting to steer a middle course, to prove herself an agreeable woman.

As for the effect of his victory on the King, Clarendon sees the esteem which he had in his heart for Catherine growing much less after her surrender, while " he congratulated his own ill-natured perseverance, by which he had discovered how he was to behave himself hereafter, and what remedies he was to apply to all future indispositions, nor had he ever after the same value of her wit, judgment, and understanding, which he had formerly."

From an engraving by W. Sherwin

BARBARA VILLIERS, COUNTESS OF CASTLEMAINE
AND DUCHESS OF CLEVELAND

CHAPTER IV

THE CASTLEMAINE ASCENDANCY

O N Sunday, September 7th, 1662, Samuel Pepys,
being alone in town—his too trustful wife having
gone on a visit to the country during the presence of
the workmen in their house—met " Mr. Pierce the
chyrurgeon," and was by him taken to Somerset House,
the palace assigned to the Queen-Mother, and recently
altered by her at a great cost. Here, in Henrietta
Maria's presence-chamber, he saw both her and, for
the first time, Queen Catherine, of whom he says :
" Though she be not very charming, yet she hath a
good, modest, and innocent look, which is pleasing."
We will let Pepys describe the rest of the company :

" Here I also saw Madam Castlemaine, and, which
pleased me most, Mr. Crofts, the King's bastard, a
most pretty spark of about 15 years old,[1] who, I per-
ceive, do hang much upon my Lady Castlemaine, and
is always with her ; and, I hear, the Queens both of
them are mighty kind to him. By and by in comes
the King, and anon the Duke and his Duchess ; so
that, they being all together, was such a sight as I
never could almost have happened to see with so much

---

[1] He was in reality only thirteen and a half, being born on April
9th, 1649.

ease and leisure. They staid till it was dark, and then went away ; the King and his Queen, and my Lady Castlemaine, in one coach and the rest in other coaches. Here were great store of great ladies, but very few handsome."

From this scene (to which Pepys gets admittance with what now seems such astonishing ease) it is clear how far the young Queen had condescended to tolerate the presence of Lady Castlemaine, whom indeed we see "abrode in the coach" precisely as described by Clarendon to Ormonde. To make the situation the more remarkable, there is the most pretty spark, Mr. Crofts, who, of course, is none other than James, afterwards Duke of Monmouth, the King's son by Lucy Walter. The eldest of Charles's illegitimate children (with the exception of the rather mysterious James de la Cloche, who after becoming a Jesuit vanished from authenticated history about the end of the year 1668), the future Duke took his temporary surname from the " Mr. Croftes, since created Lord Croftes," whom Evelyn records having met on his visit to the exiled Court in France in 1649. Appointed by Charles as guardian to the nine-year-old boy in 1658, William Crofts also lent him a name which he continued to bear until on his marriage to his heiress bride he was legally furnished with that of Scott.

Henrietta Maria's object in taking up the boy is not clear, except that he was an attractive child and that she wished to please her son. We have Clarendon's testimony that she frequently had him brought to her, while in France, and " used him with much grace."

In taking him with her to England in 1662 she was acting at the King's request. Charles was certainly making bold demands upon his wife's complacency. Having obliged her to take one of his mistresses as a lady in attendance upon her, he now introduced to her acquaintance his natural son by another mistress. He himself received the child " with extraordinary fondness," his Chancellor writes, " and was willing that everybody should believe him to be his son, though he did not yet make any declaration that he looked upon him as such, otherwise than by his kindness and familiarity towards him." This was sufficient, however, within a very short space of time to arouse the suspicions of the Duke of York, between whom and the King there was rumoured a difference before the end of this year.

Pepys, a fortnight after the Somerset House reception, bears witness again to the intimacy now evidently existing between Lady Castlemaine and the Queen; for, being in the Park on Sunday morning, he has the fortune to see Catherine going by coach to her chapel at St. James's, ready the first time that day for the Roman Catholic services for which her marriage treaty stipulated. The inquisitive Pepys " crowded after her " and succeeded in getting close to " the room where her closet is "—Her Majesty's private pew. He admired much the fine altar, the priests with their fine copes, and many other very fine things. As for the music, it might be good, he allowed, but it did not appear so to him. He noticed that the Queen was very devout. " But what pleased me best was to see my dear Lady Castlemaine, who, tho' a Protestant, did wait upon the Queen to chapel."

In spite of what Clarendon wrote early in September to Ormonde about the mistress's lodgings, she evidently continued to make use of her husband's King Street house at the beginning of October. For on the 6th of that month we find her giving a ball there, at which the King is present. Nor has Lord Castlemaine yet left England a month later, " being still in town, and sometimes seeing of her, though never to eat or lie together." It seems, therefore, as if Charles continued at this time to make a feeble outward show of keeping his promise to the Queen that the lady should never live at Court, if she would only use her as she did others. As we shall see, the Countess was not lodged at Whitehall, to public knowledge, until April, 1663.

But, wherever she was residing for the moment, Barbara's influence was all-powerful, extending even to the choice of the King's ministers. On October 17th Mr. Creed tells Pepys how at Court " the young men get uppermost and the old serious lords are out of favour." The place of Sir Edward Nicholas, Secretary of State, is given to Sir Henry Bennet, formerly private secretary to the Duke of York and later to be first Baron, and then Earl of, Arlington ; and the Privy Purse to Sir Charles Berkeley, " a most vicious person."[1] These two and Lady Castlemaine

---

[1] So says Pepys, and it was the common opinion of the day. But the King, Clarendon tells us, loved him "every day with more passion, for what reason no man knew nor could imagine." King Charles

between them have the King's ear. The two, indeed, we hear from Clarendon, " were most devoted to the lady, and much depended upon her interest, and consequently were ready to do anything that would be grateful to her." While they made a point of keeping on good terms with the Chancellor, he could not but feel that his influence over the King declined with their appointment.

In fact, a week later " Mr. Pierce the chyrurgeon " draws for Pepys a very gloomy picture of how things are going at Court. Pierce has had a promise of being made surgeon to the Queen, but is in doubt whether to take the post, since the King shows no countenance to any that belong to her. Her private physician has told Pierce that " the Queen do know how the King orders things, and how he carries himself to my Lady Castlemaine and others, as well as anybody; but though she hath spirit enough, yet seeing that she do no good by taking notice of it, for the present she forbears it in policy; of which I am very glad," adds Pepys. He notices the public discontent at the general state of affairs, " what with the sale of Dunkirk "—concluded this year at the price of five hundred thousand pistoles—" and my Lady Castlemaine and her faction at Court ; though I know not what they would have more than to debauch the King, whom God preserve from it !" But " the

wrote to his sister Henrietta in 1665 on receiving the news of the battle of Southwold Bay, at which Berkeley, then Earl of Falmouth, was killed : " I have had as great a losse as 'tis possible in a good frinde, poore C. Barckley." The *Gramont Memoirs*, strange to say, are extremely kind to Berkeley's character.

G

King is very kind to the Queen," we are told on
December 15th, Dr. Clerke on this occasion being
Pepys's informant.

It was public property, at Court at least, that the
favourite was expecting another child by His Majesty,
though Lord Castlemaine, being still in town, could
be represented as the father.   Charles kept him in
England for this very reason, in spite of his desire to
set out on his travels.

" Strange how the King is bewitched to this pretty
Castlemaine ! " exclaims Pepys, as he records another
piece of Court gossip.   Very oddly, Carte in his *Life
of the Duke of Ormonde* tells a story how Queen
Catherine actually believed that the lady had bewitched the King.   Carte is speaking of Peter Talbot
the Jesuit, who, after the royal marriage, was one of
the priests who officiated in the Queen's household.

"His busy nature did not suffer him to continue long
in that post ;   he was always telling the Queen some
story or other, and the uneasiness which she suffered
in October 1662, upon Lady Castlemaine's being put
about her, was imputed in a good measure to his in-
sinuations.   There is a Spanish word frequently used
by lovers in that country to their mistresses, and which
likewise signifies an enchantress.   Talbot had un-
happily made use of this expression in his discourse ;
and the good Queen, not being used to the language of
lovers, nor comprehending the true meaning of the
word, presently imagined the Countess of Castlemaine
to be a real sorceress.   In consequence of this notion,
and in great tenderness to the King's person, she

cautioned him against the lady, and expressed her
fears in such a manner that he was puzzled a good
while to know her meaning. But finding her very
serious in the matter, he inquired how she came to
entertain so wrong a notion; she ascribed it to Peter
Talbot, who being now involved with the Duke of
Bucks in contriving to make the mischief which at that
time distracted the Court, was ordered to depart the
kingdom."

On New Year's Eve our most useful of informants
has the happiness of seeing the Royal Ball at Whitehall.
He is taken by Mr. Povy into the room where the ball
is to be, crammed with fine ladies. "By and by comes
the King and Queen, the Duke and Duchess, and all
the great ones: and after seating themselves, the
King takes out the Duchess of York; and the Duke,
the Duchess of Buckingham; the Duke of Monmouth, my Lady Castlemaine; and so other lords
other ladies: and they danced the Bransle. After
that, the King led a lady a single Coranto; and then
the rest of the lords, one after another, other ladies:
very noble it was, and great pleasure to see. Then
to country dances; the King leading the first, which
he called for; which was, says he, 'Cuckolds all awry,'
the old dance of England. Of the ladies that danced,
the Duke of Monmouth's mistress, and my Lady
Castlemaine, and a daughter of Sir Harry de Vicke's,
were the best. The manner was, when the King
dances, all the ladies in the room, and the Queen herself, stand up: and indeed he dances rarely, and much
better than the Duke of York. Having staid here as

long as I thought fit, to my infinite content, it being
the greatest pleasure I could wish now to see at Court,
I went out, leaving them dancing."

Yet in his closing note upon the year 1662 the
diarist is not so dazzled by the scene which he has just
witnessed as to close his eyes to the ill state of affairs
at Court. He sees the King " following his pleasure
more than with good advice he would do ; . . . his
dalliance with my Lady Castlemaine being publique,
every day, to his great reproach ; and his favouring
of none at Court much as those that are the confidants
of his pleasure, as Sir H. Bennet and Sir Charles
Barkeley ; which, good God ! put it into his heart
to mend, before he makes himself too much contemned
by his people for it ! "

In the same strain he begins again his record of 1663,
after Mrs. Sarah has told him how the King sups at
least four or five times every week with my Lady
Castlemaine—we hear later that he has not supped
with the Queen for a quarter of a year and almost
every night with the lady—and how " the very
centrys " notice and speak about his going home in
the morning " through the garden all alone privately."
This and other tales make Pepys very gloomy as to the
Court morals, from top to bottom.

One of these visits of the King to his mistress
attracted particular comment, and this was paid only
a few days after Mrs. Sarah had imparted her gossip
to Pepys. The story is found in the extremely interesting collection of letters still preserved in the French
Foreign Office, sent by the various French ambassadors

at Whitehall to Louis XIV and his Foreign Secretary, Hugues de Lionne. Louis was particularly anxious to receive from his representatives in England not only diplomatic intelligence, but also " the most curious of the Court news " ; and the ambassadors, especially the Comte de Cominges (who arrived in this country at the end of 1662 and left in 1665), did their best to gratify him—to the great edification of posterity. Cominges now, writing to Lionne, tells how Madame Jaret (by whom he means Lady Gerard, wife of a gentleman of King Charles's Bedchamber) invited the King and Queen to supper at her house. " All things were ready, and the company assembled, when the King left and went off to Madame de Castlemaine's, where he spent the rest of the evening." It is not surprising to hear that this gave rise to much talk and great heart-burnings. It seems that there was ill-feeling between the Ladies Castlemaine and Gerard, and that the former chose to insult her enemy by this display of authority over the King. Two months later Pepys heard how " for some words of my Lady Gerard's against my Lady Castlemaine to the Queen, the King did the other day affront her in going out to dance with her at a ball, when she desired it as the ladies do, and is since forbid attending the Queen by the King ; which is much talked of, my Lord her husband being a great favourite."

Pepys was himself a witness on one occasion of the open way in which the King now paid his visits to the mistress. He was proceeding with Lord Sandwich on January 12th to a Navy Office Committee meeting,

under the presidency of the Duke of York. On the
way through Whitehall garden, to the Duke's chamber,
" a lady called to my Lord out of my Lady Castlemaine's lodging, telling him the King was there and
would speak with him. My Lord could not tell what
to bid me say at the Committee to excuse his absence,
but that he was with the King ; nor would suffer me
to go into the Privy Garden (which is now a through-
passage and common), but bid me go through some
other way, which I did ; so that I see he is a servant of
the King's pleasures too, as well as business."

Burnet, in one of the fragments which he did not
incorporate in his *History of my own Time*, says : " My
lady Castlemaine was now become very insolent, for
though upon the Queen's first coming over the King's
courtship of her was carried very secretly, yet she would
not rest satisfied unless she were publicly owned. So
that was done this winter "—the winter of 1662–3, he
appears to mean. Assuredly the King could scarcely
have gone further in the direction of publicly owning
her than in the instances which we have mentioned
above.

Just about this time, when the former Barbara
Villiers was at the height of her sway over the King,
her first lover made himself at least a nine days'
wonder at Court by his conduct toward his second
wife Elizabeth, his marriage with whom may have
been the cause of Barbara's " displeasure " with him
in 1661. The beautiful Elizabeth had, whether in-
tentionally or not, succeeded in attracting the attention of the Duke of York in the autumn of 1662, and

Court scandal then said that the Duchess had complained about this to the King and to her father Lord Clarendon, with the result that the lady was sent to the country. But in December she was allowed to return to Court, only for the scandal to break out again and a second banishment to follow. Pepys is favourable to the lady. His version of the affair, after a talk with Dr. Clerke, is as follows. It seems that Lord Chesterfield, he says, " not only hath been long jealous of the Duke of York, but did find them two talking together, though there were others in the room, and the lady by all opinions a most good, virtuous woman. He, the next day (of which the Duke was warned by somebody that saw the passion my Lord Chesterfield was in the night before), went and told the Duke how much he did apprehend himself wronged, in his picking out his lady of the whole Court to be the subject of his dishonour ; which the Duke did answer with great calmness, not seeming to understand the reason of complaint, and that was all that passed : but my Lord did presently pack his lady into the country in Derbyshire, near the Peake." Thither he followed her himself in May.

Gramont, always more vivacious than veracious, tells a very long and circumstantial tale about the Duke and the Countess, and some green stockings, and Lord Chesterfield's jealousy. What historical value should be attached to the tale may be gathered from two sentences in a letter written by Sir Charles Lyttelton to Viscount Hatton, on August 8th, 1671. " As

for the story of the silk stockings," says Lyttelton, " I
heare now there was no such thing but an old story
revived of the last King's time." And in a postscript
he adds : " The news I tell of the Dutch admirall is
all false ; so is that of the green stockings."

With the wife on whom he imposed a very different
code of married life from that which he followed himself, Chesterfield, according to his own account, spent
the whole of the summer of 1663 at Bretby. There
is no evidence that Lady Castlemaine felt any particular interest in His Lordship now. She was too
much occupied in other affairs to cherish any longer
the passion of her girlhood. She had, if rumours were
true, already commenced to play the King false, if
that expression be permissible in such circumstances.
The scandalmongers attributed to her a kindness toward Sir Charles Berkeley, soon to be made Viscount
Fitzharding, whom the King used as a go-between
between himself and her. And Anthony Hamilton
suggests that his eldest brother was on very friendly
terms, for a time at least, with the lady. This was
James Hamilton, Groom of the Bedchamber to the
King, described by his junior as the best-dressed man
at Court, the liveliest wit, most polished courtier, most
accomplished dancer, and most general lover—this last
point a merit of some account, he observes, in a
court entirely given up to gallantry. The *Gramont
Memoirs* also mention Henry Jermyn as already
favoured by her. Later the name of Lord Sandwich
is added to the list, and Pepys is evidently inclined to
believe the report.

It would be rash to say that Lady Castlemaine took undue risks in allowing herself to be talked about in connection with the courtiers of the King her master, for she proved that she knew eminently well how to handle Charles II to her own advantage. But it is a fact that, while these stories were beginning to circulate about her conduct, there were others just coming to birth concerning a wandering of the King's affections.

At the end of January 1663, however, the Castlemaine influence is still supreme. One Captain Ferrers, a lively blade, tells Pepys of " my Lady Castlemaine's and Sir Charles Barkeley being the great favourites at Court and growing every day more and more." On February 1st Pepys and Creed, walking in Whitehall Garden, " did see the King coming privately from my Lady Castlemaine's ; which is a poor thing for a prince to do." A week later Ferrers regales the two as they walk together in the Park on Sunday afternoon, watching people sliding on the ice, with various " Court passages "—which, in truth, were very scandalous tales. One of these introduces, for the first time in the *Diary*, the name of the lady who actually did what Pepys had vainly feared Catherine of Braganza would do, namely, " put out of joynt " my Lady Castlemaine's nose. Lady Castlemaine was represented as having, a few days before, invited " Mrs. Stewart " to an entertainment. " And at night began a frolique that they two must be married, and married they were, with ring and all other ceremonies of church service, and ribbands, and a sack posset in bed, and flinging the stocking." Ferrers concluded the story with the intervention of

the King and the downfall of " pretty Mrs. Stewart " ;
which is quite inconsistent with the prevailing belief
of a very evil-minded Court about the young lady, and
may therefore be dismissed as an effort of the imagina-
tion—as perhaps the whole story was, in spite of
another of the diarist's gossips affirming the general
acceptation of it.

But about the appearance on the scene of *la belle
Stuart* and the King's infatuation with her there is no
doubt. Frances, elder daughter of Dr. Walter Stewart
or Stuart,[1] third son of Lord Blantyre, and therefore
connected with the Royal Family, came to England
at the beginning of 1663 from Paris, where she had
lived under the protection of her mother and of
Henrietta Maria, to be a maid of honour to Queen
Catherine. She was about fifteen when she reached
the English Court and was commended to Charles by
his sister Henrietta, Duchess of Orleans, as " the
prettiest girl in the world and one of the best fitted
of any I know to adorn a Court." Of her prettiness
there can be no doubt, whether we judge by the
testimony of a multitude of her contemporaries or by
the surviving portraits of her. As to her capacity to
adorn a Court, there are more ways than one of inter-
preting this claim. Frances does not appear to have
possessed intelligence to match her looks. It was
hardly possible, say the *Gramont Memoirs* indeed,
for a woman to have less wit or more beauty. She
lived under four sovereigns without making any more

---

[1] We shall in future keep to Stewart, which was the usual spelling
of Frances's family name in her own day.

enduring mark upon the history of their reigns than by her appearance as Britannia on our copper coins. She was certainly circumspect, and as a maid of honour passed for modest. The Marquis de Ruvigny, one of Louis's agents in England, declares her to be " one of the most beautiful girls and one of the most modest to be seen," even when he is transmitting some dubious reports as to her position with regard to the King. Evelyn evidently believed her to be chaste up to the time of her marriage ; and " good Mr. Evelyn," as Pepys calls him, was quite capable of expressing himself forcibly on the subject of ladies whom he did not consider virtuous. Clarendon, who thought the King's passion to be stronger for Frances Stewart than for any other woman, says that she " carried it with that discretion and modesty that she made no other use of it than for the convenience of her own fortune and subsistence, which was narrow enough." According to the *Gramont Memoirs*, her virtue broke down before her marriage, overcome by the King's grant of her request to allow her to be the first to ride in a new carriage just arrived from France ! But these memoirs cannot be treated as good evidence unless strongly supported by other testimony. The secret of the girl's power over Charles seems to have been a combination of beauty, artless conversation, and an obduracy which piqued his vanity and attracted him by its rarity at his Court.

Frances Stewart soon begins to figure largely in the writings of the day. On February 23rd she is one of the ladies noticed by Pepys at a performance of

Dryden's first play *The Wild Gallant*, at the King's
private theatre at Whitehall. " My Lady Castlemaine was all worth seeing to-night," he says, " and
little Steward." He is unsuspicious of the coming
struggle as yet, and records, on the same date, the
omnipotence of the Royal mistress. " This day was I
told that my Lady Castlemaine hath all the King's
presents, made him by the peers, given to her, which
is a most abominable thing ; and that at the great
ball she was much richer in jewells than the Queen
and Duchess put both together." He might have
added, had he been aware of it, that it was she who
was the chief patron of Dryden's play, " so poor a
thing " though he thought it. For Dryden wrote to
thank Lady Castlemaine for her encouragement of
him at this time in an adulatory verse epistle.

For a time we only catch glimpses of Lady Castlemaine—at Whitehall, after service in the Chapel
Royal, where among the fine ladies she is " above all,
that only she I can observe for true beauty," as Pepys
quaintly expresses it ; in Hyde Park, where the King
and she, riding in separate coaches, greet one another
at every turn of the Ring, round which it was the
fashion to drive ; at St. George's Feast at Windsor,
when the newly created Duke of Monmouth was
married to the Lady Anne Scott, only child of the
second Earl of Buccleugh, with whom he got a very
large fortune. Unfortunately Pepys was not present
at the ceremony at Windsor. But Gramont, who
probably was, has a few words about it in the *Memoirs*.
" New festivals and entertainments celebrated this

marriage," he says. " The most effectual method to pay court to the King was to outshine the rest in brilliancy and grandeur. . . . The fair Stewart, then in the meridian of her glory, attracted all eyes, and commanded universal respect and admiration. The Duchess of Cleveland endeavoured to eclipse her at this festival by a load of jewels and by all the artificial ornaments of dress. But it was in vain ; her face looked rather thin and pale, from the commencement of a third or fourth pregnancy, which the King was still pleased to place to his own account ; and, as for the rest, her person could in no respect stand in com- petition with the grace and beauty of Miss Stewart."

Gramont is, as usual, very loose in his chronology, for Barbara was not to be Duchess of Cleveland for another seven years, nor by any means could Frances Stewart be described as in " the meridian of her glory " yet. The maid of honour had only very recently reached England, and the rivalry between her and the royal mistress had barely commenced. The elder woman (not yet twenty-two herself) was so far quite pleased to patronise the little Stewart, as Gramont himself bears witness later.

On the Court's return from the festivities at Windsor on April 24th, Charles took a step which must have settled the doubts of the most charitably minded persons in the kingdom as to the position of the Countess of Castlemaine at his Court. Pepys, of course, has the story early, in fact, on the very next day, how " she is removed from her own home to a chamber in Whitehall, next to the King's own ; which I am sorry

to hear, though I love her much." This news is confirmed by Dr. Pierce soon after, and was quite true,
for Lady Castlemaine had left King Street and taken
up her abode in the buildings which were included in
Whitehall Palace.

Curiously, the move to Whitehall had scarcely been
made—and also the warrant for creating Lady Castlemaine and other ladies of the Bedchamber to the
Queen passed—when there spread about still more
definite and persistent rumours of an alteration in the
King's affections. Scandal proceeds to couple Frances
Stewart's name with the mistress's, as though they
were on a similar footing with His Majesty; and,
more astonishing still, the Queen " begins to be
brisk and play like other ladies, and is quite another
woman from what she was," so that there are specula-
tions whether the King may not be made to like
her better and forsake Lady Castlemaine *and*
Mrs. Stewart. Even Pepys seems for a while shaken
in his allegiance. On June 13th he sees his idol, " who,
I fear, is not so handsome as I have taken her for,
and now she begins to decay something ! " This is
also the opinion of Mrs. Pepys, " for which I am sorry,"
says her husband. He makes handsome amends, however, a year later, when he speaks of " Mrs. Stewart,
who is indeed very pretty, but not like my Lady
Castlemaine, for all that."

From a photograph by W. J. Roberts, after a painting by Sir Peter Lely at Goodwood, reproduced by permission of the Earl of March

FRANCES STEWART

CHAPTER V

THE RIVALS

"TO Westminster Hall," says Pepys, on July 3rd, 1663, "and there meeting with Mr. Moore he tells me great news that my Lady Castlemaine is fallen from Court, and this morning retired. He gives me no account of the reason of it, but that it is so : for which I am sorry : and yet if the King do it to leave off not only her but all other mistresses, I should be heartily glad of it, that he may fall to look after business."

Next day, as he is dining with Creed very well for 12*d.* at the King's Head ordinary, "a pretty gentleman " in their company confirms the news and further tells them of " one wipe " the Queen had recently given the mistress. It appears that the latter " came in and found the Queen under the dresser's hands, and had been so long. ' I wonder Your Majesty,' says she, ' can have the patience to sit so long a-dressing ? '—' I have so much reason to use patience,' says the Queen, ' that I can very well bear with it.' " This gentleman thinks it may be that the Queen has commanded Lady Castlemaine to retire from Court, " though that is not likely " in Pepys's opinion.

Nor was it the fact. What had actually happened

is known to us from a letter which the Comte de
Cominges wrote to Louis XIV on July 5th and which
is among the correspondence from the London Embassy preserved in the French Foreign Office. " There
was a great quarrel the other day among the ladies,"
he reports, " which was carried so far that the King
threatened the lady at whose apartments he sups every
evening that he would never set foot there again if he
did not find the *Demoiselle* with her."

The lady with whom King Charles sups every
evening is, of course, Lady Castlemaine ; and the
Demoiselle is Frances Stewart. The *Gramont
Memoirs*, which do not record the falling out between
Charles and Lady Castlemaine, have a good deal to
say about the way in which the latter took up the
young maid of honour when she noticed that the
King paid attention to her. " She was not satisfied,"
writes Gramont through his biographer, " with appearing without any degree of uneasiness at a preference which all the Court began to remark ; she even
affected to make Miss Stewart her favourite, and invited her to all the entertainments she made for the
King . . . being confident that, whenever she thought
fit, she could triumph over all the advantages which
these opportunities could afford Miss Stewart ; but
she was quite mistaken."

The actual quarrel between Charles and his mistress
now was brief, and if her absence from the Royal
coaches in the Ring at Hyde Park on July 5th
was remarked, it was not because she had been banished from Court. On the contrary, according to the

story which Captain Ferrers brought Pepys some
weeks later—a story more worthy of belief than some
that he told—" her going away was a fit of her own
upon some slighting words of the King." These
would, of course, be connected with his request that
he might see Frances Stewart in her apartments if
she desired a continuance of his favour. Lady Castlemaine, in a rage, called for her coach and drove off
to her uncle's house at Richmond, whither we have
seen her fly before. But Charles, for all that he was
found by people to be stranger and colder than
ordinary to her, could not spare her. The very next
morning after her departure, he made a pretence of
going hunting at Richmond, called to see her and
make friends, and " never was a-hunting at all."

So my Lady Castlemaine was back at Whitehall,
commanding the King as much as ever and flouting
all who crossed her will. Another of the loquacious
Captain's stories shows the King still absolutely at her
beck and call. On July 21st her cousin, the Duke of
Buckingham, gave a private entertainment to Charles
and Catherine at Wallingford House (on the site of
the present Admiralty Office), and did not invite her.
She was that day at the house of her aunt, Lady
Suffolk, where she was heard to say : " Well, much
good may it do them ! For all that I will be as merry
as they." So she went home and had a great supper
prepared. Presently to her from Wallingford House
came King Charles, attended by Lord Sandwich, and
spent the night. Not long after we hear of the King
being fetched to her from the very Council-table by Sir

H

Charles Berkeley. She certainly could not complain now that she was not openly acknowledged.

Nevertheless, though she might exhibit her sway over His Majesty in this public way, one thing which she could not do was to prevent him admiring other ladies, and in particular Frances Stewart. This " cunning slut "—the expression is Lord Sandwich's— who provoked Charles so much that he once hoped to " live to see her ugly and willing," held out steadfastly against the royal offers. She refused to share Lady Castlemaine's dishonourable post, while the latter, to her mortification, was compelled to treat her as a friend and never be without her. Meanwhile she could not but know that people were beginning to compare her beauty unfavourably with that of her rival and, though she herself was but twenty-two, to talk of her decay. As soon as the King could get a husband for Mrs. Stewart, they said (and, it seems, with considerable prescience), my Lady Castlemaine's nose would really be out of joint.

We have heard Pepys's somewhat disillusioned criticism on his favourite lady's looks in the June of this year. A still more interesting passage in the *Diary*, in which he describes her and the younger beauty side by side, is to be found under the date July 13th. This day, walking in Pall Mall, he finds that the King and Queen are riding with the ladies of honour in the Park, and waits with a great crowd of gallants to see their return. Thus he describes the scene :

" By and by the King and Queen, who looked in

this dress (a white laced waistcoat and a crimson short pettycoat, and her hair dressed *à la négligence*) mighty pretty; and the King rode hand in hand with her. Here was also my Lady Castlemaine rode among the rest of the ladies; but the King took, methought, no notice of her; nor when they 'light did anybody press (as she seemed to expect, and staid for it) to take her down, but was taken down by her own gentleman. She looked mighty out of humour and had a yellow plume in her hat (which all took notice of), and yet is very handsome, but very melancholy: nor did anybody speak to her, or she so much as smile or speak to anybody. I followed them up into Whitehall, and into the Queen's presence, where all the ladies walked, talking and fiddling with their hats and feathers, and changing and trying one another's by one another's heads, and laughing. But it was the finest sight to me, considering their great beautys and dress, that ever I did see in all my life. But, above all, Mrs. Stewart in this dress, with her hat cocked and a red plume, with her sweet eye, little Roman nose, and excellent taille, is now the greatest beauty I ever saw, I think, in my life; and, if ever woman can, do exceed my Lady Castlemaine, at least in this dress: nor do I wonder if the King changes, which I verily believe is the reason of his coldness to my Lady Castlemaine."

The impressionable Pepys was, indeed, extremely smitten with Mrs. Stewart this day, as students of the *Diary* will remember.

On July 23rd the King and Queen went down to Tunbridge Wells, the latter having been recommended

by her doctors to try the none too pleasant waters
there as a cure for that which undoubtedly did more
than anything to make Charles so unfaithful to her,
her lack of children. She should have gone in May,
but so short of money was the Royal Household that
the visit could not be made until nearly the last week
in July. The King was in London again four days
later to prorogue Parliament and then returned to
the Wells, where he and Catherine are seen to be on
excellent terms. Dr. Pierce, who has just purchased
the place of Groom of the Privy Chamber to Her
Majesty, reports to Pepys that she " is grown a very
debonnaire lady, and now hugs him [the King], and
meets him gallopping upon the road, and all the
actions of a fond and pleasant lady that can be." The
King, says Pierce, " has a chat now and then of Mrs.
Stewart, but there is no great danger of her, she being
only an innocent, young, raw girl ; but my Lady
Castlemaine, who rules the King in matters of State,
and do what she list with him, he believes is now
falling quite out of favour."

Lady Castlemaine, it seems, accompanied the Court
to Tunbridge Wells, although she, unlike the Queen,
was expecting very shortly the birth of a child. But
she can have played little part in the amusements of
the Court, of which Cominges gives a glimpse in the
sheet of Court news for August, sent by him to
Louis. " One might well call these the Waters of
Scandal," he writes, " for they have come near ruining
the good names of the maids and the ladies (I mean
those who are there without their husbands). It

took a whole month, and more in some cases, for them to justify themselves and save their honour; and it is even said that a few of them have not yet got clear. This is the cause why the Court returns in eight days' time, leaving one of the Queen's ladies behind to pay for the others."

After quitting Tunbridge Wells, the Court moved to Bath for a month, in order that the Queen might continue her cure. They set out from Vauxhall on August 26th. There is no mention of the Countess of Castlemaine accompanying them. On the contrary, after a conversation with Mrs. Sarah, on September 22nd, Pepys writes : " This day the King and Queen are to come to Oxford. I hear my Lady Castlemaine is for certain gone to Oxford to meet him, having lain within here at home this week or two supposed to have miscarried."

Mrs. Sarah was usually well informed, and her very considerable error in one particular here seems to show that there was a good deal of mystery about the birth of Henry, second son of Lady Castlemaine, afterwards Duke of Grafton. Moreover, the date of the event is supposed to have been September 20th, 1663. Yet the mother starts two days later upon the journey from London to Oxford, which cannot have been easy for her at such a time, and is next heard of in lodgings near Christ Church Meadows on the morning of the 24th.

King Charles, we know, hesitated for some years to recognise Henry (Palmer or Fitzroy, as he was at first variously called) as his child. Lord Castlemaine had long ceased living with his wife, and is not heard of in England later than November 1662. Scandal suggested that the father's name was Charles Berkeley, Lord Fitzharding; and his office of go-between to the King and the lady naturally aroused such suspicions in a Court so prone to suspect.

The royal visit to Oxford, for which Lady Castlemaine left London so soon after Henry's birth, lasted a week. The King and Queen, coming from the west by way of Cirencester, dined with Lord Chancellor Clarendon, who was also Chancellor of the University, at his house at Cornbury, eight miles outside the city, on the 23rd. Arriving from the other direction, Lady Castlemaine may be assumed not to have been present (she could only have been so uninvited) at the country home of the man whom she was determined to ruin ; nor to have assisted, therefore, at the two receptions of the royal party, first by the University authorities at the last mile-stone as they entered Oxford, and then by the Mayor and other civic dignitaries. She did not see Charles take from the hands of the Chancellor the " large fair Bible," covered with black plush, bossed and clasped with silver double-gilt, etc., of which Antony Wood tells ; nor, from those of the Mayor, the purse of white satin, embroidered with the King's arms and " beset with aglets and pearles," containing £300 in gold. But she may have seen the further reception at Christ Church, when the King, arriving by torchlight through a lane made down St. Giles's by the city militia, was welcomed by the Dean, in whose lodgings he was to sleep.

At any rate, she was with Charles again early next day, for Wood has the following entry under September 24th : " The King betimes in the morning went to Xt. Ch. meed [Christ Church Meadows] to view and see where the workers were, and called upon the countess of Castlemaine, who then lay in Dr. Richard Gardiner's lodgings next to the fields. . . ." Some blotted words follow, which seem to indicate that Wood at first expressed an opinion either on the King's behaviour or on the lady's character, but afterwards expunged it.

We hear no more of Barbara during this, her first visit to Oxford. After a busy week, which included in its programme an audience to the University authorities at Christ Church, a Convocation at the Schools, a fox-hunt ending at Cornbury, and two touchings for the King's Evil in the Cathedral choir, the whole Court set off for Whitehall on the 30th. Pepys notes the return of King and Court, " from their progress," on October 1st. He also says, in a later entry, that he hears that my Lady Castlemaine " is in as great favour as ever, and that the King supped with her the very first night he came from Bath," by which he seems to mean the night of the return to Whitehall. Two other suppers he also tells of, given by Lady Castlemaine to His Majesty at this time. For one of these there was a chine of beef to roast, but her kitchen was flooded by the Thames and the cook came to tell her what had happened. " Zounds ! " said my Lady, " you must set the house on fire, but it shall be roasted ! " But, by carrying the chine elsewhither

to roast, the supper was, in the end, prepared without
burning the house.

It seems as if nothing could induce Charles to fore-
go these suppers at Lady Castlemaine's ; not even a
grief which had all the appearance of sincerity.   In
the middle of October Queen Catherine suddenly fell
most seriously ill.   What her complaint was it is
difficult to make out.   Mrs. Sarah says the spotted
fever, and that she is as full of the spots as a leopard ;
whereon Pepys remarks, not very lucidly, " which is
very strange that it should not be more known ; but
perhaps it is not so."   On the 17th the doctors gave
but little hope of her recovery.   When the King came
to see her that morning she told him she willingly left
all the world but him—at which His Majesty was much
afflicted, according to Arlington, who described the
scene in a letter to the Duke of Buckingham.   The
Gramont Memoirs supply further information :

" The Queen was given over by her physicians :
the few Portuguese women that had not been sent
back to their own country filled the Court with dole-
ful cries ; and the good nature of the King was much
affected with the situation in which he saw a princess
whom, though he did not love her, yet he greatly
esteemed.   She loved him tenderly, and, thinking that
it was the last time she should ever speak to him,
she told him that ' the concern he showed for her
death was enough to make her quit life with regret ;
but that, not possessing charms sufficient to merit his
tenderness, she had at least the consolation in dying
to give place to a consort who might be more worthy
of it and to whom Heaven, perhaps, might grant a

blessing that had been refused to her.' At these words she bathed his hands with some tears, which he thought would be her last; he mingled his own with hers; and, without supposing she would take him at his word, he conjured her to live for his sake."

Gramont, or Hamilton, cannot omit the sting in the tail of the anecdote. But Charles scarcely deserved to escape the cynical suggestion when he could give occasion for the French Ambassador to write as follows to his master:

" I am just come from Whitehall, where I left the Queen in a state in which, according to the doctors, there is little room for hope. She received extreme unction this morning. . . . The King seems to me deeply affected. He supped, nevertheless, yesterday evening at Madame de Castlemaine's and had his usual conversations with Mademoiselle Stewart, of whom he is very fond. There is already talk of his marrying [again]. Everyone gives him a wife according to his inclination, and there are some who do not look for her out of England."

If any confirmation were required of what Cominges says of the King's behaviour, there is Mrs. Sarah's report to Pepys, " that the King do seem to take it much to heart . . . but, for all that, that he hath not missed one night since she was sick, of supping with my Lady Castlemaine." Perchance, in his state of low spirits His Majesty felt more than ever the need of that company and conversation from which he once told Clarendon he would not be restrained.

The critical state of the Queen's illness, whatever it was, continued well into the second half of October, so that people began to prepare for the possibility of going into mourning. But on the 24th she was out of danger. " The Queen is in a good way of recovery," writes Pepys that day; " and Sir Francis Pridgeon [Prujean] hath got great honour by it, it being all imputed to his cordiall, which in her dispaire did give her rest and brought her to some hope of recovery." [1] The pious Queen, however, imputed her restoration to health to her husband's prayers ; and the Poet Laureate Waller to His Majesty's tears !

> " When no healing art prevail'd,
> When cordials and elixirs fail'd,
> On your pale cheeks he dropt the shower
> Reviv'd you like a dying flower."

A pathetic part of the Queen's illness was that in her delirium she raved about having given birth to an heir to the throne, whom the King was fain to humour her by declaring a very pretty boy. Another day she fancied that she had three children, of whom the girl was very like the King, and woke from sleep asking, " How do the children ? " Some at least of the tragedy of Catherine's life might have been removed had her dream about a son been true. But the King, though destined to have several more sons by other women, was never to have a child from her.

With the Queen restored to health, the old situation continues, the King being, as it were, in the midst

[1] It is not until November 10th, however, that she is quite well again and "hath bespoke herself a new gowne."

of a triangle of which the angles are the Queen, the
Countess of Castlemaine, and Frances Stewart; his
wife, his mistress, and the lady who cannot be one
and will not be the other. During the worst crisis of
Catherine's illness it was believed by many that, if
she died, the little maid of honour would become
her lawful successor. And actually we hear of a
" committee," as Lord Sandwich calls it to Pepys, of
Edward Montagu, Sandwich's cousin (afterwards
second Earl of Manchester), Sir H. Bennett, and the
Duke and Duchess of Buckingham, with " somebody
else," whose name is not divulged, " for the getting of
Mrs. Stewart for the King." But Frances, advised by
the Queen-Dowager Henrietta Maria and by her own
mother, proves a cunning slut, and the precious plot is
spoiled. Montagu and the Duke quarrel, and the
former makes up to his kinsman Sandwich, who is a
friend of Lady Castlemaine.

Dr. Pierce adds his contribution to the gossip, telling
" how the King is now become besotted upon Mrs.
Stewart, that he gets into corners, and will be with
her half an houre together kissing her to the observa-
tion of all the world." As for my Lady Castlemaine,
" the King is still kind, so as now and then he goes to
have a chat with her, but with no such fondness as he
used to do."

In this curious and disgraceful situation it may be
safely asserted that no one had more reason to be glad
of the Queen's recovery than the royal mistress. Had
Catherine died and Charles taken Frances Stewart
as his second wife, Lady Castlemaine could not have

continued to rule the King as she had done from 1661. *La belle Stuart* was no Catherine of Braganza, as is clear from her diplomatic management of her importunate royal lover, and from her holding of her own in this dissolute Court at the age of only sixteen years.

But if the Countess had grounds for gratitude to the Queen for continuing to live, there is no sign of any better relations being established between them than what may be called the armed neutrality established after the return from Hampton Court in 1662. The next step taken by Lady Castlemaine, though it brought her in a sense nearer to the Queen, scarcely commended itself to the latter, who could not believe that it was prompted by conscience. My Lady became a Roman Catholic. Cominges writes to Hugues de Lionne : " The Chevalier de Gramont's marriage [1] and Madame de Castlemaine's conversion were made public the same day. The King of England, having been begged by the lady's relatives to interfere to prevent this step, gallantly replied that, as for the soul of the ladies, he never meddled with that."

There is nothing which gives us any clue to the immediate reason of Barbara's conversion to Roman Catholicism at this present moment. In spite of Catherine's suspicion, it is difficult to discover any interested motive for Lady Castlemaine's change of faith—unless we accept the explanation given in the

[1] To the celebrated beauty Elizabeth Hamilton, sister of Antony Hamilton, Gramont's later biographer ; of James, reputed lover of Lady Castlemaine—among others; and of four more brothers besides.

From an engraving by J. Enghels, after a picture by Sir Peter Lely

BARBARA VILLIERS, COUNTESS OF CASTLEMAINE
AND DUCHESS OF CLEVELAND

scurrilous *Secret History of the Reigns of King Charles II and King James II*, that she knew that the King was covertly a Papist and " had been often heard to say that she did not embrace the Catholic religion out of any esteem that she had for it, but because that otherwise she could not continue the King's mistress : and consequently Miss of State." [1]

In the popular estimation, never favourably inclined toward her, Lady Castlemaine undoubtedly did herself enormous injury by her change, as was to be shown in the future. The Church of England, however, could hardly be expected to express much regret at the defection of such a daughter. When told of it by William Penn the Quaker, Edward Stillingfleet (preacher at the Rolls Chapel and afterwards Dean of St. Paul's and Bishop of Norwich) remarked that, if the Church of Rome had got no more by it than the Church of England had lost, then the matter would not be much !

A few months after her conversion Lady Castlemaine is seen attending service at the chapel attached to the French Embassy in the Strand. It is Holy Week and, Cominges writes to Lionne, " the King has done me the honour to lend me his French musicians, thanks to whom a number of people in society come to my chapel, Madame de Castlemaine especially, whom I mean to regale as well as I can."

---

[1] Miss Strickland suggests that Lady Castlemaine " was cunningly preparing, in case of being abandoned by her royal lover, to pave the way for a reconciliation with her injured husband by embracing his religion." This does not seem a likely explanation.

At the beginning of 1664 we continue to hear regularly of Charles's infatuation with Frances Stewart and his comparative disregard for his mistress. Dr. Pierce walks an hour with Pepys in the Matted Gallery at Whitehall on January 20th, and tells him, among other things, " that my Lady Castlemaine is not at all set by by the King, but that he do doat upon Mrs. Stewart only ; and that to the leaving of all business in the world, and to the open slighting of the Queene ; that he values not who sees him or stands by him while he dallies with her openly ; and then privately in her chamber below, where the very sentrys observe his going in and out ; and that so commonly that the Duke or any of the nobles, when they would ask where the King is, they will ordinarily say, ' Is the King above or below ? ' meaning with Mrs. Stewart : that the King do not openly disown my Lady Castlemaine, but that she comes to Court." And, according to Pierce, Lady Castlemaine consoles herself with Lord Fitzharding, the Hamiltons, and Lord Sandwich. About a fortnight later the same informant has more to tell on the same theme of Charles and the maid of honour, and how some of the best parts of the Queen's jointure are " bestowed or rented to my Lord Fitzharding and Mrs. Stewart and others of that crew." In spite of which, Mr. Pepys soon after finds " Mrs. Stewart grown fatter and not so fair as she was " !

My Lady Castlemaine, however, was not one to be easily slighted. The *Diary* records a curious scene at the theatre in Whitehall, where *The Indian Queen*, by Dryden and Sir Robert Howard, is being played.

Lady Castlemaine is in her box, next to the royal box, before Charles comes. On his arrival, " leaning over other ladies awhile to whisper to the King, she rose out of the box and went into the King's, and set herself on the King's right hand, between the King and the Duke of York ; which he [Dr. Pierce] swears, put the King himself, as well as every body else, out of countenance ; and believes that she did it only to show the world that she is not out of favour yet, as was believed."

A month later Sir Robert Paston, subsequently Earl of Yarmouth, writing to his wife to describe the scene at the prorogation of Parliament on March 2nd and Charles's departure from the House of Lords, says : " The press drive me up to the King's very elbow, and I had like to have carried my Lady Castlemaine along in the crowd, who was pleased very civilly to take notice of me." It is clear that the lady was not suffering her King to deprive her of the pleasure of close association with him in public.

Further, she is able to keep a hold upon him through his tenderness of heart, for he goes at midnight to her nurses and takes her child up and dances it in his arms—the child being the five-months-old Henry, whom he thus treats kindly, in spite of not yet accepting him as his own offspring.

About this time Lady Castlemaine is supposed to have moved into new lodgings at Whitehall Palace. On January 25th there had been a fire in her apartments, when she bid " £40 for one to adventure the fetching of a cabinet out, which at last was got to be done." The fire was put out without much damage to property, but its occurrence may have been made a reason for a move. At any rate, we learn that on May 29th, the King's birthday, Charles was " at my Lady Castlemaine's lodgings (over the hither-gate at Lambert's lodgings) dancing with fiddlers all night almost, and all the world coming by taking notice of it," which Pepys is sorry to hear.

As she is not before this stated to have resided " over the hither-gate " of Whitehall, and as " Countess of Castlemaine's kitchen " is placed in an old survey of the Palace in the Cockpit buildings, on the West side of the street running from that gate to the King Street gate of the Palace, it is thought that in the early part of this year she exchanged her former rooms for some rather nearer to the royal apartments. The evidence is not quite conclusive, but on the other hand there is a fairly good case for a change of abode. The new lodgings (if they were new) were in the gate-house built across Whitehall after Holbein's design in the reign of Henry VIII and not pulled down until 1759. This gatehouse was used by King Henry as a study. During the Commonwealth it was inhabited by Lambert, and now it was given up to a royal mistress, so that it had a varied history.

For some time after this supposed change of abode we hear very little of Lady Castlemaine. She appears at the lottery organised by Sir Arthur Slingsby in the Banqueting Hall (which was very close to the Holbein Gate); for Pepys, who manages as usual to get in here and place himself in the midst of all that is worth seeing, stands " just behind my Lady Castlemaine, whom I do heartily adore." We do not hear what luck the lady had at the lottery, which Evelyn, who was also present, says " was thought to be contrived very unhandsomely by the master of it, who was, in truth, a meer shark."

There was a very good cause for the lady not being much seen in public about this period. On September 5th, 1664, there was born at White-hall Palace, Charlotte Fitzroy, second daughter of Lady Castlemaine. So secretly did the birth take place that Pepys's *Diary* shows no knowledge of the child's existence at any date; while Pepys's friend Pierce, the doctor, surmises less than four weeks before the event something entirely incorrect about the condition of affairs, and again, on November 11th, Pepys unsuspectingly writes: " My wife tells me the sad news of my Lady Castlemaine's being now become so decayed that no one would know her; at least, far from a beauty, which I am sorry for."

Charles had, no doubt, the best of reasons for keeping Charlotte's appearance in the world from common knowledge as long as possible, for there was no chance of attributing the child to the lady's husband when he had been so long away from England. The King does not seem to have made any attempt to disown the fathership, in spite of the current scandal at Court earlier in the year, and a very affectionate letter to " my deare Charlotte " from " your kinde father," when she was of an age to appreciate a present of five hundred guineas, remains in existence to-day.

I

Only nine days after the birth of her child Lady Castlemaine entertains in her lodgings at Whitehall Madame de Cominges, the recently arrived wife of the French Ambassador. Cominges himself, seemingly without any suspicion of the lady's late experience, comments on the magnificence of the affair and tells how the King "did the honours of the house in a way befitting a host rather than a guest."

If it is curious that such an inveterate gossip and so great an admirer of Barbara as Samuel Pepys should not have heard of Charlotte Fitzroy's birth, it is still more curious that he should also have failed to hear about a very unpleasant mishap to the royal mistress a month later. Perhaps it was because the diarist was unusually occupied with his own amours at this period that he had little time to glean from his general informants the latest scandals in high society. It is from a letter of the French Ambassador to Lionne that our knowledge of the affair is derived. Writing on October 2nd, Cominges relates how two days previously Lady Castlemaine, returning home after an evening spent with the Duchess of York at St. James's Palace, and accompanied only by one lady and a little page, was met suddenly in the Park by three *gentilshommes* (so at least they seemed to be from their clothes), wearing masks, who addressed to her the strongest and harshest reprimand imaginable, going so far as to remind her that the mistress of Edward IV died on a dunghill, scorned and abandoned by all the world. "You may imagine," continues Cominges, "whether the time seemed long to her. . . . As soon as she was in her room she fainted. The King was informed of it, and running to her assistance ordered all the gates to be closed and all persons found in the Park to be arrested. Seven or eight people who happened to be there were brought in, but not identified, and have spread the story. It was desired to hush the matter up, but I think that will be difficult." It was not so difficult, apparently, as Cominges thought.

This was not the first time, as we know, that Lady Castlemaine had to endure the odious comparison of herself with Jane Shore; nor was it to be the last. Doubtless the three masked gentlemen were people about the Court, enemies of the mistress, and aware of the recent birth which had been kept so carefully concealed from the general public. If courtiers, they would have chances of escape not possessed by other people.

CHAPTER VI

POLITICS AND PLAGUE

THE outbreak of the war between England and
Holland toward the end of 1664, not officially
declared but none the less real, is doubtless the reason
why we hear less about the gaieties at Court than
usual at this period. But it took more than foreign
troubles to dissipate the frivolous atmosphere of
Whitehall, so that there is no necessity to imagine a
slackening of the furious pace of pleasure there. On
Candlemas Day (February 2nd), 1665, we have a
glimpse of the Court at its amusements. On that day
a masque was got up to surprise the King. Evelyn was
a spectator, but gives no details. Pepys, deriving his
information from Lord Sandwich's niece, tells how
" six women (my Lady Castlemaine and Duchess of
Monmouth being two of them) and six men (the
Duke of Monmouth and Lord Arran and Monsieur
Blanfort being three of them) in vizards, but most
rich and antique dresses, did dance admirably and
most gloriously." The *Gramont Memoirs* contain
some entertaining but very ill-natured details about a
masquerade organised by Queen Catherine, which has
been identified with this Candlemas Day revel. There
are several difficulties in the way of the identification,
one of which is that Gramont describes a lady as

still Mademoiselle Hamilton when she had become
his own wife more than a year before and had presented
a son to him five months before the revel ! It is true
that he was a singularly forgetful man where his wife
was concerned, the tale being famous of his attempted
departure from England after his engagement to her.
Her brothers hastened after him to Dover and, catching him, asked him : " Count, have you forgotten
nothing in London ? "—" Pardon me," replied Gramont, " I have forgotten to marry your sister. Let us
go back and finish that affair." So he returned, married
Elizabeth Hamilton, and only changed his character
so far as to become the most bare-faced liar in the
world, according to his compatriot, King Louis's
Ambassador at Whitehall.

To enliven the masquerade got up by the Queen
(whether it was that of February 1665 or not), Gramont makes Mademoiselle Hamilton " invent two or
three little tricks for turning to ridicule the vain fools
of the Court, there being two pre-eminently such ;
one Lady Muskerry, wife of her cousin-german, and
the other a maid of honour to the Duchess [of York],
called Blague." Lady Muskerry, a rich heiress, but
no beauty, with one leg shorter than the other, received
a forged invitation from the Queen to come dressed
" in the Babylonian fashion," and arrived at the entrance to Whitehall " with at least sixty ells of gauze
and silver tissue about her, not to mention a sort of
pyramid upon her head, adorned with a hundred
thousand baubles "—to the astonishment of all who
caught sight of her and to the rage of her husband, who

packed her off home before she could display her glory
in an assembly to which she had not really been invited. The trick played upon Miss Blague (sister of
the lady of whom Evelyn gives so noble and touching
a picture) was even more cruel, for it had its point in
an unrequited affection, and made her ridiculous in
the eyes of the man whom she desired to love her.

These and similar tales, of which there are many,
certainly give a vivid picture of the freedom allowed
at the Court of him whom history calls the " Merry
Monarch " ; in which freedom the ladies were not a
whit behind the gentlemen. The Countess of Sandwich
was not overstating the case when she talked to Pepys
of the " mad freaks " of the maids of honour, when
even the more innocent among them, like Elizabeth
Hamilton and Frances Jennings (heroine of the orange-
girl story told by both Pepys and Gramont), were
guilty of such extraordinary escapades. Lady Sandwich observed that few men would venture upon these
damsels for wives, and repeated a prophecy of Lady
Castlemaine's, that her daughter (the four-year-old
Anne) would be the first maid at Court that would be
married. But the former Barbara Villiers should surely
not have been a harsh critic in matters of maidenly
behaviour !

Early in 1665 the husband whom she had so much
wronged appeared again in England, and was seen by
Pepys at St. James's, where no doubt he was paying
his respects to the Duke of York. He had spent a
considerable portion of his time abroad in the company of Andrew Cornaro, Admiral of the Venetian

fleet carrying on war with Turkey in the Levant,
his experiences being embodied by him in a letter
which he wrote to the King from Venice and afterwards published. Returning home by way of France,
he was preceded by a report that he was about to make
friends with his lady again. But we hear from one
of Cominges' letters to Lionne that he was much dis-
turbed when he found, on his arrival at Court, that
his wife was the mother of two more fine children
since he had left her. It is perhaps not surprising,
therefore, that a few days after his return he set out
again with the Duke of York for the fleet to fight the
Dutch, leaving his lady to go her own way. It was
probably on the day before the husband's departure
from London that Pepys caught one of his most curious
glimpses of Lady Castlemaine, in Hyde Park. On
Sunday, March 19th, he tells how he rode with Mr.
Povy in his coach to the Park, " where many brave
ladies ; among others, Castlemaine lay impudently
upon her back in her coach asleep, with her mouth
open." It was the first day this year of the " tour "
or Ring, where the fashionable people took the air.
There was also to be seen on the same day Lady
Carnegy, Barbara's old friend Lady Anne Hamilton,
whose reputation was even worse than hers by now.

A fortnight later Lady Castlemaine is seen with the
King at the Duke's Theatre, witnessing Lord Orrery's
new play *Mustapha*. Their presence is to Pepys " all
the pleasure of the play " ; but he notices also, for
the first time in his *Diary*, " pretty witty Nell," who
is, of course, none other than the famous Nell Gwynn.

But Lady Castlemaine did not devote herself entirely to pleasure at this time. She had long taken her share in the domestic politics of Charles II, and, as we have seen, had fostered the rise of Henry Bennet and Charles Berkeley in the counsels of the King, to the discomfiture of " the old serious lords,"[1] such as Clarendon and Southampton, whom she hated for refusing to seek her favour. Since she had become a Roman Catholic, her apartments in Whitehall had more than ever been the meeting-place of the faction hostile to the Chancellor and Treasurer, and the resort particularly of Bennet, now Earl of Arlington, and his co-religionists. Foreign affairs played their part in creating a wider divergence between the rival parties. The outbreak of the quarrel with Holland, very unwelcome to the Chancellor and his friends, was popular with the Roman Catholic section of the Court ; and the Duke of York, though he showed no signs yet of any leaning toward Rome, was also a strong advocate of the war.

There was, indeed, no distinct division on religious grounds in this matter of a war with Holland. At this period a bitterly anti-Dutch feeling prevailed in England generally, due to the commercial and colonial rivalry of the two leading naval Powers of the world. On the other hand, it did not at all suit the policy of Louis XIV of France that one of these two nations should crush the other and become supreme. Louis was tied by treaty to the Dutch at present, and

[1] Otherwise "those old dotards," as Charles's other counsellors called them, according to Lord Sandwich.

at the same time was anxious to enter into closer
relations with England. He was, therefore, bent on
mediating, if possible, between the two countries, and
to this end made extraordinary diplomatic efforts,
which the friends of France at the English Court, including the adherents of the Queen-Mother Henrietta
Maria, seconded to the best of their ability. Among
the French party was Frances Stewart, whose
mother was attached to Henrietta Maria. Accordingly we find now the royal favourite and the
titular mistress of the King no unimportant figures in
the struggle for the direction of England's foreign
policy.

Louis, seeing that Cominges alone was unable to
influence Charles in the direction he desired, sent
over to help him the extraordinary mission which is
known as *la célèbre Ambassade*, including a prince of
the blood, the Duc de Verneuil. On their arrival
the envoys found the chief obstacle in the way of
carrying out their instructions to prevent an official
declaration of war between the English and Dutch
was the alliance between Lady Castlemaine and the
Spanish Ambassador, the Count de Molina. Spain,
the great military rival of France in Europe, was
naturally concerned to prevent any attempt at closer
Anglo-French relations. The Vatican was still domin-
ated by her, and, in spite of Charles's Portuguese
marriage, which seemed to commit him to hostility
against her, she had a strong hold on the sympathies
of the English Roman Catholics. Nor was she any
longer disliked by the English nation generally. Lady

Castlemaine, for once in a way, was ranged on the more popular side.

The letters sent to Paris by the representatives of France this summer bring out the attitude of the mistress about the political situation. The Ambassadors are soon compelled to recognise the difficulty of their task. They believe that the English King wants peace, but he tells them that his people are enraged against the Dutch and that he cannot recall his fleet. On June 1st Verneuil and his associates write reporting a bitter speech against the French made at Lady Castlemaine's by Lauderdale, who ruled the King as far as Scottish affairs were concerned and was growing more powerful in English affairs also. His words are quickly on every one's lips and are repeated on the Exchange every morning. Was the King at Lady Castlemaine's to hear Lauderdale's speech ? We are not told, but a day later Pepys, going to Court on a matter of business, is " led up to my Lady Castlemaine's lodgings, where the King and she and others were at supper," so that we may presume His Majesty was still constant at his suppers with the mistress.

On the day after this visit of Pepys to Lady Castlemaine's apartments was fought the great naval battle in Southwold Bay, when the English fleet under the Duke of York gained a handsome victory over Opdam and the other Dutch admirals. The chief loss on the English side was Charles Berkeley (or, as he had now lately become, Lord Falmouth), who with Lord Muskerry and another was killed on board the flagship, so close to the Duke that he was splashed with their blood and brains. The public rejoicings over the fleet's success were enthusiastic, followed by demonstrations against the French Embassy, which refrained from joining in the display of bonfires at all the street doors.

While this naval battle was taking place Queen Catherine was at Tunbridge Wells once more, drinking the waters, and the Court ladies attended upon her in their turns. " The ladies here," writes Henry Savile from London to his sister-in-law, " begin to go down to pay their duty to Her Majesty. My Lady Denham goes this night, my Lady Castlemaine and Lady Falmouth go next week." Savile does not anticipate much enjoyment for them, since he declares : " That Tunbridge is the most miserable place in the world is very certain, and that the ladys do not look with very great advantage at three of the clock in the morning is as true ! " Late hours were evidently the rule, whatever the ladies found to amuse them.

After her return from the Wells, Lady Castlemaine is next heard of at a great feast given by the Spanish Ambassador to her and his other friends. The pro-Spanish party was naturally jubilant at the result of Southwold Bay, and Molina was on the best of terms with all the world. In honour of the occasion, his hospitality was so lavish that even his servants, entertaining the coachmen and lacqueys of his visitors, made them all drunk, and when my Lady and the other guests were ready to depart they found it impossible to trust themselves to be driven by men in such a state. Molina offered the services of his own

staff, whereon the English servants in their indignation rose up and fought them—which a French Embassy official finds " the greatest and pleasantest disorder possible."

But the French refuse to lose heart. Mademoiselle
Stewart, " incomparably more beautiful " than Lady
Castlemaine, according to one of them, is very friendly
to them, and they think they see hopeful signs of a
decrease of the Castlemaine influence. On July 16th
Courtin, one of the Ambassadors, reports with satisfaction to Lionne that the mistress " has refused to
sleep at Hampton Court, saying that her apartment
is not yet ready." Meanwhile, " His Britannic
Majesty supped yesterday with Mlle. Stewart, at Lord
Arlington's " ; Lady Castlemaine " runs great risks,
and if her anger lasts may well lose the finest rose on
her hat."

The move to Hampton Court, to which Courtin
refers, was occasioned by fear of the terrible visitor
which had reached London in the summer of 1665.
During the week ending June 27th the deaths from
plague in town had numbered 267. The Court prepared to fly, and on the 29th Pepys saw at Whitehall
the waggons and people ready to go. What Lady
Castlemaine did when she refused to sleep at Hampton
Court we do not know. It is hardly likely that she
continued at Whitehall when all around the infection
was spreading. Possibly she went for a time to Richmond Palace, as we have seen her go before ; if so,
probably her retirement thither was as brief as on
the previous occasions.

But soon the plague began to extend its ravages; the London death-rate increased enormously, and a soldier on duty at Hampton Court itself was seized. So before the end of July a move further out of the danger-zone was decided on, and on the 27th the Court set out for Salisbury. Pepys, a visitor to Hampton Court that day, watches the King and Queen depart and finds it " pretty to see the young pretty ladies dressed like men, in velvet coats, caps with ribbands, and with laced bands, just like men." No ladies' names are mentioned, but both Lady Castlemaine and Frances Stewart were among those who accompanied Their Majesties and may have been among the wearers of the man-like dress, with regard to which an Oxford letter some two months later is of interest. " One cannot possibly know a woman from a man," writes Denis de Repas to Sir Robert Harley, " unlesse one hath the eyes of a linx who can see through a wall, for by the face and garbe they are like men. They do not wear any hood, but only men's perwick hats and coats."

The plague was not slow in following the fugitives to Salisbury, and in August there were deaths in the street—" an unpleasant habit which begins to spread here," writes Courtin—and closings of infected houses. It seemed necessary to make another move. Moreover, time doubtless hung rather heavily on King and courtiers alike at Salisbury, while there was the assembly of Parliament to take place in October, the appointed place for which was Oxford.

So on September 25th King Charles reached Oxford

and took up his residence as before in the lodgings of the Dean of Christ Church. The Dukes of York and Monmouth arrived the same day, the Queen the next. Lady Castlemaine possibly travelled with Her Majesty in her capacity of Lady of the Bedchamber ; but her two little sons came on the 25th and were lodged at the house of the Wood family, opposite Merton College Gate, as Antony Wood records.[1] The Queen and her ladies were assigned rooms in Merton, the Queen having those in the Warden's House which Henrietta Maria had occupied in the troublous times of the Civil War, and Lady Castlemaine, Frances Stewart, and others having rooms belonging to various Fellows and Postmasters of Merton, who were turned out of college to make room for them. The rest of the Court and the Diplomatic Body were distributed about the University, the Duke and Duchess of York being at Christ Church, the Duke and Duchess of Monmouth at Corpus, the French Ambassadors at Magdalen, the Spanish at New College, and so on.

The task of housing all these people at Oxford was a difficult one, and it is evident that the Chancellor of the University by no means relished it. He tells, in the *Continuation* of his life, how there was some unpleasantness with the Lord High Treasurer Southampton about it. Attempts had recently been made to sow the seeds of ill-will between them, and South-

---

[1] "Sept. 25, M., the lady of Castlemaine's two children began to lay at our house." Wood apparently did not feel honoured by his home sheltering the future Dukes of Southampton and Grafton.

ampton was feeling some jealousy of his old friend.
" Which," says Clarendon, " was improved by the
ladies, who did not like their lodging, and thought it
proceeded from want of friendship in him [the
Chancellor], who had the power over the University,
and might have assigned what lodgings he pleased to
the Treasurer; and he had assigned this, as the best
house in the town for so great a family."

As for the University, it certainly seems to have
felt but little pleasure at the prolonged visit of the
Court in its midst. The presence of more ladies than
scholars in chapel, which the Merton College Register
notes, did not compensate for the turning out of their
rooms of fellows and undergraduates and the conse-
quent upset of scholarly peace.[1] Then there was the
dread, fortunately unrealised, of the great epidemic
reaching the town in the train of the Court. " It
was noe better," declares Wood, " than tempting God
to bring upon us the sad judgment of the plague."
However, Denis de Repas in the above quoted letter
quaintly remarks : " There is no othere plague here
but the infection of love."

Wood's opinion of the intruders themselves is the
reverse of flattering. He sums them up thus :

" The greater sort of the courtiers were high, proud,
insolent, and looked upon scolars noe more than pedants,
or pedagogicall persons ; the lower sort also made noe
more of them then the greater, not suffering them to

[1] One Fellow of Merton sent Antony Wood sixty-nine folios to
look after for him until the King and Queen should have left Oxford.
He was no doubt wise.

see the King or Queen at dinner or supper or scarce at cards or at masse, never regarding that they had parted with their chambers and conveniences. . . . To give a further character of the Court, they, though they were neat and gay in their apparell, yet they were very nasty and beastly. . . ."

Politeness forbids us continuing the quotation ; but Woods finds the courtiers rude, rough, immoral, vain, empty, and careless. He had certainly some justification for his censure, particularly as at Merton " the Masters " had to complain of discourtesy shown to them by a royal servant on the very day after the Queen's arrival.

Nevertheless, the welcome given to the visitors was very loyal. At Merton itself, when the Queen was escorted to her lodgings by the King and the Duke of York, the College authorities met them and one of the Fellows recited sixteen lines of verse, of which two asserted that :

> " Our pious founder, knew he this daye's state,
> Would quitt his mansion to congratulate."

Walter de Merton was happily beyond reach of questions as to what he might think about the matter.

About Lady Castlemaine during this, her second visit to Oxford, we hear but little before an occurrence soon to be mentioned. Her state of health now did not allow her to appear much in public. And, unfortunately, one supposed reference to her promenading in the Lime Walk of Trinity College with a lute playing before her, and attending the chapel there " like an angel but half-dressed," turns out to be an error, the lady alluded to being really Lady Isabella Thynne, in the reign of Charles I.[1]

But if Lady Castlemaine was debarred from showing herself much abroad, she had the satisfaction of seeing her influence with the King prevailing still and his foreign policy shaped according to her desire. At the end of November, the French Ambassadors quitted Oxford, leaving with the President of Magdalen a piece of plate worth four pounds as a memorial of their visit. *La célèbre Ambassade* had failed. England was still in a fighting mood, as was shown by the early speeches of the Parliament which began its sittings in the schools at Oxford on October 9th ; and Louis, unable to stop the war and pledged by treaty to aid

---

[1] As a Trinity man I am sorry to spoil (if, indeed, I am the first to do so, which I do not know) the pleasant legend connecting Lady Castlemaine with my own college. But John Aubrey in his *Lives of Eminent Men*, writing of Ralph Kettle, D.D., tells how a certain Lady Isabella Thynne used to visit Trinity Lime Walk during the time when Oxford was the Royalist head-quarters. " Our grove," he says, " was the Daphne for the ladies and their gallants to walke in, and many times my Lady Isabella Thynne would make her entreys with a theorbo or lute played before her. I have heard her play on it in the grove myselfe, which she did rarely. . . . One may say of her as Tacitus said of Agrippina, *Cuncta alia illi adfuere praeter animum honestum.* She was most beautifull, most humble, charitable, &c., but she could not subdue one thing." Aubrey adds that this lady and " fine Mrs. Fenshawe, her great and intimate friend," were wont " to come to our Chapell, mornings, halfe dressed like angells." The late Mark Pattison, then Rector of Lincoln, writing in *Macmillan's Magazine* for July 1875, and trusting to his memory, made Lady Castlemaine the heroine of the tale. And Steinman (*Memoir of Barbara, Duchess of Cleveland, Second Addenda,* 1878, p. 4), by accepting the unidentified reference, perpetuated the error.

K

the Dutch, had to renounce for the present his scheme
for closer union with England.   There was nothing
for it but an open rupture between England and
France.   The Castlemaine-Molina alliance had won
the day, and " Mrs. Stewart " had proved a broken
reed, as far as her political influence over the King
was concerned.   No doubt the representatives of
France had over-estimated her desire to take a hand
in the game.   Clarendon, who has a high opinion of
Frances Stewart, states that she " never seemed disposed to interpose in the least degree in business " ;
" which kind of nature and temper," he adds, " the
more inflamed the King's affection, who did not in his
nature love a busy woman, and had an aversion from
speaking with any woman, or hearing them speak, of
any business but to that purpose he thought them
all made for, however they broke in afterwards upon
him to all other purposes."

About a month after the discomfiture of the French
Ambassadors, in which she had played her part, Lady
Castlemaine was delivered of her third son and fifth
child.   On December 28th, 1665, was born George,
one day to be Duke of Northumberland.   Antony
Wood made the official entry in the register of the
parish of St. John Baptist, Oxford, which reads as
follows :

" 1665, Dec. 28, George Palmer, sonne of Roger,
earl of Castlemaine, was born in Merton College ; and
was baptized there the first of January following.   His
mother's name was Barbara, daughter of —— Villiers,

since dutchesse of Cleveland. *Filius naturalis regis Caroli II.*"

In his private copy of the register he speaks of "George Palmer, base son of King Charles II." And there was never any doubt as to the fatherhood of the child, in the King's mind or that of any one else. That Oxford was scandalised may be gathered from Wood's mention of a "libell on the countess of Castlemayne's dore in Merton College" one day in January. He gives the libel, which was in both Latin and English, but the sample of scholastic scorn cannot be quoted here. It must suffice to say that it suggested that, but for the King being the father, the mother would have been ducked—which seems to have been the contemporary Oxford method of dealing with undesirable ladies. A thousand pounds was offered as a reward for the discovery of the libel's author, without effect. But Lady Castlemaine was not ashamed, and we shall see her one day claiming proudly that this son of hers was born among the scholars !

CHAPTER VII

THE STRUGGLE FOR SUPREMACY

THE plague in London having decreased very markedly, and war with France having been declared, Charles II left Oxford on January 27th, 1666, eighteen days after Pierce, lately come from there, had told Pepys that " all the town, and every boy in the streete, openly cries, 'The King cannot go away till my Lady Castlemaine be ready to come along with him.' " Whether the lady left with him we do not hear. The Queen was not able to move until February 16th, having been so unfortunate as to disappoint the hopes of the King which had been fulfilled in the case of Lady Castlemaine. This accident is said to have had a lasting effect on her husband's mind. Clarendon says that " some of the women who had more credit with the King " assured him that there had never really been any foundation for the Queen's expectation,[1] of which he suffered himself to be convinced ; and that " from that time he took little pleasure in her conversation, and more indulged to himself all the liberties in the conversation of those who used their skill to supply him with divertisements which might drive all that was serious out of

[1] As a matter of fact, hopes were aroused again in 1668 and 1669, but were again disappointed.

CHARLES THE SECOND

his thoughts." During his abode at Oxford, though he had been regular in his morning calls upon both Lady Castlemaine and Frances Stewart, he had been observed to live with more constraint and caution. Now he relaxed the effort to be an attentive husband, and, but for Clarendon's own continued presence at the head of affairs, it seems possible that in the bitterness of his disappointment Charles might have given his consideration at once to the scheme that was actually debated after the Chancellor's fall a year and a half later.

The mistress was naturally triumphant over the turn which affairs had taken, and abused her influence over the King to the utmost, especially in the matter of replenishing her purse. " Her principal business," says Clarendon, " was to get an estate for herself and her children, which she thought the King at least as much concerned to provide as she to solicit; which however she would not be wanting in, and so procured round sums of money out of the privy purse (where she had placed Mr. May) and other assignations in other names, and so the less taken notice of, though in great proportions : all which yet amounted to little more than to pay her debts, which she in a few years contracted to an unimaginable greatness, and to defray her constant expenses, which were very excessive in coaches and horses, clothes and jewels, without anything of generosity, or gratifying any of her family, or so much as paying any of her father's debts,[1] whereof some were very

---

[1] She did, however, erect to his memory the marble tomb in Christ Church Cathedral.

clamorous." He goes on to say that she procured
for herself grants of land in Ireland, because these
did not have to come before the Chancellor and
Treasurer of England, who were thus powerless to
obstruct the grants and did not even know about
them.

We shall hear more later about these grants in
Ireland, and considerably more about the money
lavished by the King upon her whom Burnet so
justifiably calls " enormously vicious and ravenous."
For the present, it may be noticed that she had hardly
returned to London from Oxford when she bought
from Edward Bakewell or Backwell, alderman, banker,
and goldsmith, two diamond rings, valued at £1100
and £900 respectively, but did not pay for them.
The Domestic State Papers of Charles II show that
this same year another jeweller, John Leroy, was
petitioning the King for " payment of £357, balance
of £850 due for a ring delivered to the Countess of
Castlemaine, which she said was for His Majesty."
Whether the other rings were for her own adornment
or to give away does not appear. But she was very
fond of personal jewelry.

The conduct of the war simultaneously against
Holland and France—it is true that the French
demonstrations against England were very languid—
had little effect on the amusements of the Court.
Dining with Pierce and his family on Easter Day,
Pepys hears all about " the amours and the mad
doings that are there." Even after the murderous
sea-fight with the Dutch, the Battle of the Downs,

on the opening days of June, domestic affairs seem to occupy most attention at Whitehall. On June 10th Pepys has another of his Sunday gossips with Pierce, and learns the details of a falling out between the King and Lady Castlemaine, of which we should otherwise have heard nothing. The Queen, says Pierce, " in ordinary talke before the ladies in her drawing-room, did say to my Lady Castlemaine that she feared the King did take cold by staying abroad so late at her house. She answered before them all, that he did not stay so late abroad with her, for he went betimes thence (though he did not before one, two, or three in the morning), but must stay somewhere else. The King then coming in and overhearing did whisper in the eare aside, and told her she was a bold impertinent woman, and bid her begone out of the Court, and not come again till he sent for her ; which she did presently, and went to a lodging in the Pell Mell, and kept there two or three days, and then sent to the King to know whether she might send for her things away out of her house. The King sent to her, she must first come and view them ; and so she came, and the King went to her, and all friends again."

While her anger lasted, however, Lady Castlemaine went so far as to threaten " to be even with the King and print his letters to her." Charles could scarcely afford to anticipate the terse answer of the Duke of Wellington to a similar threat and tell the lady to " publish and be damned," for Lady Castlemaine would probably have taken him at his word. So he was doubtless wise, if not dignified, in the course which he adopted.

A very odd petition among the Domestic State Papers of 1666 shows how much the conduct of the King with his mistress aroused public concern at this time. The document is three pages long, and concludes by stating that the petitioner " is but a woman and can only pray for His Majesty." The most interesting statement made in it is that " people say, ' Give the King the Countess of Castlemaine, and he cares not what the nation suffers.' " With what feelings, we may wonder, did Charles read this, if it ever came before his eyes ?

Some casual notices of Lady Castlemaine and Frances Stewart in the following months do not convey much information. But one entry in Pepys's *Diary* is worth quotation on account of its unusually critical tone. He went to Whitehall on the evening of October 3rd. " And there among the ladies, and saw my lady Castlemaine never looked so ill, nor Mrs. Stewart neither, as in this plain, natural dress. I was not pleased with either of them." " Plain, natural dress," was seldom worn by the Caroline ladies, and doubtless looked strange upon them.

On October 21st we hear from the same source of a matter of more interest. Attached to the Bedchamber of the Duke of York was a young man called Harry Killigrew—the same whom Henry Savile, brother of the future Marquis of Halifax, addresses in a letter as " Noble Henry, sweet namesake of mine, happy-humoured Killigrew, soul of mirth and all delight ! " while Charles II, in a letter to his sister in 1668, calls him " a most notorious lyar." Like his father, " Tom " Killigrew, who held the curiously named post of Master of the Revels to Charles II and actually had a fool's dress in his wardrobe, Harry aspired to all the verbal licence of a recognised wit.[1] On this occasion he ventured to comment, in language more caustic than humorous, on Lady Castlemaine's conduct in girlhood. The truth was not palatable to the lady, who complained to the King. Charles asked his brother to dismiss his gentleman, which the Duke did. But James was offended that Lady Castlemaine had not come to him first, instead of going to the King ; and so, in spite of an effort by the lady, calling in person, to conciliate the Duke, " ill blood is made of it." Killigrew was forgiven after a time, for in 1669 he was Groom of the Bed-chamber to Charles himself. Nine years later he offended another mistress in a drunken freak, calling at Nell Gwynn's early one morning to tell her, ostensibly from the King, that her hated rival, the Duchess of Portsmouth, had recovered from an illness that was expected to kill her. He was banished again, but nevertheless succeeded his father as Master of the Revels.

It was naturally annoying to the former Barbara Villiers to be put in mind of her first period. The last

[1] Thomas Killigrew's best effort was when he appeared before Charles dressed and booted as if for a journey. Asked by the King where he was going in such a hurry, he replied : " To Hell, to fetch up Oliver Cromwell to look after the affairs of England, for his successor never will ! "

reminders, except for the name which accompanied it, of the second period were effaced this same year. Lord Castlemaine had been in England at the beginning of 1666, for in May he received the King's leave to go abroad again. He did not depart at once, or else he paid another brief visit to England; for on December 12th Pepys hears from Sir H. Cholmly how Lady Castlemaine and her husband are now "parted for ever, upon good terms, never to trouble one another more."

The Great Fire which made this year so memorable for London, as it was prevented from reaching Whitehall, did not affect Lady Castlemaine personally ; save in so far as it gave an impetus to the bitter and unjust anti-Papist agitation which involved her later, and (we may perhaps add) because it induced John Leroy, jeweller, to send in a more pressing request for the balance of the money due to him on the ring purchased for His Majesty. But she doubtless watched the progress of the conflagration, while Charles, to his credit—unlike the legendary fiddling Nero—took an active part in the devising of schemes to fight the fire, and, as Evelyn relates, with the Duke of York " even laboured in person and was present to command, order, reward, and encourage workmen, by which he showed his affection to his people and gained theirs." The same loyal observer, it must be noticed, speaking of the general fast ordered throughout the nation on October 10th, says that the " dismal judgments " of fire, plague, and war were highly deserved for " our prodigious ingratitude, burning lusts, dissolute Court, profane and abominable lives."

It was not long before the dissolute Court which Evelyn laments resumed its gaiety and licence after the temporary quiet caused by the Fire. Evelyn's indignation against the Duke of York for the way in which he behaved with Lady Denham at Court toward the end of September is recorded by his friend Pepys; and the graver of the two diarists himself has some scathing remarks on the theatre when, against his conscience at such a time, he attends a performance of Lord Broghill's *Mustapha* at Whitehall. He sees the theatres " abused to an atheisticall liberty " and " fowle and undecent women now (and never till now) permitted to appear and act, who inflaming severall young noblemen and gallants, became their misses, and to some their wives." He does not foresee, however, how much worse things are to become, and how the " misses " are soon to threaten the position of the very mistress *en titre*, the Countess of Castlemaine, and defeat her by virtue of being yet more brazen than she.

Some more innocent revels at Court this autumn are described by Pepys on the occasion of the Queen's birthday, November 15th. The scene is so characteristic and interesting that no apology is needed for transcribing it :

" I also to the ball, and with much ado got up to the loft, where with much trouble I could see very well. Anon the house grew full, and the candles light, and the King and Queen and all the ladies

set : and it was, indeed, a glorious sight to see Mrs.
Stewart in black and white lace, and her head and
shoulders dressed with dyamonds, and the like a
great many great ladies more, only the Queen none ;
and the King in his rich vest of some rich silke and
silver trimmings, as the Duke of York and all the
dancers were, some of cloth of silver, and others of
other sorts, exceeding rich. Presently after the King
was come in, he took the Queene, and about fourteen
more couple there was, and begun the Bransles. . . .
After the Bransles, then to a Corant, and now and
then a French dance ; but that so rare that the
Corants grew tiresome, that I wished it done. Only
Mrs. Stewart danced mighty finely, and many French
dances, specially one the King called the New Dance,
which was very pretty ; but upon the whole matter,
the business of the dancing of itself was not extraordinary pleasing. But the clothes and sight of the
persons was indeed very pleasing, and worth my
coming, being never likely to see more gallantry
while I live, if I should come twenty times. . . . My
Lady Castlemayne, without whom all is nothing,
being there, very rich, though not dancing."

There had been rumours of the lady's indisposition
for some weeks before this, so that her not taking
an active part in the ball seems to have occasioned no
surprise. It is curious, however, that in a letter to
Harley a month later, Denis de Repas should say :
" Lady Castlemaine lives as retired as a nun. She has
not been seen at ball or play since the fire." Although
the eye-witness Pepys must, of course, be correct,
doubtless Lady Castlemaine may have lived in unusual

retirement at this period. Still her hold over the King and her extortions from him continued undiminished, of which a signal proof was given before the end of this year. According to what Sir H. Cholmly told Pepys on December 16th, Charles had lately paid about £30,000 to clear her debts. On the following Sunday the diarist himself went to Whitehall, and " saw my dear Lady Castlemaine, who continues admirable, methinks, and I do not hear but that the King is the same to her still as ever." But, as usual, at the end of the year Pepys grows moral and shakes his head over the " sad, vicious, negligent Court."

If 1666 closed with no alteration in the situation of affairs in Charles's heart, in the following spring the Court was suddenly struck as though a thunderbolt had fallen in its midst. Frances Stewart at the end of March eloped with her cousin Charles, Duke of Richmond and Lennox, kinsman to his namesake the King as well as to herself. The Duke had lost his second wife at the beginning of the year, and a fortnight after she was buried proposed for the hand of Frances. On March 19th they were betrothed, report said, and the next thing to be heard was that the maid of honour had been fetched by a ruse to the Bear Tavern by Southwark Bridge, got into a coach with her cousin, and fled with him to Kent without the King's leave.

Gramont, " the most bare-faced liar in the world," has a long story of the King's discovery of an intrigue between Frances and the Duke of

Richmond, led to it by Lady Castlemaine and the
infamous William Chiffinch, keeper of Charles's
backstairs, and dispenser of his most secret funds ;
with circumstantial details of the resulting quarrel
between the King and the maid.   But the un-
supported word of Gramont here is probably
about as valuable as it is anywhere else.   It is better
to rely on what Burnet says about Charles's consent
to the marriage, " pretending to take care of her,
that he would have good settlements made for her,"
as " he hoped by that means to have broken the
matter decently, for he knew the Duke of Richmond's
affairs were in disorder."   This at least is reconcilable
with what Pepys hears from Sir William Penn and
Evelyn, the latter of whom learns " from a Lord
that she told it to but yesterday, with her own mouth,
and a sober man, that when the Duke of Richmond
did make love to her, she did ask the King, and he
did the like also ; and that the King did not deny it."

That Charles was nevertheless vexed at the sudden
elopement is quite possible.   He was trying to make
the best of things and to take up a generous attitude,
but the runaway marriage snatched the matter out
of his hands, and he took what was a long time for
him to choke down his feeling of resentment.   Part
of his anger against Clarendon was supposed to be
due to his belief that the Chancellor was implicated
in the Richmond match.

One person who could not fail to be pleased at
what had happened was the mistress.   " Now the
Countess Castlemaine do carry all before her,"

Evelyn told Pepys. Her rejoicing was premature, it is true; but that was not to be manifested until some time had passed. For the present matters seemed to be going very well for her. The Richmond match removed her great rival of her own sex from her path. On May 16th death took away an object of her detestation in the Lord Treasurer Southampton— an event which Clarendon declares made a fatal breach in his own fortune, " with a gap wide enough to let in all the ruin which soon after was poured upon him." It is certain that the disappearance of one of the only two great ministers who refused to pay court to her made easier the gratification of the mistress's spite against the other, whom she hated still more.

With " the prevalence of the lady," as Clarendon calls it, naturally increased by these two happenings of early 1667, frivolity reigned at Court unchecked by domestic sorrows or public calamities. On May 23rd the infant Duke of Kendal, younger son of the Duke of York, died, while his elder brother, the Duke of Cambridge, was so ill that he was expected to go first, and, as a matter of fact, only survived him by a month. In the second week of June came the famous raid of the Dutch fleet up the Thames and Medway, the capture of the Duke's flagship, *The Royal Charles*, and the destruction of several other big warships, followed by a great panic and cries of England's betrayal by " the Papists and others about the King." Charles, going out one day to feed his ducks in St. James's Park and to stroll with Prince

Rupert, returned to find the whole of Whitehall in an uproar and the Countess of Castlemaine bewailing, above all others, that she should be the first torn to pieces. Yet " the Court is as mad as ever," says Sir H. Cholmly to Pepys ; " and that night the Dutch burnt our ships the King did sup with my Lady Castlemaine at the Duchess of Monmouth's, and they were all mad in hunting a poor moth "— a tale which makes a curious contrast with Pepys's own experience on the backstairs at Whitehall on June 13th, where he heard the lacqueys saying that there was " hardly anybody in the Court but do look as if he cried " !

Never, perhaps, was the inconsistent character of Charles II more clearly demonstrated than at this period of his life. A man so capable of rising to an occasion as he had proved himself to be had a glorious opportunity now of showing what lay beneath the surface. But all he could do apparently was to furnish his subjects with material for indignant reflection. The moth-hunting story is bad enough. What of this other, which Pepys got a few days after from Povy ?

" He tells me, speaking of the horrid effeminacy of the King, that the King hath taken ten times more care and pains in making friends between my Lady Castlemaine and Mrs. Stewart, when they have fallen out, than ever he did to save his kingdom ; nay, that upon any falling out between my Lady Castlemaine's nurse and her woman, my Lady hath often said she would make the King to make them friends, and they would be friends and be quiet ; which the King hath been fain to do : that the King is, at this day, every night in Hyde Park with the Duchesse of Monmouth, or with my Lady Castlemaine."

Truly Burnet's diagnosis of the case of Charles and Lady Castlemaine seems correct, that " his passion for her, and her strange behaviour toward him, did so disorder him that often he was not master of himself nor capable of minding business." [1]

The most noticeable evil arising from this condition of the King was the enormous demands which he made upon the revenues of his country to satisfy his Privy Purse, which by the influence of his mistress had been entrusted to the hands of Baptist May, another gentleman of the same stamp as William Chiffinch. May had the effrontery to tell the discontented Members of Parliament that £300 a year was enough for any country gentleman—" which makes them mad," Pepys hears, " and they do talk of 6 or 800,000£ gone into the Privy Purse this war, when in King James's time it arose to but £5000, and in King Charles's but £10,000 in a year." Pepys's informant also reports that " a goldsmith in town told him that, being with some plate with my Lady Castlemaine lately, she directed her woman (the great beauty), ' Wilson,' says she, ' make a note for

---

[1] The loyal Sir John Reresby makes this defence of his master in such matters : "If love prevailed with him more than any other passion, he had this for excuse, besides that his complexion was of an amorous sort, the women seemed to be the aggressors." Lady Castlemaine certainly was not lacking in aggressive spirit.

L

this, and for that, to the Privy Purse for money.'"
This plate is doubtless the same which the Domestic
State Papers show Charles II presenting to Lady
Castlemaine this summer, weighing in all 5600 ounces.

The King's lavish bounty to his mistress, on the
top of the £30,000 with which he had recently paid
off her debts, did not prevent a most violent quarrel
between them now. It seems to have had a double
cause. In the first place, it was occasioned by Lady
Castlemaine's intervention on behalf of her kinsman,
the Duke of Buckingham. She had herself been on
very ill terms with Buckingham in the previous year,
and the Duke's candid comments on Court life
(of which he was one of the leaders, when not, as he
so frequently was, in disgrace) aroused Charles's
anger against him. He got himself twice committed
to the Tower in 1666 through the violence of his
behaviour. His wit, " unrestrained by any modesty
or religion," as Clarendon says, and his social talents
reconciled him to the King, but he was soon in
trouble again, leading the opposition in Parliament,
and giving reasons for suspicion of more serious
designs against the King. He was consequently
stripped of all his offices, and once more, after some
delay, committed to the Tower.

As a Villiers herself, Barbara apparently felt called
upon to come to his rescue, and Charles, though
supposed to be ready enough to pardon him, was
annoyed at this interference. In early July there
was a great falling out, Charles and the lady parting
" with very foul words." He called her, among

other things, " a jade that meddled with things she
had nothing to do with at all " ; while she said he
was a fool, for if not a fool he would not suffer his
business to be carried on by fellows that did not
understand them, and cause his best subjects, and
those best able to serve him, to be imprisoned. So
irritated was His Majesty that it was believed he
would never restore the Duke to office again. But
in a few days came the news of Buckingham's release
from the Tower without a trial, which Pepys declares
" one of the strangest instances of the fool's play
with which all publick things are done in this age."
His restoration to his various offices only waited for
the removal of Clarendon's opposition, which was not
long in coming.

The Duke of Buckingham's pardon was attributed
to Lady Castlemaine's influence, the public being
unable to believe that the King would remain at
variance with her for any length of time. But there
was more at the bottom of this quarrel. On July
27th Pepys learns that the King and the lady " are
quite broke off, and she is gone away, and is with
child, and swears the King shall own it, and she will
have it christened in the Chapel at Whitehall so,
and owned for the King's, or she will bring it into
Whitehall gallery and dash the brains of it out before
the King's face." Soon after he has additional
details, how that when Charles said the child was not
his, " she made a slighting ' puh ' with her mouth
and went out of the house, and never come in again
till the King went to Sir Daniel Harvy's to pray her."

According to Dr. Pierce, Charles was forced to go upon his knees, asking her forgiveness and promising to offend no more, before she would make it up with him again, even to the extent of receiving his visits at Harvey's house.

The King, it was said, was convinced that the expected child, of which, by the way, we hear no more, would belong to Henry Jermyn, nephew of the Earl of St. Albans, and one of the villainous heroes of the *Gramont Memoirs*, a complete courtier and fearful rake, though anything but a handsome man. Gramont represents Lady Castlemaine as infatuated with Jermyn, and the scandal of Whitehall, which had for some time connected her name with his, supports Gramont to the full. "The King," comments Pepys, "is mad at her entertaining Jermyn, and she is mad at Jermyn's going to marry away from her"—he was reputed to be engaged to the widowed Lady Falmouth, who, from her portrait by Lely, had one of the most charming faces of her time—"so they are all mad; and thus the kingdom is governed."

The outward appearance of tranquillity, however, is restored. The lady still remains at Harvey's house, where Charles visits her. But she does not avoid Whitehall, and is seen walking in the Privy Garden on "Bab" May's arm, immediately after the King. She gets her 5600 ounces of plate, she is credited with having a maternal uncle of hers, Dr. Glemham—"a drunken, swearing rascal, and a scandal to the church"—made a Bishop, and generally

" hectors the King to whatever she will." The
courtiers laugh at Charles's very face about it. When
he rallies the Duke of York on being henpecked
by his wife, and compares him with *Tom Otter*,
Ben Jonson's type of such a husband, the elder
Killigrew asks : " Sir, pray which is best for a
man, to be a *Tom Otter* to his wife or his mistress ? "
The King's answer is not recorded, but the subject
must have been a very sore one to this slave of an
imperious beauty who denied him even the right
of decision as to who were his own children.

At some date between the 9th and the 26th of
August the mistress returned to her apartments
over the Holbein Gate, thus ratifying her peace with
the King very soon after the signing of the Treaty
of Breda, which brought peace to England, France,
and Holland, and was the last important event in
Clarendon's administration of English affairs. The
Chancellor had opposed the summoning of Parliament
before the Treaty of Breda was signed, and when
after the signature it was summoned and immediately
prorogued by the King, a violent outcry at once
arose, not against Charles, but against the Minister
who was accused of having advised this sudden
prorogation. The opportunity had come for all
Clarendon's enemies to band together to destroy
his power for ever, and they were quick to seize
upon it.

Lady Castlemaine, fresh from her own personal
triumph over Charles, figured as one of the chief
actors in a very celebrated scene at Whitehall on

August 26th, 1667. At about ten o'clock on the morning of that day the old Chancellor came to Whitehall for a conference with the King, who had decided to get rid of him, and had indeed already sent the Duke of York to request him to deliver up the Great Seal. This the Chancellor would not do until he had seen his master, and accordingly an interview was arranged, no one else being present but the Duke. Charles explained his reason for requiring the Chancellor's retirement from office, which was that he was assured of Parliament's resolve to impeach him as soon as they met again, and saw no way of saving him except by dismissal. Clarendon disputed the necessity or propriety of this, and in the course of his argument, as he relates himself, " found a seasonable opportunity to mention the lady, with some reflections and cautions which he might more advisedly have declined." The result was that " after two hours' discourse the King rose without saying anything, but appeared not well pleased with all that had been said." The Duke of York (who was, of course, Clarendon's son-in-law, and who, to his credit, made efforts both before and after this interview to save him) discovered that it was at the reference to the lady that his brother was so angered.

The King having gone, there was nothing for Clarendon to do but depart also. He made his way homeward through the Privy Garden, in which there were many watching to see him. He describes very briefly what occurred. " When the Chancellor returned, the lady, the Lord Arlington, and Mr. May looked together out of her open window with great gaiety and triumph, which all people observed." The invaluable Dr. Pierce supplements this account in one of his gossips with Pepys. When the Chancellor left, he says, Lady Castlemaine was in bed, though it was about twelve o'clock, and she ran out in her smock into her aviary, looking into Whitehall Garden. Her woman—Wilson " the great beauty," we may presume—brought her her nightgown, or what we should now call her dressing-gown. And then my Lady " stood joying herself at the old man's going away : and several of the gallants of Whitehall, of which there were many staying to see the Chancellor return, did talk to her in her bird-cage ; among others, Blancford, telling her she was the bird of paradise."

Two days after the interview Charles sent Sir William Morrice, Secretary of State, to receive the Seal from the Chancellor's hands. Morrice brought it back to the King, whereon Baptist May came in " and fell on his knees and kissed His Majesty's hand, telling him that he was now King, which he had never been before." Confirmed by his favourite advisers that he was acting rightly, Charles refused to relent, and insisted on his old and faithful friend's withdrawal from England. The ex-Chancellor left on December 3rd, never to return.

Clarendon asserts that he " could not comprehend or imagine from what fountain, except the power of the great lady with the conjunction of his known enemies, . . . that fierceness of the King's displeasure could arise." His view was shared by most other people, for example by Dr. Pierce, who told Pepys how "this business of my Lord Chancellor's was certainly designed in my Lady Castlemaine's chamber." Nor, indeed, could the Chancellor complain that he had been without warning from the mistress of his impending fate. Shortly before his fall he had stopped a grant from the King of a place worth £2000 a year (nominally to Viscount Grandison, the lady's uncle, but really for the use of her children), observing scornfully that this woman would soon sell everything. Lady Castlemaine at once sent him a message that "she had disposed of this place and did not doubt, in a little time, to dispose of his."

"The lady," against whom Clarendon had stood out so steadfastly from the first, had taken six years to accomplish her revenge ; but that revenge was complete when it was attained. She did not, it is true, have the pleasure of seeing his head upon a stake, keeping company with those of the regicides on Westminster Hall, as she is said, in the presence of the Queen, to have expressed a wish to see it. But at least he was gone an exile from his country at the age of fifty-eight, after having borne the heat of the day with the ungrateful Charles before 1660, and guided his affairs since the Restoration. The "old dotard" could thwart her no more.

Nor had she to pay any price for her vengeance. There was no public demonstration on behalf of the victim. Pepys, going to Bartholomew Fair on August 30th, finds the street full of people waiting to see Lady Castlemaine come out from a puppet-show. " I confess I did wonder at her courage to come abroad," he says, " thinking the people would abuse her ; but they, silly people ! do not know her work she makes, and therefore suffered her with great respect to take coach, and she away, without any trouble at all." She had, indeed, little reason to fear unpopularity over the latest exhibition of her power. Clarendon, at first at least, was almost without friends in the country, having to bear the odium of all the acts during his holding of the Great Seal, whether he had approved them or not. He brought this on himself, it cannot be denied. " Old Clarendon had as much power as ever Premier Minister had," says a letter written some time after his fall. His manner created this impression. He appeared unwilling to let any one else speak at the Council-table—not even the King, according to Charles himself. He was intolerant of opposition, convinced of his own correctness of judgment, scornful of intriguers, and an honest man, who had bought himself no friends. There were no mourners, therefore, at the funeral of his career.

With those who succeeded to the power which the great Chancellor had kept in his hands for seven years Lady Castlemaine, like her friend Bab May and the rest of " that wicked crew," as Pepys calls them, was on easy terms. The Duke of Buckingham in particular, after Clarendon's removal not merely readmitted to the Privy Council, but the greatest man in it, was more friendly disposed to his cousin now than at any time before or after. A common feeling of hatred for the Chancellor had united them, as it had many other not naturally harmonious persons. The sentiment was at least strong enough to keep them together until all fear of a restoration of the old regime was past.

Yet, in spite of the favourable appearance of affairs after the disappearance of her great enemy, all was not well with Lady Castlemaine's position at Court. At the very beginning of September 1667 rumours were afloat to the effect that she was " coming to a composition " with the King, to take a pension and retire to France. Pepys hears about it from four different sources in ten days, though one of his informants is incredulous about the likelihood of the wished-for event. Lord Brounker says that her demands are mighty high, and Sir William Batten speaks of a pension of £4000 a year. Povy, who does not think the composition will be successful, nevertheless believes that " the King is as weary of her as is possible, but he is so weak in his passion that he dare not do it."

There can be no doubt that the tales repeated by these courtiers were not far from the truth. The King was eager to placate Parliament after it had been offended so grievously by his sudden prorogation of it. One of his readiest ways of pleasing both Houses would be to rid his Court of some of the women in it, especially Castlemaine, before the reassembly in October. Nor can Povy's estimate of his feelings toward his mistress be far wrong. She had no longer the same sensual power over him as formerly. Possibly his passion for her had ceased entirely this year.   The habit of her ascendancy over him remained and was destined to remain almost for another ten years, to the great cost of his pocket and the nation's. But the yoke galled, and the taunts of the courtiers in this singularly free-speaking Court were constantly touching him on the raw. In his efforts to break away from his bondage he will soon be seen widening the area of his attentions, and lending to the stage a patronage which was more royal than reputable.

It is possible that some attempt was actually made to induce Lady Castlemaine to withdraw herself from Whitehall, at least while Parliament began its sittings. It is known from the *Savile Correspondence* that on September 16th she went down on a visit to Althorpe, the family seat of the Earls of Sunderland.   Robert, the second Earl, and his wife Anne (Digby) were both born intriguers, and made up to Lady Castlemaine now as later they did to the Duchess of Portsmouth. The visit to Althorpe was quite short, but it is not until nearly the end of the year 1667 that we hear of the mistress at Court again. On Christmas Eve Pepys is led by his happily insatiable curiosity to the Queen's chapel, where he " got in up almost to the rail, and with a great deal of patience staid from nine at night to two in the morning, in a very great crowd ; and there expected, but found nothing extraordinary, there being nothing but a high mass." Pepys's comments are amusing, as usual. The music he found very good indeed, but the service very

frivolous—" there can be no zeal go along with it "—
though all things very rich and beautiful.   Finally,
" all being done, and I sorry for my coming, missing
of what I expected ; which was, to have had a child
born and dressed there, and a great deal to do :
but we broke up, and nothing like it done : and
there I left people receiving the Sacrament : and the
Queen gone and ladies ; only my Lady Castlemaine,
who looked pretty in her night-clothes, and so took
my coach and away through Covent Garden, to set
down two gentlemen and a lady, who come thither
to see also and did make mighty mirth in their talk
of the folly of this religion."

A dozen years later Pepys was in serious trouble
for his supposed Papist sympathies ! But his accusers
had not the privilege of reading his *Diary*.

*From a photograph by Emery Walker, after a copy of a picture by
Sir Peter Lely in the National Portrait Gallery*

BARBARA VILLIERS, COUNTESS OF CASTLEMAINE
AND DUCHESS OF CLEVELAND

CHAPTER VIII

THE DECLINING MISTRESS

A PERIOD of great disorder, as Burnet calls it, was now opening for Lady Castlemaine. She was still at Whitehall, but her hold over the King, to whom her hectoring was so wearisome, was no longer the same in nature as it had been formerly. Frances Stewart was in London again, staying at Somerset House with her husband, and the King had already at the end of 1667 made overtures to her to return to Court. A disfiguring attack of smallpox in the following spring failed to make the Duchess less beautiful in his eyes; indeed, caused him, in his own words, to " pardon all that is past." The Richmonds were forgiven—seemingly against the Duke's own wish, and with some considerable reluctance on the part of the lady— and in July Frances was made a Lady of the Bedchamber to the Queen, who was fond of her and had earlier interceded on her behalf. In token of his affection for the wife Charles found occasion to send the husband on missions, first to Scotland and then to Denmark, on the latter of which he died. Frances was left a widow at the end of 1672, and never married again. Her reputation suffered considerably after her return to Court, and apparently with justification, though in such an age of scandal it is difficult to know how much to believe. At least, however, she was as modest in her requisitions from the Royal purse as Lady Castlemaine was exorbitant, and when she died, at the age of fifty-four, had been so far rehabilitated in character as to figure at the coronation of Queen Anne.

But it was not so much an old flame of the King's that caused Lady Castlemaine annoyance as some new flames, discovered in quite a different class of society from that of the Court. According to Burnet, it was the Duke of Buckingham who directed his master's attention to the beauties of the stage, in order to punish his cousin for opposing his scheme of persuading Charles to divorce his childless wife and marry again. That there was actually talk of putting away Catherine of Braganza, after the fall of Clarendon, her best friend, there is evidence. She was to retire to a nunnery for the remainder of her life, a divorce was to be procured, with the help of a complaisant Archbishop of Canterbury—the enemies of Gilbert Sheldon declared him ready to oblige the King—and a new wife was to be found. Whether Charles could have ever brought himself to take these steps is very doubtful, for he had a curious kind of regard for the wife he so gaily and grossly wronged ; but at least he allowed himself to consider the scheme. Lady Castlemaine, however, for once became a warm partisan of the Queen and, when she discovered who was the arch-plotter, quarrelled with Buckingham, never to be reconciled again. An unofficial rival was bad enough, but a new Queen—and this time probably an Englishwoman—threatened a death-blow to her power.

Therefore, as the story goes, Buckingham determined to undermine the influence which he could not sweep away. He made the first advance with the introduction of Mary Davis, once a milkmaid, now an actress. Reputed a daughter of one of the Howards, Earls of Berkshire, near whose Wiltshire house she was borne by a blacksmith's wife, she springs into notoriety in January 1668. Previously she is only " little Mis. Davis " of the Duke's Playhouse, whom Pepys describes to us as dancing a jig in boy's clothes and infinitely outshining as a dancer Nell Gwynn of the King's House. But it was not her dancing as much as her singing which charmed Charles's heart. Traditionally it was her rendering of a ballad, " My lodging it is on the cold ground," which raised her to a higher sphere. On January 13th there was an amateur performance of *The Indian Emperor* at Court, in which the Duke and Duchess of Monmouth and others took part. The players of the Duke's House were present, having no doubt coached the amateurs for the affair. Mrs. Pierce, who sat near them, describes Moll Davis to Pepys and his wife next day as " the most impertinent slut in the world ; and the more now the King do show her countenance ; and is reckoned his mistress, even to the scorne of the whole world ; the King gazing on her, and my Lady Castlemaine being melancholy and out of humour, all the play, not smiling once." The King, it is said, has given her a ring worth

£700, which she shows to everybody, and has furnished for her most richly a house in Suffolk Street; " which is a most infinite shame," observes Pepys. The Queen was disgusted, and at a performance in the Whitehall theatre one night she was observed to take her departure when Mrs. Davis came on to dance her jig. For the mistress, however, it was more serious to be out of request than for Her Majesty, so that we are not surprised to hear from Pepys again that she is " mighty melancholy and discontented "—especially as scandal makes Moll Davis not the only new rival, but has already begun to hint at Nell Gwynn and others.

But Lady Castlemaine did not content herself with being " mighty melancholy and discontented " over the King's bestowal of his affections in a new quarter. She promptly paid him back in his own coin. She was a well-known patron of the drama, not only of playwrights, but of performers also. She had been a great friend even to Nell Gwynn for a time. Among her other actress acquaintances was Rebecca Marshall, of the King's House, through whom she obtained an introduction to her fellow-actor, Charles Hart, great-nephew of Shakespeare, and reputed to have been the first lover of Nell Gwynn. One day Pepys is told by Mrs. Knipp of the King's—of whom Mrs. Pepys was very legitimately jealous—some " mighty news, that my Lady Castlemaine is mightily in love with Hart of their house, and he is much with her in private, and she goes to him and do give him many presents ; . . . . and by this means she is even with the King's love to Mrs. Davis."

Such a story, interesting no doubt to other members of the King's House company as well as the lively Mrs. Knipp, must soon have got around the town. It is not surprising, therefore, that among the " libertine libels " that Evelyn says were printed and thrown about now was a bold mock-petition to Lady Castlemaine, who was horribly vexed at it, according to Pepys. There had been near the end of March some riots in the low quarters of London, in the course of which a mob of holiday-making apprentices and others pulled down a number of houses of ill-repute. Some jester, who naturally took good precautions to keep his identity secret, promptly came out with a petition addressed to " The most Splendid, Illustrious, and Eminent Lady of Pleasure, the Countess of Castlemayne." This was indeed, as Pepys remarks, " not very witty, but devilish severe against her and the King." It may be permissible, however, to quote a reasonably decent part of the document, of which a copy is preserved in the British Museum to-day. The victims of the late riots are made to say :

. . . " We being moved by the imminent danger now impending, and the great sense of our present suffering, do implore your Honour to improve your Interest, which (all know) is great, That some speedy Relief may be afforded us, to prevent Our Utter Ruine and Undoing. And that such a sure course may be taken with the Ringleaders and Abetters of these evil-disposed persons, that a stop may be put unto them before they come to Your Honours Pallace, and bring contempt upon your worshipping of *Venus*, the great

M

Goddess whom we all adore. . . . And we shall endeavour, as our bounden duty, the promoting of your Great Name, and the preservation of your Honour, Safety, and Interest, with the hazzard of our Lives, Fortunes, and Honesty.

" And your Petitioners shall (as by custom bound) Evermore Play &c.

" Signed by Us, Madam *Cresswell* and *Damaris Page*, in the behalf of our Sisters and Fellow-Sufferers (in this time of our Calamity) in Dog and Bitch Yard, Lukeners Lane, Saffron Hill, Moor-fields, Chiswell-street, Rosemary-Lane, Nightingale-Lane, Ratcliffe-High-way, Well-close, Church-Lane, East-Smith-field, &c., this present 25th day of March, 1668."

A month later there was a pretended reply published called " The Gracious Answer of the most Illustrious *Lady* of *Pleasure* the *Countess* of *Castlem* . . ." and dated " Given at our Closset in King Street, Westminster,[1] die Veneris April 24 1668." As an indication of the state of the public mind toward the royal mistress at this period, some of this is of interest.

" Right Trusty and Well-beloved Madam *Cresswell* and *Damaris Page*, with the rest of the suffering Sisterhood," it begins, " . . . We greet you well, in giving you to understand our Noble Mind, by returning our Thanks, which you are worthy of in rendring us our Titles of Honour, which are but our Due. For on

---

[1] Which might be taken to show that the lady was residing in her husband's house again ; but "the Street " which ran through Whitehall Palace and over which the Countess lived in her gatehouse was practically a continuation of King Street.

Shrove-Tuesday last, Splendidly did we appear upon
the Theatre at W. H. being to amazement wonderfully
deck'd with Jewels and Diamonds, which the (abhorr'd
and to be undone) Subjects of the Kingdom have
payed for. We have been also Serene and Illustrious
ever since the Day that *Mars* was so instrumental to
restore our Goddess *Venus* to her Temple and Worship;
where, by special grant we quickly became a famous
Lady : And as a Reward of our Devotions soon created
Right Honourable, the Countess of *Castlemain*."

Lady Castlemaine is made to go on to explain that
she has become a convert to the Church of Rome—
rather a belated announcement !—where worthy
fathers and confessors declare that certain things
" are not such heynous Crimes and crying Sins, but
rather they do mortifie the Flesh." She is made to
allude to the story of the Fire of 1666 being due to
" the Good Roman Catholicks " and to threaten :
" But for our Adversaries with the Rebellious Citizens,
Let them look to it when the French are ready (who
as yet drop in by small parties, and lie *incognito* with
the rest of the Catholicks) we shall deal with them, as
we did with their Brethren in Ireland."

A certain skill in the drawing up of this precious
" Answer " and its language and allusions suggest that
it was composed by some one in Court circles. Courtiers
were fond of gratifying their malice in writing such
libels, though most often in verse. No one, however,
came forward later to father either the " Petition "
or the " Answer," so that the authorship of both must
remain a mystery.

It is curious that the " splendid appearance " of the
lady at the Theatre at W(hite) H(all) on Shrove Tuesday is attested by Evelyn, though his language is less
complimentary than that of the libel. The entry in his
Diary for February 4th, 1668, is as follows :—

" I saw the tragedy of ' Horace ' (written by the
virtuous Mrs. Phillips) acted before their Majesties.
'Twixt each act a masq and antiq daunce. The
excessive gallantries of the ladies was infinite, those
especially on that . . . Castlemaine esteem'd at
£40,000 and more, far outshining the Queene."

Of Lady Castlemaine's large expenditure on jewelry
we have heard before. She may have been particularly
reckless now, in the " disorder " to which Burnet sees
her driven by the loss of the King. She was also
gambling heavily at this time, risking £1000 and £1500
on a single cast, winning £15,000 one night and losing
£25,000 another. And then there were her presents to
Hart. We do not know their extent, but she was wont
to be very generous to her later favourites, and doubtless was so to Hart now.

A handsome gift from the King this spring scarcely
lessened her debts; or, more probably, added to her
expenses. He gave her a house, which she proceeded
to furnish herself. Coupled as it was with his renewed
attentions to Frances, Duchess of Richmond, and his
infatuation with Moll Davis, Charles's removal of his
titular mistress out of his own immediate neighbourhood had something ominous about it. But the house
was undeniably a fine one and cost him, it appears,

£5000, which was the sum that passed the Privy
Seal for it. It was Berkshire House, standing in ex-
tensive grounds (which included the present Green
Park) to the north-west of St. James's Park, on the
further side of the Palace. Formerly the London
residence of the first two Earls of Berkshire, it had
been recently occupied by the Lord Chancellor
Clarendon. It was strange that the next owner should
be the lady for whom the grant for £5000 could
scarcely have been even suggested in the imperious
old Chancellor's time.

With her departure from Whitehall Lady Castlemaine takes a less prominent place in the public eye ;
that is, if we can judge by the eye of Samuel Pepys.
He only records one vision of her between December
1667 and December 1668. This is on May 5th at
the Duke of York's Playhouse, where Shadwell's
The Impertinents is being performed. Pepys sits in
the balcony-box—" where we find my Lady Castlemaine and several great ladies "—close to " her
fine woman Wilson," with whom he gets into conversation, no doubt to his great satisfaction. He
is, indeed, in as close touch with the admired one
as at any time in his life. What he finds to remark
on, however, is rather unromantic : " One thing
of familiarity I observed in my Lady Castlemaine :
she called to one of her women, another that sat
by this [Wilson], for a little patch off her face, and
put it into her mouth and wetted it, and so clapped
it upon her own by the side of her mouth, I suppose
she feeling a pimple rising there ! "

Not until December 21st in the same year is the lady seen again. On that day Pepys is once more at the Duke's and witnesses a performance of *Macbeth*. " The King and Court there ; and we sat just under them and my Lady Castlemaine, and close to the woman that comes into the pit, a kind of loose gossip that pretends to be like her, and is so, something. . . . The King and Duke minded me, and smiled upon me, at the handsome woman near me : but it vexed me to see Moll Davis, in the box over the King's and my Lady Castlemaine's head, look down upon the King, and he up to her ; and so did my Lady Castlemaine once, to see who it was ; but when she saw her, she looked like fire ; which troubled me."

The theatre occupied a good deal of the Court's attention at this period, apart from its connection with the King's amours. In the middle of January there was a great disturbance at Whitehall Palace, " even to the sober engaging of great persons," according to the *Diary*, " and making the King cheap and ridiculous." A certain actress, Mrs. Corey, playing the part of *Sempronia* in *Catiline's Conspiracy*, took it on herself to imitate Lady Harvey, wife of Lady Castlemaine's host in the summer of 1667.[1] This Lady Harvey was by birth Anne Montagu, sister of Ralph (of whom we shall soon hear much) and cousin of the two Edward Montagus, Lord Sandwich and

---

[1] It would appear that there was some sort of connection between the Harveys and the Castlemaines, for the Earl of Castlemaine in 1668 accompanied Sir Daniel Harvey on the mission to the Porte mentioned below

the Earl of Manchester.   The Earl of Manchester
was Lord Chamberlain, and to him Anne naturally
appealed in her indignation.   The Lord Chamberlain
promptly put the offending actress in prison ; where-
upon Lady Castlemaine, for some reason at enmity
with her former hostess, insisted on the King ordering
Mrs. Corey's release and performance of the part of
Sempronia before his own eyes.   Lady Harvey, in
her turn, provided people to hiss and to fling oranges
at the actress.   The Court was divided in its sympathies,
taking the affair very seriously ; but unfortunately
we hear no more about it.

The mistress's successful intervention in this matter
shows her still able to rule the King, in spite of the
fact that politically the Duke of Buckingham was all
in all and that she and he were now mortal enemies.
In her hatred for her cousin she drew closer to the
chief opponents of the Buckingham interest at Court,
the Duke and Duchess of York, who, it should be
noted, were her closest neighbours in St. James's
Park.   Buckingham, having failed in his scheme for
the divorce of Catherine of Braganza and a remarriage
of the King, was eager for Charles to legitimise the
Duke of Monmouth and make him the heir to the
throne, so cutting out the Duke of York from the
succession.   Thus, though the mistress had contributed so much to the ruin of Clarendon, the
Duchess's own father, the Yorks were induced to
enter into an alliance with her as their best resource
at need.

How powerful an ally she was is abundantly plain.

Povy sums the situation up admirably for Pepys on January 16th, 1669: " My Lady Castlemaine is now in a higher command over the King than ever—not as a mistress, for she scorns him, but as a tyrant to command him." All in vain had Charles sent the lady to Berkshire House. Her iron grip was on him still, however much he might try to disguise the fact from himself. For he did try. We read in a letter written to Louis XIV by Colbert, his new Ambassador at Whitehall, on January 14th, that it is inadvisable to lavish handsome gifts upon Madame Castlemaine [1] to buy her support for France, since then " His Majesty may think that, despite his assertions to the contrary, we fancy that she rules him, and may take it ill." *Tom Otter* was sensitive !

Pepys had the good luck to be eye-witness on one occasion of the close relations of Lady Castlemaine and the Yorks this spring. He and Sir Jeremiah Smith went on March 4th to Deptford, where the Duke and Duchess were on a visit to the Treasurer's house. Here, after a dinner by invitation with the Duchess's maids of honour (" which did me good to have the honour to dine with and look on "), they go upstairs and " find the Duke of York and Duchess,

---

[1] We hear, however, of one handsome gift. On May 3rd, 1669, Ralph Montagu writes from Paris to Lord Arlington : "I went to Martiall's to look for gloves, and I saw a present which I am sure must cost a thousand pounds packing up. I found since that it is for my Lady Castlemaine, which you will quickly know there. I asked him who it was for, but he could not or would not tell me. I asked him who paid him ; he told me, the King of France, and that he had an order from Mr. Colbert for his money, to whom he is to give the things."

with all the great ladies, sitting upon a carpet, on the
ground, there being no chairs, playing at ' I love my
love with an A, because he is so and so ; and I hate
him with an A, because he is this and that ' ; and some
of them, but particularly the Duchess herself, and my
Lady Castlemaine, were very witty."

We could wish that Pepys had thought fit to set
down some examples of the wit. But unfortunately
he did not. And, more unfortunately still, the never-
equalled *Diary* comes to an end three months later,
to the incalculable injury of posterity. In the case of
Lady Castlemaine, its cessation means the loss of
those hundred little intimate details which bring the
person described vividly before us. Only once more
before he ceases to delight us does Pepys mention the
great lady in whom he is so interested. On April 28th
Sir H. Cholmly, calling upon him about some Navy
Office accounts, proceeds to other talk and tells him
of his proposals for a league with France in return for
a sum of money, which have been supported by such
various people as the Duke and Duchess of York, the
Queen-Mother, and Lord Arlington, though he is of
the Buckingham faction. And, also, " my Lady Castlemaine is instrumental in this matter, and, he says,
never more great with the King than she is now."

The *Diary* takes leave of the royal mistress with
her political power vigorous and using it (no doubt
for a sufficient consideration, even if diplomacy made
the givers discreet) on behalf of the country whose
ambassadors she had, five years previously, succeeded
in thwarting. At this moment, before the appearance

on the scene of the lady who ousted her from her position of mistress *en titre*, we may conveniently pause to consider the condition of her affairs in general.

Thanks to the King's generosity, combined with his desire to keep her at a safer distance than when she was in apartments next his own at Whitehall, the Countess, having reached the age of twenty-eight, was residing at Berkshire House, standing in its own grounds, with no nearer neighbours than St. James's Palace. Her three youngest children, Henry, Charlotte, and George, were possibly living with her. The two eldest, Anne and Charles, aged eight and seven respectively, are known to have been in Paris now, receiving such education as was thought fit for them. The unfortunate Lord Castlemaine was still out of the country. After his final separation from his wife in December 1666—" never to trouble one another more "—he had gone abroad, to remain there for eleven years without a visit to England, as far as is known. In 1668 he was a member of the mission sent by Charles to Turkey, and he continued to travel for his own pleasure until 1677.

To maintain the mistress in the independent position in which he had placed her Charles, about this time, bestowed upon her a regular income. We have seen that as early as the beginning of September 1667 there had been rumours of an intended pension, possibly £4000 a year, to be paid on condition that she withdrew to France. She had not withdrawn to France, though the expectation of her doing so was occasionally revived. She obtained her pension, how-

ever, without such a sacrifice. A grant was made out
of the revenues of the Post Office of a sum of £4700
a year.   In accordance with former precedents, to
make the transaction less notorious, the grant was not
in the lady's own name, but in those of her uncles Viscount Grandison and Edward Villiers.

Such a sum, indeed, was inadequate to meet her
extravagant expenditure, which is no doubt the reason
why she is found soon after to have sold Berkshire
House, keeping only part of the grounds on which
to erect a new mansion. But at least it enabled
her to gratify some of her desires, such as the bestowal
of presents upon favourites. The disorder of her life
was increasing. Acting upon her determination to be
even with the King, she had descended from Charles
Hart the actor to Jacob Hall the rope-dancer, whom
Pepys sees at Bartholomew and Southwark Fairs in
the autumn of 1668 and finds " a mighty strong man."
Granger, writing a century later and therefore not
from personal acquaintance, says that " there was a
symmetry and elegance, as well as strength and agility,
in the person of Jacob Hall, which was much admired
by the ladies, who regarded him as a due composition
of Hercules and Apollo."   Gramont, as might be
expected, has something to say on the subject, the
gist of which is that Lady Castlemaine's fancy was
notorious, " but she despised all rumours and only
appeared still more handsome."   She went so far as
to pay the rope-dancer a salary, according to Granger.
She certainly had her portrait painted with him, for
the picture is still in existence. " You know as to love

one is not mistriss of one's self," she wrote to Charles
eight years later. She proved this amply in her own
case, it cannot be denied.

It would seem that the scandal did not fail to produce the effect which the lady desired. The King
appreciated the indignity of his mistress entering into
a contest with him in which the weapons were the
degradation of the combatants. But, characteristically,
beyond a sarcastic comment,[1] his only punishment for
Lady Castlemaine's offence was to bestow a new
honour upon her.

[1] See p. 188.

CHAPTER IX

SUPPLANTED

EARLY in 1670 Louis XIV achieved his desire of binding England to France in close political union. Negotiations had been proceeding for a long time, forwarded, as we have seen, by a variety of persons in this country, including the royal mistress to a certain extent. To hasten their conclusion Louis sent to England Charles's sister, the Duchess of Orleans, whom Charles had often declared to be the only woman who had any hold upon him. This Louis did much against the wishes of his brother Orleans, who was apparently afraid that his wife was too well inclined to the young and handsome Duke of Monmouth, her nephew, and asked Charles to send him on a visit to Holland during her stay in England. The story of the Orleans mission has much tragedy in it, and a little comedy. On May 16th Henrietta landed at Dover, bringing in her train as maid of honour a young lady of twenty-one years of age called Louise Renée de Keroualle, who at once attracted the ever roving eyes of Charles. Unconsciously perhaps at first, France had discovered the means of securing the English King's affections, as well as interests, on her side. Instead of buying the

English mistress, which would be a difficult and expensive matter, she sold him a French one. Charles's passion for Barbara Palmer was doubtless dead and buried before Louise de Keroualle set foot in England ; but the latter's appearance shortened the remaining empire over the King of her who had ruled him so long. It was impossible to keep two such harpies simultaneously in the immediate neighbourhood of the Privy Purse, though not impossible (as it was unfortunately discovered) to have one of them, as it were, installed on the table in the Palace and the other hovering outside at no great distance, ready to swoop in and carry off the side-dishes.

Louise de Keroualle did not immediately step into her disreputable position. In June the Duchess of Orleans returned to France, after a secret treaty had been signed at Dover on the 1st, by which Charles bound England to engage with France in war against Holland, in return for a subsidy of three million francs a year, with an extra two million for declaring himself a Roman Catholic. With the Duchess returned her maid of honour, but not before Charles had gallantly intimated how much he would like to keep her at the English Court. On June 29th the Duchess, after having been welcomed back most graciously by Louis and his Queen, but very sourly by her husband, died so suddenly that there were at first suspicions of foul play, and the relations between the English and French Courts became rather cool. To remedy this, somebody, perhaps Colbert, one of the astutest of ambassadors, suggested that the charming maid of

From a mezzotint engraving after the painting by Sir Peter Lely

BARBARA VILLIERS, COUNTESS OF CASTLEMAINE
AND DUCHESS OF CLEVELAND

honour should be sent to London. It was said also
that the Duke of Buckingham, whom Charles
despatched to Paris to thank Louis for his con-
dolences on Henrietta's death and to strengthen
the harmony between the two Powers, had represented to his King that it would be very fitting for
him now to look after the interests of his late
sister's young attendant.[1] Buckingham, it must be
remembered, was now actively hostile to the mistress
in possession and was eager therefore to see her deprived of her remaining power. Louise made a show
of reluctance, but finally gave way and crossed the
Channel in charge of Ralph Montagu, the English
Ambassador in Paris. On November 4th, 1670,
Evelyn saw at Court for the first time " that famous
beauty, but in my opinion of a childish, simple, and
baby face, Mademoiselle de Querouaille, lately Maide
of Honor to Madame, and now to be so to the
Queene." On her arrival in England Louise still
proved very coy, to the alarm of Louis's representative
at Whitehall, who feared that the plan of binding
Charles firmly to the French side by means of the
lady might miscarry. Almost another year had to pass
before the beauty would give way. No doubt she

---

[1] The Marquis de Saint-Maurice, Savoy's Ambassador in Paris,
writing to the Duke Charles Emmanuel II on September 19th, says :
"The Duke of Buckingham has taken with him Mlle. de Keroualle,
who was attached to her late Highness ; she is a beautiful girl, and it
is thought that the plan is to make her mistress to the King of Great
Britain. He would like to dethrone Lady Castlemaine, who is his
enemy, and His Most Christian Majesty will not be sorry to see the
position filled by one of his subjects, for it is said the ladies have great
influence over the mind of the said King of England."

understood the game better than even Colbert. Certainly, when once she stooped to conquer, she established herself in her position for the remainder of the King's lifetime.

As Louise de Keroualle did not even reach England until the autumn of 1670, Charles's gift of a new and higher title to the Countess of Castlemaine in the summer of that year cannot be regarded in the light of a consolation to the mistress whom he was replacing by another. It was on August 23rd that he created her Baroness Nonsuch, Countess of Southampton, and Duchess of Cleveland. It is significant that in the patent the remainder is granted to Charles and George Fitzroy, described as her first and second sons, the paternity of Henry thus being still disowned by the King. Henry had to wait another two years for recognition.

The *Gramont Memoirs* give an extraordinary reason for Charles's bestowal of the new honour upon Lady Castlemaine at this moment. According to them, it was the result of a violent quarrel between King and lady over her continued infatuation for Henry Jermyn. Charles, says Gramont, " did not think it consistent with his dignity that a mistress whom he had honoured with public distinction, and who still received considerable support from him, should appear chained to the car of the most ridiculous conqueror that ever was. His Majesty had frequently expostulated with the Countess upon this subject, but his expostulations were never attended to. It was in one of these differences that, when he advised her to bestow her favours upon Jacob Hall the rope-dancer, who was able to return them, rather than lavish her money upon Jermyn to no purpose, since it would be more honourable to her to pass for the mistress of the former than for the very humble servant of the latter, she was not proof against his raillery. The impetuosity of her temper broke forth like lightning." Reproaches against his promiscuous and low amours, floods of tears, and Medea-like threats of destroying her children and burning his palace followed. The King, who only wanted peace, was in despair how to obtain it. So Gramont (he says) was called in as mediator by mutual consent. He drew up a treaty by which he managed to please both parties. This ran as follows :

" That Lady Castlemaine should give up Jermyn for ever ; that, as a proof of her sincerity and the reality of his disgrace, she should agree to his being sent into the country for some time ; that she should rail no more against Mlle. Wells [one of the maids of honour who had attracted the King] or Mlle. Stewart ; and this without any constraint on the King's behaviour to her ; that in consideration of these condescensions His Majesty should immediately give her the title of Duchess, with all the honours and privileges appertaining thereto, and an addition to her pension to enable her to support the dignity."

The proceedings at the Court of Charles II were certainly extraordinary, but not quite so extraordinary as to induce us to credit a tale like this in its entirety. It is, however, not improbable that there was some

N

such quarrel between the King and his mistress as the *Memoirs* describe, and that the latter exacted as the price of peace the rank of Duchess. Charles was never grudging with titles.

The choice of the names Cleveland and Southampton is unexplained. An earlier Cleveland peerage had lapsed three years previously when Thomas Wentworth, Earl of Cleveland, one of the heroes of the Battle of Worcester, died leaving only a granddaughter, Lady Henrietta Wentworth, afterwards mistress of the Duke of Monmouth. Southampton was the first title of Barbara's old enemy the Lord Treasurer—Thomas Wriothesley, Earl of Southampton and Chichester; and it is curious to notice that Charles Fitzroy, who was now, as first heir to his mother, created Earl of Southampton, was three years later made Duke of Southampton and Earl of Chichester. The grant of the barony of Nonsuch no doubt indicated that the King had already decided on the gift of Nonsuch House, which he made five months later.

The assumption of her new rank was followed by the Duchess's bestowal of the name of Cleveland House on the residence she was building on the unsold portions of the Berkshire House estate. Cleveland House, described by Evelyn as " a noble palace, too good for that infamous . . ." (here words fail him), was pulled down and replaced by Bridgewater House in the middle of the nineteenth century, but its memory is preserved in the present-day Cleveland Square and Row, Westminster. It was perhaps for the decoration of the grounds of her new house that the Cupid was intended which is mentioned in the last letter in the Chesterfield collection addressed to the " Dutches of Cleaveland," dated 1670. Lord Chesterfield, a year ago married for the third time, boasts of his obedience to the least of the Duchess's commands, having as soon as he came to town bespoken a figure for her fountain, a Cupid kneeling on a rock and shooting from his bow a stream of water up towards heaven. " This may be interpreted by some," he writes, " that your ladyship, not being content with the conquest of one world, doth now by your devotions attack the other. I hope this stile hath to much gravity to appear gallant ; since many years agoe your ladyship gave me occasion to repeat those two lines :

" Vous m'otes tout espoir pour vous, belle inhumaine,
Et pour tout autre que vous vous m'otes tout désir."

Doubtless Her Grace reflected, as she read the closing words of this letter, on the existence of Lady Chesterfield number three—for whose loss, by the way, her husband evinced considerable sorrow when she died in 1678.

In this year of fresh honours to her Lady of the Bed-chamber, there seems to have been a revival of the rumours of the coming divorce of the unhappy Queen. Burnet is our authority for the prevalence of talk about the probability of Catherine " turning religious " and a bill being brought before Parliament to legalise a divorce. With his usual readiness to attribute the worst to Charles himself,[1] he makes him the originator of the scheme. " It was believed," he continues, " that upon this the Duchess of York sent an express to Rome with the notice of her conversion ; and that orders were sent from Rome to all about the Queen to persuade her against such a proposition, if any should suggest it to her. She herself had no mind to be a nun, and the Duchess was afraid of seeing another Queen ; and the mistress, created at that time Duchess of Cleveland, knew that she must be the first sacrifice to a beloved Queen ; and she reconciled herself upon this to the Duchess of York."

There is no reason to doubt that the divorce rumours were actually current again in 1670, to whomever the revival of the scheme was due. Once more the Queen had disappointed her husband's hopes in the previous year, and he might well despair now of ever seeing a legitimate heir from her. As for the alliance between the Duchess of Cleveland and the Yorks, the reasons for their opposition to the idea of a new queen were as good as ever. We do not know, apart from what Burnet says, of any necessity for " reconciliation " between the two Duchesses. Her Royal Highness seems to have become a Roman Catholic at heart as early as 1668, but it was not until

---

[1] In return Charles impugned the Bishop's truthfulness. The then exiled Queen (Mary of Modena), meeting George Granville, first Baron Lansdowne in Paris at the time when Burnet's *History* appeared, told him that she well remembered Dr. Burnet and his character; "that the King and the Duke, and the whole Court, looked upon him as the greatest liar upon the face of the earth, and there was no believing one word that he said."

two years later that she was actually received into
the Church. The Duke of York's conversion is placed
by Sir John Reresby in the same year. According to
his *Memoirs*, when Henrietta of Orleans paid her
momentous visit to England, she " confirmed His
High Highness the Duke in the Popish superstition,
of which he had as yet been barely suspected ; and it
is said to have been his grand argument for such his
adherence to those tenets, that his mother had, upon
her last blessing, commanded him to be firm and
steadfast thereto." James, from his own *Memoirs*,
appears not to have withdrawn from the Church
of England until 1672. Both he and his wife, however, were in feeling Roman Catholics considerably
before their respective conversions and had therefore
a bond of sympathy with the royal mistress, poor
ornament though she might be to any church.
Buckingham's strong Protestantism, on the other
hand, made him still more bitterly hostile to his cousin
and the Yorks as he saw them drawn closer together.
It also forced the King to keep him, like Lauderdale
and Ashley—all members of the ruling " cabal "—
actually ignorant, when they signed a treaty with
France on the last day of 1670, that there was the
secret Treaty of Dover already in force seven months
ago ! We need not suppose that the Duchess of
Cleveland had any knowledge of this stupendous piece
of duplicity, although the Duke of York (and therefore possibly his wife) had. Charles was not so foolish
as to commit so ruinous a secret to the keeping of a
lady with a temper and a tongue like Barbara's.

The ever-rising French influence, even before the
establishment of Louise de Keroualle as mistress,
doubtless accounts for the very few public appearances
of Lady Cleveland of which we hear in 1671. She is
seen at a ballet at Court in February " very fine in a
riche petticoat and halfe skirte, and a short man's coat
very richly laced, a perwig cravatt, and a hat : her hat
and maske was very rich." About the same time also
she drives in Hyde Park in a coach with eight horses,
and rumour attributes to her the intention of having
twelve horses. On March 2nd Evelyn has an interesting entry. He walks through St. James's Park to the
Privy Garden, " where I both saw and heard a very
familiar discourse between [the King] and Mrs.
Nellie as they called an impudent comedian, she looking out of her garden on a terrace at the top of the
wall and [the King] standing on the greene walke
under it. I was heartily sorry at this scene," continues
Evelyn. " Thence the King walked to the Duchess
of Cleveland, another lady of pleasure and curse of
our nation." It seems to have been impossible for
Evelyn to mention the lady's name without recording
his detestation of her, just as Pepys could seldom do
so without a note of admiration. Yet the two diarists
were excellent friends !

As though to console her for her supersession as a
political influence, the King was lavishly generous to
the Duchess of Cleveland in the year 1671. He began
with a grant in January of Nonsuch House and Park,
near Epsom—the complement of the lowest of the
three titles conferred upon her in the previous

August. Nonsuch House or Palace had been built by
Henry VIII as a hunting-box. After it had passed
temporarily into private hands Elizabeth had purchased it back for the Crown, and her successors
had used it as an occasional residence, Charles I having
taken Henrietta Maria thither after their quarrel over
his dismissal of her French attendants, and afterwards
settling it upon her. In spite of the damage done to it
during the Commonwealth and its use as the office
of the Exchequer during the period of the Plague in
London, it had come down to this date in excellent
preservation. Evelyn, who visited it on January 3rd,
1666, praises it highly, with its plaster statues and
bas-reliefs inserted between the timbers and pun-
cheons of its outer walls, " which must needs have
been the work of some celebrated Italian " ; its in-
genious arrangement of slate scales on wood, " the
slate fastened on the timber in pretty figures, that has,
like a coate of armour, preserved it from rotting " ;
and its " mezzo-relievos as big as the life, the storie is
of the Heathen Gods." As for the grounds, " there
stands in the garden two handsome stone pyramids,
and the avenue planted with rows of faire elmes, but
the rest of these goodly trees . . . were felled by
those destructive and avaricious rebells in the late
warr, which defaced one of the stateliest seates His
Majesty had." Alas ! a worse fate was now to befall
it. The new owner pulled down the old palace of
Henry VIII and turned the park into farm-land, in
order to extract fuller cash-value from her acquisition.

This grant was made in the names of Viscount

Grandison and of Henry Brounker, a creature of the King's, justly called by Pepys " a pestilential rogue." A letter survives, written by Charles to Brounker on August 25th, in which His Majesty refers to the changes at Nonsuch. "The Dutches of Cleaveland," he says, " has satisfied me it is both for her advantage and those in the reversion that Nonsuch should be suddenly disparked, to avoid all sutes and contests between her and the Lord Berkeley, and that she intends to let it out at a rent which is to be reserved to her Grace," &c.

We hear of enormous money gifts later in the year. Writing on August 9th to a friend travelling in Persia, Andrew Marvell tells how the House of Commons has grown " extreme chargeable to the King and odious to the people." Lord St. John, Sir Robert Howard, Sir John Bennet, and Sir William Bucknell the brewer, all members of the Commons, have " farmed the old customs, with the new Act of Imposition upon Wines and the Wine Licenses, at six hundred thousand pounds a year, and have signed and sealed ten thousand pounds a year more to the Duchess of Cleveland, who has likewise near ten thousand pounds a year out of the new farm of the county excise of Beer and Ale ; five thousand pounds a year out of the Post Office, and, they say, the re-version of all the King's leases, the reversion of all places in the Custom House, the Green Wax, and what not ! All promotions, spiritual and temporal, pass under her cognizance." Near the end of the same letter he relates how " Barclay," i.e. Baron

Berkeley of Stratton, Lord-Lieutenant of Ireland, has been compelled to come over to England to pay ten thousand pounds rent to his landlady Cleveland." What precisely Berkeley is paying rent for is not clear— though Berkeley's name is also mentioned in Charles's letter above. But we know that some time later the Duchess of Cleveland appears as the recipient of estates in Ireland sufficient to produce a revenue of £1000 a year to compensate her for a promise which Charles had made her and not kept. How this came about is told by Carte in his *Life of the Duke of Ormonde*. Explaining why the Duchess always did Ormonde all the ill offices that were in her power, he says :

" She had obtained of the King a warrant for the grant of the Phœnix Park and House near Dublin, which was the only place of retirement in the summer season for a chief governor ; and the more necessary at that time, when His Grace coming over found the castle of Dublin so out of repair, and in such a miserable condition, after the neglect of it during the late usurpation, that it did not afford him sufficient accommodation. The Lord Lieutenant refused to pass this warrant, stopped the grant, and prevailed with His Majesty to enlarge the park by the purchase of four hundred and fifty acres of land adjoining in Chapel Izod of the Lord Chancellor Eustace, and to fit up the house for the convenience of himself and his successors in the government of Ireland. This incensed the Lady Castlemaine so highly that upon His Grace's return to England, meeting him in one of the apartments about Court, she without any manner of regard to the place or company, fell upon him with a torrent of abusive language, loaded him with all the reproaches that the rancour of her heart could suggest, or the folly of her tongue could utter, and told him in fine that she hoped to live to see him hanged. The Duke heard all unmoved, and only made her this memorable reply : That he was not in so much haste to put an end to her days, for all he wished with regard to her was that he might live to see her old."

The Duchess, nevertheless, forgave Ormonde sufficiently to ask a favour of him many years later, as will be seen.

Marvell, in his above-quoted letter, we may suppose, is summarising for the benefit of his friend in Persia all the Duchess's recent acquisitions, not merely those of the year 1671. It is a fact, however, that in the following February yet another grant was made by the King to Viscount Grandison, Henry Howard, and Francis Villiers of a number of manors and advowsons in Surrey, two-thirds of which they proceeded to declare they would hold in trust for the Duchess of Cleveland.

Even if Marvell's list be a summary to date, therefore, it is plain that the Duchess was in possession of enormous resources soon after her acquisition of the title. As to the manner in which she dissipated much of her wealth there is no doubt. Reckless gambling and reckless expenditure on favourites accounted for vast sums. Of her gifts to Hart and salary to the rope-dancer we have already heard. She added a more aristocratic client to her list. The *Gramont Memoirs*, with their usual disregard for dates, place the beginning of her intrigue with John Churchill in the year when the Court visited the West of England—1663, at which time Churchill was but thirteen ! This is obviously absurd. That extraordinary person, Mrs. Mary de la Riviere Manley, who disputes with Mrs. Aphra Behn the palm for feminine literary indelicacy in the Restoration era, seems to place it in 1667. But Mrs. Manley did not make the acquaintance of the Duchess of Cleveland until twenty-six years later, indeed was not born for another three years, and she is not, therefore, a first-hand authority concerning her temporary patroness's doings in 1667. The fact that Pepys has no mention at all of John Churchill in the *Diary* is a very strong argument against his association with the Duchess previous to May 1669. All that we can be certain of, however, is that they were acquainted before the end of 1671, since their daughter Barbara was born in the July of the following year.

Mrs. Manley in *The New Atalantis* attributes the introduction of the young ensign to the royal mistress to a chance meeting at Cleveland House. Churchill's maternal aunt was " surintendant of the family of the *Dutchess De l'Inconstant*, Sultana Mistress to *Sigismund the Second*," and her nephew used to visit his aunt and fill himself with sweetmeats. " The Dutchess came one day unexpectedly down the back stairs to take chair, and found 'em together ; he had slip'd away, for fear of anger, but not so speedily but she had a glimpse of his graceful person. She ask'd who he was; and being answer'd, she caus'd him to be call'd. . . . The Governess, knowing the Dutchess's amorous star, was transported at the happy introduction of her nephew," etc.

Perhaps this must be dismissed as romance based on gossip related to Mrs. Manley after her quarrel with the Duchess in 1694. But doubtless the Duchess when she first met Churchill was immediately smitten. The fourth Lord Chesterfield, writing to his son, says that Marlborough's figure was beautiful, his manner irresistible by either man or woman. The Duchess did not attempt to resist, and the affair was soon known to the King. Churchill has been identified with the hero of Burnet's story of how an intrigue, " by the artifice of the Duke of Buckingham, was discovered by the King in person, the party concerned leaping out of the window." Charles was indignant, as he had been in the case of Jermyn; not jealous over the lady falling in love, but angry at the exhibition which she made of it. As will be seen, his desire, after he had pensioned her off, was that she should make the least noise she could.

On the present occasion he took no steps to punish the offenders. He dismissed Churchill with nothing worse than the cynical " I forgive you, for you do it for your bread ! " The sting of this was that the Duchess of Cleveland had been lavishly generous to the young man, whether or not she had at this time already presented him with that famous £5000 which Churchill, showing thus early in life the appreciation of the value of money which marked him so strongly later, invested profitably in the purchase of an annuity of £500 a year. This present from the Duchess was, as both Lord Chesterfield and Boyer remark, the foundation of Churchill's subsequent fortune. His gratitude, however, for the lady's generosity was small. Mrs. Manley in her *roman à clef*, *The Adventures of Rivella* relates how " from *Hilaria* she received the first ill-impressions of *Count Fortunatus*, touching his ingratitude, immorality, and avarice ; being herself an eye-witness when he deny'd *Hilaria* (who had given him thousands) the common civility of lending her twenty guineas at Basset ; which, together with betraying his master, and raising himself by his sister's dishonour, she had always esteem'd a just and flaming subject for satire." [1]

In *The New Atalantis* she describes the same scene of the refusal in graphic detail. The Duchess, she says, had oftentimes not a pistole at command, " solicited the *Count* (whom she had rais'd) by his favour with the Court that her affairs might be put into a better posture, but he was deaf to all her intreaties ; nay, he carried ingratitude much further ; one night at an assembly of the best quality, when the Count tallied to them at Basset, the Dutchess lost all her money & begged the favour of him, in a very civil manner, to lend her twenty pieces ; which he absolutely refused, though he had a thousand upon the table before him, and told her coldly, the bank never lent any money.

[1] *Rivella* is Mrs. Manley herself, *Hilaria* the Duchess of Cleveland, *Count Fortunatus* the Duke of Marlborough.

Not a person upon the place but blamed him in their hearts : as to the Duchess's part, her resentment burst out into a bleeding at her nose, and breaking of her lace ; without which aid, it is believed, her vexation had killed her upon the spot."

Churchill " could refuse more gracefully than other people could grant," says Lord Chesterfield in the above-mentioned letter to his son. His refusal of the Duchess's request for a loan is scarcely an instance of this !

To supply Churchill with the £5000 without inconvenience to herself the Duchess is credited with having got double the amount out of the notorious spendthrift and rake, Sir Edward Hungerford, who founded Hungerford Market some years later on the site of his town house, burnt in 1669, and after selling the market, like some thirty manors which were once his, died in comparative poverty two years after the Duchess. This affair with Hungerford explains Pope's allusion to the lady

> " Who of ten thousand gulled her Knight,
> Then asked ten thousand for another night ;
> The gallant too, to whom she paid it down,
> Lived to refuse the mistress half-a-crown."

Boyer, in his obituary notice of the Duchess, after speaking of her affair with Churchill, says : " I had rather draw a Veil over the Life this Lady led from henceforward. . . . Indeed it would be too tedious to enter upon a Detail of her other Amours." To a certain extent we may follow Boyer's discreet example, since there is little interest beyond mere curiosity in

many of the lady's rapidly increasing love-affairs.
But one calls for attention, since the other person involved in it was the celebrated dramatist Wycherley,
who owed not a little of his early success to the
patronage of Her Grace. Some time in the early spring
of 1671, it would appear, he had produced at Drury
Lane Theatre his *Love in a Wood, or St. James's Park*,
his first written and first acted play. The Duchess
of Cleveland went to a performance, with a result
which the dramatist could not have anticipated. John
Dennis, the friend of Wycherley, Congreve, Dryden,
and other wits, in his *Familiar Letters* describes what
happened on the very next day following the Duchess's
visit to Drury Lane. As Wycherley was going, he
says, through Pall Mall towards St. James's in his
chariot, he met the lady in hers. She, thrusting half
her body out of the chariot, cried out aloud to him,
" You, Wycherley, you are the son of a ——," at the
same time laughing heartily. Wycherley, we are told,
was very much surprised, but soon apprehended that
the allusion was to a song in *Love in a Wood*, suggesting,
in language almost as coarse as the Duchess's own, that
the mothers of great wits had always a bad character.
The rest may be told in Dennis's words :

" As during Mr Wycherley's surprise the chariots
drove different ways, they were soon at a considerable
distance from each other, when Mr. Wycherley, re-
covering from his surprise, ordered his coachman to
drive back and to overtake the lady. As soon as he
got over against her, he said to her : ' Madam, you
have been pleased to bestow a title on me which

generally belongs to the fortunate. Will your Ladyship be at the play to-night ? ' ' Well,' she reply'd,
' what if I am there ? ' ' Why, then I will be there
to wait upon your Ladyship, tho' I disappoint a very
fine woman who has made me an assignation.' ' So,'
said she, ' you are sure to disappoint a woman who has
favoured you for one who has not.' ' Yes,' reply'd he,
' if she who has not favoured me is the finer woman
of the two. But he who will be constant to your
Ladyship, till he can find a finer woman, is sure to die
your captive.' The lady blushed and bade her coachman drive away. . . . In short she was that night in
the first row of the King's box in Drury Lane, and
Mr Wycherley in the pit under her, where he entertained her during the whole play."

Wycherley was a very handsome man, as his contemporaries tell us and his portrait by Lely proves,
and it is not to be wondered at, therefore, that the
Duchess of Cleveland took a great fancy to him. She
not only favoured him with her own society but
introduced him also to Court and King. Wycherley,
in his turn, when he printed his *Love in a Wood*, pre-
faced it with a dedication to " Her Grace the Duchess
of Cleveland," which is not only important for fixing
the date of his first play's appearance, but also an
interesting document in itself, as a few extracts will
show :

" Madam," says Wycherley,
    " All authors whatever in their dedication are
poets ; but I am now to write to a lady who stands as
little in need of flattery, as her beauty of art ; other-

W. Wycherley
Ætat. Suæ 28

Quantum mutatus ab illo Virg

From a mezzotint engraving by I. Smith, after a painting by Sir Peter Lely

WILLIAM WYCHERLEY

wise I should prove as ill a poet to her in my dedication as to my readers in my play. I can do your Grace no honour, nor make you more admirers than you have already; yet I can do myself the honour to let the world know I am the greatest you have. . . . I cannot but publicly give your Grace my humble acknowledgements for the favours I have received from you : this, I say, is the poet's gratitude, which, in plain English, is only pride and ambition; and that the world might know that your Grace did me the honour to see my play twice together. Yet, perhaps, my enviers of your favour will suggest 'twas in Lent, and therefore for your mortification. Then, as a jealous author, I am concerned not to have your Grace's favours lessened, or rather my reputation; and to let them know you were pleased, after that, to command a copy from me of this play ;—the only way, without beauty and wit, to win a poor poet's heart."

The dedication closes with a panegyric on the lady. " You have that perfection of beauty (without thinking it so) which others of your sex but think they have ; that generosity in your actions which others of your quality have only in their promises ; that spirit, wit and judgment, and all other qualifications which fit heroes to command and would make any but your Grace proud. . . . In fine, speaking thus of your Grace, I should please all the world but you ; therefore I must once observe and obey you against my will, and say no more than that I am, Madam, Your Grace's most obliged and most humble servant

" WILLIAM WYCHERLEY."

The irregularity of the ex-mistress's life was no doubt one of the reasons why the King reduced the

o

amount of his merely friendly acquaintance with her. On February 22nd, 1672, we find Charles Lyttelton writing to Viscount Hatton that "the King has of late forebore visiting my Lady Cle[veland]; but some two days since was with her againe and I suppose will continue to goe sometimes, though it may not be so often." Again, on March 22nd, "The King goes but seldom to Cleveland House." On the other hand, according to Lyttelton, "Mdlle. Keerewell is infinitely in favour, and, to say truth, she seems as well to deserve it, for she is wondrous handsome, and, they say, as much witt and addresse as ever anybody had." Mdlle. Keerewell, also popularly known as Madam Carwell, or Carewell, is, of course, Louise de Keroualle whose ascendancy over the King is now established. In the previous October Charles had gone to Newmarket for the "autumnal sports" in the company of "jolly blades, racing, dauncing, feasting, and revelling, more resembling a luxurious and abandoned rout than a Christian Court," as Evelyn, who lodged first with the surely uncongenial Henry Jermyn and then with the Arlingtons at Euston, sadly exclaims. The chief sporting event was a race between His Majesty's *Woodcock* and Tom Eliot's *Flatfoot*, before many thousand spectators. But a more important affair was the presence, as the guest of Lord and Lady Arlington, of "the famous new French Maid of Honour Mlle Querouaille, now coming to be in great favour with the King." His Majesty, indeed, came to Euston almost every second day and frequently slept there. Colbert was also a guest at the

house, and with his benevolent aid, no doubt, matters
were arranged to Charles's desire. " 'Twas with confidence believed," Evelyn says, that the lady was
" first made a misse, as they call these unhappy creatures, with all solemnity at this time." And in token
of her shame the Duchess of Cleveland's successor
on October 19th appeared at the races in the royal
coach and six. The visit to Newmarket fulfilled
Colbert's hopes. The King's affections were secured,
especially when it was known that the baby-faced
maid of honour was going to present him with a child.

By a curious coincidence in the same month of
July 1672 there were born Barbara Palmer, on the 16th,
and Charles Lennox, on the 29th. The latter was the
King's son by Louise de Keroualle, the former the
first of the known offspring of the Duchess of Cleveland
that was certainly not the King's—being universally
credited to Churchill.

The King showed not the slightest displeasure over
the appearance of the little Barbara. A fortnight
later he graced with his presence the formal marriage
of the Duchess's second son Henry to Isabella Bennet,
only daughter of the Earl of Arlington. This is the
union so ornately celebrated by Nahum Tate in his
second part of *Absalom and Achitophel* :

> " His age with only one mild heiress blest,
> In all the bloom of smiling nature drest ;
> And blest again to see his flower allied
> To David's stock, and made young Othniel's bride."

Young Othniel, otherwise Henry Fitzroy, was only
nine, Isabella five, so that the ceremony was rather

of the nature of a betrothal and was repeated seven
years later. Evelyn, who was present as a friend of
the Arlingtons, " tooke no great joy at the thing for
many reasons." The bride to him appears now " a
sweete child if ever there was any," and on a subsequent occasion " worthy for her beauty and virtue
of the greatest Prince in Christendom." His opinion
at the time of the second marriage we shall see
later.

The presence of the King and " all the grandees,"
as Evelyn records, at the marriage and the officiation
of the Archbishop of Canterbury show that His
Majesty had at last determined to recognise Henry
as his son, especially as on August 15th he conferred
upon him, " our second naturall son by ye Lady
Barbara," &c., the titles of Baron Sudbury, Viscount
Ipswich, and Earl of Euston ; before his younger
brother George, whom the King always acknowledged,
had received such an honour. Henry's wedding,
too, was celebrated with a splendour that had been
totally lacking in the case of his elder, Charles Fitzroy.
In the previous year Charles, aged nine, had been
contracted to a child bride, Mary Wood, seven years
of age, daughter of Sir Henry Wood, a clerk of the
Green Cloth. Possibly the King had not approved
of so undistinguished an alliance. But the Duchess
of Cleveland, with her eye on Mary's considerable
fortune for her son, had obtained forcible and illegal
possession of the little girl and insisted on an immediate
marriage and conveyance of the dowry.

With regard to George, we find a grant of £500

made, in the names of Grandison and Edward Villiers, to him and his heirs male. Before the end of the year the King had granted all three boys arms, crests, and supporters ; and two months later their sisters were also furnished with arms.

Clearly, therefore, to whatever extent the French mistress had taken the place of the Duchess of Cleveland, and however annoyed the King was at the latter's indiscretions, he had no intention of stopping his bounty to her or of slighting their children. That this was universally recognised is clear from the alliances which these children were able to make, both the sons and the daughters. As early as the autumn of 1671 Lord Howard confided to Evelyn his project of marrying his eldest son to one of the daughters of the King and Duchess, " by which he reckoned he should come into mighty favour." This scheme was not carried out. The young lady Anne Palmer came back to her mother from Paris in the autumn of the following year, escorted by her uncle Grandison, but when she married, in 1674, it was a Lennard, not a Howard, she took as her husband.

The year 1672 was associated with death as well as marriage. Before its close the Duchess of Cleveland lost her grandmother, Dame Barbara Villiers. Previously she had lost her mother, but except that it occurred later than March 1671 the date of her death is unknown. So little is the former Mary Bayning heard of that one cannot but suspect that she and her daughter were on unfriendly terms during the latter's ascendancy over Charles II. She had taken a third husband, Arthur Gorges, and survived him like the other two. Otherwise her doings are unknown.

That the grandmother, too, did not die on the best of terms with her granddaughter seems probable from the smallness of her legacy to her—£50 with which to buy a mourning ring. The old lady may have considered that it was not money but respect that the Duchess lacked.

CHAPTER X

THE PORTSMOUTH SUPREMACY

ON April 4th, 1672, Evelyn made the following
entry in his *Diary*. " I went to see the fop-
peries of the Papists at Somerset House, and York
House, where now the French Ambassador had
caused to be represented our Blessed Saviour at the
Paschal Supper with his Disciples, in figures and
puppets made as big as the life, of waxwork, curiously
clad and sitting round a large table, the roome nobly
hung, and shining with innumerable lamps and candles :
this was exposed to all the world, all the City came to
see it : such liberty had the Roman Catholics at this
time obtained."

It is strange to read this when we know that eleven
months afterwards the Test Act passed the House
of Lords, whereby all Roman Catholics were debarred from holding any office under the Crown
or post in the Royal Household. Extreme bitterness
of feeling in England against Popery had indeed
begun to make itself felt as early as 1666. The Great
Fire was attributed variously to the Dutch, the
French, and the native Roman Catholics, but especially to a plot between the two last-named. Out-
rages against foreigners and Romanists occurred
before the Fire itself was subdued. To the flourish-

ing of the legend two years later the mock answer
of Lady Castlemaine to the libellous petition of
March 1668 bears witness. But the French alliance,
followed by a large influx of French visitors into the
English Court, produced its natural effect, and what
Marvell twice in his letters calls " the insolence of
the Papists "—which was little more than the open
avowal of their beliefs—was constantly on the increase.

The news of the conversion of the Duchess of
York before her death in March 1671, coupled with
the widespread belief that the Duke had also gone
over already, served to aggravate popular hostility
toward Rome. So strong had the prejudice grown
before the end of 1672 that the Protestant members
of the Cabal extorted the King's most reluctant
consent to a Test Act. The first result of this was
that the Duke of York, though not yet a declared
Roman Catholic, refused to take the required oath
and laid down all his offices, including that of Lord
High Admiral, which was dear to him. An instructive
letter preserved among the collection addressed to
Sir Joseph Williamson, Keeper of the King's Paper
Office, while he was acting as plenipotentiary for
England at the Congress of Cologne in 1673, shows
what effect this had on the public. " Its not to be
writt," says Henry Ball, Williamson's chief clerk
at the Paper Office, " the horrid discourses that
passes now upon His Royall Highness surrendring ;
they call him Squire James and say he was alwayes
a Romanist." A little later Ball declares the talk
of the town to be as bad against the Duke as ever

it was against his father in the height of his troubles;
and again of the town's "averseness to both France
and Popery, the latter of which is the generall eccho
of every place." The remarriage of the Duke to
Mary Beatrice d'Este (Mary of Modena), "a stiffe
Roman Catholique," makes things worse than ever.
Talk is "undecent and extravagent"; and "never
did the common streame run swifter against the
Recusants than now." In the November of the same
year Charles Hatton writes to his brother of the
incredible number of bonfires on the 5th, the Pope
and his cardinals being burnt in effigy in Cheapside—
a fact which is also noticed by Evelyn, and attributed
by him to displeasure at the Duke for altering his
religion and marrying an Italian lady.

One of the sufferers through the Test Act was the
Duchess of Cleveland, who was compelled to resign
that post of Lady of the Bedchamber to the Queen
which had cost such a struggle eleven years before.
Possibly she did not come in for such obloquy now
for her religious beliefs as the reigning mistress;
it was for Louise de Keroualle, this year created
Duchess of Portsmouth, that Nell Gwynn was one
day mistaken as she was driving through the streets
of London and had to jump out of her coach and
explain to the "good people," who were proposing
to mob her, that she was the Protestant mistress.

The French beauty's patent, making her Duchess
of Portsmouth, Countess of Farnham, and Baroness
Petersfield, was ready in July 1673, but there was
some difficulty about passing it before she was

naturalised an English subject. This being sur-
mounted, there was now a second peeress who owed
her title solely to her complaisance to the King.
Rumour would have it that there was going to be
a third—no other than "Madam Gwynn," who " is
promised to be Countess of Plymouth as soon as
they can see how the people will relish itt." The
general public would doubtless have relished it far
more than they relished the Cleveland and Portsmouth peerages ; but Nell Gwynn got no nearer to
the ranks of the aristocracy than by the creation of
her son, Charles Beauclerc, first Earl of Burford
and then, in 1684, Duke of St. Albans.

As if to appease the former mistress for the dignity
about to be conferred upon her successor, the King
was very prodigal with his grants to the Duchess
of Cleveland and her children in the first half of
1673.   In January he invested the young Earl of
Southampton with the Order of the Garter.   In
February he made the already mentioned grant of
arms to the Fitzroy girls.   In April he appointed
the Earl of Euston Receiver-General and Comptroller
of the Seals of the Courts of King's Bench and
Common Pleas.   In June there were warrants issued
for a grant to Viscount Grandison and Edward
Villiers of moneys arising from rents, etc., in the
Duchy of Cornwall ; for a free gift of £5000 to
Grandison ; and for the reversion of certain manors
in Huntingdonshire to Grandison and Villiers and
their heirs—all for the benefit of the Duchess in
reality.   And in July the revenue of the wine licences

were charged with a pension of £5500 a year to Lord Grandison for the Duchess of Cleveland's life, and after her decease to the Earl of Southampton and his heirs male, etc. Finally, in November a letter from one Derham to Sir Joseph Williamson states that " there was brought into the House [of Commons] an account of foure hundred thousand pounds given away since last Session, of which the Duchesses of Cleavland and Portsmouth had the greatest share."

The Williamson letters, from which most of these details are taken, are extraordinarily informing as to the domestic affairs of 1673, the head of the Paper Office having taken good care, with the help of his correspondents, to keep himself in touch with Court news while he was absent from England. On July 14th Ball reports that " a pleasant rediculous story is this week blazed about, that the King had given Nell Gwinn 20,000*l*., which angrying much my Lady Cleaveland and Mademoiselle Carwell, they made a supper at Berkshire House, whither she being invited was, as they were drinking, suddenly almost choaked with a napkin, of which shee was since dead ; and this idle thing runs so hott that Mr. Philips askt me the truth of it, believing it, but I assured him I saw her yester night in the Parke."

Her Grace of Cleveland, being now outwardly amicable to Her Grace of Portsmouth, was probably at the fête mentioned in Ball's letter of July 25th, when " the King, Duke, and all the young Lords and Ladyes, went up to Barn Elmes, and there intended to have spent the evening in a ball and supper

amongst those shades, the trees to have been en-
livened with torches, but the report of it brought
such a traine of spectators that they were faine to
go dance in a barne and sup upon the water ; the
treate was at the cost of Madamoselle Carowell." [1]

From another correspondent we learn that " since
my Lady Dutchesse of Portesmouth's creation few
nights have escaped without balles ; it falls this night
to my Lord of Arlington's turne at Goring House,
where all things will bee very splendid." The French
Ambassador entertained the King and whole Court
at Chelsea, the Duke of Monmouth at his residence,
and so on. The summer season in London this year,
in fact, was very gay and unusually prolonged, to
the detriment of the King's health. On October
10th Ball writes : " Indeed now they lett not his
sacred person alone neither, but say (and that every
body) that he has had lately 3 sad fitts of an apoplexy,
the first whereof tooke him in the Duchesse of Portsmouth's presence, who has since begged he would
not come to her att nights. On Tuesday, they say,
he had a 3d fitt in the Privy Garden, so that many
people are much concerned and have begged His
Majesty to be adviced by his phisitians, who tell
him he must a little refraine company, etc."

Soon after these alarming fits Charles was called
upon to arbitrate between the Duchess of Cleveland
and Lord Arlington, who had fallen out concerning
the upbringing of the Earl of Euston. After the
marriage of August 1672 the Lord Chamberlain

---

[1] Yet another Anglicisation of Keroualle.

wished to have some control of his son-in-law's education. He therefore obtained the King's permission to take him with him to Euston, his Suffolk seat, of which Evelyn's *Diary* has an elaborate description. When Henry Fitzroy was created Earl of Euston it was understood that he was one day to occupy the " palace " there with his bride. But the Duchess of Cleveland absolutely refused to put the boy under Arlington's charge. " Shee will not part with him," says a contemporary letter, " nor cares for any education other than what nature and herselfe can give him, which will bee sufficient accomplishment for a married man." The last statement we may take to be an echo of the Duchess's own words. Whether she gained the day or not does not appear.

For some considerable time now the Duchess's name is only heard of in connection with the affairs of her children. Two of these, in spite of their tender years, were already married. In 1674 two more weddings took place, those of Anne, aged thirteen, and Charlotte, aged nearly ten. The husbands provided for them were Thomas Lennard, fifteenth Lord Dacre, soon created Earl of Sussex,[1] and Edward Henry Lee, just made Earl of Lichfield, both of them Gentlemen of the Bedchamber to His Majesty. An account survives of the Dacre wedding, which took place at Hampton Court on August 2nd. From it we learn how Dacre was brought at nine in

---

[1] His mother was Elizabeth Bayning, a daughter of the first Viscount and therefore a sister to Barbara's mother.

the morning to the Duchess's apartments, and found
the child-bride awaiting him there. A little after
noon the King arrived from Windsor and led the
procession from the Duchess's, through the Gallery,
to the ante-camera of his own bedchamber. Charles
walked first, holding the bride's hand; next came the
bridegroom, next the Duke of York and the Duchess
of Cleveland, and then Prince Rupert, followed by
the ladies of the two contracting families. The
ceremony was performed by the Bishop of Oxford,
in the presence of those already named, together
with the Duke of Monmouth, " Don Carlos "—
Charles's natural son by Catherine Peg, now Lady
Green, who died at Tangier five years later—the
Earls of Suffolk (as Barbara's uncle by marriage), Arlington, Danby, and the Lord Keeper Finch. The
service being over, the King kissed the bride, and
" by and by the bride-cake was broken over her head "
—a proceeding which doubtless sounds more alarming
than in reality it was. Finally there was a dinner
in the Presence Chamber, at which the King had
the bride on his right and her mother on his left.
Soon after the wedding the little Countess was
assigned rooms in Whitehall Palace, the same suite
which had once been her mother's.

There is no similar account of Charlotte Fitzroy's
wedding with the Earl of Lichfield, and owing to her
very tender age this daughter was kept by her mother
to live with her for several years more. The King,
however, provided for both girls with great generosity,
giving a dowry of £20,000 with Anne and one of

£18,000 with Charlotte, and allowing their husbands a pension of £2000 a year each. He was also called upon to pay, ten years later, some large sums incurred for the wedding trousseaus by the Duchess of Cleveland. Among the *Secret Services of Charles II and James II* in 1684–5 occur a number of entries, of which the following, on July 19th, and December 12th, 1684, are typical :

" To Richard Bokenham, in full, for several parcells of gold and silver lace, bought of Wᵐ Gostling and partners on 2nd May 1674 by the Dutchess of Cleavland, for the wedding cloaths of the Lady Sussex and Lichfield . . . . . . 646*l*. 8*s*. 6*d*."

" To John Dodsworth, husband of Katherine Dodsworth, al's Eaton, admˣ of the goods and chattels of John Eaton, unadministred, in part of 1,082*l*. 8*s*. 10*d*. for lace and other things bought of the said John Eaton, for the wedding cloaths of the Ladys Litchfield and Sussex by the Dutchess of Cleaveland . . 182*l*. 0*s*. 0*d*."

The entries prove that Charles ultimately paid at least £1599 18s. od. against nearly £3000 claimed against the Duchess by five creditors in connection with the Dacre and Lichfield weddings. Her Grace had as usual left her bills unpaid.

The flow of Charles's generosity to the Duchess and her children continued unabated by his establishment of a new mistress or by her own flagrant indiscretions. In October he made her a grant, in the names of her uncles Grandison and Edward Villiers, as so often before, of £6000 a year from the excise revenues, with remainder to her sons; made grants from the same source of £3000 a year to each of these and their heirs male; and raised to the peerage the only untitled one of them, the eight-year-old George, whom he created Baron Pontefract, Viscount Falmouth, and Earl of Northumberland. In the September of next year he promoted Charles and Henry to the rank of Dukes, of Southampton and Grafton respectively; a counterpoise to his creation of the reigning mistress's son Duke of Richmond and Lennox in August.

Barbara had therefore among her children two Dukes, an Earl, and two Countesses, all handsomely provided for. Only her namesake, the infant Barbara, reputed daughter of John Churchill, was without a token of the Royal bounty; and, boldly grasping as Lady Cleveland was, perhaps even she could scarcely demand that the King should provide for this witness to her infidelity as a mistress.

To the Duchess's views on the proper education for her children we have already had an allusion in connection with Henry Fitzroy. Some interesting light on her desires about her other two sons is shed by a letter written on September 17th, 1674, by Humphrey Prideaux, at that time tutor of Christ Church, Oxford, and afterwards Dean of Norwich, to his friend John Ellis. Ellis was credited with being a lover of the Duchess somewhere about this time. But the worthy

Prideaux certainly shows no sign of being aware of the fact in his letters.

" Tuesday night," writes Prideaux, " the Dutchesse of Cleveland lodged here in town, and sent for Mr Dean to her lodgings, whom she treated with much civility, and desired him to take her son into his care, whom she will send here next weeke, and leave the whole disposal of him to Mr Dean, as for the appointing of his tutors, lodgeing, allowance, and all other things whatsoever. Her third son was with her, who beeing, she told Mr Dean, born in Oxford among the schollars, shall live some considerable time among them, especially since he is far more apt to receive instructions than his elder brother, whom she confesseth to be a very kockish idle boy. The morneing before she went she sate at least an hour in her coach, that every body might se her."

" Mr. Dean " is the celebrated Dr. John Fell, whose death, as bishop of Oxford in 1686, Evelyn declared to be " an extraordinary losse to the poore church at this time." As on the occasions of her former visits, so now Barbara does not seem to have impressed the scholars favourably, in spite of her honeyed words. But Mr. Dean accepted the charge of the " kockish idle boy," Charles, Earl, and soon to be Duke, of Southampton—a married man of the mature age of fourteen, it should be remembered. It was arranged that before he came into residence he should travel abroad for a while. A tutor was selected for him in the person of Edward Bernard, scholar of St. John's College, with whom he set out for the Continent in the follow-

P

ing spring. How little to his taste Bernard found his job can be gathered in a letter from Prideaux to Ellis in February 1677. " My friend Mr. Bernard, who went into France to attend upon the two bastards of Cleveland, hath been soe affronted and abused there by that insolent woman that he hath been forced to quit that imployment and return."

Bernard apparently undertook the tuition of George as well as Charles Fitzroy. The latter came up to Oxford in the winter term of 1675. " Harry Aldrich is to be his tutor," writes Prideaux ; " what he will get by him I know not. It is the generall desire among us that he come not." A year later he confirms his unfavourable expectations about the young Duke. He " is kept very orderly, but will ever be very simple, and scarce, I believe, ever attain to the reputation of not beeing a fool." We shall see that Mrs. Manley, when she met the Duke about eighteen years later, found the Oxford tutor's prediction fulfilled.

In making arrangements for the guardianship of her sons, the Duchess of Cleveland had no doubt in mind her often discussed withdrawal from England into France. Owing partly to the fact that it was now on Portsmouth rather than on Cleveland that the unfriendly public gaze was turned, and partly to the comparative dearth of letters furnishing us with intimate Court news in 1675–6, we are without precise information about the exact circumstances which led to the deposed mistress's retirement nine years after the idea of her going was first suggested. There is no reason for connecting her departure with the

arrival in England of another celebrated beauty at the
end of 1675, although the coincidence is remarkable
in view of the intimate association of the new-comer's
name with those of the Duchesses of Castlemaine and
Portsmouth at the end of King Charles's life. Undoubtedly there was a plot in connection with the
introduction to Whitehall of Hortense Mancini,
Duchess of Mazarin ; but it was directed against the
reigning mistress, not against her discarded rival,
whose influence was now no longer feared except in
so far as she was still able to extract money from the
Privy Purse. Portsmouth, on the other hand, had
been able to compass the ruin of the once all-powerful
Duke of Buckingham, whose influence over the King,
his cousin had never managed to impair seriously ;
and the other leaders of the Cabal were on the look-
out for a means of striking at her supremacy when an
instrument presented itself to them, which may have
looked heaven-sent, but was probably discovered by
the diabolical Ralph Montagu.

In the last month of 1675, Hortense Mancini
crossed the Channel. Cardinal Mazarin's third and
perhaps most beautiful niece was not unknown to
Charles. When she was but ten years old and he was
still only a king in exile he had been an unsuccessful
suitor for her hand. Now at the age of twenty-nine,
married for fifteen years to a pious husband whom she
found most uncongenial and enriched by her uncle's
will with an enormous fortune of over a million and a
half pounds, after wandering about Europe and indulging in the wildest exploits she came to England

to escape her husband's society and doubtless also
with other intentions. Being aunt to the young
Duchess of York, she was welcomed at Court, and
apartments were assigned to her at St. James's Palace.
She was soon the talk of the day. On April 25th, 1676,
we find Charles Hatton writing to his brother : " The
Dutchesse of Portsmouth is not well : her sicknesse,
it is said, is encreased at somebody's visiting the
Dutchesse Mazarine at my Lady Harvey's house."
For the second time my Lady Harvey shows her friendship for " somebody " when the bounds of Whitehall
are all too narrow for the prosecution of his affairs.

In September Evelyn sups at the Lord Chamberlain's,
where he meets " the famous beauty and errant lady the
Dutchesse of Mazarine," the Duke of Monmouth, and
the Countess of Sussex. From other sources we know
that the brilliant French beauty had quite won the
heart of the thirteen-year-old Countess, to the discontent of her husband, who took steps to put an end to
acquaintance. A letter written by Lady Chaworth
on November 2nd of the same year, speaking of Lady
Sussex, reports : " They say her husband and she will
part unless she leave the Court and be content to live
to him in the country, he disliking her much converse
with Madam Mazarine and the addresses she gets in
that company." Lord Sussex did not at once take
her away from Whitehall, for we hear at the end of
December how " she and Madam Mazarine have
privately learnt to fence, and went downe into St.
James's Park the other day with drawne swords under
their night gownes, which they drew out and made

several fine passes, much to the admiration of severall
men that was lookers-on in the Parke." A few weeks
later, however, the Countess is at her husband's country
seat. Here, after a brief illness, she recovers and,
writes Lady Chaworth, is "mightily pleased with
fox-hunting and hare-hunting, but kisses Madame
Mazarine's picture with much affection still."

Little more than a year later Anne was to cause her
mother most furious pangs of jealousy, which showed
that Lord Sussex's fears of the bad effects of the
addresses of the flighty young girl got in the Duchess
of Mazarin's company were not unfounded. But for
the present my Lady Cleveland was removed from
her daughter's neighbourhood. At some time in 1676
she had at last betaken herself to Paris.[1] A letter
written by Lord Berkeley in Paris on April 8th of that
year mentions her as looking out for a monastery in
which to live during her stay there.

> "Fair beauties of Whitehall, give way,
> Hortensia does her charms display,"

wrote St. Evremond, the Duchess Mazarin's devoted
admirer, who after her death could never hear her
name mentioned without tears. The Duchess of
Cleveland, in seeming anticipation of St. Evremond's
advice (for he wrote these lines in a funeral panegyric
upon his idol in 1699), had departed from a country
where no further triumphs appeared within her power.

---

[1] A letter from Lady Chaworth to Lord Roos, dated simply May 4,
has been assigned to this year. Lady Chaworth writes: "Lady
Cleaveland is not, they say, much satisfied in France because the
greatest ladies doe not visit her."

CHAPTER XI

THE DUCHESS IN PARIS

WITH her removal to Paris, the Duchess of Cleveland entered upon what was to prove a very stormy period in her life. By quitting England she doubtless relieved King Charles's mind of the apprehensions which he always had of a sudden outburst of his former mistress's temper ; but it was not very long before he discovered that the Channel was powerless to quench the flames of her rage. For the present, however, he was thankful and, as if in proof of his gratitude, made a new grant to her of the offices of Chief Steward of Hampton Court and Keeper of the Chace. This sounds a very inappropriate gift, but in those days, when offices were every day sold with the King's permission, and had a certain market value, it promised her a good revenue, which was secured to her for her lifetime and after her death to her third son, the Earl of Northumberland.

That she was in possession of ample funds, even in spite of her extravagant ideas about the spending of money, is shown by her handsome gift now of a thousand pounds to the English nuns of the Convent of the Immaculate Conception of our Blessed Lady to help them to build a new chapel. This appears to be her only recorded present for a religious purpose,

From a mezzotint engraving, after a painting by H. Gascar

BARBARA VILLIERS, COUNTESS OF CASTLEMAINE AND DUCHESS OF CLEVELAND, AND HER DAUGHTER LADY BARBARA

but she was on excellent terms with the dignitaries of the Church in France; on too good terms, according to the scandalous insinuation of Humphrey Prideaux. In a letter of which we have already quoted part above, Prideaux writes to John Ellis on February 2nd, 1677, that the " Dutchess driveth a cunneing trade and followeth her old imployment very hard there, especially with the Arch Bishop of Paris, who is her principal gallant." The Archbishop in question was François de Harlay de Champvalon, a man who, disappointed of his ambitions of becoming a Mazarin, was declared by his critics to be better with precept than with example where holiness of life was concerned. Madame de Sévigné in more than one letter attacks Harlay's private life. There may therefore have been some ground for Prideaux's insinuation. As a matter of fact, as will be seen, the Duchess, having rather unsuccessfully invoked his aid in a difficult matter later on, in her anger gave none too good a character of him to Charles II.

Lady Cleveland seems to have taken two of her daughters with her to Paris. Barbara, who was still little more than an infant, she placed with the English nuns who have been already mentioned. As for Charlotte, in February 1677, at the age of twelve and a half, she was remarried to the Earl of Lichfield and, in defiance of the traditions of her family, made him a good wife. A favourite alike with her father and with her uncle James, she seems to have deserved affection. She was fortunate in being so early removed from her mother's care.

In place of Charlotte the Duchess of Cleveland
before long had the society of Anne, the perplexed
Earl of Sussex having perhaps, in despair of managing
his young wife, handed her over to her mother's
charge.   In December 1677 Lady Chaworth writes
to her brother that the Duchess has put her daughter
into a religious house, and "she means certainly to
come hither in the spring to either ajust things better
between her and her lord, or get his consent that her
daughter may go into orders."

While awaiting the arrival of spring, the Duchess
settled down in Paris to amuse herself.   This never
proved a difficult task to her.   To assist her she found
the English Ambassador, Ralph Montagu, brother of
the lady with whom she had once had so violent a
quarrel.   Montagu bore her no grudge for the outrage
against his sister seven years ago.   Well described by
Swift as being " as arrant a knave as any in his time," he
crowned a chequered and treacherous career by being
made an Earl by William of Orange, a Duke by Anne.
His success in obtaining the Paris ambassadorship from
Charles II was somewhat of a mystery to his contemporaries at Court, but Lord Dartmouth furnishes
an explanation.   " Montagu," he says, " told Sir
William Temple he designed to go Ambassador to
France.   Sir William asked him how that could be,
for he knew the King did not love him, and the Duke
[of York] hated him.   ' That's true,' said he, ' but
they shall do as if they loved me.'   Which, Sir William
told, he soon brought about, as he supposed by means
of the ladies, who were always his best friends for

some perfections that were hid from the rest of the world."

For all we know, Lady Castlemaine may have been one of the ladies who helped Montagu to his post in Paris in 1669. Their acquaintance was now soon very intimate, as all the world noticed and as is shown by two short messages written by her to him and still preserved. They run as follows, the original spelling being retained : [1]

" *friday*. before I reseued yours I was in expectation of seing you to daye, but the ocation that hinders your comming I am extremly sorry for, being realy and kindly consarned for you and all that relats to you. I doe ashuer you I am as much afflicted for your garls ilnes as if she ware my one, and shall be as unease

---

[1] The fearful spelling seems to prove that Lord Chesterfield, as has been suggested above, when he transcribed Barbara Villiers's youthful love-letters in his celebrated collection, revised the orthography. For had Barbara at fifteen spelt so well as she is made to in those letters she could surely not have spelt quite so badly at the age of thirty-seven. But the mere fact that she should make such gross errors is not surprising. The ladies of the day were truly astonishing in this respect ; not only the English ladies, but the French also. See, for instance, a letter from the Duchess of Portsmouth to Henry Sidney on March 8th, 1689 (quoted in *Letters to Sir Joseph Williamson*, II, 19). Nor were many of the gentlemen much better. There survives a humorous letter to Williamson by Sir Nicholas Armorer in October 1673, of which one sentence runs : "This weeke is arrived your good frinde Mauris Justace [Maurice Eustace], to the great joye of Miss Lockett, and I thinke off few els off our nation, that knows his late proceedings ; for take him for what you pleasse heare, I know what hee is on the other side of the watter ; hee has beene too coning for himselfe, and the Dutches of Cleveland will be too hard for him." It was a rare accomplishment to be able to spell in one's own language or to speak another. Cominges, French Ambassador at Whitehall, never knew a word of English.

till I heare she is better ; I was yesterdaye at Paris,
but not hauing the Pleausher of seing you thar mayd
me dislik it more then euer."

" tusday. I will yeld the disscret part to you thoue
not the other for notwithstanding the but, I doe
ashuer you the ten days will be more griuos to me
then to you."

The affair proceeded very smoothly for some time,
during which Montagu, if what the lady says after
the quarrel is to be believed, made her the confidante
of his nefarious schemes and his contemptuous opinions
of the King and the Duke of York. Then the Duchess
aroused her lover's jealousy. The first Gentleman of
the Chamber to Louis XIV was a certain Alexis Henry,
Marquis de Chastillon or Chatillon, who is described
to Lord Hatton by his sister as a person of quality,
young and handsome, but with no estate. This young
man was attracted by the Duchess, or she by him, and
Montagu became aware of the intrigue. It seems
probable that he gave information of it to Whitehall even before he, by some means, got possession of
the compromising letters from the lady of which we
shall hear below. Now in the spring of 1678 the
Duchess paid her intended visit to England, leaving her daughter Anne in a nunnery at Conflans, where also was the country-seat of the Archbishop, near, but outside the walls of, Paris. She
parted on friendly terms with Montagu, not being
aware yet of his betrayal of her intrigue with Chatillon;
while he, on his part, was supremely unconscious of
the pit he was digging for himself. This is evident

from a letter which he wrote from Paris, some time in May, to one of his very numerous cousins, Henry Sidney, afterwards Earl of Romney. " I am glad to hear my Lady Cleveland looked so well," said Montagu. " I do not wonder at it. I will always lay on her side against everybody. I am a little scandalised you have been but once to see her—pray make your court oftener for my sake, for no man can be more obliged to another than I am to her on all occasions, and tell her I say so, and, as my Lord Berkeley says, give her a pat from me. If you keep your word to come in June, I fancy you will come together, and I shall not be ill pleased to see the two people in the world of both sexes I love and esteem the most."

Who could have been more unsuspicious of ruin than the Ambassador at this moment ? His eyes were very soon opened. The Duchess returned to Paris earlier than she was expected, indeed before the end of May, but with no " pat " for Montagu. On the contrary, she dealt him the hardest blow he had ever received. In a letter dated July 17th, 1678, Mary Hatton, who was living in a nunnery in Paris, wrote to her brother :

" What I have to acquaint you withall of Paris news is our cosin Montagues being gon last Monday post towards Ingland, opon my Lord Sunderland's being sent hither ambassador, which bussness they say my Lady Cleavland has intrigued, out of revenge to the ambass. for being soe jealous of her for one Chevalier Chatillon as to wright it wheire he thought it might doe her most prejudice, which she being advertised of, and attributing to it the cold reception she found when she was laitly in Ingland, has, as they say, acussed him of not being faithfull to his master in the imployment he gave him here; to which there is another particular that dus much agravate her, and that is that, whillest she was in Ingland, the ambas. was every day with her daughter Sussex, which has ocationed such jealousy of all sides that, for the saffty of my Lady Sussex, it is reported the ambass. advised her to a nunnery, and made choice of Belle Chase for her, where she is at present and will not see her mother."

Another letter to Lord Hatton, from his brother Charles, shows that Montagu had reached London before July 11th to vindicate himself against accusations brought against him by the Duchesses of Portsmouth and Cleveland, from which it looks as if Her Grace of Cleveland in her fury condescended to make common cause with her supplanter. But we will now let Barbara speak for herself.

Two extremely long letters addressed by her to Charles after her return to Paris have survived the destruction of time and are preserved, the first among the Harleian MSS., the second among the British Museum Additional MSS. Both are so extraordinary and give so vivid a picture of the writer's mind that it seems impossible to mutilate or paraphrase them. With a hope, therefore, that the reader will display sufficient patience to digest them as they stand, we give them in their entirety. It may assuredly be said that there is not their like in the correspondence of kings.

The first, which is dated " Paris, Tuesday 28 78," i.e. May 28th, 1678, must have been sent off almost immediately after the Duchess's arrival, as soon as she discovered Montagu's capture of her letters to Chatillon (at least one of which was obviously written by her when on her visit to England), and runs as follows :

" I was never so surprized in my holle life-time, as I was at my comming hither, to find my Lady Sussex gone from my house & monestrey where I left her, and this letter from her, which I here send you the copy of. I never in my holle lifetime heard of suche government of herself as She has had, since I went into England. She has never been in the monestrey two daies together, but every day gone out with the embassador ; and has often layen four daies together at my house, & sent for her meat to the Embassador, he being allwaies with her till five a'clock in ye morning, they two shut up together alone, and w^d not let my maistre d'hostel wait, nor any of my servants, onely the Embassadors. This has made so great a noise at Paris, that she is now the holle discours. I am so much afflicted that I can hardly write this for crying, to see that a child that I doated on as I did on her, sh^d make so ill a return, & join with the worst of men to ruin me. For sure never any malice was like the Embassador's, that onely because I w^d not answer to his Love, & the importunities he made to me, was resolv'd to ruin me. I hope y^r majesty will yet have that justice & consideration for me, that tho I have done a foolish action, you will not let me be ruined by y^s most abominable man. I do confess to you that I did write a foolish letter to the Chevalier de Chatilion, wch letter I sent enclosed to Madam de

Pallas, and sent hers in a Packet I sent to Lady Sussex by Sir Henry Tychborn; wch letter she has either given to ye embassador, or else he had it by his man, to whom Sir Harry Tychborn gave it to, not finding my Lady Sussex. But as yet I doe not know wch of the waies he had it, but I shall know as I have spoke wth Sir Harry Tychborn. But the letter he has, and I doubt not but that he either has or will send it to you. Now all I have to say for myself is, that you know, as to love, one is not mistriss of one's self, & that you ought not to be offended wth me, since all things of y^s nature is at an end wth you and I; so that I could do you no prejudice. Nor will you, I hope, follow the advice of y^s ill man, who in his hart, I know, hates you, & were it for his interest w^d ruine you too if he could. For he has neither conscience nor honour, and has several times told me, that in his hart he despised you and y^r Brother; and that for his part, he wished wth all his hart that the Parliament w^d send you both to travell, for you were a dull governable Fool, and the Duke a willfull Fool. So that it was yet better to have you than him, but that you allwaies chose a greater beast than y^rself to govern you. And w^n I was come over, he brought me two letters to bring to you, wch he read both to me before he seal'd them. The one was a man's, that he sayd you had great faith in, for that he had several times foretold things to you that were of consequence, and that you believed him in all things, like a changeling as you were. And that now he had writ you word, that in a few months the King of France, or his son, were threatned wth death, or at least a great fit of sickness, in wch they w^d be in great danger, if they did not dye; and that therefore he counsell'd you to defer any resolutions of war or peace till some months were past; for that, if this happen'd, it w^d make a great change in France. The Embassador, after he had read this to me, sayd, ' Now the good of this is,' says he, ' that I can do w^t I will wth this man; for he is poor, & a good summe of money will make him write w^{t}ever I will.' So he proposed to me that he & I should join together in the ruining my Ld Treasurer and the Dutchess of Portsmouth, which might be done thus. The man, tho he was infirm and ill, sh^d go into England, and there, after having been a little time, to sollicite you for money; for that you were so base, that tho you employd him, you let him starve. So that he was obliged to give him 50 ll., & that the man had writ several times to you for money. O, says he, w^n he is in England, he shall tell the King things that he foresees will infallibly ruin him; & so wish those to be removed, as having an ill star, that w^d be unfortunate to you if they were not removed : but if that were done, he was confident you would have the gloriousest reign that ever was. This, says he, I am sure I can order so, as to bring to a good effect, if you will. And in the mean time, I will try to get Secretary Coventry's Place, wch he had a mind to part with, but not to Sir Willm Temple, because he is the Treasurer's creature, and he hates the Treasurer; and I have already employ'd my sister to talk wth Mr Cook, and to send him to engage Mr Coventry not to part with it as yet, and he has assured my Lady Harvey he will not. And my Ld Treasurer's lady and Mr Bertie are both of them desirous I sh^d have it. And w^n I have it, I will be damn'd if I do not quickly get to be Lord Treasurer; and then you & y^r children shall find such a friend as never was.

And for the King, I will find a way to furnish him so easily with money for his pocket & his wenches, that we will quickly out Bab. May, & lead the King by the nose.' So when I had heard him out, I told him I thank'd him, but that I w^d not meddle in any such thing ; and that, for my part, I had no malice to my Lady Portsmouth, or the Treasurer, and therefore I would never be in any Plot to destroy them, but that I found the character the world gave of him was true ; which was, that the Devil was not more designing than he was. And that I wonder'd at it ; for that sure all these things working in his brains must make him very uneasy, and w^d at last make him mad. 'Tis possible you may think I say all this out of malice. 'Tis true he has urged me beyond all patience ; but what I tell you here is most true ; & I will take the Sacrament of it when ever you please. 'Tis certain I would not have been so base as to have informed against him for what he sayd before me, had he not provoked me to it in this violent way that he has. There is no ill thing that he has not done me, and that without any provocation of mine, but that I would not love him. Now, as to what relates to my Daughter Sussex, & her behaviour to me, I must confess that afflicts me beyond expression, & will do much more, if what she has done be by your orders. For tho I have an intire submission to your will, and will not complain whatever you inflict upon me, yet I cannot think you would have brought things to this extremity with me, & not have it in your nature ever to do no cruel things to any thing living. I hope therefore you will not begin with me ; and if the Embassador has not rec^d his orders from you, that you will severely reprehend him for this inhumane proceeding. Besides, he has done what you ought to be very angry with him for; for he has been with the King of France, & told him that he had intercepted Letters of mine by your order, who had been informed that there was a kindness between me and the Chevalier de Chatilion, & therefore you bid him take a course in it, & stop my Letters ; which accordingly he has done. And that upon this you order'd him to take my children from me, & to remove my Lady Sussex to another monastery. And that you were resolved to stop all my Pensions, & never have any regard to me in any thing. And that if he w^d oblige your Majesty, he sh^d forbid the Chevalier de Chatillon ever seeing me, upon the displeasure of losing his Place, & being forbid the Court ; for that he was sure you expected this from him. Upon which the King told him that he could not do anything of this nature, for that this was a private matter, & not for him to take notice of. And that he could not imagine that you ought to be so angry, or indeed be at all concerned ; for that all the World knew, that now all things of Gallantry were at an end with you and I ; that being so, & so publick, he did not see why you sh^d be offended at my Loveing any body. That it was a thing so common nowadays to have a Gallantry, that he did not wonder at any thing of this nature. And when he saw the King take the thing thus, he told him that if he w^d not be severe to the Chevalier de Chatillon upon your account, he supposed he would be so upon his own, for that in the letters he had discoverd, he found that the Chevalier had proposed to me the engageing of you in the mariage of the Dauphin and Madamoselle,[1] and

---

[1] Marie-Louise, daughter of the Duke of Orleans, and therefore niece to Charles II.

Q

that was my greatest busyness in England. That before I went over, I had spoke to him of the thing & would have ingaged him in it ; but that he refused it, for that he knew very well the indifference you had whether it were or no, & how little you cared how Madamemoselle was married. That since I went into England 'twas possible I might engage somebody or other in this matter to press it to you, but that he knew very well, that in your hart you cared not whether it was or no, that this busyness setting on foot by the Chevalier. Upon which the King told him, that if he wᵈ shew him any Letters of the Chevalier de Chatillon to that purpose, he shᵈ then know what he had to say to him ; but that till he saw those Letters, he wᵈ not punish him without a proof for what he did. Upon which the Embassador shewd a letter, which he pretended one part of it was a Double Entendre. The King said he cᵈ not see that there was any thing relating to it, & so left him, & said to a Person that was there, ' Sure the Embassador was the worst man that ever was, for because my Lady Cleveland will not love him, he strives to ruine her the basest in the world, and would have me sacrifice the Chevalier de Chatillon to his revenge, which I shall not do till I see better proofs of his having medled with the marriage of the Dauphin and Madamoselle than any yet that the Embassador has shewed me.' This, methinks, is what you cannot but be offended at, and I hope you will be offended with him for his whole proceeding to me, & let the world see that you will never countenance the actions of so base & ill a man. I had forgot to tell you, that he told the King of France, that many people had reported that he made love to me, but that there was nothing of it, for he had too much

respect for you to think of any such thing. As for
my Lady Sussex, I hope you will think fit to send for
her over, for she is now mightily discours'd of for the
Embassador. If you will not believe me in this, make
inquiry into the thing, & you will finde it to be true.
I have desired Mr Kemble to give you this letter, &
to discourse with you more at large upon this matter,
to know your resolution, & whether I may expect that
justice & Goodness from you which all the world does.
I promise you, that for my conduct it shall be such,
as that you nor nobody shall have occasion to blame
me ; and I hope you will be just to what you said to
me, which was at my House, when you told me you
had letters of mine ; you said, ' Madam, all that I
ask of you, for your own sake, is, live so for the future
as to make the least noise you can, & I care not who
you love.' Oh ! this noise that is, had never been,
had it not been for the Embassador's malice. I cannot
forbear once again saying, I hope you will not gratify
his malice in my ruine."

Before we give the second letter, it is advisable
to explain the allusion in the first to the man whom
Charles " had great faith in." According to Burnet,
" the King had ordered Montagu . . . to find out
an astrologer, of whom it was no wonder he had
a good opinion, for he had long before his restoration
foretold that he should enter London on the 29th of
May, 1660. He was yet alive, and Montagu found him
out, and saw that he was capable of being corrupted,
so he resolved to prompt him to send the King
such hints as could serve his own ends ; and he was
so bewitched with the Duchess of Cleveland that
he trusted her with this secret. She, growing jealous

of a new amour, took all the ways she could to ruin him, reserving this of the astrologer for her last shift; and by it she compassed her ends. For Montagu was entirely lost upon it with the King, and came over without being recalled."

Certainly the letter of May 28th was well calculated to inflame the mind of Charles II against a man whom already he did not love, when he heard himself described by him as "a changeling" (!) and "a dull governable fool," who always chose a greater fool than himself to govern him. How satisfactory to the wrathful Duchess was his reply to her demands can be gathered from her second letter, dated "Paris, friday 3 a clocke in the afternoun":

"I reseued your Ma^{ty} letter last night with more joy then I can expres, for this prosiding of yours is so jenoros and obliging that I must be the werst wooman alive ware I not sensible; no S^r my hart and soule is toucht with this genoriste of yours and you shall allways find that my conduct to the world and behavior to your childeren shall allways render me worthy of your protecktion and favor, this pray be confydent of; I did this morning send your letter to my Lady Sussex by my Jentleman of the hors who when he cam to the grat asket for her: her wooman cam and told him her lady was aslep: he sayd he would stay till she was awake, for that he had a letter to give into her owne hands from the King and that he would not deliver it but to her self: her wooman went into her and stayd above half an hower, which I beleve was whilest she sent to the Embasodor, for he cam in as Lachosse was thar:

her wooman cam owet and sayd that her lady had binne ill to days and had conultion fits and knue nobody : upon which Lachosse said that since she was in that condition he would carry backe the letter to me : the wooman ansard that if he would leave the letter with her she would give it her lady when she came to her self but that nowe she knue nobody and calld all that ware abowet her my Lord Embasodor and my Lady, and spocke of nothing but them ; as soone as I heard this I sent to the Arch Bishop of Paris to let him knowe that haveng sent to Bellchas to specke with my daughtar and to send her a letter of consaren from the King I heard that she was extrem ill and could not com to the Parloyer, wherefor I desiered he would send to the Abbes to let one of my weemen goe in to speck with her : he immedietly writ, on which I sent Pigon [1] with : when she went to the Abbesse she sayd that my Lady Sussex was not so ill as that thar was a nesesety of opening the dores of the monestry, and that if she would com at seven a clocke at night my Lady Sussex would be at the Parloyer, but that nowe she could not com becaus she had binne just let blood, and that for comming in she would not permit her : uppon this I sent agan to the Archbishop and sent your letter to him, which I mad to be put into french that he might se why I prest him so earnestly, and desierd him to send a more positive command to the Abbes : he read the letter and sayd he was very much surprisd but he would send a Prist along with my wooman and him to specke to the Abbess, but that Prist should goe in his coach : all this was to

---

[1] Mrs. Pigeon (?), evidently a successor to "her fine woman Willson" of whom Pepys tells us.

gane time that he might send as I beleve to my
Lady Sussex whoe he visits very often : and this
monestry whar she is is cald the Bishops monestry
and has none of the best reputations ; when Pigion
cam to the monestry the Prist talket with the Abbess
abowet half an hower and then cam to her and told
her that my Lady Sussex was at the Parloyer : she
went thar and found my Lady Sussex siting thar with
the Embasodor : she gave her the leter : the Embasodor
turnd to her and told her, ' Mes Pigion, the King,
has som of your letters.' She made him a cursy and
sayd, ' has he, my Lord, I am very glad of it.' My
Lady Sussex sayd, ' Mes Pigion, if the King knue the
reasons I have for what I have don he would be more
angre with my lady then with me, for that I can
justyfy to the King and the world why I have don
this, and though I have conseald it all this whill
owet of respect to my Lady, I will satisfy the King,
and I dowet not but he will turne his angre from
me to my Lady.' Pigion told her, ' these ware thinges
she did not enter into and that she had only orderes
from me to aske her for the letter when she had read
it that I might sattisfy pepell that it was not by the
Kinges order she was thar.' She sayd ' noe, she would
not give the leter backe ' : uppon which the Embasodor
stood up and sayd, ' my Lady Sussex, doe not give
the letter backe ' : ' No, my Lord,' says she, ' I doe
not intend it ' : with that the Embasodor rise up
and sayd, ' Mes Pigion, doe you knowe whoe my
Lady Sussex is that you should dare to dissput withe
her the delivering the leter.' She sayd, ' my Lord, I
hop I have don nothing unbecomming the respect
I aught to pay my Lady Sussex.' ' Yes,' says he,
' you se she is not well and you argue with her.'

'My Lord,' says she, 'I only aske her for the leter again as my Lady commanded me.' 'The King,' says he, 'has Letters both of yours and your ladys.' 'My Lord,' says she, 'what letters I have writ I doe not at all aprehend the Kinges seing, and for my Lady she is very well inforamd of all that is past.' 'Mes Pigion,' says he, 'my Lady Sussex being the Kinges daughter it was not fit for her to live with my Lady Duchess whoe lead so infamos a life, and therfor she removed, and if annybody askes whoe counseld her to it you may tell them it was I.' ' 'Tis anof, my Lord,' says Pigion, and so mad a curse and cam awaye ; this I thought fite to give you an acount of with all sped that you may se howe this ill man sekes to ruen her : he made her goe to court with my Lady Embasodris, and she was at the hotell de ville of St Jhons day at the fyer and the super, and has mayd a great manny fyn clothes and tacken thre weemen to wayet one her, of the Embasodors prefering, and a swise to stand at her Parloyer dore, and thar is furneture a making for her apartment and she is tacking more footmen, for as yeat she has but one ; I dowet not but that the Embasodor will invent a thousan lyes for her and himself to writ to you of me : but beleve me uppon my word if thay tell truth thay can have nothing to say of my conduckt, for I have both before I went into England and since I cam back lived with that resarvednes and honnor that had you your self market me owet a life I am sure you would have orderd it so : and had it not binne for that sely Leter his malis could not have had a pretentian to have blasted me, and thous leters can never be knowen but by him and my Lady Sussex : pray if your Ma^ty has them send them to me

that I may se if thay ar all and the originales: if
not I bege of you to oblige them to deliver them to
you, for I knowe not what ill use thay may make of
them ore wether the Embasodores malis may not
forge letters I never writ: if you will let me se thous
you have I will aquant you wether ore noe thay be
all; you ar pleasd to command my Lady Sussex to
stay in the monesstery at Conflans: I bege of your
Ma^{ty} not to command her that for it must be very
uneasy to her and me to, ever to live together aftar
such a prosiding as she has had to me, and though
I am so good a Christen as to forgive her, yeat I
cannot so fare conquer my self as to se her dayly,
though your Ma^{ty} may be confydent that as she is
yours I shall allways have som remans of that kindnes
I had formerly, for I can hate nothing that is yours;
but that which I would propos to you is that you
would writ a letter in french which may be showed
to the Arch Bishop of Paris, in which you desier
she may be put into the Monestry of Portroyall at
Paris, and that she maye have to nuns given her to
wayet on her, and that she cares no sarvants with
her, that she stires not owet nor reseaves no visits
what so ever withowet a leter from me to the Abbes:
for whar she is now all pepell visits her and the
Embasodor and others careys consorts of museke
every day to entertan her: so that the holle disscores
of this place is nothing but of her, and she must be
ruend if you doe not tacke som spedy cores with her:
this Portroyall that I propos to you is in great reputation for the piete and regularety of it, so that I
think it much the best place for her: and for Conflans
ware it not for the reasons I have given you before
that place would not be proper for her, for she has

by great presents that she has mad the Abbess gand her to say what she will: for when I cam over she would have conseald from me my Lady Sussex frequent goeng owet of the monestry, but that it was so puplike she could not doe it long: and when she sawe that she sayd that my Lady Sussex told her she went owet for afares of min that I had orderd her to doe in my absance: this being, Conflans is of all places the most unfit for her and would be the most uneasse to me: therfor I doe most humbly bege of your Ma^{ty} not to command her that place."

It is in this letter that the Duchess of Cleveland, as has already been pointed out, speaks of her daughter Anne as if there were no possible doubt of the King being her father. We do not know whether Charles now yielded to the mother's demand that she should be sent to Port Royal instead of Conflans, or whether she was brought back to England now, in spite of her " conultion fits." But already attempts had been made to persuade Lord Sussex to receive her again, and sooner or later she rejoined him. Although she bore him an acknowledged daughter before the end of Charles's reign, her reputation continued to be evil, as might have been expected from so bad a beginning. She separated from the Earl again, and after the abdication of James II went to live at Saint Germain. In 1703 her mother is found writing to Sir Thomas Dyke (one of the trustees of the Sussex marriage settlement), expressing concern for the position of her "daughter Sussex and her childerne," threatened with ruin by Lord Sussex's extravagance. In 1715 His Lordship died. In 1718 his widow found in Lord Teynham another man bold enough to marry her. He shot himself, however, five years later at his house in the Haymarket in a fit of madness, whereon the widow married a third time. Losing this husband, the Hon. Robert Moore, less than three years after the wedding, Anne resigned herself to her fate, and lived another twenty-seven years without a spouse, dying finally in 1755.

Whoever was her father, Anne certainly proved her descent from her mother, as was recognised readily by the libellous verse-writers of the day, who coupled their names together in unpleasing doggerel.

As for the wicked ambassador, his career as a diplomatist was at an end as long as Charles remained on the throne. He left Paris without waiting to be recalled. On reaching England he found himself no longer of the Privy Council, and denied even a hearing by the King. Until Charles's death he remained a man whose acquaintance was dangerous to the reputation of a courtier. James II unwisely admitted him to favour, and in return found him one of the first to desert to William of Orange.

Victory in the Montagu affair undoubtedly remained with the Duchess of Cleveland, but she had not won it without a loss on her side. Charles found it hard to forgive her disregard of his injunction that she should "live so as to make the least noise she could," and his generosity which she so fulsomely acknowledged did not extend so far as to

allow her to return to England until another fourteen
months had elapsed.

Moreover, there was another reason against her
return. Lord Castlemaine had come back to England
in the summer of 1677, and had taken up his residence
in London again. We last saw him, after his mission
in the company of Sir Daniel Harvey to Turkey,
travelling on his own account. Now some affairs
connected with his property brought him back,
and he found no longer any reason of honour why he
should not stay.

If she remained in France, however, the Duchess
of Cleveland retained her interest in her sons' affairs
at home. In the *Savile Correspondence* there is a
letter written by Henry Saville in Paris to his elder
brother on September 21st, 1678, which certainly
must refer to the Duchess of Cleveland. " As for
the question you ask," says Savile, " concerning
Her Grace and her son's pretensions to my Lady
B. P., that is a matter she has had very long in her
wishes, but has fail'd in all the attempts of carrying
it further, and is at last tired with the King's non-
chalance in the prosecution, which could hope for
success from nothing but his vigour in it. However,
the young lord stays this winter in England, to be at
least in the way, and if any method can be found
to set the business on foot, I will take upon me the
part of minding the King to be a little more vigorous
now it is near than he was when it was at a further
distance, which possibly was the occasion of his taking
so little care in it."

"My Lady B. P." is without a doubt Lady Elizabeth (Betty) Percy, only daughter and heiress of the last Earl of the old Northumberland line, Joceline Percy. Some have identified the son of Her Grace here referred to with Charles, Duke of Southampton; but the evidence is in favour of George Fitzroy, or even of Henry. George was the first of the new Northumberland line, and was still unmarried. Charles had been married for seven years, and, imperious as was the Duchess of Cleveland, she could scarcely have hoped to undo now that marriage which she had forced on with such violence in 1671. Henry Fitzroy, too, was a more likely candidate than Charles, for we do know that the Duchess endeavoured to upset the half-completed contract with the daughter of the Arlingtons. Indeed Lady Chaworth writes positively to Lord Roos on December 18th, 1677, that the Duchess of Cleveland "designes to get the King to break her son the Duke of Grafton's marriage to Lord Arlington's daughter, and then hopes to make a match between him and Lady Percy, and her son Northumberland and Mis Anne Mountagu, which double marriage they say Lady Northumberland and her husband aproove." Perhaps the match-making Duchess offered the choice of her sons Henry and George.

Betty Percy's guardians, of whom the chief was her grandmother, decided, however, in favour of Henry Cavendish, Earl of Ogle, son of the Duke of Newcastle, to whom they married her in 1679. Ogle died in a year, and Betty was next contracted (or sold, as people said) by her grandmother to the extremely wealthy commoner, Thomas Thynne, friend of the Duke of Monmouth and once suitor for Anne Fitzroy's hand, it seems.   Although she now expressed her disapproval of George Fitzroy on account of his parentage, the young lady was far from having a liking for Thynne, and she fled in aversion immediately after the private celebration of her wedding. To anticipate events, on February 12th, 1682, Thynne was brutally murdered in Pall Mall by Count John von Konigsmark, brother of the hapless Sophia Dorothea's lover, and two accomplices, leaving Elizabeth at the age of fifteen again a widow. As we shall see, the Duchess of Cleveland once more tried to secure her hand for her son—and once more failed.

If she had been absent from England at the remarriage of her daughter Charlotte to the Earl of Lichfield in 1677, the same was not the case at the remarriage of her son Henry, Duke of Grafton, to Isabella Bennet in November 1679.   In fact, the Duchess was back in London four months previously, for Narcissus Luttrell, whose quaint diary of events from this time onwards helps us with occasional references to Barbara, has the following entry under July of that year : " The latter end of this month the Dutchesse of Cleaveland arrived here from France.   About this time Mrs. Gwyn, mother to Madam Ellen Gwyn, being in drink, was drowned in a ditch near Westminster." [1]

[1] The date of the Duchess's return is also approximately fixed by an amusing letter written on July 31st by Edward Pyckering to Lord

The Duchess of Cleveland had attempted to break off the alliance with the Arlingtons, but, finding herself unable to do so, figured among the principal guests at the wedding on the evening of November 6th, 1679. Evelyn, who was present, has the following account :

" The ceremonie was performed in my Lord Chamberlaines (her fathers) lodgings at Whitehall by the Bishop of Rochester, His Majesty being present. A sudden and unexpected thing, when every body believ'd the first marriage would have come to nothing ; but the measure being determin'd I was privately invited by my Lady, her mother, to be present. I confesse I could give her little joy, and so I plainely told her, but she said the King would have it so, and there was no going back. This sweetest, hopefullest, most beautifull child, and most vertuous too, was sacrific'd to a boy that had been rudely bred, without any thing to encourage them but His Majesty's pleasure. I pray God the sweete child find it to her advantage, who, if my augury deceive me not, will in a few years be such a paragon as were fit to make the wife of the greatest Prince in Europe. I staied supper, where His Majesty sate betweene the Dutchesse of Cleaveland (the mother of the Duke of Grafton) and the sweete Dutchesse the bride ; there were several

Montagu. " The Duchess of Cleveland is lately come over," he says, " and will shortly to Windsor, if not there already. His Majesty gave the Commissioners of the Treasury fair warning to look to themselves, for that she would have a bout with them for money, having lately lost £20,000 in money and jewels in one night at play." Charles had not lost his dread of the harpy's claws !

greate persons and ladies, without pomp. My love to my Lord Arlington's family and the sweete child made me behold all this with regret, tho' as the Duke of Grafton affects the sea, to which I find his father intends to use him, he may emerge a plaine, usefull, and robust officer, and were he polish'd, a tolerable person, for he is exceeding handsome, by far surpassing any of the King's other natural issue."

To signalise the return of the ex-mistress to England there appeared, in the very month of the Grafton wedding, a virulent libel upon her and the Duchess of Portsmouth, forming part of an effusion entitled *An Essay on Satire*. Nine lines of this were as follows :

> " Yet sauntering Charles, between his beastly brace,
> Meets with dissembling still in either place,
> Affected humour, or a painted face.
> In loyal libels we have often told him
> How one has jilted him, the other sold him ;
> How that affects to laugh, how this to weep,
> But who can rail so long as he can sleep ?
> Was ever Prince by two at once misled,
> False, foolish, old, ill-natured, and ill-bred ? "

The authorship of these uncomplimentary verses was attributed to the Earl of Mulgrave and John Dryden in collaboration. The King took in good part the censure administered to him, and only expressed his amusement. Certainly he had been very lightly treated in comparison with the ladies. In the lines—

> " How that affects to laugh, how this to weep,
> But who can rail so long as he can sleep ? "

the laugher and railer is Cleveland, the weeper
Portsmouth, whose most effective argument was said
always to be tears. Yet, strange to say, on this occasion, it was the weeping lady who was the one
to take action. We hear of no move on the part of
the Duchess of Cleveland, but the ruling mistress
hired a gang to waylay and beat Dryden for his
insolence.

Perhaps the authors of this libel were inspired
to be so bold by the recent more than usual kindness
of the King toward his wife. For in the summer of
this year the Countess of Sunderland had written
to Henry Sidney that the Queen " is now a mistress,
the passion her spouse has for her is so great."

Charles, however, had no intention of reforming.
My Lady Portsmouth continued her sway, and
the Duchess of Mazarin and Madam Gwynn, the
latter recently bereaved in the painful way described
by Luttrell, had their shares in his affections still.
If the Queen had no reason for hope, neither had
the Duchess of Cleveland. She returned to Paris,
though the date of her departure is unknown, beyond
that it was probably before December 4th, when
Cleveland House is known to have been occupied by
some one else.

CHAPTER XII

THE LAST YEARS OF CHARLES II

APART from the uselessness of attempting to reconquer Charles's heart, even if she wanted to, the Duchess of Cleveland could not have found England a very pleasant place to live in at the end of 1679. Since she had first withdrawn to Paris the " No Popery " cry had enormously swollen in volume. Demonstrations of hatred for the Pope were common occurrences throughout the country. No doubt Lady Cleveland could have witnessed one on the eve of her son's wedding had she visited the City that day. Such pretty scenes as are described by Charles Hatton to his brother were not confined to one year. Hatton writes, in November 1677, of " mighty bonfires and the burning of a most costly pope, caryed by four persons in divers habits, and the effigies of two divells whispering in his eares, his belly filled full of live catts who squawled most hideously as soone as they felt the fire ; the common saying all the while, it was the language of the Pope and the Divel in a dialogue betwixt them."

But the violence of feeling against the Roman Catholics was not confined in its expression to such ghastly fooleries as this. The hideous Titus Oates

and his allies had now invented what Luttrell calls,
and probably quite honestly believed to be, " a
hellish conspiracy contrived and carried on by the
papists," of which the chief object was to murder
the King—himself a Roman Catholic, little as Oates
and company suspected it! Although the worst
days of the persecution were still to come, it was
already very unsafe to be known as a Papist. One
of the early sufferers was Lord Castlemaine, who
had been committed to the Tower in the autumn
of 1678, and, after being released, was put back
again at the very time of his former wife's presence
in England, Dangerfield having in October sworn
that Lords Arundel of Wardour and Powis had
offered him £3000 to kill the King and that Lord
Castlemaine had blamed him for not accepting
the money for so glorious a work. Lord Powis,
who was Castlemaine's first cousin, being the son
of the first Lord's son, as Castlemaine was son of
his daughter, had gone to the Tower in 1678, to
spend most of his time there since. His wife, before
marriage Lady Elizabeth Somerset, daughter of the
Marquis of Worcester, was sent thither, too, in the
autumn of 1679, three months after Samuel Pepys.

It was impossible to prove Popish sympathies
against Pepys, as all readers of his *Diary* will understand. But the Powises and Castlemaine were well-
known Roman Catholics, and had great difficulty
in rebutting the charges of conspiracy against the
King's life, supported by some swearing as hard as
has ever been heard in a court of law. In the case

of Castlemaine it was the infamy of the witness Dangerfield's character which served him best and led to his acquittal in June 1680.

Had the Duchess of Cleveland remained in the country she might also (unless her very lack of reputation would have saved her) have been the object of persecution like her former husband and so many other highly placed Roman Catholics. Even the mistress *en titre* could not entirely escape. Attacks on her in Parliament in April 1679 were repeated at the end of the year, and an attempt was made to compel the King to exile her from Court. Indeed, she was so alarmed that she herself was for a time anxious to leave England. The ex-mistress escaped such terrors and, safe in France, witnessed similar tyrannical oppression there of the Protestants.

For nearly two years now we lose sight of the Duchess, but in the middle of September 1681 she was expected on another visit to England, Luttrell recording that her house was at that time preparing for her reception. During her last absence in Paris it would appear that she had let Cleveland House, for Evelyn records dining with Lords Ossory and Chesterfield " at the Portugal Ambassador's, now newly come, at Cleaveland House." Of the reason for this visit in 1681, if it was actually paid, we are not told, but it may possibly have been in connection with an honour about to be bestowed upon the Duke of Grafton, who was in high favour with the King. On December 30th at a review in Hyde Park of the Household Troops the Duke was publicly presented by His Majesty with a commission as Colonel of the Foot Guards.

Perhaps, however, the contemplated visit did not actually come about until the spring of the next year, when we know Her Grace came over. A libellous poem entitled *A Dialogue between the D. of C. and the D. of P. at their meeting in Paris with the Ghost of Jane Shore* seems to show that she was in the French capital in March, if it is based on the actual simultaneous presence there of the two Duchesses. Lady Portsmouth left Whitehall with her little son on March 4th, 1682, on her way to Paris, whence she went to the waters of Bourbonne for the benefit of her health. And on April 20th Viscountess Campden writes to her daughter the Countess of Rutland : "Lady Cleaveland is come over. Yesterday I heard the King had not yet given her a visit, and to-day I hear has visited her five times a day."

On reaching England the Duchess of Cleveland took up again her scheme for the marriage of her youngest son George, Earl of Northumberland, to the heiress of the Percies. The wealthy little beauty Elizabeth had been made a widow for the second time by Thynne's murder in February, and two of her former suitors had lost no time before presenting themselves again, the Duke of Somerset and the Earl of Northumberland. The Duke was much the older of the two, being thirty as against his rival's seventeen. The son of the King had no doubt a Dukedom like his brothers' in sight ; but

Charles Seymour was sixth Duke of his line by legitimate inheritance. Elizabeth had already expressed
her prejudice against " a bastard " and had been
confirmed in it by her grandmother, quoting passages
of Scripture to reinforce the argument. So the
marriage with Somerset was quickly arranged and
on May 30th, 1682, Elizabeth took the Duke as
her third husband in the course of three years.

To console the slighted Earl of Northumberland
the King made him a Duke within a year's time
(April 6th, 1683) and a Knight of the Garter nine
months later.

From the time of her arrival in England with
the Duke of Grafton in April 1682 until just before
the death of Charles II, the history of the Duchess
of Cleveland is extremely vague. Luttrell, as we
have seen, makes her come to Whitehall, but in
his notices of the Court's doing in the following
month he never mentions her name. He records
Lady Portsmouth's return to England in July and the
expectation of the arrival that month of the Comtesse
de Soissons, Olympia Mancini, sister of the Duchess
of Mazarin. But neither in London, at Newmarket,
or elsewhere does he give a hint of the presence of
the Duchess of Cleveland. Nor does Evelyn speak of
her being in England again until 1685. But Mr.
Steinman discovered a letter in the Bodleian Library
at Oxford which shows that she was in London in
March 1684. From here she writes to the Duke
of Ormonde, in full confidence of his forgetfulness
of their former violent disagreement, and asks for

his support in connection with certain petitions to him. " I doe not dowet," she writes, " your favorable reporte tharuppon, which I shall tacke as a marke of that frindshippe you allways ownd to have for her that is My lord your Ex[ce]ll[ency's] most faithfull humblle sarvant CLEAVELAND."

Thirteen days after this letter was Easter Sunday, March 30th, 1684, when Evelyn witnessed the remarkable scene which he thus describes in his *Diary* : " The Bishop of Rochester preached before the King ; after which His Majesty, accompanied with three of his natural sonns, the Dukes of Northumberland, Richmond, and St. Albans (sons of Portsmouth, Cleaveland, and Nelly), went up to the Altar ; the three boys entering before the King within the railes, at the right hand, and three Bishops on the left. . . . The King kneeling before the Altar, making his offering, the Bishops first received and then His Majesty ; after which he retired to a canopied seate on the right hand."

It is possible, therefore, that the Duchess of Cleveland was in London when Charles made this wonderful display of himself, in a church which he had secretly long deserted, in the company of her son and those of two of her rivals—three of the six Dukes whom he had added to the peerage from among his natural children. It may be noted that Evelyn thinks Northumberland " the most accomplished and worth the owning " of the six, " a young gentleman of good capacity, well-bred, civil and modest . . . extraordinary handsome and well shaped."

Of all Charles's numerous sons, Northumberland was the one who most resembled him in appearance, being described by John Macky as " a tall black man like his father the King." A verse libel on him a few years later speaks of " his beautiful face and his dull stupid carriage." Northumberland scarcely fulfilled Evelyn's hopes about him. Nor from his only two notable exploits—the kidnapping of his wife in 1685 and his prompt betrayal of the flight of James II and desertion to William in December 1688—should we have judged him to deserve Macky's verdict, " He is a man of honour, nice in paying his debts, and living well with his neighbours in the country " ; or Swift's manuscript note thereon, " He was a most worthy person, very good natured, and had very good sense."

Northumberland was perhaps a little more estimable than his brother Grafton, though Evelyn, owing to his respect for the young Duchess, was on good terms with the latter, and Burnet considered him, if rough, the most hopeful of all Charles's children and, but for his premature death, likely to have become a great man at sea. In recognition of his naval abilities Charles made him Vice-Admiral of England at the end of 1682, in succession to the late Prince Rupert. Indeed the father amply atoned for his early unwillingness to recognise him as his son, and heaped honours on him toward the end of his reign. James II was equally generous to him, in return for which Grafton deserted him even earlier than did Northumberland.

As for Southampton, no one ever discovered merit in him. His first wife, the little Mary Wood, died in 1680, aged only sixteen. The next we hear of the Duke is five years later, when he brings an action in Chancery against her uncle, Dr. Wood, Bishop of Lichfield, suing (as next of kin through her to the deceased Sir Henry Wood) for £30,000. This was adjudged to him as being part of Mary's rightful portion. After this new triumph over justice, Southampton relapsed into obscurity for a few years more.

In connection with two of these sons there is introduced now into the story of the Duchess of Cleveland's life a new and remarkable person. Since the explosion caused by the publication of her affairs with Montagu and Chatillon in 1678 there was a period of silence concerning the Duchess's intrigues. Perhaps, alarmed by what had happened then, she had for a time been endeavouring to obey Charles's injunction to live so as to make the least noise she could. But it is certain that she had not changed her manner of life in any other respect. Boyer, when " drawing a Veil over the Life this Lady led," [1] cannot refrain from mentioning nevertheless that " she descended to the embraces of a Player, a Highwayman, and since an Assassine, Evidence, and *Rennegadoe*." The individual whose character Boyer thus pleasantly sums up is a certain Cardonell Goodman, a gentleman by birth, but something very different by conduct. Colley Cibber tells us that he was

[1] See p. 190.

From a mezzotint engraving by Beckett

HENRY FITZROY, FIRST DUKE OF GRAFTON

styled by his enemies " Scum " Goodman.   The
nickname seems not inappropriate.   A parson's son,
he went to St. John's College, Cambridge, and took
his B.A. degree in 1670, when he was about twenty-
one.   Expelled by the University for his implication
in the defacement of the Duke of Monmouth's
portrait, he came to London and received or perhaps
bought a place as Page of the Backstairs to the King—
whose backstairs certainly did not demand persons
of high moral worth.   But he lost this position by
neglect of his duties and turned from Court to stage,
joining the King's Company at Drury Lane when
about twenty-eight.   As he was soon playing leading
parts (including the title rôle of Shakespeare's *Julius
Cæsar*) he must have had histrionic ability.   It was
after he had become an actor that he made the acquaintance of Lady Cleveland, but the date is uncertain.   Probably it was at the time of one of her
visits to London during her residence in Paris, and
presumably it was before the autumn of 1684, since
his conduct then could not have introduced him
favourably to her notice.

On October 27th, 1684, Narcissus Luttrell records
that " Mr. Goodman the player (who was sometime
since committed for the same) pleaded not guilty
at the Court of King's Bench to an information for
conspireing and endeavouring to hire one Amidee
to poyson the Dukes of Grafton and Northumberland."   On November 7th we are told that he was
" tryed at the nisi prius at Westminster . . . and found
guilty," and on the 24th that " he came to receive

his judgment ; which was, to pay £1000 fine and find
sureties for his good behaviour for life." Earlier
in his London career he had come in for a fortune of
£2000 on his father's death. This, however, had
been squandered before he took to the stage, and
in those days of small salaries he certainly could not
have paid his fine from what he made as an actor.
He tried his hand accordingly at highway robbery,
but was caught and convicted. He must have had
influence of some sort, for he was pardoned by James II
and once more adorned the stage.

We shall hear of Goodman again. For the present,
we may note that the attempt to poison the two
young Dukes did not permanently alienate their
mother's affections from the villain. After his escape
from the gallows, according to Oldmixon, " the fellow
was so insolent upon it that one night, when the
Queen was at the theatre and the curtain, as usual,
was immediately ordered to be drawn up, Goodman
cried, ' Is my Duchess come ? ' and, being answered
no, he swore terribly the curtain should not be
drawn till the Duchess came, which was at the instant, and saved the affront to the Queen."

The year of Goodman's first trial, which may
have been also that of his earliest acquaintance with
his Duchess, saw the large payments out of Charles's
secret funds against the debts incurred by Lady
Cleveland ten years before on account of her daughters' weddings. Her demands on the Privy Purse
had been outdistanced by the Duchess of Portsmouth,
who, it has been calculated, had already in 1681 re-

ceived as much as £136,668 from her royal lover,
and knew as well as her predecessor in Charles's
favour how to make money in addition to what
she was given by the King. "So damned a jade,"
the very free-tongued Countess of Sunderland declared her, that " she will certainly sell us whenever
she can for £500." It seems impossible to compute
with any approach to accuracy the extent of the
Cleveland extortions.

Apart from this payment against the bills for
Sussex and Lichfield trousseaus, the gift of the Hampton Court stewardship, etc., is the last known grant
from Charles to his ex-mistress, but there is a story
of Lord Essex in 1679 being deprived of his post at
the Treasury because he refused to pay over a gift
of £25,000 from the King to the Duchess of Cleveland. Arthur Capel, Earl of Essex, brother-in-law
of Lord Chesterfield's first wife, was an upright
and straightforward man. While acting as Lord-
Lieutenant of Ireland in 1672-7 he had followed
Ormonde's example in resisting the Duchess of Cleveland's claim to Phœnix Park. After retiring from
this post in Ireland he was, on the Lord-Treasurer
Danby's fall early in 1679, put at the head of the
commission appointed to administer the Treasury.
The "discoverers" of the Rye-house plot endeavoured to implicate Essex in the pretended conspiracy, and, after vainly trying to persuade Charles
to summon Parliament, he resigned on November
19th of the same year. Now in a letter written to
Sir Ralph Verney by a kinsman at Court eight days

later there is the following explanation of Essex's motive in leaving the Treasury :

" Some say the E. of Essex went out on this score. The King had given Cleveland £25,000, and she sending to him for it he denied the payment, and told the King he had often promised them not to pay money on these accounts while he was so much indebted to such as daily clamoured at their table for money ; but if His Maj. would have it paid he wisht somebody else to do it, for he would not, but willingly surrender his place, at which the King replied, ' I will take you at your word.' "

Lawrence Hyde, younger son of the former great Chancellor, succeeded Essex at the head of the Treasury Commission, made no difficulty, it was said, over paying the money which his predecessor had refused and his own father would have died rather than pay. But " that Duchess was ever his friend and kept him in," says Sir Ralph Verney's correspondent.

The day of these rapacious harpies, however, was nearly at an end. The year 1685 had scarcely opened when Charles was overtaken by the fate which had been threatening him for some time. In the summer of 1679 he had a series of ague fits which were sufficiently severe to induce him to fetch back the Duke of York from his exile in Holland, in case anything serious might occur. Again in May 1680, when the Duchess of Cleveland was hiding a somewhat diminished head in France, there had been another scare caused by a fit which came upon the King at Windsor, and compelled him to take to his bed.

His physicians diagnosed his malady as ague again, and treated him with " Jesuits' Powder."[1] His Majesty quickly recovered, and in no way abated his usual manner of life. When the end arrived it took both him and the nation by surprise. But it was something worse than ague which had been coming upon him.

At the time of the King's last illness the Duchess of Cleveland was in England, whether or not she had remained here since the previous March. On January 25th, 1685, was witnessed the famous scene recorded for posterity in Evelyn's *Diary*. The day was a Sunday, and Evelyn writes : " Dr. Dove preached before the King. I saw this evening such a scene of profuse gaming, and the King in the midst of his three concubines, as I had never before seen. Luxurious dallying and prophanenesse." A week later Evelyn adds further details.

" I can never forget," he says, " the inexpressible luxury and prophanenesse, gaming and all dissoluteness, and as it were total forgetfullnesse of God (it being Sunday evening) which this day se'nnight I was witnesse of, the King sitting and toying with his concubines, Portsmouth, Cleaveland, and Mazarine, &c., a French boy singing love songs, in that glorious gallery, whilst about twenty of the greate courtiers

---

[1] *I.e.* quinine. Sir William Temple, writing of this drug in his *Essay on Health and Long Life*, says : " I remember its entrance upon our stage, and the repute of leaving no cures without danger of worse returns : but the credit of it seems now to be established by common use and prescription, and to be improved by new and singular preparations."

and other dissolute persons were at Basset round a large table, a bank of at least 2000 in gold before them, upon which two gentlemen who were with me made reflexions with astonishment. Six days after was all in the dust ! "

There are numerous accounts of King Charles's fatal seizure. That given by Sir Charles Lyttelton in a letter written on February 3rd, 1685, is perhaps less familiar to the general reader than some others. " Yesterday," says Lyttelton, " as the King was dressing, he was seized with a convulsion fit and gave a greate scream and fell into his chaire. Dr. King happening to be present, with greate judgment and courage (tho' he be not his sworn phizitian), without other advise, immediately let him blood himself. He had 2 terrible fits, and continued very ill all day, and till 1 or 2 a clock at night. He had several hot pans applied to his head, with strong spirrits. He had the antimoniall cup, which had no greate effect ; but they gave him strong purges and glisters, which worked very well ; and they cupped him and put on severall blistering plasters of cantharides. It took him abt. 8 a clock, and it was eleven before he came to himself. He was not dead, for he expressed great sense by his grounes all ye time. At midnight there was little hopes ; but after, he fell a sleepe and rested well 3 or 4 howers, and Sr Ch. Scarboro [Sir Charles Scarborough, the physician] told me he thinkes him in a hopefull way to doe well. His plasters were taken of this morning, and the blisters run very well ; only one is yet on his leg,

which is very painfull.   He found himself ill when he
rose ; and those abt. him perceived it (but he said
nothing) by his talking and answering not as he used
to doe ; and Thom. Howard desired Will Chiffing
to goe to him, but he would not let him come in, and
as soone as he came out the convulsion seized him,
and he fell into his chaire."

On the 3rd Charles was " twice let blood since
noone," after which the doctors thought he was in
a condition of safety.   But on the night of the 5th
Lyttelton wrote again to Lord Hatton that he had
been very ill almost since the previous midnight.
Hopes of amendment had been dashed, " his disease
being, as is supposed, fallen upon his lung, which
makes him labor to breath, and I see nothing but
sad lookes come from him."   The relentless physicians
drew more blood from the dying man ; twelve ounces
in the early morning of the 6th, as Evelyn tells.
" It gave him reliefe, but it did not continue, for
now being in much paine, and struggling for breath,
he lay dozing, and after some conflicts, the physitians
despairing of him, he gave up the ghost at halfe an
houre after eleven in the morning, being 6 Feb. 1685,
in the 36th yeare of his reigne, and 54th of his age."

" He spake to the Duke of York," adds Evelyn a
little later, recording the King's last wishes, " to
be kind to the Dutchesse of Cleaveland, and especially
Portsmouth, and that Nelly might not starve."
*The Secret History of the Reigns of King Charles II
and King James II* says that " all the while he lay
upon his death-bed, he never spoke to his brother to

put him in mind of preserving the laws and religion of his people; but only recommended to him the charitable care of his two concubines, Portsmouth and poor Nelly." The author of *The Secret History* must indeed have been well informed if he knew all that was said by Charles upon his long and agonising death-bed! It is not, however, in order to refute this imputation against the dying King that we have made this quotation from a work full of crude and reckless charges against both Charles and James, but to call attention to the fact that only "Portsmouth and poor Nelly" are mentioned in this version of the commendation of the ladies to the care of the Duke of York. Similarly Burnet says that Charles "recommended Lady Portsmouth over and over again" to his brother. "He said he had always loved her, and he loved her now to the last; and besought the Duke, in as melting words as he could fetch out, to be very kind to her and to her son. He recommended his other children to him: and concluded, Let not poor Nelly starve; that was Mrs. Gwyn." Barillon, the French Ambassador, also speaks only of a recommendation of the Duchess of Portsmouth and "poor Nelly" to James's care.

It is curious that enemies of Charles II like Burnet and the author of *The Secret History* should omit the name of the Duchess of Cleveland in their accounts of the dying charge, when Charles's connection with her certainly did him as much injury as that with the Duchess of Portsmouth and more than that with Nell Gwynn. Since Evelyn, however, is a most conscientious recorder of what he sees and hears, and is not likely to have inserted the name of Cleveland through any desire to depreciate the King, of whom he is a most tender-hearted censor, we are justified in crediting his version rather than that of the hostile bishop and the libellous pamphleteer, even though these are supported by the French Ambassador. We know that Charles appealed to his brother on behalf of his natural children, except the Duke of Monmouth, who was in disgrace and an exile in Holland. He is not likely to have forgotten, therefore, the mother of five of them.

We shall not yield to the temptation to add yet another to the innumerable character-sketches of Charles II. But it will not be out of place to make a few observations upon his treatment of the lady with whom he linked his name during the whole of his actual reign of twenty-five years. Evelyn is not making an unwarrantable assertion when he says, in his character of Charles, that he " would doubtless have been an excellent Prince, had he been less addicted to women, who made him uneasy and always in want to supply their unmeasurable profusion, to the detriment of many indigent persons who had signally served both him and his father." Ingratitude is a grievous fault in a prince—though cynics find it their commonest failing—and Charles's reputation has suffered enormously from his apparent readiness to forget services and betray friends. Yet his letters and reported speeches do not show him by any means lacking in grateful feeling toward those to whom

s

he considers himself indebted. It is true that it is
the Charles Berkeleys rather than the Clarendons
to whom he shows genuine attachment. But Clarendon for a long time had little cause for complaint.
Burnet, who does not like the Chancellor, sees
Charles so entirely trust him " that he left all to his
care and submitted to his advices as to so many
oracles." Clarendon himself, while finding excuses for
his King's seeming ingratitude to others early in his
reign in the behaviour of the Royalists, grasping
at favours and fighting among themselves, when
it comes to his own betrayal can only attribute His
Majesty's " fierce displeasure " with him to " the
power of the great lady," united with the efforts of
his personal enemies. There is every reason for
supposing that Clarendon was right, and that it was
Lady Castlemaine, as she then was, who brought
about his ruin in revenge for his unceasing opposition
to her power since first Charles elevated her to the
position of official mistress.

It is scarcely necessary to go beyond the case of
Clarendon to show that the King gave the lady
a scandalous licence of interference with the internal
government of the country ; and in the influencing
of England's foreign policy we have seen her take
her share in 1665-6, when she was one of those
who forced on the war which Louis XIV was so
anxious to avoid. As to the extent to which Charles
allowed his mistress to govern him up to the time
when she left Whitehall for Berkshire House there
can be **no doubt**. In spite of his fond belief that

women did not rule him, Lady Castlemaine's hand
was in all his affairs, political and financial.

The financial power of that hand excited more
indignation than its political workings. The precipitation of a war with the unpopular French and
the ruin of an autocratic Chancellor were watched
without much concern. But the outpouring of
vast sums from the country's revenues to gratify
the tastes of " an enormously vicious and ravenous
woman " stirred up the wrath of all but the gang
who shared the spoils with her. It was in vain that
the King tried to disguise his grants by making out
the patents to obliging relatives of hers and friends
of his. It is not possible to reckon up the sum in
hard cash which he made over to her between 1660
and 1685. But everyone was aware that it amounted
to many thousands of pounds a year, and that but
for the advent of Louise de Keroualle, another beauty
as ravenous if not as vicious as Barbara herself, it
might have reached much greater figures.

But it was not the case that Charles's reckless
generosity to his first official mistress ceased when
he deposed her from her post, as we have seen. When
his passion for her was exhausted, which perhaps
occurred as early as 1664, he still took a long time to
break off the habit of his intimacy with her. He
managed to banish her honourably from her Whitehall
apartments in 1668, but it was another eight years
before she took her departure to France. All this
time she was receiving fresh sources of revenue
which made the position of discarded mistress more

lucrative still than that of ruling favourite. Even
the disgrace which befell her in connection with
the Montagu affair did not dry up the stream of gold.
At the very time of his death, Charles's secret funds
were going to the settlement of some of her old debts.
In fact, it might be said that even in the tomb Charles
did not close his purse to her. He died on February
6th, and nine days later, the morrow of his funeral,
sums amounting to £305 11s. were paid from his
secret funds to various tradesmen in connection with
the unsettled debts for the Sussex and Lichfield
trousseaus.

Truly, if Charles, as he told Clarendon, liked
the company and conversation of Barbara Villiers,
and felt that, having undone her and ruined her
reputation, he was "obliged in conscience and
honour to repair her to the utmost of his power,"
he had made in the course of the twenty-five years
of their acquaintance very handsome amends for
the ruin of such a reputation as was hers when he
met her. The price of real virtue in His Majesty's
estimation would be incalculable if Barbara's was
worth so much.

CHAPTER XIII

" HILARIA "

THE personal history of the Duchess of Cleveland is even more vague during the brief reign of James II than during the closing years of his brother's reign. We have seen Evelyn's notice of her on January 25th at Whitehall, in the company of Charles and the Duchesses of Portsmouth and Mazarin. In the upset following the King's unexpected death the earliest of the three mistresses appears to have escaped public notice. Not so the Duchess of Portsmouth. Luttrell, after mentioning the report that " His Majesty, the night before he was taken ill, was to visit the Dutchesse of Portsmouth," tells how that lady " since His late Majesties death hath sent her goods and is retired to the French ambassadors ; but 'tis said a stopp is putt to her goeing beyond sea by His Majestie till she hath paid her debts, which are very great : 'tis said she hath also many of the crown jewells, which some are apt to think she must refund before she goe beyond sea." She was not, indeed, allowed to leave until about two years after Charles's death, for as late as March 1687 she " is said to be returning to France."

As for the Duchess of Mazarin, she owed so much money in London that it is doubtful whether she could have gone to France, even had she desired to do so. She preferred the country of her adoption, however, to her country by marriage, and continued to reside in London during King James's reign and the next, in spite of a request from the House of Commons to William that she should be banished. And it was in London that, in the last year of the seventeenth century, she " died seriously, with Christian indifference towards life," as Saint-Evremond declares.

While two of the three Duchesses are thus known to have remained in the country, one for the greater part of, and the other throughout, the year, the action of Her Grace of Cleveland in 1685 is unknown. Seeing that her former husband was in very high favour with the new King, it might have been expected that she would withdraw for a time. In early May Lord Castlemaine was one of the important witnesses against Titus Oates in his trial for perjury at the King's Bench Bar, as were his kinsfolk the Earl and Countess of Powis at Dangerfield's trial a week later. The Roman Catholic triumph which followed on James's accession, bringing about the well-deserved ruin of Oates and Dangerfield and some startling conversions among well-known people,[1] did not, of course, do any harm to Lady Cleveland, a Roman Catholic of twelve years' standing. But the lack of any mention of her presence in England for the

[1] Evelyn, on January 19th, 1686, writes : "Dryden the famous playwriter, and his two sonns, and Mrs. Nelly (Misse to the late [King]) were said to go to masse ; such proselytes were no greate losse to the church."

whole of the first year of James's reign would suggest that she returned to Paris, were it not for one little piece of scandal mentioned in a letter written to the Countess of Rutland by her uncle Peregrine Bertie in April 1686. According to this letter " the gratious " Duchess of Cleveland had just given birth to a son, " which the towne has christained Goodman Cleveland," attributing the fatherhood to Cardonell Goodman. We hear no more of this child, and there may, of course, have been nothing but malice in the story. But at least it argues that the Duchess was in London in March 1686, and had been there nine months previously.

The one personal mention of Barbara between King Charles's death and the Revolution is contained in a letter written by some unknown person to John Ellis on July 31st, 1688. This correspondent relates that the Duchess of Mazarin, her sister the Duchess of Bouillon (Marie Mancini), and the Duchess of Cleveland " went down the river on board an East Indiaman, and were, it seems, so well satisfied with their fare and entertainment that Their Graces stayed two or three days." This was certainly a rather remarkable proceeding on the part of the three ladies. Perchance they were endeavouring to keep up their spirits in the midst of the agitation caused by the daily expected invasion of England by the Prince of Orange.

Apart from the chronicling of this trip down the Thames, what little we hear about the Duchess of Cleveland at this period is in connection with her sons. Of these the Duke of Grafton was the most prominent. At the Coronation of James II on April 23rd, 1685, he was present as Lord High Constable of England. In the following June he proceeded to the West of England in command of part of the King's army against the Duke of Monmouth, and had a narrow escape from death. He was drawn into an ambuscade near " Phillipsnorton," Luttrell recounts, " where a pretty many were killed, with hazard of the Duke himself, had he not been timely relieved by some of the King's forces." After the crushing of the rebellion at Sedgemoor, where he commanded the foot and with the rest of James's army "behaved himself with all imaginable resolution and bravery," Grafton is next prominent in February 1686. Luttrell says that on the second of that month he " fought a duel with one Mr. Talbott, brother to the Earl of Shre[w]sbury and killed him "—a coroner's inquest subsequently bringing in a verdict of manslaughter ; Evelyn, that on the 19th the Duke " killed Mr. Stanley, brother to the Earle of [Derby], indeede upon an almost insufferable provocation," though he hopes that " His Majesty will at last severely remedy this unchristian custome." We have no clue as to what was this almost insufferable provocation, nor indeed any details of either affair. For neither does Grafton appear to have suffered any harm, since next month he is not only at liberty, but is involved in an extraordinary escapade with his brother Northumberland.

The youngest of the sons of King Charles and

the Duchess of Cleveland, after his unsuccessful wooing of Betty Percy, remained unmarried until some time in 1685 or early 1686, when, as one of John Ellis's correspondents wrote to him, he was "bubbled into marriage with Lucy's widow, to the disgust of the King." This "Lucy's widow" was Catherine, the relict of a certain Thomas Lucy, but by birth the daughter of a poulterer who may have made a fortune—although the Countess of Northampton writes that the lady was "rich only in buty, which tho much prised will very hardly mentaine the quality of a Duchess." According to a doggerel poem of the period, it was a case of—

> "Lucy into bondage run,
> For a great name to be undone;
> Deluded with the name of Duchess
> She fell into the Lion's clutches." [1]

Grafton appears to have helped his brother to this match, and when the King's disgust was made known he further helped him in that attempt to "spirit away his wife" of which Evelyn speaks in his *Diary* on March 29th, 1686. On April 6th someone writes to Ellis to the effect that "the Graces Grafton and Northumberland are returned from Newport"—*sc.* Nieuport in Flanders—"and put the lady in a monastery; but the King says it is not fit she should stay, nor is it believed she will."

Grafton's influence on his brother in this affair

---

[1] One is reminded of what Congreve once wrote to John Dennis: "I have often wondered how these wicked writers of lampoons could crowd together such quantities of execrable verses, tag'd with bad rhimes."

and King James's anger are borne witness to by
another poem of the time, which says :

> " Since His Grace could prefer
>   The poulterer's heir
> To the great match his uncle had made him,
>   'Twere just if the King
>   Took away his blue string
> And sewed him on two to lead him.
>   That the lady was sent
>   To a convent in Ghent
> Was the counsel of kidnapping Grafton ;
>   And we now may foretel
>   That all will go well
> Since the rough blockhead governs the soft one."

What was " the great match his uncle had made
him " appears from a letter of Peregrine Bertie to the
Countess of Rutland. " I have but jest time," he tells
his niece, " to send your Ladyship word of the Duke of
Northumberland owning himself married to Captaine
Lucy's widow. The King was very angry with him
about it, for they had treated a match for him with
my Lord Newcastle's daughter, and all the particulars
agreed." But no steps seem to have taken to break
the marriage. At any rate Northumberland did not
divorce his wife, and on June 17th, 1686, we read in
another letter from Peregrine Bertie to the Countess
that " the Dutchess of Northumberland went yesterday
to waite on the Queen at Windsor, some say to bee
declared Lady of the Bedchamber."

This escapade had no effect on the Duke of Grafton's
advancement, for little more than a year later he is
found entrusted with the honourable mission of
escorting the Princess Palatine from Rotterdam to

Lisbon, on her way to be married to the King of
Portugal.   Of his illegitimate nephews Grafton
appears to have been the favourite of James II.

In the year following that in which the Dukes
of Grafton and Northumberland carried out their
remarkable abduction, the man to whose honour their
birth had done so great a wrong reached the highest
point in his career.   In January 1687 he was sent
by the King as Ambassador Extraordinary to the Pope,
with a mission to " reconcile the kingdoms of England,
Scotland, and Ireland to the Holy See from which,
for more than an age, they had fallen off by heresy."
Castlemaine proceeded to Rome, and at once began
to assert the dignity of his post.   Letters reached
England telling of his setting up " the armes of the
Pope and His Majestie over his pallace, with several
devices of the catholick religion triumphing over
heresy " and of " the great splendor and magnificence
of his reception." [1]   But suddenly there came about
a change in the news, and at the beginning of March
he " is talkt of to come home," leaving his secretary
behind him in Rome as ambassador.   Innocent XI
apparently found his pretensions too high, and treated
him with scant courtesy, being " seasonably attacked
with a fit of coughing " when the envoy attempted
to discuss his business with him.   So says Wellwood,
whose *Memoirs*, however, it must be remembered, are
entirely coloured by his prejudice against the Jacobite

[1] " His publick entry into Rome," Boyer says in his obituary
notice on Castlemaine in 1705, " was pompously printed with a great
many curious copper cuts, at King James the 2d's charge."

party. " These audiences and fits of coughing," says
Wellwood, " continued from time to time, while
Castlemaine continued at Rome, and were the subject
of diversion to all but a particular faction at that
Court." At last Castlemaine, in disgust, threatened to
leave Rome, when the Pope sent him a recommendation to " rise early in the day and rest at noon, since
it was dangerous in Italy to travel in the heat of the
day." Thereon he departed for England. The
editor or compiler of King James's own *Memoirs* says
that the English envoy " being of a hot and violent
temper, and meeting a Pope no less fixed and positive
in his determinations, they jarr'd in almost every point
they went on."

But Castlemaine, even if recalled, was not dis-
graced. On the contrary, in September he was
sworn of the Privy Council, as his cousin Powis had
been the year before. Powis was also created a
Marquis, and his wife on June 10th, 1688, the day
of the birth of James Francis Edward, Prince of
Wales, was made " lady governess of their Majesties'
children." Among the loyal adherents of James II
there were none of higher character than Castlemaine and the Powises, and it is a melancholy fact
that James's bestowal of signal honours on them
was made within fifteen months of the landing in
England of his successor on the throne. Had he not
relied so much on people of a very different stamp,
James might never have had to abandon that throne.

The Earl of Castlemaine and his cousins did not
betray their King. The Powises left for France,

THE EARL OF CASTLEMAINE AT THE FEET OF INNOCENT XI

the Marquis being condemned in his absence next
year for being in arms with King James in Ireland ;
while Castlemaine, remaining in England, was captured in the country and sent to the Tower.   On
the other hand, one of the earliest of those actually
holding office under James to desert to the invader
was the Duke of Grafton, who joined the Prince
of Orange before the end of November.   What was
thought of his conduct even at the time when London
was preparing to welcome the Prince may be gathered
from the fact that as he was riding along the Strand
on December 14th at the head of his regiment of
foot he was shot at by a dragoon near Somerset House.
The pistol missed fire, and the man was immediately
shot dead by one of the Duke's soldiers.

His brother Northumberland was almost as prompt
to turn his coat, and Southampton followed their
examples.   Their mother's uncles, Sir Edward Villiers
and Lord Grandison, were both found on the same
side very early, the former being escort to the Princess
of Orange on her journey from Holland in February
1689, while the latter retained his post as captain of
the Yeomen of the Guard until March.   William,
indeed, seems to have been particularly fascinated by
the Villiers family.   One of them, Elizabeth, daughter
of Sir Edward, he honoured by making his mistress.

Whatever may be thought of the conduct of
her sons and her uncles, who all owed so much to
the family of Stuart, it was not to be expected that
the Duchess of Cleveland would let considerations
of loyalty guide her.   She was forty-seven years

of age when the change of dynasty took place, and her most pressing anxiety was naturally about her pension. Life in exile at Saint-Germain was not for her. As early as July 13th, 1689, she is found writing to the new Lords of the Treasury to the following effect :

" My Lords,

"I am extremely sensible of your justice in renewing my dormant warrant to the Postmaster-General or Governour of the Post Office for the receipt of my rent charge established by two Acts of Parliament on that Branch. But I am very much surprised to find that since some objections have been made (upon pretence of what Major Wil[d]man refuses payment) and the consideration of it left to his Majesties Councill, I cannot obteyne a report, my request is that your Lordsh'pps will be pleased to expedite that justice on my behalfe in hastening the report, which may continue me alwayes.

" Your Lords'pps most humble

" Ser't,

" CLEAVELAND."

This letter did not have the desired effect. Their Lordships at first refused altogether to order Major Wildman to pay their most humble servant, and at the end of the following January only relented so far as to give orders for the payment of one quarter's pension while the question was being referred to Kensington Palace, recently purchased from the Earl of Nottingham to serve as a royal residence. And, though she made a piteous appeal on August 1st, 1692, alleging that her creditors' clamour forced her to write so insistently, apparently it was not until another five years had gone by that the Duchess received satisfaction of her claims. It does not seem to have weighed much with William that he had found such useful supporters in the lady's family. The chief of these, however, was soon removed by death. After taking part in the naval battle off Beachy Head in June 1690, Grafton proceeded to Ireland, and was mortally wounded at the siege of Cork in October, leaving a son to inherit his title, and, in later days, to afford some protection to the lady to whom they both owed their distinguished place in the world.

It is not certain whether the Duchess of Cleveland was in England at the time of King James's retirement from Ireland in 1690. But that she was back in London again in the spring of the following year, and residing at Cleveland House for a time, may be supposed from an occurrence there on March 30th, 1691. On that day there was born a son to the Lady Barbara " Fitzroy," who thus before she was nineteen gave a proof of her appreciation of her mother's example. Herself the reputed daughter of John Churchill, she owed her son to James Douglas, Earl of Arran, eldest son of the third Duke of Hamilton, who had in January 1688 married Lady Ann Spencer, daughter of Lord Sunderland. He is described by Evelyn as " a sober and worthy gentleman," although the connection with the Lady Barbara is poor testimony to his sobriety or worthiness. At the time of his natural son's birth he was a prisoner in the Tower

for the second time since the throne changed hands.
He was arrested on the first occasion because, it was
said, he waited on the Prince of Orange soon after his
arrival and told him that he did so by command of
His Majesty the King. Released shortly afterwards,
he was re-arrested on the charge of corresponding
secretly with the French Court, and kept in custody
for over a year, during which period Barbara Fitzroy's
child was born. His own family being disgusted
with him, a condition made by their desire, when he
was let out upon bail, was that the young lady should
be despatched out of England. She was accordingly
sent as a nun to the convent of Pontoise, where she
ultimately died. The father retired to Scotland, and
was finally acquitted of conspiracy—to die in 1712 by
the sword of the ruffianly Lord Mohun, or of his
second, General MacCartney, in the duel introduced
by Thackeray into the closing chapter of Part I of
Esmond. The son, who was given the name of Charles
Hamilton, was left from his birth in the care of his
grandmother Cleveland, with whom we shall hear of
him again later.

The Lady Barbara, as we have seen, bore her son
at Cleveland House in March 1691, and from this
it has been assumed that the Duchess of Cleveland
was also at that time at the residence which Charles
II had presented to her. If so, she was soon compelled by lack of ready money to quit Cleveland
House. We know that she was without cash from the
letter addressed to the Treasury on August 1st, 1692,
She had moved to a house in Arlington Street,

Piccadilly—a street which had then been built only
two years—in order to save the upkeep of Cleveland
House, for which she no doubt again found a tenant.

After her move to Arlington Street, the Duchess
of Cleveland is once more brought vividly before our
eyes, owing to a chance acquaintance which she
made about 1692–3. This was with Mary de la
Riviere Manley, already alluded to above in connection with the story of the Duchess's intrigue
with John Churchill. Her autobiographical romance,
The Adventures of Rivella, and, in a less degree,
her unsparing or (to use an expression of her own)
" flaming " satire, *The New Atalantis*, provide much
information about the Duchess, some at least of
which looks to contain as much truth as can be expected from the pen of one woman writing about
another with whom she has quarrelled.

De la Riviere Manley, as she is generally called,
was one of the three daughters of Sir Roger Manley,
whom Charles II made Lieutenant-Governor and
Commander-in-Chief of the castles, forts, and forces
in Jersey as a reward for his loyalty. Sir Roger died
in 1688, when his celebrated daughter was only
about sixteen years of age. He left her a small legacy
in his will, but apparently with no sufficient guardian to
look after her. At any rate she soon came to grief.
After having been entrapped into a mock-marriage
by a cousin (supposed to have been John Manley, son
of the Cromwellian Major Manley, and afterwards
Member of Parliament), she was deserted by him
and left to shift for herself. She spent, according

T

to herself, three solitary years after her betrayal, apparently in London, and must have been about twenty-one when she came in contact with the Duchess of Cleveland.

We will let Mrs. Manley tell the tale her own way; after mentioning that *The Adventures of Rivella* are cast in the form of a narrative by *Sir Charles Lovemore* to the young *Chevalier D'Aumont* concerning a charming and much-wronged lady *Rivella*, who is, of course, De la Riviere Manley herself. A " compleat key " to the *Adventures* (published with the third edition in 1717, three years after the appearance of the first), states that *Lovemore* was Lieutenant-General Tidcomb. But he is of no importance except as the narrator. After explaining to the Chevalier that he had known the lady in her girlhood in Jersey, had been smitten by her charms, had lost sight of her after her father's death, and had sought for her determinedly, he continues :

" One night I happen'd to call in at Madam Mazarin's, where I saw *Rivella* introduced by *Hilaria*, a Royal mistress of one of our preceding Kings. I shook my head at seeing her in such company. . . . I accepted the offer she made me of supping with her at *Hilaria's* house, where at present she was lodg'd ; that Lady having seldom the power of returning home from play before morning, unless upon a very ill run, when she chanced to lose her money sooner than ordinary." [1]

[1] The Comte de Soissons, descendant of Hortense Mancini's sister, Olympe, Comtesse de Soissons, has kindly given me the following note : " 'The playing is but moderate, and it is the only entertain-

Hilaria, as has been explained in chapter IX, is the Duchess of Cleveland. In the following paragraph " the lady who liv'd next door to the poor recluse " (*Rivella*) is stated in the Compleat Key to be " Mrs. Rider, Sir Richard Fanshaw's daughter."

" *Hilaria* had met with *Rivella* in her solitary mansion, visiting a lady who liv'd next door to the poor recluse. She was the only person that in three years *Rivella* had conversed with, and that but since her husband was gone into the country. Her story was quickly known. *Hilaria,* passionately fond of new faces, of which sex soever, us'd a thousand arguments to dissuade her from wearing away her bloom in grief and solitude. She read her a learned lecture upon the ill-nature of the world, that wou'd never restore a woman's reputation, how innocent soever she really were, if appearances prov'd to be against her ; therefore she gave her advice, which

ment,' says Saint-Evremond in his description of the pleasures of hospitality at the Duchesse de Mazarin's. When Hortense's friend employs the adjective ' moderate ' to qualify the gambling, for which Hortense's apartments in London were so famous that it was popularly known as *la banque* of the Duchesse de Mazarin, he is not exact ; he is the only historian who attempted to exculpate Hortense from the accusation of being a gambler. It is true that at the beginning of her life at St. James's Palace conversation and wit prevailed in her drawing-room, but this was changed. A *croupier* by the name of Morin ran away from Paris to London and succeeded in sneaking into St. James's Palace, where he made the game of *bassette* (basset) fashionable, and for this game Hortense neglected witty and learned conversations. In vain Saint-Evremond protested in his prose and verse against the rage for gambling, which competed with conversation as does bridge-playing in our time. He remained *vox clamantis in deserto.* Morin drove away from Hortense's drawing-rooms the whole witty Areopagus which had once frequented them."

she did not disdain to practise ; the English of which was, To make herself as happy as she could without valuing or regretting those by whom it was impossible to be valued.   The lady at whose house *Rivella* first became acquainted with *Hilaria*, perceiv'd her indiscretion in bringing them together.   The love of novelty, as usual, so far prevail'd that herself was immediately discarded, and *Rivella* persuaded to take up her residence near *Hilaria's ;* which made her so inveterate an enemy to *Rivella* that the first great blow struck against her reputation proceeded from that woman's malicious tongue : She was not contented to tell all persons who began to know and esteem *Rivella*, that her marriage was a cheat, but even sent letters by the penny-post to make *Hilaria* jealous of *Rivella's* youth, in respect of him who at that time happen'd to be her favourite."

There is a delightfully modern touch in this use of the penny post for the transmission of anonymous letters, which was hardly to be expected.   Next follows the passage which has already been quoted in an earlier chapter [1] concerning *Count Fortunatus* and his " ingratitude, immorality, and avarice."   The story then proceeds :

" *Rivella* had now reign'd six months in *Hilaria's* favour, an age to one of her inconstant temper ; when that Lady found out a new face to whom the old must give place, and such a one, of whom she could not justly have any jealousie in point of youth or agreeableness ; the person I speak of was a kitchin-maid married to her master, who had been refug'd

[1] See p. 189.

with King James in France. He dy'd, and left her
what he had, which was quickly squander'd at play;
but she gain'd experience enough by it to make
gaming her livelihood, and return'd into England
with the monstrous affectation of calling herself
a French-woman; her dialect being thenceforward
nothing but a sort of broken English: This passed
upon the Town, because her original was so obscure
that they were unacquainted with it. She generally
ply'd at Madam Mazarin's basset-table, and was also
of use to her in affairs of pleasure; but whether
that lady grew weary of her impertinence and strange
ridiculous airs, or that she thought *Hilaria* might
prove a better bubble; she profited of the advances
that were made her, and accepted of an invitation
to come and take up her lodgings at *Hilaria's* house,
where in a few months she repay'd the civility that
had been shewn her, by clapping up a clandestine
match between her patroness's eldest son, a person
tho' of weak intellects, yet of great consideration,
and a young lady of little or no fortune."

The Duke of Southampton had, in fact, made a
second marriage, no more illustrious than his former
one. His new wife, whom he wedded in November
1694, was Anne, daughter of Sir William Pulteney,
formerly Member of Parliament for Westminster
and Commissioner of the Privy Seal under the new
regime. With her he settled down to quiet domestic
life, dying finally at the age of sixty-eight, and leaving
a son to bear his title. We now come to *Rivella's*
estimate of her former patron's character, from
which it will be gathered that the young lady was,

by the time when they parted, heartily tired of her
acquaintance, and that when she published her
Adventures, five years after the Duchess's death, she
felt bound by no considerations of gratitude for any
favours in the past to respect her memory. " *Hilaria*,"
she writes, " was querilous, fierce, loquacious, excessively fond or infamously rude. When she was
disgusted with any person, she never fail'd to reproach
them with all the bitterness and wit she was mistress
of, with such malice and ill-nature that she was
hated not only by all the world, but by her own
children and family ; not one of her servants but
what would have laugh'd to see her lie dead amongst
them, how affecting soever such objects are in any
other case. The extreams of prodigality and covetous-
ness ; of love and hatred ; of dotage and adversion,
were joyn'd together in *Hilaria's* soul."

Hilaria had now made up her mind to get rid
of *Rivella* in favour of the ex-kitchenmaid. But
just for a few days, pretending a more than ordinary
passion, she " caused her to quit her lodgings to come
and take part of her bed " in Arlington Street.
Rivella was not deceived. She attributed this action
to *Hilaria's* desire to make it more difficult for her
to see the man she herself was in love with—who,
the Compleat Key informs us, was none other than
Goodman the actor. This agreeable personage is
known to have left the stage by 1690 and to have
betaken himself to heavy and successful gambling,
which made another bond of sympathy between him
and the Duchess.

According to the *Adventures* Goodman was not
faithful, having a mistress in the next street whom
he kept in as much grandeur as his lady. *Rivella*,
however, he did not like at all. His feelings towards
her were hatred and distrust, as he feared that *Hilaria*
would learn about his intrigue round the corner
through " this young favourite, whose birth and
temper put her above the hopes of bringing her into
his interest, as he took care all others should be that
approached *Hilaria*." So he told *Hilaria* that
Rivella had made advances to him—which confirmed
the news sent by the penny post. But *Hilaria*,
not yet being provided with anyone to take *Rivella's*
place at once, dissembled her feelings and threw in
Rivella's way one of her own sons—we are not told
whether it was Southampton or Northumberland—
leaving them alone together upon various plausible
pretences. " What might have proceeded from so
dangerous a temptation," says the supposed narrator,
" I dare not presume to determine, because *Hilaria*
and *Rivella's* friendship immediately broke off upon
the assurance the former had receiv'd from the broken
French-woman that she would come and supply her
place."

" The last day she was at *Hilaria's* house just as
they sat down to dinner, *Rivella* was told that her
sister *Maria's* husband was fallen into great distress,
which so sensibly affected her that she could eat
nothing ; she sent word to a friend, who could give
her an account of the whole matter, that she would
wait upon her at six a clock at night, resolving not

to lose that post, if it were true that her sister were in misfortune, without sending her some relief. After dinner several ladies came into cards. *Hilaria* ask'd *Rivella* to play; she begg'd Her Ladyship's excuse, because she had business at six a clock; they persuaded her to play for two hours, which accordingly she did, and then had a coach sent for and return'd not till eight : She had been inform'd abroad that matters were very well compos'd touching her sister's affairs, which extreamly lightned her heart; she came back in a very good humour, and very hungry, which she told *Hilaria*, who, with leave of the first Dutchess in England that was then at play, order'd supper to be immediately got ready, for that her dear *Rivella* had eat nothing all day."

At the supper-table, *Rivella* having again mentioned how hungry she was, her hostess threw out an insinuation as to the reason for this, and, on being challenged, introduced her son's name in a very pointed way. She continued :

" ' Nay, don't blush, *Rivella*; 'twas doubtless an appointment, I saw him to-day kiss you as he led you thro' the dark drawing-room down to dinner.' ' Your Ladyship must have seen him attempt it,' answer'd *Rivella* (perfectly frighted with her words), ' and seen me refuse the honour.' ' But why,' reply'd *Hilaria*, ' did you go out in a hackney-coach, without a servant ? ' ' Because,' says *Rivella*, ' my visit lay a great way off, too far for your Ladyship's chairmen to go : It rain'd, and does still rain extreamly ; I was tender of your Ladyship's horses this cold wet night ; both the footmen were gone on errands ;

I ask'd below for one of them, I was too well manner'd
to take the Black, and leave none to attend your
Ladyship ; especially when my Lady Dutchess was
here. Besides, your own porter paid the coachman,
which was the same I carried out with me ; he was
forc'd to wait some time at the gate, till a guinea
could be chang'd, because I had no silver ; I beg
all this good company to judge whether any woman
would be so indiscreet, knowing very well, as I do,
that I have one friend in this house that would not
fail examining the coachman where he had carried
me, if it were but in hopes of doing me a prejudice
with the world and your Ladyship.'

"The truth is, *Hilaria* was always superstitious
at play ; she won whilst *Rivella* was there, and would
not have her remov'd from the place she was in,
thinking she brought her good luck. After she was
gone her luck turn'd ; so that before *Rivella* came
back, *Hilaria* had lost above two hundred guineas,
which put her into a humour to expose *Rivella* in
the manner you have heard ; who briskly rose up
from table without eating anything, begging her
Ladyship's leave to retire, whom she knew to be so
great a mistress of sense, as well as of good manners,
that she would never have affronted any person at
her own table but one whom she held unworthy of
the honour of sitting there. Next morning she wrote
a note to *Hilaria's* son, to desire the favour of seeing
him. He accordingly obey'd. *Rivella* desir'd him
to acquaint my Lady where he was last night, from
six till eight. He told her at the play in the side-
box with the Duke of —— whom he would bring to
justify what he said. I [that is to say, *Lovemore*, the
supposititious narrator] chanc'd to come in to drink

tea with the ladies. *Rivella* told me her distress.
I was moved at it, and the more because I had been
myself at the play, and saw the person for whom she
was accus'd set the play out. In a word *Rivella* waited
till *Hilaria* was visible, and then went to take her
leave of her with such an air of resentment, innocence,
yet good manners, as quite confounded the haughty
Hilaria.

" From that day forwards she never saw her more ;
too happy indeed if she had never seen her. All the
world was fond of *Rivella*, and enquiring for her
of *Hilaria* she could make no other excuse for her
own abominable temper and detestable inconstancy,
but that she was run away with —— her son, and
probably would not have the assurance ever to appear
at her house again."

We have quoted *The Adventures of Rivella* at
considerable (but, it is trusted, not at excessive)
length, because there is no other work except Mrs.
Manley's which throws any light on her patroness's
doings at this period, and because it seemed a pity
to abridge to any great extent the account given in so
amusing, but now so little read, a work.

CHAPTER XIV

IN LOW WATER

WITH the help of Mrs. Manley we have been able to see something of the life at Arlington Street of the Duchess of Cleveland after she had passed her fiftieth year. One last quotation from the same gall-dripping pen will serve to complete the picture. " The Dutchess," says *The New Atalantis*, " by her prodigality to favourites fell into an extream neglect. Her temper was a perfect contradiction, unboundedly lavish and sordidly covetous, the former to those who administered to her particular pleasures, the other to all the rest of the world. When Love began to forsake her, and her charms were upon the turn, because she must still be a bubble, she fell into gamesters hands, and play'd off that fortune *Sigismund* had enrich'd her with ; she drank deep of the bitter draught of contempt, her successive amours, with mean ill deformed domestics, made her abandoned by the esteem and pity of the world ; her pension was so ill páy'd that she had oftentimes not a pistole at command. . . ."

The portrait, it is to be feared, is scarcely overdrawn. The Duchess's want of money, her extreme greed for it, and her abandonment to the gambling

passion require no proving, nor does her prodigality
to those to whom she took into her favour. The
worse charges were freely circulated against her in
many lampoons published while she was still living.
The grossness of these verse-tributes to her "execrable
name" forbids their reproduction here, and it
must suffice to say that they bear out Boyer's description of the Duchess as "this second Messalina."
No doubt there is to be seen in the ferocious onslaught
upon her the accumulated rage of thirty years,
the bitter memory of the stream of gold which
Charles II had poured into her lap ; and the period
was not one to let considerations of age or sex weigh
aught when there was a chance offered for exacting
vengeance. To represent the lady of " the withered
hand and wrinkled brow "—though the Duchess's
portrait by Kneller in the reign of Anne, unless it
was a mere piece of flattery, shows that she really
retained her good looks to a wonderful extent—
condemned to seek for pleasure in the meanest of
company gave the satirists the keenest delight. Nevertheless, the whole tenor of the Duchess's life en-
courages the belief that there was not only smoke,
but also much fire.

Of one lover, whom the spiteful tongue of Mrs.
Manley perhaps intended to include among the
" mean ill deformed domestics," though actually
he was nothing of the sort, the Duchess of Cleveland
was robbed in the eighth year of William's reign.
In February 1695 a number of arrests were made
of Jacobites said to be implicated in an " Assassination

Plot " against the life of the monarch. The alleged leaders were Robert Charnock and Sir John Fenwick, who were convicted of high treason and executed in March 1696 and January 1697 respectively—Fenwick having avoided capture for some time. Among those arrested on the first discovery of the plot was Cardonell Goodman. His sympathies with King James were well known. Indeed, he had already got into trouble less than a year before. On June 11th, 1695, Luttrell writes :

" Yesterday being the birthday of the pretended Prince of Wales, several Jacobites mett in several places, and particularly at the Dogg tavern in Drury Lane, where with kettle drumms, trumpets, &c. they caroused, and having a bonfire near that place, would have forced some of the spectators to have drank the said princes health, which they refusing, occasioned a tumult, upon which the mobb gathering entred the tavern, where they did much damage, and putt the Jacobites to flight, some of which are taken into custody, viz. captain George Porter, Mr Goodman the late player, Mr Bedding, Mr Pate, &c."

Whether Goodman suffered any punishment for his riotous behaviour on this occasion, we do not hear. But about the following February 22nd he was again arrested and sent to Newgate. It looks as if some attempt were made to connect the Duchess of Cleveland with the plot, for on April 7th Luttrell says : " Mr Gisburn, of the band of pentioners extraordinary, is taken into custody, there being found in his custody a chest of carabines, and another of pistolls, which he said were sent him by the Dutchesse of Cleveland to be kept soon after Goodman was apprehended, and is committed to the Gatehouse."

The Duchess's character must surely have protected her from all suspicion of risking anything on behalf of James II. Goodman, too, soon revealed the nature of his convictions. After his examination on April 16th it was observed that he returned to Newgate without irons or a military escort, and it was generally believed that he had informed against the Earl of Ailesbury. Soon after he and " Mr Porter " (? the Captain George Porter of the Drury Lane riot) gave evidence against another conspirator, Peter, son of Sir Miles Cook. An attempt was made by some persons to get Porter to fly to France, but Porter betrayed his would-be bribers, who were committed to Newgate. Then on November 16th " Goodman and Porter swore positive against Sir John," as Luttrell tells us. The result to Fenwick was that he lost his head on Tower Hill. Goodman, having served his end as an informer, was allowed to escape to France. The English Jacobites were said to have helped him to get away, to prevent further disclosures. The move was not, however, to his advantage ; for on February 11th, 1697, Luttrell says : " Several letters from France advise that the French King had caused Goodman to be committed to the Bastille and put into irons, designing to break him upon the wheel for what he swore against Sir John Fenwick." He avoided this fate, but two years later succumbed to a fever while still in France.

" Scum " Goodman had quitted his Duchess without damaging her character as far as politics were
concerned. Nor, even if the " Goodman Cleveland "
of Peregrine Bertie's letter was a fact, can he
be said ever to have damaged her character much
otherwise, for the simple reason that it was beyond
his power to damage when he first met her.

While her actor lover was ending his miserable
career, one who stood in a very different position
to the Duchess was also suffering for his connection
with the Stuarts. The Earl of Castlemaine, however,
was in trouble sooner, and after enduring it longer
escaped without dishonour. He was arrested at
Oswestry in January 1689; and after seven or eight
weeks there was brought to London. On October 28th,
according to Luttrell, he " attended the House of
Commons, and being charged with goeing ambassador
to Rome he excused it by the late King's positive
command for that purpose: however, they committed
him to the Tower for high treason." In the May of
the following year he and the Marquis of Powis
were among the thirty specially exempted from the
Act of Indemnity. But although Castlemaine was,
unlike his cousin, within the clutch of his enemies,
he was not treated with the full rigour of the law.
An inexplicable system of petty persecution was,
instead, put into effect against him. On June 2nd,
1690, he appeared at the Court of King's Bench and
was discharged. In August he was again seized,
and on October 23rd he is found appealing, with
some others, either to be tried or bailed out according

to the Habeas Corpus Act. On November 28th
the petitioners were admitted to bail, which was
renewed in the following January. Then on May
22nd, 1691, Luttrell writes : "At the Exchequer was
a tryal between the King and the Earl of Castlemaine
for 4000*l*. worth of plate, which he had of King James
when he went on his embassy to Rome ; the Earls
council insisted on a privy seal from the late King
James, which they produced in Court, dated 8 Dec.
1688, whereby the plate was given to his own use ;
but the witnesses not being positive whither it past
the seal really before or after the abdication of King
James, the jury found for the King, and gave £2,500
damages, the value of the plate."

After this severe blow to his purse, Castlemaine
seems to have departed to live at Saint-Germain
for some years, for in the parish registers there his
name occurs on three occasions between December
1692 and August 1694 as godfather at the baptism
of three children born at the Court of King James.
Once more his private affairs caused him to risk
returning to England. On September 3rd, 1695,
we read that " Bills of high treason are found at
the sessions against 23 persons, most Romanists,
who have absented the kingdom, as sir Edward Hales,
Earles of Castlemain and Middleton, &c., who, if
they doe not appear, will be proceeded against by
way of outlawry, in order to extend their estates."
Castlemaine must have appeared, in order to save
his estate, and have been once more arrested and imprisoned, for we find him on July 18th, 1696, " dis-

charged out of the Tower, on condition he goe beyond sea." He went back to Saint-Germain to find Lord Powis, created by his exiled master Duke, Knight of the Garter, and Lord Chamberlain to his household, dead and buried just before his own release from the Tower. He settled down once more at James's Court for a time, but returned again to his native land, possibly after the decease of both James and William. Boyer makes him "live retiredly in Wales" at the last. At any rate, death overtook him at Oswestry on July 21st, 1705. In his will, which was dated November 30th, 1696, and was therefore drawn up subsequently to his banishment from England, he appointed as his trustees "my Lady Ann, now Countess of Sussex, and John Jenyns, of Heys, in the county of Middlesex, Esq.," leaving to Anne (though he does not call her his daughter) his property in the Savoy and his leaseholds in Monmouthshire, together with his plate, jewels, and other personalty. His body was buried, by his desire, in the family vault of the Powises at Welshpool, Montgomeryshire. So ended a life ruined by an infatuation with a beautiful face.

We have been anticipating events, and must now return to the Duchess of Cleveland at her Arlington Street house, occupying her time with intriguing, gambling, and evading the demands of her creditors, while striving hard to persuade William's Government to continue the payment of the pension which she had received from Charles and had continued to draw under James. We have

U

heard of her urgent appeal in August 1692 and of its
lack of success.   When 1697 opened she was still
unpaid, and in desperation she prepared a memorial,
which was read on March 22nd before the Lords of
the Treasury.   In this she represented that by an
Act of Parliament of the fifteenth year of Charles II
the revenue of the Post Office was settled on the
Duke of York, the King having power to charge
it with a sum not exceeding £5382 a year; that
Charles had granted to Lord Grandison and others,
in trust for her, £4700 a year from that revenue;
that in James's reign she had an order to receive
payment of £500 a week to satisfy arrears, which
then amounted to more than £1300; and that she
had been compelled to borrow money at interest,
and now owed nearly £10,000.   She therefore prayed
for a warrant empowering her to receive the rents
due to her from her annuity.

     This appeal was rejected at first.   But William
seems to have considered that justice demanded
he should recognise the grants of his predecessors,
and accordingly, when the Lords of the Treasury
at the end of July applied to his Secretary for direc-
tions during his absence on the Continent, on August
5th the answer was received that His Majesty desired
a payment to be made to the Duchess on the
arrears of her pension proportionable to what had
been paid to other great persons.   The Lords on
the 24th ordered the Postmaster-General to " satisfie
the Dutchess of Cleveland's want of £2350 by
£100 a week for twenty-three weeks, and £50

the last week, the first payment to be made this week."

The struggle of nine years was crowned with victory, and Her Grace of Cleveland had succeeded in emulating the Vicar of Bray. As changes of reign made no difference to his position, so too she under Charles, James, and William, and soon under Anne, drew her pension of £4700 from the Post Office. It is true that she had the debt of £10,000 to pay off, but debts troubled her not at all so long as she had a supply of ready money for present needs and the gratification of her desires. She could afford now the presents which she loved making to her favourites, and was free to indulge her passion for gambling without humiliating appeals to an avaricious and ungrateful Churchill.[1]

Another period of obscurity, if no longer of indigent obscurity, follows. During the last years of William the Duchess is not found figuring in public. She might "still be a bubble," as Mrs. Manley says, but on the top of a muddy pool of her own choosing, not on the surface of high society, and the polite writers of the day neglect her until the time is reached of her curious second experiment in matrimony.

[1] A late reference to the Duchess as a gambler may be seen in a letter written on August 29th, 1704, when Her Grace was nearly sixty-three. Stanley West at Tunbridge Wells tells his friend Robert Harley in London: "Here are few persons of quality. . . . The Lords George Howard, Petre, and Fanshaw are still remaining, and also the Duchess of Cleveland who is a constant player with the gentlemen only, and hath had bad success."

CHAPTER XV

THE DUCHESS AND BEAU FEILDING

A S was only to be expected from her personal character, the Duchess of Cleveland had a faculty for making the acquaintance of people whose reputations were more peculiar than edifying. Among all those with whom she came into contact during her long life not one, with the exception perhaps of Cardonell Goodman, was more extraordinary than the man whom she made, for the briefest of periods, her second husband. When their paths met Robert Feilding was already remotely connected with her, through William Feilding, first Earl of Denbigh, who married Susan Villiers, Barbara's great-aunt. The precise relationship of Robert to the Denbighs does not appear, but he was on very friendly terms with George, third Earl and younger son of the first. The Feildings were descended from the Hapsburghs, and were Counts of the Empire; and the Beau did not fail to have the spread eagle emblazoned on his coach and to claim the countship on occasions. His father, George Feilding, of Hill-field Hall,[1] Solihull, Warwickshire (now on the edge of

[1] The Beau changed its name to Feilding Hall. By the courtesy of the present occupier, Mr. Samuel Boddington, I have been allowed to inspect this charming old mansion. The front and a

From an engraving by M. Van der Gucht

ROBERT FEILDING

Greater Birmingham), married a daughter of Sir Thomas Shirley, and their son was well provided for when he reached years of indiscretion. He is said by some to have been at Queen's College, Oxford, and to have served for a time in the army of the Emperor Leopold I, commanding a regiment. Another account of his early days makes him come up to London to study law, but quickly abandon the idea when pleasure and fashion had their influence upon him, spending his money upon his personal adornment, and cutting a great dash with his fine clothes and his footmen in yellow liveries with black sashes and black-plumed hats. James Caulfield, who is responsible for this account, says that he paid for his profligacy by disgraceful means, for " the contributions which he raised from some of the sex he lavished upon others."

Some said King Charles first called him " Handsome Feilding " ; others, the ladies who admired him.

good deal of the rest of the house remain much in the state in which they were when the Feildings owned the place. The Feilding arms are to be seen on the wall above the window of the dining-room, and are also on a stained-glass window which was removed from the Hall to Solihull parish church. In a book *Solihull and its Church*, written by the Rev. Robert Pemberton and privately printed, it is stated that the Hall was built in 1576 by one William Hawes. On the death of his son, some time after 1653, it passed into the possession of George Feilding, who was parish bailiff. He died in 1671, and his son Robert sold it to the Rev. Henry Greswold, rector of Solihull. The date of the sale Mr. Pemberton places about 1676, but he admits that there is no direct evidence to show that the Greswolds owned Hillfield Hall until 1709. In his will the Beau describes himself still as "Robert Feilding, of Feilding Hall in the County of Warwick, Esq."

Addison contributed to the *Tatler* in 1709 the following description of him under the disguise of *Orlando
the handsome* :

" Ten *lustra*[1] and more are wholly passed since
Orlando first appeared in the metropolis of this
island : his descent noble, his wit humorous, his
person charming.   But to none of these recom-
mendatory advantages was his title so undoubted
as that of his beauty.   His complexion was fair, but
his countenance manly ; his stature of the tallest,
his shape the most exact ; and though in all his limbs
he had a proportion as delicate as we see in the works
of the most skilful statuaries, his body had a strength
and firmness little inferior to the marble of which
such images are formed.   This made *Orlando* the
universal flame of all the fair sex ; innocent virgins
sighed for him as Adonis ; experienced widows
as Hercules. . . . However, the generous *Orlando*
believed himself formed for the world, and not to
be engrossed by any particular affection."

Feilding was taken into favour by James II, who
made him a grant of £500.   He repaid the King
better than did many whose characters were more
highly esteemed, since he did not, like the Fitzroys,
Villierses, Churchills, etc. etc., desert to William of
Orange at the first opportunity.   On the contrary,
he first raised a regiment on James's behalf in Warwickshire, and later accompanied him on his invasion
of Ireland after the Revolution, sat in his Irish

[1] This is incorrect, for Feilding was only about sixty-one when he
died in 1712.

Parliament as member for Gowran, co. Kilkenny, in 1689, and went back to Saint-Germain with him. At the exiled Court he was one of those rarities, a man with money, having brought with him a sum of £4000, doubtless part of his second wife's dowry. He became reconciled somehow with the Williamite Government, possibly through the Denbigh influence, for he was living in England again at the beginning of 1696. On January 11th of that year Luttrell tells how " Sir Henry Colt and Beau Feilding fought a duel near Cleveland House; the former was run thro the body, tho' not mortal, and the latter disarmed and escaped."

It was not over the Duchess that the duel was fought, in spite of the curious coincidence with regard to its locality and the subsequent Feilding-Cleveland marriage. A week later Luttrell says that Sir Henry Colt, having recovered from his wound and come to the House of Commons, "was ordered to bring in a bill to ascertain the wages of servants, and more easy recovery thereof, it being about that which occasioned the quarrel between him & Mr Feilding, for the apprehending of whom a proclamation was this day ordered, offering a reward of £200 to any that shall seize him, for assaulting Sir Henry Colt, a justice of the peace, in execution of his office."

It is difficult to imagine how Feilding could be so particularly interested in the servants' wages question as to fight a duel about it. Yet this is all we know. He was arrested early in March, but seems to have escaped serious punishment. A fine should not have inconvenienced him greatly, for he had married in succession two rich women ; the first the Honourable Mary Swift (daughter of Viscount Carlingford and a relative of the Dean), who left him a widower in 1682, and the second the lady of whom we have already heard as Viscountess Muskerry, one of the lively Elizabeth Hamilton's victims at the Court masquerade described by Gramont. She was a daughter of Lord Clanricarde, and, in spite of her ungainly appearance, had already before she met Feilding married first Lord Muskerry (the husband who had objected to her "Babylonian" fancy dress), and on his death a doubtfully legitimate Villiers, Robert, by courtesy third Viscount Purbeck, and by assumption "Earl of Buckingham." This Villiers was slain in a duel in 1684, leaving his widow to prove again the power of money by taking to herself a third partner. Through his second wife's influence, perhaps, the Beau became a Roman Catholic. She died in 1698, and for seven years after this he remained unmarried, while he ran through her fortune, no difficult feat for so raffish a person as he.

Before he made his match with the Duchess of Cleveland he came into notoriety again over a quarrel in the theatre. On December 15th, 1702, Luttrell writes: " Last night Beau Feilding was dangerously wounded in the playhouse by one Goodyer, a Herefordshire gentleman." Swift, not predisposed to love Feilding for having married and spent the fortune of a kinswoman of his own, adds a little to our scanty knowledge of this affair. In a fragment upon the subject of *Mean and Great Figures* he speaks of " Beau Feilding at fifty years old, when in a quarrel upon the stage he was run into his breast, which he opened and showed to the ladies that he might move their love and pity ; but they all fell a-laughing." Sir Walter Scott in his edition of Swift's works has a note to the effect that Feilding received his wound at Mrs. Oldfield's benefit. " The combat took place betwixt him and Mr. Fullwood,[1] a barrister, whose foot he had trodden upon in pressing forward to display his person to most advantage. His antagonist was killed in a duel the very same night, having engaged in a second theatrical quarrel. The conduct of the hero might be sufficiently absurd ; but a wound of several inches' depth was an odd subject of ridicule."

A curious work entitled *Cases of Divorce for Several Causes*, published early in the eighteenth century, contains some prefatory " Memoirs of Robert Feilding Esq." Here it is stated that " Major-General Feilding was undoubtedly one of the Leaders of Cupid, if not of Mars " ; and it must be admitted that, in spite of his high military rank (which was possibly conferred on him by King James in Ireland, if not merely assumed by himself), it was more as a lover than as a warrior that he made his name ; and his violence toward the old Duchess, Mary Wadsworth and Mrs. Villars, described later, argues in him the heart of a bully rather than a man of courage.

Owing to the rapidity of pace with which affairs

[1] The discrepancy between the names Goodyer and Fullwood is odd.

usually progressed with such ardent spirits as Feilding
and the Duchess of Cleveland, it seems safe to assume
that it was not before the second half of the year
1705 that they made each other's acquaintance.
The lady was then nearing her sixty-fourth birthday,
and had just lost her unhappy first husband. Feilding
was ten years younger and was eagerly looking out
for a third heiress-bride. About the same time the
names of two promising candidates occurred to him.
One was a young widow, Anne Deleau, the possessor
of a fortune of £60,000 ; the other the famous ex-
mistress of Charles II. He had no difficulty in getting
to know the latter. According to Addison in the
Tatler, his first speech on meeting " the beauteous
Villaria " was to this effect : " Madam, it is not only
that Nature has made us two the most accomplished
of each sex and pointed to us to obey her dictates in
becoming one ; but that there is also an ambition in
following the mighty persons you have favoured.
Where kings and heroes as great as Alexander, or
such as could personate Alexander,[1] have bowed,
permit your General to lay his laurels."

In reply to this fine speech, the *Tatler* says in the
language of Milton :

> " The Fair with conscious majesty approved
>   His pleaded reason."

It was not so easy to scrape an acquaintance with
Mrs. Deleau, who had a father still living to look

[1] " Such as could personate Alexander," i.e. Goodman, one of
whose famous parts was Alexander the Great.

after her interests. Feilding invoked the assistance
of one Mrs. Streights, who suggested the employment
of a certain Charlotte Henrietta Villars, a person
of no repute (as he was to be called upon to show),
but able to get access to ladies of quality in the capacity
of a dresser of hair. Feilding readily agreed—he is
soon afterwards found to be calling Mrs. Villars by
the familiar name of "Puggy"—and confided the
matter to her care. Before long, with her assistance,
he introduced himself, as he imagined, to Mrs. Deleau,
representing himself to her as Earl of "Glascow,"
Viscount Tunbridge, and Major-General Feilding,
though, of course, he had not even the shadow of a
claim to the two first titles. He proceeded to take
the remarkable step of marrying both widows in the
course of sixteen days. We will not anticipate the
account of the first marriage, which is set forth very
fully in the evidence of the great bigamy trial below,
further than by saying that he was united with the
supposed Anne Deleau on November 9th, 1705,
in the lodgings which he had recently taken in Pall
Mall, the ceremony being privately performed by
a priest from the Austrian Embassy. Then on November 25th he was married to the Duchess of Cleveland, also privately, at her house in Bond Street,
to which she had moved after leaving Arlington Street.
The priest on this occasion was Father Remigius,
alias Deviett, chaplain to the Portuguese Ambassador.

Two allusions to Feilding's marriage to the Duchess
are to be found in the correspondence of the day.
One is in a letter written by Lady Wentworth to

her son, Lord Raby, then in Berlin, on December 14th, 1705. "The old Boe Feelding is maryed to the Dutchis of Cleevland," she says, "and she owns it and has kist the Queen's hand sinc[e]." This is interesting as showing that the scandalous Duchess was not debarred from the Court of Anne now.

The other letter was sent on December 17th to Dr. Atterbury by Lord Stanhope, son of the Lord Chesterfield of whom we have heard so much earlier in this book. "I had a letter from you this day," wrote Stanhope, "with a diverting one enclosed from a mad imaginary general, who is so happy as to be fond of that which my father, and all the world besides himself, were weary of long ago. I think him (as Dryden says of the last Duke of Buckingham) a happy madman; since he can at this time be pleased with Cleveland . . . without so much as calling back the idea of *quantum mutatus ab illo*."

After his second wedding the Beau transferred his abode to the Duchess's house, though secretly keeping up his lodgings in Pall Mall, in order to meet the supposed Anne Deleau there. Toward the Duchess of Cleveland he soon showed himself in his true colours. "She payed dear for her fancy," says Boyer; "for he used her very ill, and not being content with the plentiful allowance she made him out of her constant income of a hundred pounds a week, paid her out of the Post Office, he would have divested her of all, even to the necessary furniture of her house, had not her sons, and particularly the Duke of Grafton, her grandson, stood by her."

But worse was to come. In May 1906 Grafton came to her and informed her that two women had been to his house and told him that Feilding had already made a marriage sixteen days before the Bond Street ceremony. It is with no wonder that we read in Luttrell on May 11th : " The Dutchesse of Cleeveland is given over by her physitians." The violence of the old lady's rage now may be imagined from what Mrs. Manley tells of her state on the occasion of Churchill's refusal of a loan.

The house in Bond Street cannot have been a pleasant home for the Beau after the discovery of his perfidy, and it is difficult to believe that he continued to reside in it while the Duchess remained there. Before the end of June we find him prematurely consigned to the grave. Luttrell on the 29th writes : " Handsome Feilding, who married the Dutchesse of Cleveland, died yesterday." So far was this from being a fact, however, that on July 24th Feilding was committed to Newgate, the Duchess having " sworn the peace against him." It is clearly to this that Lady Wentworth alludes when on July 29th she writes to Lord Raby from Twickenham : " Just as I came down hear I hard that the Dutchis of Cleeveland's Feeldin was dead, and she in great greef for him ; but it was no such thing, for instead of that she has gott him sent to Newgate for thretning to kill her twoe sons for taking her part, when he beet her and broack open her clösset doar and toock fower hundred pd. out. Thear is a paper put out about it. He beat her sadly and she cryed out murder

in the street out of the windoe, and he shott a blunder-
bus at the people."

On the day after his committal to Newgate, however, Feilding was released on bail, he finding £1000
and the Duke of Devonshire and Earl of Denbigh
£500 each. During his brief absence in jail the
Duchess seized the opportunity of leaving Bond
Street and seeking the protection of either her son
Northumberland or her grandson Grafton. On
his release he published the following remarkable
advertisement in a broadside, of which an example
has been preserved among the Harleian MSS. :

" Where as the most Noble and most Illustrious
Princess *Barbara*, Dutchess of *Cleveland*, did on
the 25th of *July*, or thereabouts, make a spontaneous
Retreat from the Dwelling House of her Husband,
Major-General *Robert Feilding*, near *Piccadilly*, taking
with her, or sending and conveying before her Elopement, Goods, consisting of Money, Plate, Jewels,
and other things, amounting to the Value of Three
Thousand Pounds, or upwards, the Goods and
Chattels of her said Husband, and which was own'd
by herself to be removd by her Order, with a solemn
promice of restoring the said Goods the next day ;
But so it is, that as yet there has been no Restoration
made of any thing : And notwithstanding her Husband
did, by the Earl of Denbeigh, invite her the said
Dutchess to return to her Co-habitation with him,
she has absolutely refus'd it, by alledging, that she
had put herself under the Protection of her Children ;
and that she defy'd her said Husband, and would
Justify her Elopement. For these causes, and others

no less considerable, her Husband thinks fit solemnly
to give Notice to all Tradesmen and others, upon
no Account whatever to Trust, or give Credit, to
the said Dutchess, whose debts he will in no wise
satisfy."

The sublime impudence of Beau Feilding is admirably illustrated in this claim on the property
of the woman he had deceived so grossly. But
Nemesis was awaiting him with no slow foot now.
On September 3rd, as Luttrell tells, " the bench of
justices at Hicks Hall granted a warrant against
Handsome Feilding for beating a person since he
was bound over." Who was the person assaulted
on this occasion we do not know. Next, on October
4th he was " taken out of his coach by baylifs, near
Temple Bar, and carried to Newgate for debt."
Then on October 23rd, the first day of the legal
term, the Duchess appeared in the Court of Queen's
Bench and preferred an information against him for
abusing her. " It's said," adds Luttrell, " the grand
jury at Hicks Hall have found a bill against him for
having two wives, for which he is to be tried next
session at the Old Bailey." [1]

The Duchess of Cleveland, in her fury, was not
content to proceed against the evildoer in one way

[1] A newsletter of November 2nd, 1706, says : "The Duchess of
Cleveland was introduced by Grafton, Northumberland, and Quarendon
the first day of the term, when for continuing of the bail she swore she
feared personal hurt, and for a proof of her not having malice she said
she had married him who had nothing. Feilding answered that she
had no malice when she married him, but his having now £50 per
week, etc. However, his bail was continued."

only. She was determined to make him suffer all the ignominy possible. She therefore had him arraigned at the Old Bailey for felony, while she sued in Doctors Commons for divorce and nullity of marriage. The first case is a celebrated example of a bigamy trial two hundred years ago, and the report of it throws an immense amount of light upon one side of life in those days. We shall endeavour to give enough of it to make clear the conduct of Feilding, the Duchess of Cleveland, and Mary Wadsworth in this extraordinary affair.

The trial opened on Wednesday, December 4th, 1706, at the Sessions House in the Old Bailey, the indictment against Feilding being that he, on the 9th day of November [1705], at the parish of St. James's, Westminster, took to wife one Mary Wadsworth, spinster, and the same Mary Wadsworth then and there had for his wife ; and that afterwards, viz. on the 25th day of the same month, at the parish of St. Martin's-in-the-Fields, did feloniously take to wife the most noble Barbara, Duchess of Cleveland (the said Mary Wadsworth his former wife, being then living), " against the peace of our Sovereign Lady the Queen, her crown and dignity, and against the form of the statute in that case made and provided."

The counsel for the Queen were Mr. Raymond and Sir James Montague. Feilding perforce defended himself, the law not allowing him the assistance of counsel on such a charge.

The important part of Montague's opening speech was as follows, slightly abbreviated here and there :

"About a year ago there was a young lady left a widow by Mr. Deleau and reputed a great fortune. Mr. Feilding had a design upon this lady and in August 1705 applied himself to one Mrs. Streights to contrive some method how he might have access to this widow. Mrs. Streights had no acquaintance with her, but knew Mrs. Villars used to cut her hair. So they thought the best expedient was to make Mrs. Villars their friend, that by her interest he might have admittance to Mrs. Deleau ; not questioning but if once she had a sight of his very handsome person she would have the same affection for him that he had met with from other ladies. Mrs. Villars was promised £500 to bring this about ; and though she doubted whether she could ever accomplish it, yet by these means she might perhaps make a penny of it to herself. Therefore she promised Mrs. Streights to use her endeavour to serve the Major-General (meaning Mr. Feilding), though she could not be sure such an overture would be well received by Mrs. Deleau. But being acquainted with one Mary Wadsworth, who was somewhat like the widow, she imagined it would be no difficult matter to set her up to represent Mrs. Deleau. And accordingly it was done, and Mr. Feilding proved so intent upon the matter that he went to Doctors-Commons to examine Mrs. Deleau's will, and found that she was left very considerable "—to the extent of £60,000, it was stated later in the trial.

"Soon after he went to Tunbridge and after two or three days' stay there returned and called at Waddon, where Mrs. Deleau resided, with a pretence to see the house and gardens, but in reality to see the widow. It happened that the lady would

x

not be seen herself, but her servants were permitted
to show him the gardens, and he fancied that he had
a sight of Mrs. Deleau too ; for, a kinswoman of
her looking out of window into the garden, he concluded it could be nobody but Mrs. Deleau admiring
Beau Feilding. About three days after his return
from Tunbridge, he told Mrs. Villars of his calling
at Waddon, and that he had acquainted the Duchess
of Cleveland of the fine gardens that were there,
which she expressed a great desire to see, and therefore
directed Mrs. Villars to go in Her Grace's name to
ask the favour of seeing the house and gardens.
Accordingly Mrs. Villars went down to Waddon ;
and Mrs. Deleau treated her very civilly and told
her whenever Her Grace pleased she should see her
house and gardens ; but as she was a widow she could
not attend upon her. Though the Duchess was
expected after this, she did not go, for indeed she
did not know anything of the message.

" The next time Mr. Feilding attempted to see
Mrs. Deleau was at a horse-race at Banstead Downs,
but he was again disappointed. After this he sent
a letter to her house, but the servants when they
saw the name to it, knowing the character of Mr.
Feilding, threw it into the fire.

" When Mrs. Villars found that the Duchess of
Cleveland knew nothing of her being sent to Waddon
and that it was only a contrivance of Mr. Feilding's
to get an opportunity of seeing Mrs. Deleau, and
that in truth he had never seen her, she resolved
to play trick for trick with him and thereupon
proposed the matter to Mary Wadsworth, whom
Mr. Feilding did not know, and one that could not
worst herself much by such an undertaking, whether

it succeeded or not. Mrs. Wadsworth readily em-
braced the offer, and thereupon Mrs. Villars went to
Mr. Feilding and told him she had proposed the
matter to Mrs. Deleau, who had at last given a
favourable ear to it, and that she did not fear but
if matters could be prudently managed his desires
might be accomplished.

" A little before Lord Mayor's Day, 1705, Mrs.
Villars told Mr. Feilding that she had at length
obtained of the lady a promise of an interview,
and that she was shortly to bring her to his lodgings ;
but he must take care not to let her know they were
his lodgings or to give her the least cause to suspect
he had anything to do there. Accordingly Mrs.
Villars, the evening of Lord Mayor's Day, brought
Mrs. Wadsworth, in a mourning coach and widow's
dress, to the lodgings. He was not within at the
time they came, but being sent for came soon after
and was extremely complaisant. At length, in spite
of the caution he had received, he could not forbear
showing her his fine clothes and what furniture he
had, and sent for Mrs. Margaretta Galli to sing to her,
and pretended that he was extremely taken with her,
and that nothing would satisfy him but being married
that night. She, with a seeming modesty, checked
his forward behaviour and made a show of going
away in displeasure ; but before they parted he prevailed on her to promise not to put off their marriage
longer than Wednesday seven-night.

" The appointed day being come, to make him the
more eager and shun suspicion through too much
forwardness on her part, the lady put it off again
till Friday, November 9th; at which time Mrs.
Villars and she came again to Mr. Feilding's lodgings,

where he received them with extraordinary transports of joy. The lady still putting him off and making as if she would be gone, Mr. Feilding, to make things sure, locking them in his apartment, drove in a hackney-coach directly to Count Gallas's, the Emperor's envoy, in Leicester Fields, and returned with one Don Francisco Drian, a Popish priest [attached to the Roman Catholic chapel in the Fields], styled The Father in Red, on account of a red habit he wore. On his arrival the marriage took place."

Counsel went on to say that after the wedding-night the supposed widow Deleau went away with Mrs. Villars to Waddon, as Feilding thought, to which place he addressed letters to her, calling her The Countess of Feilding, best of wives, etc. She visited him again twice at his lodgings before November 25th (the reason for this secrecy being that the heiress's father must not know of the marriage, having a portion of her fortune in his hands). Once more after his marriage with the Duchess of Cleveland she paid him a visit. "During all this time he made her presents, furnished her with money, and treated her as his wife, until the cheat was found out, which was in the following May. Then finding how he had been served, that instead of marrying a fortune of £60,000 he had been imposed upon and had married one not worth so many farthings, he discarded her in great wrath."

The first and principal witness called for the prosecution was Mrs. Villars, who bore out what had been said about her share in the business, and stated that when the supposed Mrs. Deleau had paid her second visit after the wedding-night, Feilding kept writing to her to come again soon, as he was going to leave his lodgings altogether and be with Her Grace the Duchess of Cleveland.[1] Mrs. Wadsworth therefore came; but neither Feilding nor his man-servant were at the lodgings. The latter, however, came in later and said he had brought his master's night-gown and slippers from the Duchess of Cleveland's. Apparently this did not open Mary Wadsworth's eyes yet, for Mrs. Villars explained thus the manner in which she was enlightened with regard to the Beau's proceedings. At the beginning of May 1706 Mrs. Wadsworth sent to him for money, which, of course, betrayed to him, with his knowledge of the Deleau will, that she could not be what she had pretended to be. He thereupon sent for Mrs. Villars to come to the Duchess of Cleveland's. When she arrived he demanded to have his presents returned, beat her, and taking " a thing made of

---

[1] In the "Articles exhibited against Robert Feilding, Esq.," in the case in Doctors Commons, the 24th Item says that, after the marriage with Mary Wadsworth, " the said Robert Feilding, Esq. did tell and declare to the said Mary his Wife, that the most noble Barbara, Duchess of Cleaveland, had settled all, or the greatest Part of her Estate on him the said Robert. And that if she heard of his aforesaid Marriage, he feared she might alter her Mind, or retract what she had done, and not be so kind to him. The said Robert, for the Reasons aforesaid, desired that his Marriage to the said Mary his wife might be kept private." In the fifth of the seven letters to Mary Wadsworth after her marriage, put in as evidence against Feilding at both trials, he writes: "I have not lain at my lodgings since I saw my dear wife; and this week shall leave them altogether, to lye at Her Grace's. However, I shall always keep the conveniency to meet you there."

steel at one end and a hammer at the other," vowed
that if she would not unsay what she said of his
marriage with the false widow Deleau he would slit
her nose off! According to the Articles against
him in the second case, Feilding " did beat and abuse
her in a most barbarous and cruel way." He also
sent for Mary Wadsworth, whose real identity he
had now discovered, to meet him at the lodge at
Whitehall, also called Whitehall Gate. What happened here is described by one of the subsequent
witnesses as follows : " Mr. Feilding came to Whitehall Gate in a chariot, he lit out of it. There was a
hackney-coach brought two women ; one of these
women got out of the coach and came up to M^r
Feilding. Mr. Feilding called her ' Bitch.' The lady
called him ' Rogue ' and said she was his lawful wife.
At that, Mr Feilding having a stick, he punched it
at her ; it happened upon her mouth and made her
teeth bleed. He ordered the sentry to keep her till
he was gone, and he would give him a crown." It
was in revenge for this brutality that Mary Wadsworth and Mrs. Villars paid that visit to the Duke of
Grafton of which we have already heard, and so revealed
the true state of affairs to the Duke's grandmother.

After some other people, including the real Mrs.
Deleau, had been put into the box to establish the
case for the prosecution, Boucher, Feilding's man
at the time of the two weddings, was examined.
From his evidence, given in true valet style and
wonderfully modern in its ring, in spite of the
two hundred years which have elapsed since these

events took place, it appeared that soon after November 25th he " understood by some of the Duchess
of Cleveland's servants that Mr. Feilding was married
to my Lady Duchess." Yet " about or on the 5th
of December, says he, ' Boucher, get my lodgings
in order again, for I expect Mrs. Villars and the lady
to be there ' ; which accordingly I did. I was sent
from the Duchess of Cleveland's with his night-
gown, cap, and slippers. Mrs. Villars and the lady
came accordingly that night, and had a boiled chicken
for supper." The lady stayed the night and went away
next morning in a hackney-coach. This was the
last time Boucher saw her at his master's lodgings.

There is much that is amusing in the course of
examination of the various minor witnesses, but
considerations of space do not permit the quotation
here of what is outside the limits of our story. Two
short passages, however, may be permitted to intrude.
Mrs. Martin, sister of Mrs. Heath, Feilding's Pall
Mall landlady, was called to corroborate the circumstances of the Wadsworth wedding, having been
present in the house at the time. The following
dialogue occurred :

Counsel : " Did you ever see any body come
whilst they were there, in an extraordinary habit, red
gown, &c. ? "
Mrs. Martin : " There was a tall man knocked at
the door in a long gown, blue facing, and fur cap, with
a long beard."
Counsel : " Do you remember the supper that night? "
Mrs. Martin : " I remember a dish of pickles."

May we be allowed to wonder why ?

Mrs. Heath herself, who said that Major-General Feilding took lodgings at her house " about the beginning of October last was a twelve-month," when asked whether she had heard or believed that Feilding and Mary Wadsworth were married, replied : " I did not believe it was a marriage but a conversion ; because his man came down into the parlour and asked for salt and water and rosemary ; which occasioned these words. ' Lord,' said I, ' I fancy they are making a convert of this woman ' ; because they said it was a priest above."

When it came to Feilding's turn to defend himself, he rested his case upon two points ; first, the bad character and untrustworthiness of Mrs. Villars ; and second, that Mrs. Wadsworth was married before, to one Bradby—a Fleet marriage. When he produced his witnesses, the counsel for the prosecution replied that they had no occasion to defend Mrs. Villars's reputation, which they did not pretend was very good. They could, indeed, hardly do that, seeing that she had been in the Bridewell on one occasion. But they insisted that Feilding had been imposed on and had married Mary Wadsworth. As for his plea of an earlier marriage on her part, they pointed out that all he had adduced was a register-book from the Fleet, in which the supposed marriage with Bradby was entered in a different hand from the rest of the entries ; no Bradby, no witnesses to the ceremony, and not even the writer of the entry ! Great use was made of Feilding's own letters (far from decent, it may be remarked) to " Anne Countess of Feilding " at Waddon—Anne being the Christian name of Mrs. Deleau, whom he believed Mary Wadsworth to be.

Mr. Justice Powel, at the end of a long summing up, made the following remarks to the jury : " Gentlemen, it is a very great charge upon Mr. Feilding, it is true, if there be evidence to maintain it. It does not really depend upon Mrs. Villars's evidence ; for if her evidence were to stand alone no credit should be given to it. But as it is supported by concurring evidence, I leave it with you whether it be not sufficient to find Mr. Feilding guilty. But if you think that Mrs. Wadsworth's marriage to Bradby is proved sufficiently, then although you think Mr. Feilding's marriage with Mrs. Wadsworth sufficiently proved, yet you are to find for the defendant."

The jury having withdrawn for some time brought in Feilding guilty of the felony of which he stood indicted. Hereupon it is added in *Cases of Divorce* :

" Mr. Feilding (in case he was found guilty) had obtained the Queen's warrant to suspend execution of the sentence ; and then by his counsel took exception to the indictment, and moved in arrest of judgment ; but they were answered by the Council for the Queen. But Mr. Feilding having obtained a suspension of the execution, the judges, by a *cur advisare vult* (as the form is) suspended giving judgment till the next sessions, and accepted bail of Mr. Feilding then and there to appear."

At the next sessions Feilding's counsel waived

their exception, and on his being asked what he had
to say why the Court should not proceed to judgment
he " craved the benefit of his clergy." [1]   Then judgment was given, the usual penalty being imposed,
which was that he should be burnt in his hand.
As, however, Feilding had the Queen's warrant to
suspend execution, he was admitted to bail. The
cruel sentence was never carried out, Queen Anne
exercising her clemency and pardoning him. Possibly
she thought that he had suffered enough for his
offence in being dragged into such unpleasant pub-
licity at the Old Bailey.   Moreover, there was still
pending against him the other suit brought by the
Duchess.

The proceedings in Doctors Commons resulted
in sentence of the Court being read on May 23rd,
1707.   There were present at the reading the Dukes
of Northumberland and Grafton, the Earls of Lichfield, Sussex, Jersey, etc., to see the triumph of the
vindictive old lady over the Beau.   The sentence
was to the effect that Robert Feilding and Mary
Wadsworth, being free from all contract and promise
of marriage with any other when they contracted
and solemnised marriage on November 9th, 1705,
were man and wife ; that, Robert Feilding not having
the fear of God before his eyes and having on November 25th, 1705, contracted a pretended marriage
with the most noble lady, Barbara Duchess of Cleve-

---

[1] " The privilege of exemption from the sentence which, in the case
of certain offences, might be pleaded on his first conviction by every
one who could read."—*Oxford English Dictionary.*

land, this pretended marriage or rather show of marriage was, from the beginning, void and of no force in law ; and that therefore the said most noble lady " was and is free from any bond of marriage with the said Robert Feilding, and had and hath the liberty and freedom of marrying with any other person."

Two days later Feilding renounced all right of appeal from the sentence, " for," as he wrote to his proctor, " I shall proceed no farther therein." One might have thought that the Duchess would now rest content ; but she claimed that the Court should deliver up to her a gold ring (the posy ring, with the motto *Tibi soli*, with which Feilding had wedded the supposed Anne Deleau) and the seven letters addressed to " the Countess of Feilding." Why she should have these is not evident. Nevertheless, the Court assented, and ring and letters were handed over to Her Grace. Possibly her thirst for vengeance was now at last satisfied. At any rate, she troubled Feilding no more. He survived her about three years, but never recovered from the blow she had dealt him. The memoir of him in *Cases of Divorce for Several Causes* denies the *Tatler's* " conclusion of his venting his dolors in a garret," saying that " his fortune never threw him so low as to be obliged to mount so very high in his abode." Nevertheless it admits that " from this time the affairs of our heroe declined from bad to worse, till at last his creditors were pleased to bring their actions upon him, against which his only refuge remained of putting himself into the Fleet, where the scene changed from gallantry to drunkery, which soon brought him to his end." "Drunkery," it appears from the same authority, had never been a vice of the Beau's in early life. Drink and gambling alike he had avoided.

Feilding did not die in the Fleet prison. He succeeded in compounding with his creditors, and went to live in lodgings in Scotland Yard—doubtless the garret to which the *Tatler* refers—until his death on May 12th, 1712. His chief consolation at the end of his life was a reconciliation with Mary Wadsworth. He left her the sole executrix of his will, calling her "my dear and loving wife Mary Feilding," and devised to her nearly the whole of what remained of his estate, while to his brother, nephew, and two married sisters he left a shilling apiece.

At the end of a work entitled *An Historical Account of the Life, Birth, Parentage, and Conversation of that celebrated Beau, Handsome Fealding* is to be found an "epitaph", which may be quoted as an example of what some thought humorous in those days :—

> "If F—g is Dead,
>   And lies under this Stone,
> That he is not alive,
>   You may bet two to one;
> But if he's alive,
>   And do's not lie here,
> Let him live till he's hang'd,
>   For no Man do's care."

CHAPTER XVI

LAST YEARS AND DEATH

AS the result of the Feilding trial, the Duchess of Cleveland, at the age of sixty-six, was declared free from any bond of marriage with the Beau and at liberty to marry again. But Her Grace is not recorded to have shown any inclination to try her fortune a third time. Perhaps at last even she felt it to be time to rest. She withdrew from the heart of town, and retired to the then quiet Middlesex village of Chiswick, taking with her the little Charles Hamilton, her doubly illegitimate grandson. Strange to say, of all the children who had the fortune or misfortune to be brought up by her, with the exception of Charlotte Countess of Lichfield, Charles Hamilton was the only one to do her credit. On his grandmother's death he was sent to France and put under the care of Charles, Earl of Middleton, whom James II had made Secretary of State before the Revolution and, after reappointing him to that post in exile, created shortly before his own death Earl of Monmouth. As has been said, Hamilton was with his father at the fatal duel with Mohun in 1712. Indeed he himself crossed swords on the occasion with MacCartney, Mohun's second, and was arrested and made one of the principal witnesses at Mohun's trial. On his release from Newgate, after a vain attempt to obtain satisfaction from MacCartney, whom he accused of foul play against his father, he took up his residence permanently abroad, where he bore the title of the Count of Arran, and devoted himself to literature. He married and had a son, called like himself Charles Hamilton, who wrote from notes collected by his father a work entitled *Transactions during the Reign of Queen Anne.*

With this grandchild, then, the Duchess of Cleveland went to Chiswick. Here she spent the last two years of her life. Researches into the question of her place of abode there have not succeeded in proving conclusively where it was. The Rev. L. W. T. Dale, who was vicar of Chiswick at the time when Steinman was writing his *Memoir*, could find no record of her residence in the church rate-books, so that apparently she could only have been the occupier of a furnished house. In the years 1723–8 the Duke of Cleveland and Southampton (Charles Fitzroy, on her death, added her title to his own) figures as a contributor to the church-rates to the extent of 30s., from which it seems as if he continued the occupancy of his mother's house. Mr. Dale favoured Walpole House, which is still standing in the Mall at Chiswick, as the home of the Duchess.

Before the time when Mr. Dale communicated his suggestion to the author of the *Memoir of Barbara Duchess of Cleveland*, all connection of the famous lady with Walpole House seems to have been for-

From a photograph by Emery Walker, after a painting by Sir Godfrey Kneller in the National Portrait Gallery

BARBARA VILLIERS, COUNTESS OF CASTLEMAINE
AND DUCHESS OF CLEVELAND

gotten. Faulkner in his *History and Antiquities of Brentford, Ealing, and Chiswick*, published in 1845, merely says of the place : " Walpole House on the Mall takes its name from having been the residence of the noble family of that name, several members of whom are buried in the church. About sixty years ago it was occupied by Mrs. Rigby as a boarding-house, and here Mr. Daniel O'Connell resided for several years whilst he was studying for the bar. This family mansion has lately been put into a state of repair, and is now occupied by Mr. Allen as a classical and commercial academy."

Walpole House has been identified with the Misses Pinkerton's select establishment for young ladies in *Vanity Fair*, although in Thackeray's description extraneous features have been introduced which are not to be traced in the original. Had Thackeray known of the notorious Duchess's residence in the place, could he have housed those chaste scholastic ladies there ?—particularly when, as a modern writer, Mr. Allan Fea, tells us, the ghost of Her Grace is supposed still to haunt the house !

There is little more to be told about the old Duchess of Cleveland. At Chiswick she lived without any scandal that has come down to us. When she moved thither she was about the same age as Catherine the Great of Russia when she died, and she may be said to have shown herself fully a peer of that ab-normal woman—who like her was branded with the name of " Messalina "—on the infamous side of her character. Catherine remained a victim of her extraordinary mania to the last. In the case of Barbara there is no evidence. Her presence at Court to kiss Queen Anne's hand in December 1705 argues a certain acquired respectability at the age of sixty-six, but we hear of no repentant death-bed such as her rivals of Portsmouth and Mazarin made. In fact, though she would have been an interesting penitent, no one apparently took the trouble to record anything at all about her death-bed except Boyer, and his account is meagre. Having referred to the Feilding case, he says :

" The Duchess, having lived about two years after this, at length fell ill of a dropsie, which swelled her gradually to a monstrous bulk and in about three months' time put a period to her life, at her house at Cheswick, in the county of Middlesex, in the 69th year of her age."

The actual date of the death was Sunday, October 9th. The funeral took place at Chiswick parish church four days after, being carried out by the Duke of Grafton " in a manner privately," Boyer says. The same writer gives the names of the pall-bearers as " the Dukes of Ormond and Hamilton, the Earls of Essex and Grantham, the Earl of Lisford and the Lord Berkley of Stratton."

The choice of pall-bearers seems rather curious. James, second Duke of Ormonde, was the grandson of Barbara's old opponent, whom she had in her rage hoped to see hanged. Hamilton was her illegitimate son-in-law, if we may so call him.

Algernon Capel, second Earl of Essex, inherited his title as eldest surviving son of the man who left the Treasury in 1679 rather than pay the £25,000 claimed from it by the Duchess of Cleveland. Grantham—Henry d'Auverquerque, son of a naturalised Dutchman who fought under the Prince of Orange—must have owed his acquaintance with her to the young Ormonde, whose sister, Lady Henrietta Butler, he married. By the Earl of " Lisford " Boyer appears to mean Frederic William de Roye de la Rochefoucauld, one of William's supporters at the Battle of the Boyne, and created by him Earl of Lifford in the Irish peerage. His connection with the Duchess of Cleveland cannot be traced. As for Lord Berkeley of Stratton—William the fourth Baron, who succeeded to his father's title after both his elder brothers had borne it in turn—he, like Ormonde and Essex, might have been supposed to have hereditary reasons for hostility rather than friendship toward her late Grace ; for we have seen how she and the first Baron had been at variance about a large sum of money. With Barbara, however, as with many of her kind, enmity was usually a caprice. She could be a most bitter foe for a moment, and then forget and forgive. Only against Clarendon and Southampton does she seem to have cherished a lifelong hatred ; and their attitude made all approach impossible.

By her will, which was dated August 11th, 1709, the Duchess of Cleveland made her grandson the Duke of Grafton residuary legatee. She had but little to leave except her property at Nonsuch.

Y

This went to Charles Fitzroy together with her title of Cleveland. In 1722 the Duke sold the remains of Nonsuch, already ruined by his mother soon after she acquired it. With the alienation of this property, the extinction of the Cleveland and Southampton peerage on the death of Charles's son William in 1774, and the pulling down of Cleveland House in the middle of last century, disappeared the last visible traces of the multitudinous gifts to his mistress from King Charles II.

The Duchess was buried in Chiswick Church, but her tomb is unknown, as no stone was raised to mark the place. Perhaps her descendants thought that no monument was required beyond the memory of her name which is preserved in literature. And who can say that they were wrong? Barbara Villiers is scarcely likely to be forgotten while the combination of a face of eminent beauty and the heart of an utter rake has any attraction for weak mankind.

NOTES

Page 1, line 3. In a poem entitled *A Faithful Catalogue of our most Eminent Ninnies* (1686).

Page 1, line 6. Burnet, *History of My Own Time,* Supplement published in 1902, p. 65. Miss H. C. Foxcroft, who edits the Supplement, assigns this fragment to the year 1683.

P. 1, l. 11. Some sentences of this passage in the *History* are quoted elsewhere. For the benefit of those who are not familiar with it, however, it is here given in full : " The ruin of his reign, and of all his affairs, was occasioned chiefly by his delivering himself up at his first coming over to a mad range of pleasure. One of the race of the Villiers, then married to Palmer, a papist, soon after made earl of Castlemaine, who afterwards, being separated from him, was advanced to be duchess of Cleveland, was his first and longest mistress, by whom he had five children. She was a woman of great beauty, but most enormously vicious and ravenous, foolish but imperious, ever uneasy to the king, and always carrying on intrigues with other men, while yet she pretended she was jealous of him. His passion for her, and her strange behaviour towards him, did so disorder him, that often he was not master of himself, nor capable of minding business, which, in so critical a time, required great application ; but he did then so entirely trust the earl of Clarendon that he left all to his care, and submitted to his advices as to so many oracles."—1897 edition, Vol. I, pp. 168–9.

P. 2, l. 23. Letter of June 25th, 1745, in Clarendon Press edition of *Walpole's Letters* (1905), Vol. II, p. 108.

P. 2, l. 29. We should perhaps add Boyer, who, in his obituary notice of the Duchess of Cleveland in *Annals of Queen Anne's Reign,* after speaking of her beauty, says : " Her other qualities of good nature, liberality, &c., we shall not here expatiate upon." He has, however, just called her " this second Messalina."

P. 3, l. 13. Reported from Pope's conversation, in Spence's *Anecdotes.*

P. 6, l. 24.   Clarendon, *History of the Rebellion* (1826 edn.), VII, 151–2.

P. 7, l. 23.   Aubrey, *History of Surrey*, I, 47.

P. 13, l. 19.   *Letters of Philip, Second Earl of Chesterfield* (1829), pp. 77–81.

P. 14, l. 22.   *Ib.*, 86.

P. 15, l. 9,   *Ib.*, 87.

P. 16, l. 4.   *Ib.*, 88.

P. 17, l. 5.   Pepys, *Diary*, March 19th, 1665, and April 6th, 1668, has even worse to tell of the lady.   And Cosmo de' Medici, when he visited England in March 1669, wrote in a letter to a friend : " I am truly not the man to be taken by the charms of a Lady Carnegie [that was then her title], nor could I ever submit to participate in such widely distributed favours."

This same Cosmo de' Medici admired Lady Castlemaine sufficiently to commission Lely to paint her portrait, along with those of three other Caroline beauties, to be sent to his home in Tuscany.   Later he had a collection of sixteen pictures of beautiful English women.   The *Historical MSS. Commission, Report 12, Appendix, Part 9*, mentions among the MSS. of Mr. R. W. Ketton an unsigned one headed " Concerning Florence " and dated October 3rd, 1693.   In this the writer speaks of seeing the sixteen pictures at the Poggio Imperiale. "The Dutchess of Cleaveland's," he says, " obscured all the rest."

P. 17, l. 6.   *Letters*, 88–9.

P. 17, l. 20.   *Ib.*, 90.

P. 18, l. 3.   *Ib.*, 93.

P. 18, l. 9.   *Ib.*, 93–4.

P. 18, l. 12.   " Cromwell and his partisans " had " shut up and seiz'd on Spring Garden, which till now had been the usual rendezvous for the ladys and gallants at this season."—Evelyn, *Diary*, May 10th, 1654.   With regard to Hyde Park, Mr. Wheatley, in his edition of Pepys, notes that in 1656 there was published a work entitled " The Yellow Book, or a serious letter sent by a private Christian to the Lady Consideration the first of May 1656, which she is desired to communicate in Hide Park to the Gallants of the Times a little after sunset " !

P. 18, l. 29.   *Letters*, 91.

P. 19, l. 10.   *Ib.*, 92.

P. 19, l. 22. *Ib.*, 96–7. Chesterfield calls her Lady Essex ; but, as a matter of fact, Lord Capel, her husband, was not Earl of Essex until 1661.

P. 20, l. 7. *Letters*, 99.

P. 20, l. 31. *Ib.*, prefatory memoir, p. 19.

P. 22, l. 1. The capital letters with which Boyer and his contemporaries garnish their writings will usually be omitted from henceforward.

P. 24, l. 12. It is from the locality of this, probably the bride's parish church, that Lord Anglesea's house is placed in the neighbourhood of Ludgate Hill, which fits in well with the appointment made by the two girls in their letter to Chesterfield on p. 17.

P. 24, l. 16. Jesse, *Memoirs of the Court of England during the Reign of the Stuarts*, IV, 85.

P. 24, l. 31. *Memoirs of the Court of Charles II by Count Gramont*, chap. VI.

P. 26, l. 13. *Letters*, 102–3.

P. 27, l. 8. *Ib.*, 103.

P. 27, l. 28. *Ib.*, 104.

P. 28, l. 17. Or January 16$\frac{5}{6}\frac{9}{0}$, as it is written to show that at this time the year was still commonly reckoned to begin on March 25th, although many persons already made January 1st the first day, as Mr. Wheatley points out that Pepys did. See his first footnote to the text of the *Diary*.

P. 28, l. 25. In Rugge's *Diurnal*, which gives an account of the duel.

P. 29, l. 5. *Letters*, 105–6.

P. 29, l. 15. *Ib.*, 112–13. "The newse I have from England concerning your ladyship makes me doubt of everything ; and therefore let me entreate you to send mee your picture," etc. This news from England cannot have been, as the editor of the *Chesterfield Letters* supposes, "respecting the intimate connection between herself and King Charles "—unless the news came from Holland *via* England and referred to that meeting between Barbara and Charles of which Jesse and Mrs. Jameson speak.

P. 29, l. 29. Jesse, *Memoirs*, IV, 85.

P. 30, l. 18. Mrs. M. A. Everett Green, *Calendar of State Papers, Domestic Series*, 1660–1661, p. 104.

P. 30, l. 25.   *Diary*, May 16th, 1660.

P. 31, l. 7.   Pepys certainly speaks as if the King only gained his way with the lady later.   From the similarity of language it seems that Boyer, writing his obituary of the Duchess of Cleveland after her death in 1709, must have had the Williamite tract of 1690 before his eyes.   Boyer says : "Whatever shews of piety this Prince made at Breda, in order to impose upon some Presbyterian divines that attended him there, it was confidently affirm'd that this lady was prepar'd for his bed the very first night he lay at Whitehall."   *The Secret History*, p. 22, says : "Soon after he arrived in England, where he was received with all the pomp and splendour and all the demonstrations of joy that a nation could express, but then, as if he had left all his piety behind him in Holland, care was taken against the very first night that His Sacred Majesty was to lie at Whitehall to have the Lady Castlemain seduc'd from her loyalty to her husband and entic'd into the arms of the happily restored Prince."

P. 32, l. 24.   *Continuation of the Life of Edward, Earl of Clarendon* (1827), I, pp. 353, 357-8.

P. 34, l. 4.   *Calendar of State Papers (Domestic)* 1661-1662, p. 165.   Another petition from Roger Palmer, dated March ?, 1662, asks for "the reversion after George, Earl of Norwich, and Hen. Wynne, of the secretaryship of the business and affairs of Wales, mortgaged by the Earl for £23,000, which debt was sold to the petitioner" (*Ib.*, p. 303).

P. 35, l. 10.   *Diary*, October 14th, 1660.

P. 35, l. 19.   *Camden Society Publications*, No. 39 (New Series), p. 26.

P. 36, l. 5.   In an address to the London Topographical Society on May 6th, 1911, Lord Welby discussed the site of the Cockpit, which, he said, formed a very important part of the "sporting apparatus" of Whitehall Palace and therefore gradually gave its name to the adjacent buildings.   He assigned its location to the site now chiefly occupied by the rooms of the Permanent and Financial Secretaries of the Treasury.   During the interregnum first Cromwell and then Monk had their apartments in the Cockpit buildings.

P. 37, l. 11.   Lord Dartmouth, in his annotations to Burnet's *History of My Own Time*, speaks of "the late Countess of Sussex, whom the King adopted for his daughter, though Lord Castlemaine always looked upon her to be his, and left her his estate when he died, but she was generally understood to belong to another, the old Earl of Chesterfield, whom she resembled very much both in face and person."

P. 37, l. 20.   *Letters*, 116–18.

P. 40, l. 1.   Quoted by G. S. Steinman, *Memoir of Barbara Duchess of Cleveland*, p. 28.

P. 42, l. 13.   Burnet, *History*, Supplement, pp. 65–6.

P. 42, l. 22.   Clarendon, *Continuation*, II, 172.

P. 43, l. 12.   *Ib.*, II, 177.

P. 43, l. 29.   A curious light is thrown upon the lady's opinion, a few years later, of the value of Irish peerages. In a letter in the collection of Sir R. Graham, dated February 20th, 1665, a certain George Walsh writes: "Ralph Sheldon . . . would marry Mrs. Win Wells provided the King would make him an Irish Viscount, which I suppose will not be denied, for (according to the Lady Castlemaine's estimation) that honour is not valued at above 1000*l*." *H. M. C., Rep. 6, App.*

P. 44, l. 6.   Boyer, *Annals of Queen Anne's Reign*, obituary of Lord Castlemaine.

P. 44, footnote.   *Continuation*, II, 171.

P. 47, l. 27.   *Chesterfield Letters*, prefatory memoir, p. 21.

P. 48, l. 7.   *Letters*, 123.

P. 49, l. 3.   Lord Dartmouth's note on Burnet, *History*, I, part 2, p. 307. Legge, according to his son, never approved of the match.

P. 49, l. 6.   Jesse, *Memoirs*, III, 387 *ff.*, collects some interesting and amusingly diverse descriptions of Catherine of Braganza, the cruellest being Lord Dartmouth's: "She was very short and broad, of a swarthy complexion, one of her fore-teeth stood out, which held up her upper lip; had some very nauseous distempers, besides exceedingly proud and ill-favoured."

P. 49, l. 14.   *Continuation*, II, 165. The remaining quotations in this chapter from Clarendon are all from the following pages of the *Continuation*, and the references will therefore be omitted.

P. 51, ll. 1–6.   Evelyn, May 30th, 1662; Pepys, May 25th, 1662.

P. 52, l. 23.   Boyer, in his obituary notice of the Earl (*Annals*, July 1705), explicitly states that he was "bred a Protestant" and only turned Roman Catholic after "the misfortunes of his bed." Burnet, as we have seen, calls him "Palmer, a papist," as if he had always been one.

P. 57, l. 19.   This letter appears in Lister's *Life of Clarendon*, III, 193.

P. 58, l. 10.   Letter of January 18th, 1681.

P. 61, l. 16.   *Lansdowne MSS.*, 1236.

P. 70, l. 13.   Steinman, *Memoir*, p. 205, from the Dorney Court Muniments.

P. 74, l. 33.   *Diary*, July 26th, 1662.

P. 78, l. 14.   That is to say, unless he was really son of Colonel Robert Sidney, as many people believed, including apparently Evelyn.

P. 79, l. 8.   *Continuation*, II, 252–3.

P. 79, l. 15.   Pepys, *Diary*, December 24th, 31st, 1662.   On October 27th Pepys believes "the Duke of York will not be fooled in this of three crowns."

P. 79, l. 17.   *Ib.*, September 21st, 1662.

P. 80, l. 7.   *Ib.*, October 6th, 1662.

P. 80, l. 9.   *Ib.*, November 3rd, 1662.

P. 80, footnote.   For one opinion of the real source of Berkeley's greatness see Pepys, *Diary*, December 15th, 1662.

P. 81, l. 2.   *Continuation*, II, 230.

P. 81, l. 10.   *Diary*, October 24th, 1662.

P. 81, l. 22.   *Diary*, October 31st, 1662.

P. 81, footnote.   Letter of June 8th, 1665.

P. 82, l. 11.   *Ib.*, December 15th, 1662.

P. 82, l. 13.   *Life of the Duke of Ormonde*, edition of 1851, IV, p. 368.   Carte's work was first published in 1735–6.

P. 85, l. 9.   This letter from Cominges was first published by Lord Braybrooke in the Appendix to his edition of Pepys's *Diary*. Concerning Cominges, see M. J. J. Jusserand, *A French Ambassador at the Court of Charles II*.

P. 85, l. 21.   *Diary*, March 7th, 1663.

P. 86, l. 12.   *History*, Supplement, p. 73.

P. 87, l. 8.   *Diary*, January 19th, 1663.

P. 87, l. 30.   *Hatton Correspondence*, I, 64.   The editor, Sir E. Maunde Thompson, finds the story itself unsuitable for publication.

P. 89, l. 24.   Pepys repeats the expression on December 26th, 1667, when Frances, now Duchess of Richmond, was expected back at Court.

P. 90, l. 6. *Diary*, February 17th, 1663.

P. 90, l. 18. Letter of January 4th, 1663.

P. 91, l. 2. Pepys, *Diary*, February 25th, 1667. Cp. Allan Fea, *Some Beauties of the Seventeenth Century*, pp. 92–3. Mr. Fea points out that on the copper coins of Charles II Britannia reveals much of her leg ; and Frances Stewart was proud of her legs !

P. 91, l. 5. Ruvigny to Louis XIV, June 25th, 1663.

P. 92, l. 20. *Diary*, March 1st, 1663.

P. 92, l. 22. *Ib.*, April 4th, 1663.

P. 92, l. 30. *Gramont Memoirs*, chap. xi.

P. 94, l. 2. *Diary*, May 11th, 1663.

P. 94, l. 27. *Ib.*, May 2nd, 1664. Cp. in the entry for May 29th : " Mrs. Stewart, very fine and pretty, but far beneath my Lady Castlemaine."

P. 97, l. 1. *Ib.*, July 22nd, 1663.

P. 97, l. 15. *Ib.*, May 10th, 1663.

P. 98, l. 7. *Ib.*, November 6th, 1663.

P. 100, l. 1. The waters *sont vitriolées et par conséquent excitent le vomissement*, according to Cominges' Court news-sheet sent to Louis in August, 1663, quoted by M. Jusserand in the Appendix to his *French Ambassador*. But Burr, a hundred years later (*An Historical Account of Tunbridge Wells*, p. 72), declares their taste " pleasingly steely."

P. 100, l. 12. *Diary*, August 11th, 1663.

P. 102, l. 3. Pepys, *Diary*, February 8th, 1663. One of Captain Ferrers' choice stories actually hints at this.

P. 102, ll. 17 *ff.* Wood, *Life and Times* (edited by A. Clark), I, 491 *ff.* Wood, after describing how the Mayor's Council discussed the reception of the royal visitors, writes : " [They determined] after that was done to present the Queene with the richest pair of gloves that could be made ; then a payre of gloves for the Duke of York and his dutchess ; then another paire to the . . ." Here follows a blank. Mr. Clark says it was suggested to him that the words to be supplied are " Countess of Castlemaine," or " King's mistress " : but he inclines, no doubt rightly, to the more charitable view that Wood had not been given the list of nobles to whom gloves were to be presented by the City. In his description of the presentation, Wood again writes : " Then the maior presented to the Queen a paire of rich gloves, and to . . .", with the same blank in the MS.

P. 103, l. 8.   See Mr. Clark's note on Wood, I, 494.

P. 103, l. 27.   *Diary*, October 13th, 1663.

P. 103, l. 28.   This was a not unfrequent occurrence at Whitehall. On December 7th of this same year Pepys tells of the greatest tide that was ever known in the Thames the night before and of "all Whitehall having been drowned."

P. 104, l. 9.   *Diary*, October 20th, 1663.

P. 104, l. 17.   Letter of October 17th, 1663, quoted by Lord Braybrooke in his note on Pepys, October 17th, 1663.

P. 104, l. 18.   Chap. VIII.

P. 105, l. 9.   Jusserand, Appendix, pp. 220-1, where this letter from Cominges to Louis is dated November 1st, 1663.   According to Lord Braybrooke it is dated October 25-29.   Pepys on October 19th speaks of Catherine having "the extreme unction given her by the priests, who were so long about it that the doctors were angry "; and by October 24th " the Queen is in a good way of recovery."

P. 105, l. 24.   *Diary*, October 20th, 1663.

P. 106, l. 19.   *Ib.*, October 26th, 27th, 1663.

P. 107, l. 8.   *Ib.*, November 6th, 1663.

P. 107, l. 19.   *Ib.*, November 9th, 1663.

P. 108, l. 16.   Cominges to Lionne, December 31st, 1663, quoted in Jusserand, Appendix, p. 224.

P. 109, l. 7.   "Miss of State."   Cp. Evelyn, *Diary*, January 9th, 1662 : "The Earle of Oxford's *Misse* (as at this time they began to call lewd women)."

P. 109, l. 14.   The " great Stillingfleete " of Pepys, *Diary*, April 16th, 1665.   Oldmixon, who tells this story in his *Critical History of England* (1730), II, 276, anticipates events by making Stillingfleet already Dean of St. Paul's, and Barbara already Duchess of Cleveland.

P. 109, l. 23.   Letter of April 17th, 1664, quoted by Jusserand, p. 118.

P. 110, l. 20.   Pepys, *Diary*, February 8th, 1664.   On July 10th it is recorded that Lady Castlemaine gives Lord Sandwich her portrait—"and a most beautiful picture it is."

P. 110, l. 27.   *Diary*, April 1st, 1664.   But contrast what is said on July 15th.   Pepys seems to think that Frances Stewart is one whose beauty varies with her dress.

P. 110, l. 29. *Ib.*, February 1st, 1664.

P. 111, l. 12. *H.M.C. Rep. 6., App. MSS. of Sir Henry Ingilby.*

P. 112, l. 17. Steinman, in his *Memoir of Barbara Duchess of Cleveland*, argues the case well for the change of apartments. He places the first set in that part of Whitehall Palace buildings which is "separated from the main buildings by 'the street,' a connecting link between King Street and Whitehall . . . and enclosed at either end by a gate"; *i.e.* in the Cockpit buildings, on ground now covered by the Treasury. It is here that in Vertue's map of 1747, based on John Fisher's survey of 1680, is marked "Countess of Castlemain's kitchen." It may be noted that this site does not answer very well to Pepys's "chamber in Whitehall next the King's own" (*Diary*, April 25th, 1663, as quoted on p. 93 above), for not only "the street," but also the Privy Garden separated the Cockpit buildings from those in which the King and Queen lived; but perhaps we must treat Pepys's description as merely a loose one. As for the apartments over "the hither-gate," there is no doubt as to situation of the Holbein gate-house at the northern end of "the street" opening into Whitehall, close to the modern Horse Guards. Steinman writes (*Second Addenda*, p. 2): "That it had now fallen to the use of Lady Castlemaine is clearly shown, and this fact goes far to assure us that she had sometime before removed from her original suite of apartments on the west side of the Street to those of her northern neighbour, whence, we may readily believe, it might be approached by her Ladyship without venturing her fair person in the air."

We cannot, however, feel sure : (1) that Lady Castlemaine did not occupy the gatehouse apartments from the first, for it adjoined the Cockpit buildings, and was only separated from the "kitchen" marked in Vertue's map by one suite of lodgings marked "Duke of Ormond" —and Ormonde was in Ireland from 1662 to 1669, so that his apartments might have been occupied by someone else; or (2) that the lady, if she made a move early in 1664, was not before that actually in some "chamber in Whitehall next the King's own," as Pepys says, that is to say, east of the Privy Garden. The Duchess of Portsmouth was later lodged on the east side "at the end of the gallery."

P. 113, l. 28. In the possession of Mr. Ambrose Lee. It is quoted by Allan Fea, *Some Beauties of the Seventeenth Century*, p. 184.

P. 114, l. 18. Cominges to Lionne, September 15th, 1664. Jusserand, Appendix, 229.

P. 117, l. 4. From the *Memoirs* it appears that Gramont, when dictating them, entirely forgot the year of his marriage, which he only mentions in his last paragraph. This marriage had been assigned to the year 1663, as Gramont's son was born on September 7th, 1664. Within two months after the latter date he took wife and child to France. On January 28th, 1665, Cominges tells Lionne that the Chevalier has been in London again for two months and has become *le plus effronté menteur du monde*. The wife's return is not mentioned, though to be present at the Candlemas Day revel she must have come back, at the latest, about the time when Cominges was writing to Lionne.

P. 118, l. 4. *Diary*, September 9th, 1678, and elsewhere.

P. 118, l. 17. Pepys, *Diary*, February 21st, 1665; *Gramont Memoirs*, chap. x.

P. 118, l. 27. Pepys, *Diary*, March 13th, 1665. *Calendar of State Papers (Domestic)* reports on March 3rd, 1665, that Lord Castlemaine has landed at Dover and gone to London.

P. 119, l. 5. So Lady Sandwich told Pepys (*Diary*, February 21st, 1665).

P. 120, footnote. Pepys, *Diary*, May 15th, 1663.

P. 121, l. 4. See his instructions of April 4th, 1665, to *la célèbre Ambassade*, quoted in Jusserand, *French Ambassador*, Appendix, pp. 233-4. The ninth chapter of M. Jusserand's book is of great interest on this period.

P. 122, l. 2. "We do naturally love the Spanish and hate the French," says Pepys, October 10th, 1661.

P. 122, l. 7. Letter to Louis, April 23rd, 1665.

P. 123, l. 9. Henry Savile to Lady Dorothy Savile, June, 1665 (*Savile Correspondence*).

P. 124, l. 3. Bigorre to Lionne, July 9th, 1665 (Jusserand, Appendix, 243).

P. 124, l. 7. Courtin to Lionne, July 9th (Jusserand, App., 243).

P. 125, l. 17. *H.M.C. Rep. 14, App., Pt. 2.* Letter of October 2nd, 1665.

P. 125, l. 25. Letter to Lionne, August 30th, 1665.

P. 125, l. 31. Concerning this royal visit to Oxford see Mr. A. Clark's edition of Wood's *Life and Times* and the Hon. G. C. Brodrick's *Memorials of Merton College*.

P. 127, l. 2. *Continuation*, II, 450.

P. 130, l. 10. *Ib.*, III, 61.

P. 132, l. 14. *Ib.*, III, 60.

P. 133, l. 15. *Ib.*, III, 61–2.

P. 133, l. 20. "Mr. May," *i.e.* Baptist or Bab May, of whom we shall hear again.

P. 134, l. 14. Steinman (*Second Addenda*, p. 4) discovered that the £2000 incurred for these rings was among the £30,000 worth of debts paid for Lady Castlemaine by the King at the end of this year. Concerning the huge transactions between Bakewell and the King see Mr. Wheatley's note on Pepys, *Diary*, July 11th, 1665.

P. 134, l. 16. *Calendar of State Papers (Domestic)*, 1666, uncertain month, petition of John Leroy. In September Leroy petitions again for the money, saying that he has had great losses by the burning of his house in the Fire.

P. 136, l. 30. Letter quoted in *Savile Correspondence*, p. 301 *n.*

P. 138, l. 4. *Calendar of State Papers (Domestic)*, May 23rd, 1666.

P. 138, l. 23. Evelyn, *Diary*, September 6th, 7th, 1666.

P. 139, l. 8. Pepys, *Diary*, September 26th, 1666.

P. 139, l. 10. Evelyn, *Diary*, October 18th, 1666.

P. 140, l. 24. Pierce's theory as to the lady's condition, however (Pepys, October 15th, 1666), does not seem to have been correct. At any rate, there was no child born that is ever heard of.

P. 141, ll. 24 *ff.* Pepys, *Diary*, March 20th, April 3rd, 1666.

P. 142, l. 14. Penn, on March 18th, 1667, told Pepys that he had that day brought in an account of Richmond's estate and debts to the King. Evelyn gave Pepys "the whole story of Mrs. Stewart's coming away from Court" on April 26th, 1667. Among other arguments which Evelyn used to prove that Frances Stewart was honest to the last was that founded on the King's keeping in with Lady Castlemaine, "for he was never known to keep two mistresses in his life."

P. 143, l. 8. *Continuation*, III, 228.

P. 143, l. 31. Coke, *A Detection of the Court and State of England* (1719), pp. 155–6. Coke was himself in the Park on this day, June 10th.

P. 144, l. 22. *Diary*, June 24th, 1667.

P. 145, l. 6. *History*, I, 169.

P. 145, l. 20. *Diary*, July 7th, 1667.

P. 146, l. 3. *Calendar*, August 29th, 1667.

P. 146, l. 31. Pepys, *Diary*, July 12th, 1667. He gets his information from Sir H. Cholmly. Sir Thomas Crew confirms it the same day.

P. 147, l. 28. *Diary*, July 29th. Next day Mr. Cooling, my Lord Chamberlain's secretary, being in drink, furnishes Pepys with still more details, couched in most plain and vigorous language—part of the vigour being due to Lady Castlemaine, who was no stickler in her talk. Pierce's story is told by Pepys on August 7th.

P. 148, l. 10. See, for example, *Memoirs*, chap. vi. Jermyn is also the *Germanicus* of Mrs. Manley's *New Atalantis*.

P. 148, l. 16. *Diary*, July 29th, 1667.

P. 149, l. 1. *Ib.* Pierce, on August 7th, also says that she "hath nearly hectored him [the King] out of his wits."

P. 149, l. 3. Pepys, *Diary*, July 30th, 1667.

P. 149, l. 5. In *Epicene, or the Silent Woman*.

P. 150, l. 1. *Continuation*, III, 291 *ff*.

P. 151, l. 20. *Ib.*, III, 294. Pepys hears the same story, November 11th, 1667.

P. 151, l. 28. *Ib.*, III, 323.

P. 152, l. 2. *Diary*, August 27th, 1667.

P. 152, l. 7. Pepys, *Diary*, September 8th, 11th. Part of this tale was told by a Mr. Rawlinson, who had it from "one of my Lord Chancellor's gentlemen."

P. 152, l. 21. Carte, *History of the Duke of Ormonde*, IV, 152. Carte says : "The Countess of Castlemaine, whose understanding bore no proportion to her power, and who would have been able to do great mischiefs if her egregious folly had not often defeated her measures, was so outrageous in her opposition to the Chancellor that she openly expressed her malice against him in all places, and did not scruple to declare in the Queen's Chamber in the presence of much company that she hoped to see his head upon a stake, to keep company with those of the regicides on Westminster Hall. The occasion of this fury was that he would never let anything pass the Great Seal in which she was named, and often by his wise remonstrances prevailed with the King to alter the resolutions which she had persuaded him to take."

P. 153, l. 15. Sir Peter Pett to Antony Wood (? in 1693), Aubrey's *Letters of Eminent Men*.

P. 154, l. 14.   Pepys, *Diary*, September 1st, 5th, 8th, 10th, 1667.

P. 157, l. 11.   In a letter to his sister, Duchess of Orleans, on May 7th, 1668.   On August 26th of the previous year he had written to the same : " You may think me ill-natured, but if you consider how hard a thing 'tis to swallow an injury done by a person I had so much tendernesse for you will in some degree excuse the resentment I use towards her."

P. 159, l. 12.   Pepys, *Diary*, March 7th, 1667.   See Lord Bray-brooke's instructive note there.

P. 160, l. 26.   *Diary*, April 7th, 1668.

P. 161, ll. 5, 8.   Evelyn, April 2nd ; Pepys, April 6th, 1668.

P. 164, l. 16.   Pepys, *Diary*, February 14th, 1668.

P. 166, l. 20.   *Ib.*, January 15th, 1669.

P. 168, footnote.   *H.M.C., Buccleugh and Queensberry MSS., Vol. I.*

P. 175, footnote.   *Lettres sur la Cour de Louis XIV (1667-70)*, with introduction and notes by Jean Lemoine.

P. 176, l. 10.   Charles declared his intention with regard to the new honours for Lady Castlemaine and two of her sons more than a month before this.   See an amusing letter from Henshaw to Sir Robert Paston, July 16th, 1670 (*H.M.C., Rep. 6, App., Ingilby MSS.*).

P. 176, l. 18.   *Memoirs*, chap. x.

P. 178, l. 26.   Evelyn, *Diary*, December 4th, 1696.

P. 179, l. 3.   *Letters of Chesterfield*, 159.

P. 179, l. 27.   *History*, I, 474.

P. 180, footnote.   *Lansdowne's Works*, II, 173.

P. 181, l. 3.   Reresby, *Memoirs*, p. 81.

P. 182, l. 5.   *H.M.C., Rep. 12, App., Pt. V.*   Lady Mary Bertie to Katherine Noel, February 23rd, 1671.

P. 184, l. 3.   *H.M.C., Rep. 5, App., Hatherton MSS.*

P. 185, l. 11.   Carte, II, 152-3.   It appears from Carte as if the King's attempted grant of Phœnix Park to the lady was about 1663.

P. 187, l. 1.   *Memoirs*, chap. xi.   Gramont goes on to say that " this intrigue had become a general topic in all companies when the Court arrived in London " from the West, and that "some said she had already presented him with Jermyn's pension and Jacob Hall's salary." Such chronology is very Gramontian.

P. 187, l. 22.   *New Atalantis*, I, 22.

P. 188, l. 10.   Letter of November 18th, 1748.

P. 188, l. 15.   Burnet, *History*, I, 370.

P. 189, l. 4.   The fourth Lord Chesterfield, in the letter quoted above, says that the Duchess of Cleveland, struck by Churchill's graces, "gave him £5000, with which he immediately bought an annuity for his life of £500 a year of my grandfather Halifax, which was the foundation of his subsequent fortune." It appears that this annuity was bought in 1674 for £4500, nine years' purchase being Lord Halifax's usual price. (See *Savile Correspondence*.) Boyer, in the obituary of the Duchess in his *Annals of Queen Anne's Reign*, speaks of her "generous rewarding of the caresses of a handsome young gentleman of the Court" with the sum of £6000, "which lay the foundation of his after fortune." And Mrs. Manley in *The New Atalantis* says that the Duchess gave 6000 crowns for a place in the *Prince of Tameran's* (Duke of York's) Bedchamber for *Count Fortunatus* (Churchill) and procured for him a rise in the Army, while taking his "fair and fortunate sister" to attend on herself. *Fortunatus* then persuaded her to have his sister transferred to the *Princess of Tameran's* (Duchess of York's) household. Later he was given by the Duchess of Cleveland 140,000 crowns in cash alone, besides having honours and places of profit procured for him. It is with little surprise that we read Lord Somers's opinion of Marlborough, in answer to Queen Anne's request for it, that he was "the worst man God ever made" (Macpherson's *History*, Vol. VIII, Carte's *Mem. Book*). Cp. what Macaulay says of the Duke's venality, *Hist.*, chap. XIV.

P. 190, l. 20.   Pope, *Sermon against Adultery*.

P. 191, l. 7.   On the date of production of *Love in a Wood* see Mr. G. A. Aitken's article in the *Dictionary of National Biography*. He shows fairly conclusively that it was first acted in the early spring before its registration at Stationers' Hall (with the dedication) on October 6th, 1671.

P. 191, l. 12.   Dennis, *Familiar Letters* (edition of 1721), pp. 216-7. Macaulay, in his essay on Wycherley, gives only the tamer (and very pointless) version which the Rev. Joseph Spence took down from the conversation of Alexander Pope. Pope told the tale thus : " Wycherley was a very handsome man. His acquaintance with the famous Duchess of Cleveland commenced oddly enough. One day, as he passed that duchess's coach in the ring, she leaned out of the window, and cried out loudly enough to be heard distinctly by him :

'Sir, you're a rascal ; you're a villain ! ' Wycherley from that instant
entertained hopes. He did not fail waiting on her the next morning :
and with a very melancholy tone begged to know how it was possible
for him to have so much disobliged her Grace ? They were very
good friends from that time ; yet, after all, what did he get by her ?"—
Spence, *Anecdotes*, p. 16.

P. 191, l. 21. *Love in a Wood*, Act I, Scene 2. The last two
lines of the song run :

> " Great Wits and Great Braves
> Have always a Punk to their Mother."

P. 194, l. 2. In *Hatton Correspondence*, Vol. I.

P. 194, l. 9. *Ib.*, letter of January 18th, 1672.

P. 194, l. 22. Evelyn, *Diary*, September 10th, 1672.

P. 195, ll. 3, 7. *Ib.*, October 9th, 21st, 1672.

P. 196, l. 13. Perhaps we should say that he had already done so
before the marriage ; since the reversion of the grant of June 5th,
1672, is to Charles Fitzroy and his heirs male, and in default to Henry
Fitzroy and his heirs male.

P. 197, l. 19. Evelyn, *Diary*, October 17th, 1671.

P. 200, l. 21. *Letters to Sir Joseph Williamson* (*Camden Society's
Publications*).

P. 201, l. 10. *Hatton Correspondence*.

P. 201, l. 27. Nell Gwynn used a coarser word.

P. 202, l. 5. *Letters to Williamson*, August 25th, 1673.

P. 205, l. 4. Evelyn, *Diary*, September 10th, 1677.

P. 205, l. 10. Derham to Williamson, November 5th, 1673.

P. 205, l. 27. First published by Steinman, *First Addenda* (1874)
from Ashmolean MSS. 837.

P. 207, l. 5. *Camden Society's Publications* (Old Series), No. 52.

P. 208, l. 27. *Letters of Humphrey Prideaux, Camden Society's
Publications* (New Series), No. 15.

P. 210, ll. 11, 13. *Ib.*, Letters of November 8th, 1675, and October 31st, 1676.

P. 212, l. 13. Evelyn, *Diary*, September 6th, 1676.

P. 212, l. 20. *H.M.C., Rep. 12, App., Pt. V.*

P. 213, l. 16. *H.M.C., Rep. 4, App., Bath MSS.*

z

P. 214, l. 10.   Grant of April 7th, 1677.

P. 217, l. 7.   First printed by Steinman, *Memoir*, pp. 154–5, from the originals in the possession of Earl Stanhope.   They are undated, but obviously belong to this period.

P. 219, l. 21.   *Hatton Correspondence*, I, 168.

P. 220, l. 10.   The Convent of the Holy Sepulchre, rue Neuve de Bellechase, Saint-Germain, within the walls of Paris.

P. 220, l. 12.   *Hatton Correspondence*, I, 167.

P. 220, l. 14.   In *The Adventures of Rivella* there is a somewhat different version of the Montagu affair : " During the short stay *Rivella* had made in *Hilaria's* family, she was become acquainted with the *Lord Crafty*.   He had been Ambassador in France, where his negotiations are said to have procured as much advantage to your King "—the supposed narrator of *The Adventures*, it must be remembered, is conversing with a young French Chevalier—" as they did dishonour to his own country.   He had a long head turn'd to deceit and over-reaching. If such a thing were to be done two ways, he never lov'd the plain, nor valu'd a point if he could easily carry it.   His person was not at all beholding to nature, and yet he had possessed more fine women than had the finest gentleman, not less than twice or thrice becoming his master's rival.   When *Hilaria* was in France he found it extreamly convenient for his affairs to be well with her, as she was mistress, and himself Ambassador.   For some time 'tis supposed that he lov'd her out of inclination, her own charms being inevitable ; but finding she was not very regular, he reproach'd her in such a manner that the haughty *Hilaria* vow'd his ruin.   She would not permit a subject to take that freedom she would not allow a monarch, which was, prescribing rules for her conduct.   In short, her power was such over the King, tho' he was even then in the arms of a new and younger mistress, and *Hilaria* at so great a distance from him, as to yield to the plague of her importunity with which she fill'd her letters.   He consented that *Lord Crafty* should be recall'd, upon secret advice that she pretended to have received of his corruption and treachery.   The Ambassador did not want either for friends in England, nor in *Hilaria's* own family, who gave him very early advice of what was design'd against him.   He had the dexterity to ward the intended blow, and turn it upon her that was the aggressor ; *Hilaria's* own daughter betray'd her to the Ambassador. He had corrupted not only her heart, but seduced her from her duty and integrity.   Her mother was gone to take the Bourbon waters, leaving this young lady the care of her family, and more immediately of such letters as a certain person should write to her, full of amorous raptures for the favours she had bestow'd. These fatal letters, at least several of them with answers full of tenderness under *Hilaria's* own hand, the Ambassador proved so lucky as to make himself master of. He return'd with his credentials to England to accuse *Hilaria* and acquit himself. The mistress was summon'd from France to justify her ill conduct. What could be said against such clear evidences of her disloyalty? 'Tis true, she had to deal with the most merciful Prince in the world, and who made the largest allowances for human frailty, which she so far improv'd as to tell His Majesty there was nothing criminal in a correspondence design'd only for amusement, without presuming to aim at consequences; the very mode and manner of expression in French and English were widely different; that which in one language carried an air of extream gallantry meant no more than meer civility in t' other. Whether the Monarch were, or would seem persuaded, he appear'd so, and order'd her to forgive the Ambassador; to whom he return'd his thanks for the care he had taken of his glory, very much to *Hilaria's* mortification, who was not suffer'd to exhibit her complaint against him, which was look'd upon as proceeding only from the malice and revenge of a vindictive guilty woman." [The *Lord Crafty* in the above is, of course, Ralph Montagu.]

For Montagu's attempted defence of himself when he got back to London see a long letter dated July 6th, 1678, from Sir Robert Southwell to the Duke of Ormonde, which is among the MSS. of the Marquess of Ormonde (*H.M.C., Ormonde MSS.*, Vol. IV.). Among other things Montagu says that, King Charles having entrusted to him the compassing of a marriage between Northumberland and Lady Elizabeth Percy, the Duchess of Cleveland and his wife became friends of a sort. "But his Lady being (on a visit to the Duchess) forbid admission because Monsieur Chattillean [*sic*] was with her, she returned in high resentment, so that he, seeing the designed marriage in danger, took on him to expostulate very roundly with the Duchess for her licentious course of life with the said Monsieur"—with the result that might be expected. To protect himself, therefore, he had six of her letters stolen, whereof some abounded with gross and unseemly things, some with disrespect to His Majesty, etc. In fact, the mischief was all due to the Duchess and Chatillon. Montagu had no chance of telling Charles this, however, for as soon as he began the King cut him short, saying that he knew already too much of it, and forbade him the Court.

P. 221, l. 1. *Harleian MSS.*, 7006, pp. 171–6. This is taken from a copy made by the Rev. George Harbin in 1731 from the original letter, then in the possession of the Earl of Berkshire. The punctuation follows Harbin, with a few modifications. It is clearly not the Duchess's own. See next note.

P. 228, l. 13. *British Museum Additional MSS.*, 21, 505. This being the original letter, the Duchess's spelling has been carefully preserved. With regard to the punctuation, the full stops, the colons, and the commas have been added for the sake of clearness; as also a few quotation-marks for the speeches reported. The writer used no stops at all except ten semicolons! [In the cases of both this and the other letter from Paris I have consulted the actual MSS. in the British Museum, so that the transcripts may claim to be more accurate than those which have appeared hitherto in print, previous editors having taken some liberties with the text.—P.W.S.]

P. 232, l. 20. The Abbey of Our Lady, Port Royal des Champs, near Versailles.

P. 236, l. 16. *H.M.C., Rep. 12, App., Pt. V.*

P. 237, l. 3. *H.M.C., Rep. 7, App.* W. Denton to Sir Ralph Verney, September 14th, 1671 : "I hear Thin is laid siege to Lady Cleveland's daughter."

P. 237, l. 21. *A Brief Historical Relation of State Affairs from September, 1678, to April, 1714.* This diary of Narcissus Luttrell is by no means as ponderous as its title would indicate. This will be clear from our quotations.

P. 237, footnote. *H.M.C., Buccleugh and Queensberry MSS.*

P. 240, l. 13. Letter of August 16th, 1679.

P. 241, l. 13. *Hatton Correspondence*, Letter of November 22nd, 1677. Compare what Dorothy, wife of Sir William Temple, writes to her father in 1684 : "If papa were near, I should think myself a perfect pope, though I hope I should not be burned as there was one at Nell Gwynn's door the 5th of November, who was set in a great chair, with a red nose half a yard long, with some hundreds of boys throwing squibs at it."

P. 242, l. 10. The *Tower Bills* show that Lord Castlemaine was in the Tower in the Christmas quarter of 1678, the Christmas quarter of 1679, and the Lady Day and Midsummer quarters of 1680.

P. 242, l. 13. *Hatton Correspondence*, I, 200.

P. 243, l. 23. Evelyn, *Diary*, December 4th, 1679. It is now that he declares Cleveland House "a noble palace, too good for that infamous . . .," as already quoted on p. 178.

P. 244, l. 15. *H.M.C., Rep. 12., App., Pt. V.* But see also a letter from the Countess of Northampton on June 10th.

P. 245, l. 2. *H.M.C., Rep. 12, App., Pt. V.* Letter dated 1681, November 15, from Chaloner Chute to the Countess of Rutland.

P. 245, l. 27. Steinman, *First Addenda*, pp. 11, 12. The letter is dated March 17th, 1683, *i.e.* 168¾, or, as we now write, 1684.

P. 246, l. 27. Evelyn, *Diary*, October 24th, 1684.

P. 247, l. 3. *Memoirs of John Macky*, p. 39, quoted by Jesse, *Memoirs of the Court of England during the Reign of the Stuarts*, IV, p. 62. With regard to his betrayal of James II, the King on the night of December 11th confided to the Duke his determination to fly, desiring him to keep it a profound secret. He left Whitehall Stairs by boat about 3 a.m., and when the door of the royal bedchamber was thrown open at the usual hour of the levee, the Duke came out and told the crowd waiting in the antechamber that James had fled. "Having performed this last act of kindness for his sovereign," says Jesse (IV, 414), "the Duke . . . immediately placed himself at the head of his regiment of guards and declared for the Prince of Orange."

P. 248, l. 29. See the article on Goodman in *Dictionary of National Biography*.

P. 249, l. 6. Luttrell in August 1685 describes how "the picture of the late Duke of Monmouth, which was drawn by Sir Peter Lely, and given to the University of Cambridge when he was their chancellor [elected in 1674], is lately, together with the frame, burnt by order before the schools of the University."

P. 250, l. 16. *History of England during the Reign of the Royal House of Stuart*, II, 576.

P. 251, l. 5. Anne, Countess of Sunderland, to Henry Sidney, January 8th, 1680.

P. 251, l. 9. The following is a rough list of the chief ascertainable gifts from Charles II to Barbara :—

> February, 1663. All the King's Christmas presents from the peers (p. 92).
>
> (?) 1663. Phœnix Park, Dublin, afterwards withdrawn (see below).

December, 1666.   £30,000 to pay her debts (p. 141).

August 29th, 1667.   5600 oz. of silver-plate (p. 146).

April, 1668.   Berkshire House (p. 64).

1669.   £4700 a year out of the Post Office revenues (p. 171).

January, 1671.   Nonsuch House and park (p. 182).

(Before August 9th) 1671.   "£10,000 a year more " from the Customs ; "likewise near £10,000 a year out of the new farm of the county excise of beer and ale " ; and various reversions (p. 184).

February, 1672.   Manors, etc., in Surrey.   Large grants to her children in this and the following years (pp. 186, 196, 202).

July, 1673.   A (? new) pension of £5500 from the wine licence revenue, and other minor gifts (pp. 202–3).

1674.   Large grants to her daughters on their marriages (p. 206).

October 9th, 1674.   £6000 a year from the Excise (p. 208).

1676.   Compensation for the withdrawn grant of Phœnix Park (p. 185).

April 7th, 1677.   Chief Stewardship, etc., of Hampton Court (p. 214).

1679.   Gift of £25,000 which Essex refused to pay, but his successor paid (p. 252).

1684–5.   Payment of £1599 out of the secret services fund of Charles II (p. 250, 251).

P. 251, ll. 13, 30.   See article on Essex by Mr. Osmund Airy in *Dictionary of National Biography*.   The letter is in *H.M.C.*, *Rep.* 7, *App.*, 477 b.   (John Verney to Sir Ralph Verney, Nov. 27th, 1679.)

P. 253, l. 6.   Dr. Raymond Crawfurd, in his painfully interesting monograph, *The Last Days of Charles II*, says : " One may assert, with considerable confidence, that his death was due to chronic granular kidney (a form of Bright's disease), with uræmic convulsions, a disease that claims the highest proportion of its victims during the fifth and sixth decades of life."

P. 254, l. 8.   *Hatton Correspondence.*

P. 256, l. 6.   Lord Chesterfield, writing to the Earl of Arran on February 7th, 1685, says in his decidedly touching account of King Charles's deathbed (he was present for two whole nights and saw him expire) : " Lastly, he asked his subjects' pardon for anything that had been neglected, or acted conterary to the best rules of a good government."—*Letters*, p. 279.

P. 256, l. 14.   Burnet, *History*, II, 461.

P. 258, l. 6. *Ib.*, I, 169.

P. 261, l. 10. Luttrell, February 2nd, 1685.

P. 264, l. 9. Luttrell, June, 1685.

P. 264, l. 14. News-letter of July 7th, 1685, among the Rutland MSS. (*H.M.C., Rep. 12, App., Pt. V.*)

P. 265, l. 4. *Ellis Correspondence*, Letter of March 15th, 1686.

P. 265, l. 9. *H.M.C., Rep. 12, App., Pt. V.* Letter of March 13th, 1686.

P. 265, l. 12. *Poems on Affairs of State*, II, 54.

P. 266, l. 2. "A song to the old tune of Taking of Snuff is the Mode of the Court," in *Poems on Affairs of State*. Jesse, *Memoirs*, IV, 63, quotes both this and another entertaining poem, "The Lovers' Session," which contains the line about Northumberland's "beautiful face and dull stupid carriage" and goes on :

> "But his prince-like project to kidnap his wife,
> And a lady so free to make pris'ner for life,
> Was tyranny to which the sex ne'er would submit,
> And an ill-natured fool they liked worse than a wit."

P. 266, l. 16. *H.M.C., Rep. 12, App., Pt. V.* Letter of March 13th, 1686.

P. 267, l. 15. Luttrell, February, 1687.

P. 267, l. 27. Wellwood, p. 185.

P. 268, l. 10. *Memoirs*, II, 78.

P. 270, l. 5. *Original Treasury Papers*, IV, 3, quoted by Steinman, *First Addenda*, p. 15.

P. 271, l. 28. Evelyn, August 18th, 1688.

P. 272, l. 2. Reresby gives a different reason, that he "had, at a meeting of the Scotch nobility in London, proposed to recall King James."

P. 272, l. 17. In *Esmond* Viscount Castlewood takes the place of the Duke of Hamilton.

P. 273, l. 1. Cunningham, *Handbook of London*.

P. 276, l. 31. The "kitchin-maid," according to the Compleat Key, is "pretended Madam Beauclair."

P. 280, l. 13. "The first Dutchess in England," *i.e.* the Duchess of Norfolk.

P. 284, l. 5. See quotation from the Earl of Dorset's poem at the head of chapter 1.

P. 284, l. 17. Kneller's picture in the National Portrait Gallery.

P. 288, l. 17. See C. E. Lart, *Jacobite Extracts from the Parish Registers of St. Germain-en-Laye* (1910), Vol. I.

P. 290, ll. 3, 24 *ff.* Steinman, *First Addenda*, pp. 16–18, from *Treasury Papers.*

P. 291, footnote. *H.M.C., Rep. 14, App., Pt. II.*

P. 293, l. 13. James Caulfield, *Portraits, Memoirs, and Character of Eminent Persons,* on Beau Feilding. This is not an authoritative work, but its compiler had access to information now lost.

P. 294, l. 1. *Tatler,* No. 50 (August 4th, 1709).

P. 297, l. 18. First edition, 1715 ; second and enlarged edition, 1723.

P. 297, l. 24. He appears as "Colonel Robert Fielding" in *A Jacobite Narrative of the War in Ireland,* his regiment being one of those sent to France in the April of 1690, in exchange for some French regiments which James had asked Louis to send him (pp. 89, 92). The *Narrative* does not say whether the Colonel accompanied his regiment or not.

P. 298, l. 14. *Tatler,* No. 50.

P. 299, l. 31. *Wentworth Papers,* p. 50.

P. 300, l. 7. *Atterbury's Correspondence,* II, 31. As a matter of fact, Dryden calls *Zimri* "Blest madman!"

P. 301, l. 23. *Wentworth Papers,* pp. 58–9.

P. 302, l. 12. Pasted in *Harleian MSS.,* 5808, p. 135. Quoted by Steinman, *Second Addenda,* p. 14.

P. 304, l. 7. See Howell, *State Trials,* XIV, cols. 1327–72, for a report of the whole proceedings ; and *Cases of Divorce* for a part account.

P. 304, l. 28. As Montague put it in his opening speech, "though the law doth not take away from him that shall be convicted thereof [bigamy, a crime amounting to felony] the benefit of his clergy, yet it is such a crime as doth take away from the prisoner the assistance of counsel."

P. 309, footnote. The "Articles" are given in full in *Cases of Divorce,* as are the seven letters from Feilding to Mary Wadsworth.

P. 316, l. 9. *Tatler*, No. 51 (August 6th, 1709): "*Orlando* now raves in a garret, and calls to his neighbour skies to pity his dolors and find redress for an unhappy lover."

P. 317, l. 21. See articles on Charles Hamilton and James Douglas, fourth Duke of Hamilton, in *Dictionary of National Biography*. Mr. Martin Haile in his *James Francis Edward, the Old Chevalier*, pp. 128–9, sets out well the reasons for thinking that the killing of the Duke of Hamilton was a treacherous murder by those whom Swift calls " the two most abandoned wretches that ever infested this island "—Mohun and MacCartney. Had the Duke gone to France as Queen Anne's ambassador (which he was on the point of doing) the Jacobite cause might have been saved. And young Hamilton, in his evidence at the trial, charged MacCartney with thrusting at his father as he lay on the ground wounded. In 1719 MacCartney was rewarded with the governorship of Portsmouth.

P. 319, l. 3. Thomas Faulkner, *History and Antiquities of Brentford, Ealing, and Chiswick*, p. 384. Mr. Lloyd Sanders, in his *Old Kew, Chiswick and Kensington*, says that Walpole House was a school for young gentlemen as early as 1817 and that Thackeray was one of the pupils there.

P. 319, l. 21. Fea (*Some Beauties*, etc., p. 190) states that "the spirit of the once lovely Barbara is said to haunt a room in the upper part of the building [Walpole House] wringing her hands and bemoaning the loss of her beauty "—which, he points out, is an unreasonable thing for the spirit to do, seeing that Kneller's portrait of her in the National Portrait Gallery shows that she retained her good looks.

P. 321, l. 13. On the Lifford peerage see G. E. C[okayne], *Complete Peerage*, Vol. V, p. 77. Frederic William appears to have been created Earl in July, 1698, but no patent seems to have been enrolled.

ADDENDUM

P. 122, l. 12. On Lauderdale's acquaintance with Lady Castlemaine Mr. John Willcock, in *A Scots Earl in Covenanting Times* (p. 117), writes: "We are told on good authority that friendship is impossible among the wicked, so it is certain that the alliance in question was a purely mercenary contract. As the royal mistress was ravenously greedy, one is not surprised to find that before Lauderdale had been long associated with her he was in straits for ready money. From some quarter he must have obtained a fresh supply, for the Countess was unfailing in her support of him against all his enemies."

INDEX

www.ingramcontent.com/pod-product-compliance
Lightning Source LLC
Chambersburg PA
CBHW030352030726
47497CB00002B/300